Heart & Soul

Heart & Soul

JAMES PEEVEY

HEART & SOUL

iUniverse books may be ordered through booksellers or by contacting:

iUniverse
1663 Liberty Drive
Bloomington, IN 47403
www.iuniverse.com
1-800-Authors (1-800-288-4677)

ISBN: 978-1-4917-7275-1 (sc)
ISBN: 978-1-4917-7276-8 (e)

Library of Congress Control Number: 2015911409

Print information available on the last page.

iUniverse rev. date: 08/11/2015

Contents

Chapter 1

Adventurous writer

John William Davis, an author of action-adventure and survival books for the last ten years, was experiencing a problem trying to come up with something new for his main character to do in the next book. His character JD was a man who used his wits and survival skills to stay alive in the wilderness. He faced new challenges in every book, and then figured out a way to solve them.

John wanted his character to experience new challenges to hook his readers while they read his book. Then they would buy the new book when it came out to see what JD faced next. With no new idea of how to start his book, the JD character might have to end. Never experiencing this problem before, he had no other choice but to reach out to the man who could give him some good advice, his best friend and publisher, Michael Parnell. Eventually, Michael would be calling him for an update on his new book wondering how it was coming along.

Michael owned Parnell publishing company in New York. They were schoolmates while growing up. John trusted and respected this man more than anyone else in his life. He always went to him for his advice and help on solving a problem, knowing he would come up with some kind of idea or solution. No matter how busy he might be, Michael always found time to help John. Not because John's books sold well, he enjoyed helping his good friend when the opportunity arose, challenging himself to come up with a solution. Of course, it did not hurt all of John's books being bestsellers, which made them both a lot of money over the years.

"Michael, for some strange reason I cannot come up with something new for my next book. I think it might be time to end the JD character and move on to something else." John said. "Wait a minute John. Before you end the character that has been very good to us, I want you to try something for me." Michael said. "I am all ears old friend." "My advice is to go out and get a new perspective on things. Go to a movie or out to dinner, or do both. If that does not work, plan a short trip to a surrounding city and get out among the people. This might give you a chance to see something new and then want to write about in the book. I think you need to change up your routine." "You might have something there, Michael. I will go out tomorrow and see what happens, thanks for the advice." "Always here to help. If you need anything else, you know where to find me." "I know in your office. I think you should take some of your advice and take a long vacation." "Can't, unlike you, I have a business to run." "I will call you later in the week and let you know how things turned out. Bye Michael and thanks again."

The next day, John got up early to work in some training and play time with his dog Suzie. She was a two-old-German Shepherd that John had raised from a pup. Every day, Suzie would follow her master throughout the house, waiting patiently for their playtime to begin. She knew John's writing had to come first, and her time was second. They had spent every day together and never had been apart. That is until today when John left for his outing later that day.

After their one-hour work out, John and Suzie went inside for some refreshments, Suzie to her water bowl and John to the refrigerator for a bottle of water. John then showered and changed to start his outing. He felt guilty leaving Suzie behind, even if it was for a few hours, to do his research. After checking the newspaper for a few things, John closed the front door with Suzie standing there watching him and not understanding what was happening. He refused to look back, knowing it would break his heart.

John decided to have a quick lunch and go see a movie. He picked one that had his favorite actor Jill Amber Green in it. Busy writing all the time, John had missed some of her movies, and thought it was a perfect time to see one. Even his local newspaper gave the movie a good review; why not go see how her movie career had progressed. He had watched Jill on her television series, and enjoyed the character she portrayed on the show, knowing at the time, she would make the jump to movies if given the chance. Jill had showed great talent growing her acting abilities over the years on that show. John wanted to see how she had aged over the years, having a secret crush on the woman.

After getting to the theater and sitting down in the dark room, John's expectations began building waiting for the movie to start. Then the previews began, which even had one of Jill's future movies that were supposed to come out later in the year. John watched and was not impressed, by what he saw. To him it looked like something similar Jill had done in one of her earlier movies. Moments later, the movie he came to see began. John sat back and got comfortable, ready to watch Jill work, hoping she would impress him for the next hour and a half.

As the movie progressed, John watched intently the character Jill portrayed to see how much she had grown over the last eight years. Like so many other movies, this story was all about the leading actor, Jill. After thirty minutes, John realized the movie had no real substance or plot and poor acting. In his opinion, the movie was a dud and not worth seeing. He could not believe Jill had agreed to be in it.

John should have stayed home and not missed time being with Suzie. He could have saved his eight dollars and watched re-runs on TV. Instead, now he sits watching this mind numbing movie his paper called a must see. Unknown to John at the time, the studio was trying to recover some of the money on one of Jill's bad movies by a limited release to certain small movie theaters throughout the country.

John watched in disbelief until the movie was finally over. While leaving, he could not believe the movie he just watched had Jill Amber Green starring in it. In his mind, Jill had mailed in her performance and put forth any acting effort what so ever, only going through the motions saying her lines and waiting for her next scene. John felt robbed by the newspaper, the studio and finally Jill Amber Green.

Later, while having dinner in a local restaurant, John could not get his mind off that movie, not understanding why Jill had agreed to do it. Maybe the studio had paid her so much money; she had no choice but to accept the role knowing the outcome. John thought something must have changed in her life and he wanted to know what.

After stopping to get Suzie a new chew rope after leaving her all alone, John now back on the road, started thinking of reasons why Jill had become what he called a sellout, doing a poor job and still getting paid for it, not caring what people thought while doing the sub-par work. He thought a person should always use their full potential if they were paid. John said to himself, "Maybe Jill should do the public a favor by going into early retirement. She could start a career doing television commercials. At least they did not cost eight dollars to watch."

John took Suzie out to play with her new toy. While she was trying to pull him all around in the front yard, John kept thinking about Jill and her poor performance. He needed some answers about what had happened to Jill, and knew exactly who to call, his good friend Michael.

The next morning before calling Michael, John decided to do some research on the movie he had seen and why the newspaper had endorsed it so highly. Soon learning that Planet Studios own his local newspaper, the maker of the movie. Evidently, the newspaper had to write whatever the studio wanted even if it was not true. Only it did not help the movie receipts, they were below expectations. After researching further, he found out Jill's other movies over the last two years were in a steady decline. In John's mind, the studio had not blamed Jill yet, but they soon would. If her movies kept losing money, the studio would need to find ways to cut costs, then her. The bottom line is the only thing the studio cares about and what have you done for me lately, good or bad determines the employee's outcome.

In his mind, John began seeing a way to solve his problem by maybe helping Jill with hers along the way. To do this, he needed Michael's help and connections in the movie industry to start his next project.

After playing and feeding Suzie, John called Michael for his help. "I have no idea how you came up with this plan, John. But if it will help you solve your problem, I will email all the information to you sometime later today." Michael said. "The idea came from the advice you gave me. Now I have an idea of what to write about." John said. "What, an actress on her way out?" "No. You are a good publisher, but like most of your kind, a terrible judge of people's true gifts in life. Trust me. Jill was born to be an actor." "It is your time. I will handle things on my end." "Fair enough. Look forward to receiving that information."

In the meantime, John did some research of his own. First, he looked up all the titles of Jill's past movies since she left the television series, so he could buy them either on line or in town. After getting into town, bringing Suzie with him this time, John bought everything he could find on Jill in movies and magazines. Like before writing a book, John was preparing himself by gathering all the information before he started writing.

At home, John spent the rest of the day watching Jill's movies and taking notes on each one of them. He would pause the movie when he needed to write something down in order to have a reference as to why the certain scenes did not work in his opinion. It was a slow process but an effective one to use.

Later that day, John read all the magazine articles about Jill to find out about any of her future movie projects. He watched all the extra features on the DVDs, to get more information on how each movie was made from the director's and Jill's point of view. The last thing John did was go on line to watch any interviews Jill had done on television or promoting her movie at the time. He needed to know why people still loved this woman after making so many subpar movies the last few years.

A week later, after Michael sent him everything he could find out about Jill and her studio situation, John started moving forward with his plan. He had two months before Jill's contract was up, which gave him time to write his new book and then try to make contact with her. Now that John had seen and read everything he could find about Jill, an idea popped in his head. A perfect character she could portray to show her true acting abilities and the potential that was deep inside her, which was never exposed.

John's new book was going to be about the fashion industry. Jill had told a reporter in one of her interviews that was her second love. John had watched it on line earlier in the week and later the idea came to him about writing this book, which Michael thought, sounded daring. John remembered as the reporter asked, "Jill, if your acting career ended tomorrow, what would you like to pursue next in life?" Jill said, "It would definitely be something in fashion. As a girl, I dreamed of designing clothes that every average woman can wear."

John thought his new character in the book needed to be strong on the inside like JD was on the outside. Jill would have to grow this character from within to show everyone her true acting strengths, which he thought she could do with the right script and effort on her part. That way the public could see something true and real, a character that had heart and soul. If the plan worked, Jill could turn his book into a movie that she could star and direct. First things first, write the book and wait for a response from Jill.

John used his notes from Jill's past movies to build the right character to use in his book. He wanted to become her toughest critic, but thought she had enough acting talent to overcome any obstacles put before her. John had found out in the latest movies, the directors never gave her a chance to explore her roles, to develop as the movie progressed. He knew how to change all that, knowing a book can go as far and as long as you want, where a movie has time restraints, giving the characters only so much time to make an impression on its viewers

Now that John had a character and story to write about, his writing pages filled up fast. First, he made Jill's character a little timid and weak, unsure of herself and abilities. By the middle and end of the book, she had found her true self and could take on any challenge that came her way. This character reminded John of his friend Michael, except for her sex. It took John six weeks to finish the book, which was faster than anything he had written before. Also, in his opinion, better than anything except his first book with the JD character. Excited about what he had written, John immediately sent the book to Michael through his computer so he could read and give his opinion.

Two days later, Michael called John to discuss the book. Michael said, "When do we go to print?" John said, "So you liked it?" "I think it could be your best work John. The editing department has already gone through it and made a few minor changes. As usual, you have written something I can publish." "Not just yet. First, I need to make contact with Jill." "Good luck with that part of your plan. Let me know when I can move forward." "It will not be long. I am sending Jill the message today." "Good. I heard from one of my contacts that she is going to her studio to discuss a new contract." "What? Why didn't you tell me?" "I just did, John. I found out a few hours ago myself." "I need to let you go. I have a message to send. Talk to you soon Michael."

An hour later, John was ready to send the very important message to Jill's blog. One he hoped would get her attention and a quick response after reading it. He knew from his research Jill never chatted with her fans, thinking it might be the only way he could approach her. First, he wrote out his message on paper, to make sure it had the right things to get her attention. Then he typed it into the computer and was ready to send it to Jill. The final step was to find a catchy screen name to make Jill curious enough to answer his message with an email. Thinking she might have hundreds to go through before reading his, John hoped he was not too late. A minute later, the perfect name came to him, "The Play-Doh Man". He thought that name would definitely get a response from Jill. Since it was noontime, John thought Jill would email him sometime later tonight, thinking she would definitely want to see who sent the message and why.

While waiting, John spent time getting more information on Jill in case she had questions of her own for him to answer. He wanted to be ready for anything she might ask him and be prepared to answer with quick responses. He thought there would only be one chance to chat with her and did not want to blow it by not being prepared. After getting everything ready, he took Suzie out for an extra playtime to help him think of anything he might have forgotten. Playing fetch with his dog helped his thinking process and he needed to be at the top of his game tonight.

Early that evening, there was still no response from Jill. A few doubts entered into John's mind; maybe his whole plan was for nothing. Then he remembered the two-hour time difference between them. He decided to fix dinner for Suzie and him to take his mind off things. John said, "Let's go get our dinner girl." Before he could move, Suzie was already in the kitchen waiting on her master to fill her bowl. After hearing the word dinner, Suzie knew exactly where to go and why.

Chapter 2

Troubled Hollywood Actress

An actor in Hollywood needed to be careful not to be type cast in the movies she starred in by taking the easy way out; doing whatever the studio offered an actor for their movie projects and never questioning or refusing to do any of them. Jill Amber Green had done exactly that, never realizing the consequences it would cost her career until today. Jill's last three movies were remakes of some of her earlier films and not worth seeing according to the box office numbers, which is why she had been called to a meeting at the studio to discuss her new contract and meet the new president recently hired there. Jill thought if her new movies did not screen well, there might not be a new contract or a job at Planet Studios after this meeting.

Jill was sitting all alone at a huge white table; waiting for everyone to show up to start the meeting. Even her agent Miss Paul was late giving Jill something else to worry about as time passed so slowly and the eagerness grew inside her. Then the door opened and Miss Paul walked in the room and took a seat next to her. She could see right away how nervous Jill was and began giving her words of encouragement, to reassure her there was nothing to worry about. Jill felt like a high school student waiting to see the principal after doing something wrong. With three subpar movies and three up in the air, someone had to pay and she knew the blame would fall on her, since she was the one everyone was coming to see.

Jill expressed her concerns to her agent of how she felt. "Do not worry my dear; I will handle these negotiations with this new president. Everything will work itself out, you will see." Miss Paul said.

Jill trusted her agent in all business deals; she decided to take her advice and let her handle things as usual. The woman seemed to know exactly what to say in order to get the best deal for her clients. Even if she did talk her into doing those last three movies hoping for a good outcome for everyone involved. With Jill starring in them, her fans going to see them, and the studio making a profit on them.

Miss Paul kept up giving Jill positive things to think about while she kept shifting in her seat, waiting on the big wigs to show up to get this meeting started. "You are a wonderful actress and a real asset to this studio; they would be foolish to get rid of you." Miss Paul said. Jill smiled at her after hearing that. Still thinking in hindsight, she should have waited and not done those last three movies. By getting pressure from both sides, meaning her agent and the studio, she did the films and received compensation for them. It could be too late to fix the trouble she was in and her career at Planet Studio might be over.

Jill thought being a bad actor was the same as being a bad student, now waiting to receive whatever punishment the studio decided to give her? Now with the executives being late for the meeting, she was definitely in trouble and could feel it while waiting on them to come through that office door.

"I think the studio will want to renegotiate the length and definitely the pay in my new contract." Jill said. "Before jumping to any conclusions, let's wait and see what they offer us. Try to stay positive dear and think what you have accomplished here in the last eight years." Miss Paul said. "I also think the studio will try to recoup their losses from my last three movies." "I believe you pay me to handle these things for you dear. All you need to do is listen and let them speak first and express their concerns. Then we can decide on what we will do next. How does that sound, dear?" "Whatever you think is best, you know I trust you." "Good to hear. Things will turn out right for us. You will soon see."

Jill decided to stay quiet and let her agent handle these negotiations, working her magic the way she had in the past. The only problem with this philosophy, Jill never did any movie roles that could show her true acting abilities as an actor and expand on them. Then Jill's work could be recognized and appreciated by fans and peers; instead being criticized by both for doing subpar movies the last four years. She had dreamt many times about doing a role that no other actor had tried before to show her true capabilities. Unfortunately, the studio was not interested in letting that happen, and were using her for their own financial gains and only cared about the bottom line and the profits they could make while Jill was poplar in the public eye.

All of her earlier films did very well at the box office because of the popularity of the television sitcom she had done. The public had fallen in love with her from the beginning and wanted to see her work in motion pictures. Now her new movies were remakes and not worth releasing to the public, she thought. It was a mistake on her part never questioning the directors as why her scenes had been shorten in the last six movies by following her agent's advice. To follow exactly what the director asked; her job was to do the scenes. Now it was time to pay the price for that decision. Only hoping her new movies did not go straight to DVD, which is a career killer in the industry for any actor.

With Miss Paul controlling all the conversation, Jill started tapping on the huge table with her fingernails to pass the time by while waiting for the executives to make an appearance.

She was anxious to get this meeting started and then find out her outcome.

A few minutes later, the door opened and three men that Jill had never met entered the room. She immediately stopped tapping her nails and sat straight up in her chair, showing the men she was ready to start this meeting. The three men sat down on the other side of the table across from Jill and Miss Paul. The man sitting in the middle introduced himself by saying, "I am Bill Turner, the new president of Planet Studios. The two men to my left and right are my vice presidents here. I am sorry for being late, but we needed time to finish watching one of your latest films, Miss Green. And I have to say, we were not pleased at what we saw." Jill was right; they were going to blame her. "I am very sorry to hear that. To be honest, I did the best job I could with the material and direction given to me. I am happy to hear any suggestions you might have to rectify the situation." Jill said. Miss Paul did not say a word, so she decided to speak up for herself. She was not going to sit back and let this new president put all the blame on her without some fight.

Jill thought having never met this man before, it would be smart to feel him out first and see what type a person he might be. A boss you can get along with or an asshole you would like to walk out on and never look back. For some reason, Jill thought the latter of this man after just meeting him.

"I don't think we have time to go over every bad scene you did, Miss Green. Then explain to you exactly what you did wrong and try to fix it. You see, the studio hired me to make them money. That is what I do best, by cutting out what does not work and saving them money. If need be, I will get rid of anyone or anything that prevents me from doing my job. Do you understand what I am telling you, Miss Green?" "Yes, please continue." I was right, an asshole and I am in big trouble Jill thought.

"We understand perfectly, Mr. Turner. How can we help with the problems you are having? Miss Paul said. "Good to hear, my two vice presidents have come up with some ideas to go over with the both of you." The VP to Bill's right asked, "You have worked here for eight years, is that right Miss Green?" Jill nodded her head yes to the man. Then the VP said, "Time sure flies doesn't." Again, Jill nodded her head yes to the man while waiting for a real question to come out of his mouth, if he had one. Now the other VP said, "You have made fifteen films here at the studio, is that right?" Jill was happy to correct the VP and said, "Sixteen to be exact. Which includes the last three that I just finished."

Bill chimed in by saying, "Well, we have some good news and some bad Miss Green, which one would you like to hear first?" Jill said, "The bad if you don't mind, I would like to get that part over with." "Okay, I have decided to send your last three movies straight to DVD. We here at the studio, cannot afford to lose any more money on your movies and think it is time for some major changes." "Are you sure that is the best way to handle things? My career will take a big hit and any future movies I do will be in question. People might not go see any of my new movies." In her mind, if all three movies went straight to DVD, it would be a death sentence to her career as an actor. "After watching one of those movies today and getting my VP's opinion of the other two, it is definitely the right thing to do. After you did the first one, someone should have stopped the other two from being made, and I guess that is why I was hired." Jill knew then nothing was going to change Bill's mind. She decided to keep quiet for the time being.

Now thinking to herself, only B-list actors go straight to DVD and not on the big screen; she was in that category and did not know how to change it. At least there is still the good news to come. Since she brought it up, Bill decided to go over all the reasons why the studio decided to take her movies to DVD. While this went on, Miss Paul never said a word in Jill's defense. Even if she did have a part in her doing all those bad movies. Bill kept talking about all the costs of making the last three movies, and that studio could lose millions if they released the movies to the public. Jill was thinking about all the ways the studio used her to get every dollar out of what they thought was a sub-par movie.

1. Only movie released that weekend, eliminating competition.
2. Only release the movie to a limited number of cities.
3. Limit the number of movie screens showing the movie.
4. Limit the time the movie is showing.
5. Last, the movie goes straight to DVD.

Debating this with Bill would be a waste of her time. Her last three movies were going straight to DVD. Now in hindsight, she thought those big paychecks for doing the bad movies were not worth it, if you had to sit through this shit storm while being bullied by these three men. Listening to Bill berating her work as if she had no acting experience at all. She had not pick the scripts, directors or the other actors she had to work with, the studio did. Only one person was getting the blame here, her. Jill almost got up and walked out, but before she did, Bill said something she wanted to hear, the good news. "We at the studio have decided to sign you to a new contract. One year instead of three years. I know all your other contracts were for three, but you have to agree that one year is better than being fired and if your work shows improvement, we can renegotiate your contract."

One of the VPs started explaining the new conditions in more detail to Jill. Like getting better actors to work with her in future movies. Another one of the conditions would be cutting her screen time along with her pay. All three men were talking to Jill as if her career was already over and she was dead. Even though she was still breathing right in front of them. That is why this whole experience reminded her of high school and going to the principal's office. Like a good girl, Jill remained quiet as Bill and the VPs went on explaining all the new conditions to her. Only nodding a few times to show them she was paying attention, Jill wanted to be anywhere else except here. Finally, the three men left the room so Jill and her agent could discuss her options.

"Well, what do you think I should do?" asked Jill. Miss Paul said, "I don't like any of these new terms any better than you do, but what choice do we have. I think you should sign the new contract and keep working here for one more year. Then make a decision on what you want to do after this new contract is up. Don't forget, I too am taking a pay cut as well my dear." "40% is a huge pay cut to take. Not to mention the screen time I will be losing." "Yes, I agree. With your three new movies going to straight to DVD, we do not have much to bargain with this time. At least you will stay in the public eye by signing the new contract." "Why didn't you say something in my defense while those three men were ganging up on me? I kept waiting for you to say something to defend me. I believe that is what I pay you for." "It would not have done any good. You could see they had their minds made up. In my opinion, you can accept their terms or they will fire you, Jill." "I think they are already starting to phase me out. First, by the lack of work and reducing my pay. Then they will find someone to replace me. I believe a younger version of myself. Even before this new contract is up."

Now came the million-dollar decision, did Jill want to do the bit parts they were offering her or quit. "I think you should take the deal and sign the new contract. Leave here when you are ready and on your own terms. Who knows, you might be on Broadway next year my dear." "I don't think doing any stage work in front of a live audience is in my future." "Then we need to accept what the studio is offering us. They have been good to us over the years, now it is our turn to return the favor." "If that is what you think, then I will agree to sign the contract, but only with a 30% pay cut. We should at least negotiate a little. All this is not my fault." "I agree. Now let me explain it to them and get that 10% for us. We have next year to get you back where you belong, one of Hollywood's top leading actors." She then smiled at Jill, and she smiled back at her. Thinking her agent was in the room looking out for her best interest. The thought never entered her mind that Miss Paul had other reasons to get Jill to sign the new contract.

The men returned to the room right on time like they had been listening at the door. They sat down in the same seats right across from Jill and Miss Paul. Bill started things off by asking, "Well, what have you decided Miss Green?" Jill looked over at the man and said, "It would be a pleasure to continue working here at Planet Studios for one more year but at a 30% pay cut." "I see. The contract we have will have to be changed, this will take another day." "If I walk now, what will it cost you for future movies without me. Well, what have you decided Mr. Turner." "I see we have a tough negotiator here." The VPs laughed at what Bill said. "Alright, I will have the new contract drawn up later today for you to sign tomorrow morning. Will 10:00 be okay for you to come in?" "That will be fine by me. See you at 10:00 sharp." This time she did not want to be the only one in the room waiting for everyone to show up.

Jill thanked everyone and got up to leave when she noticed Miss Paul was not gathering her things. She asked, her agent, "Are you not coming with me?" "No dear, I need to stay behind to discuss another client of mine with Mr. Turner. You go ahead without me. I will see you tomorrow morning to get your contract signed." She did get up to give Jill a hug goodbye. Jill left the room, not thinking anything might be wrong. A red flag should have popped in her mind. Instead, she was thinking about the extra 10% she got for herself in the new contract.

On the drive home, Jill called her BFF Carrie on her Bluetooth. She trusted Carrie in all her business decisions. The two of them had been best friends for 14 years and started their careers in television together. The show they worked on lasted six years and they became very close friends. After Jill made the move to movies, Carrie decided to stay in television by doing some writing and producing on other TV shows. Later, Carrie got her own television series, which just finished wrapping up its first season. She was waiting to hear if the network would pick it up for another year. The answer would come sometime that week.

Jill started the conversation by catching Carrie up on her meeting at the studio. Telling her all the details about the new contract and meeting the asshole, Bill Turner. Telling Carrie, she had decided to sign the new contract with the reduced pay and shortened screen time, thinking her future in the movie industry might be over soon. At least another year would keep her in the public eye. Well, that was what her agent, Miss Paul recommended. Carrie said, "I thought all your contracts were for three years, not one." "They were. Now the studio is only offering me one. Now my last three movies are going straight to DVD. After watching them, they have decided not to release them on the big screen. If things do not improve in my future movies, they will let me go." "What did Miss Paul say about all this?" "Surprisingly, very little. During the meeting while the three assholes gave me hell about my movies, she never said a word. Then when it was time to decide about my new contract, she told me to accept their terms and sign the contract." "In front of the three assholes?" "No, they had left the room so we could discuss the contract in private. Miss Paul thinks we can improve my situation over the next year and I will be back on top as a leading actress." "Well at least you still have a job, Jill. My television show has not been picked up for another year." "I still have tonight to think about my deal. Maybe it is time to move on and find something else to do with my life. The news media is going to have a field day with all these updates with my career. They will probably label me the "DVD Queen"."

Carrie knew what it meant when a movie went straight to DVD; Jill did not have to explain that part to her. She also could tell in Jill's voice, her friend was hurting about her situation. She tried to cheer her up by saying, "Jill, everyone has a few bad movies in their career. Do not let this bother you, girl. The studio is offering you another year." Jill said, "I agree, but three bad movies in a row. Talk about bad luck. In the old days, the studio would shelve the bad movies. At least my diehard fans will get to see what I have been up to lately even if it is on DVD." "Hey, why don't you come over here and have dinner with us. David and Molly would love to see you."

Carrie was trying to cheer her friend up by offering the dinner invitation. Jill was thinking over the invite when Carrie added this, "Jill, we can get drunk afterwards like the old days and forget about your bad day, girl." "Thank you for the dinner invite – drunk fest dear friend, but I think I need to go home and get in the tub for a long hot soak, and forget about this horrible day. A bubble bath with a large glass of wine should do it for me." Jill said. "Okay then, I guess we will be drinking alone in different places tonight. If you need anything girl, you know where we are."

Unknown to Jill at the time her life was about to change forever by answering a simple message sent by an unknown fan.

Chapter 3

The Chat

After arriving home, Jill was in no mood to cook herself dinner. Instead, she heated up some left overs out of the fridge to save time. Then she opened a bottle of her favorite wine to let it breathe. After that meeting, a bottle of wine should put her in a non-caring mood and able to relax and forget all about the troubles she faced today.

While her dinner cooled off a bit, Jill went into the bathroom, lit a few candles and prepared her bubble bath. When she finished eating her dinner and cleaned up the kitchen, Jill returned to the bathroom with the bottle of wine and a glass that she put on the side of the tub. She checked the temperature of her bath water, finding it just right. With the water ready, she poured herself another glass of wine and then got undressed to slip into the waiting tub with her wine glass in hand. Which by the way was not a normal size glass, it only took three fill ups to empty the large bottle.

About twenty minutes later, Jill filled her glass a third time all the way to the rim, careful not to spill a precious drop. She thought to herself, maybe I could get a job at a winery if my movie career ends. I do believe I am an expert in filling up a wine glass if I say so myself. While all the hot water was working to relax her muscles, the wine she drank did the same to her brain. Letting her feel no pain at the time and enjoying her bubbles without a care in the world.

After the water started turning cold, and all the bubbles were almost gone, Jill decided to get out of the tub to dry off and then go work on her computer before going to bed. She was feeling a little drunk at the time and in a much better mood than an hour ago. After putting on her nightgown, she turned on her computer to check her fan website, to see what her true fans had written. Sometimes the messages sent could change her mood from bad to good after reading them. Making her feel proud of what she had accomplished in her career over the years. Her fans knew exactly what to say to cheer her up when she was having a bad day like this one. Jill had one rule about answering them, never to carry on chats with any of her fans. She only gave quick and short responses making sure she kept her distance, knowing that there were crazy people in this world that could do her harm. She did not want to get too close to any of them for that to happen.

In the past, there used to be hundreds of messages sent each day; but now with her career slipping, there were fewer for her to respond back to the last two years. Jill thought box-office receipts of her movies were not the only thing that had been shrinking; her fan base also was in decline. Carrie had told her, everyone has setbacks in their careers and maybe this was her time. Even though she felt it was something more than setbacks. With having one failed marriage and a few bad relationships, her personal life was not fairing any better than her professional one. Jill thought by answering some of the messages, her mood had to get better than what she was feeling before coming home. Little did she know in a matter of minutes, everything in her life was about to change forever. Her future was only a few clicks away as she began typing on her laptop answering her fans.

All the messages were saying the same things, about how much her fans loved her movies and could not wait to see her next one. None of them knew at the time her next three movies were going to be on DVD instead of in movie theaters. Then she would know how much her fans truly loved her work. Some fans would ask when her next movie going to be out. Was she going to do another comedy or something different in her next movie? Jill kept answering them with quick responses. Thinking to herself, that these fans still loved her and her work, even though they had not seen her last three movies yet. They were her true diehard fans; thinking even if she portrayed Jane Fonda as "Hanoi Jane" in a movie, they would still pay to go see her in it. All these emails were very uplifting and had Jill on a different kind of high than the wine she had drank earlier. The feeling was short-lived, now she started reading a very different kind of message altogether. A first one of its kind that had ever appeared on her computer before.

This message expressed exactly how this person felt about her past, present and future work in the movie industry. It gave a list of reasons of why this person was so disappointed in her for doing so many bad movies lately; and knew the next three she just finished were going straight to DVD, which was not public knowledge. Jill had only found that out today in her meeting at the studio. This person did not understand how she could do such a poor job in each one of her movies, and thought it was inexcusable because of the expense to go see them. The message went on to explain that she had failed to do a good job as an actor in some of her latest movies. It was so unprofessional of her choosing to do them in the first place, only to receive a huge payday on them. This person was glad that her next three movies were going straight to DVD. With her having such great talent and doing such subpar work was where the three movies belonged and needed to go.

To portray Jill in such a manner only hurt her as an actor and showed poor judgment. If she only did it for the money, we know what that makes her, a complete sellout. The message ended by giving an email address if Jill wanted to respond to any or all comments. If she might want to justify herself for all her past work at being a so-called Hollywood actor, she could reply at any time with her response.

The message that John sent was his way of getting Jill to break her own rule on emailing her fans to have a chat. He knew how harsh he had to be in order to get a response from her. By insulting Jill and her work, he thought his plan of getting an email response should work. She would want to defend herself and her work. John knew from his research, that Jill was a proud person; her career was her life.

Jill could not believe what she had read from this last message. It hurt her to the core even if some of it was true. Thinking how negative and hurtful this person was who sent her this message. She read it over again to make sure she did not miss anything. One part she did miss, which was about accepting roles that were beneath her acting abilities. She could not stop herself; it was like a drug that was making her read it, taking in every word involving her life and career. For the first time someone had actually told her about how they felt and why. Not trying to hide anything, the message was harsh, very hurtful, and to the point. That was why Jill kept on reading it; thinking about the statements that were right in front of her. She felt her movies were bad, there was no questioning that, but to call her a sellout was only being hurtful. Even if it was straight and to the point, this person could not understand what she had been though to get where she was today. One statement said, what was she thinking doing those movies, or was she? Finally, Jill read what was at the bottom of the page. Which said, if you care to respond I am at your service, the

"Play-Doh Man". He would be waiting for a response from her if she felt like giving one.

While Jill was reading this very constructive message, John was on the phone with Michael getting some last-minute information about Jill's contract signing at the studio. Michael explained to him everything he had found out through his contacts at Planet Studios about Jill's meeting today. Then John told him to keep the information coming, anything he could find out might help his plan succeed if not now, than maybe later. Even though Michael still did not know John's entire plan, he agreed to help him out as usual. Later, John would fill him in on the rest of his plan. At least, they were working on something together and both seemed to be having some fun while doing it. Michael was glad to see his friend excited about something besides his writing and his dog learning a new trick. John now felt like he had a connection with Jill, which gave him something new in his life.

Back in Hollywood, Jill was staring at her computer screen, still very upset with the message sent by this so-called Play-Doh Man. It was the first time someone had ever attacked her personally with such strong abusive words that made her feel worthless like a piece of trash you throw away every day. Her good mood was now gone and so were the effects of all the wine she drank earlier. She was sitting there not sure how to respond or if she wanted to after reading it one more time. Already upset she said what the hell. I will break my one rule and answer this critical son of a bitch. Before she did, Jill opened another bottle of wine in case she might need it during her chat with this Play-Doh Man. She was ready to answer some of his questions and had a few of her own for him to answer as well. Now we will see if he has the guts to respond to some of my questions. Jill thought as she poured her fourth glass of wine and began typing her email to this Play-Doh Man.

John looked at his computer screen and saw he had a new email from the one and only, "Starlet". He knew it was from Jill Amber Green. She had made up her own screen name to go with his. John could not help but smile when he saw it. Now his plan could go in motion and their fun could begin. Thinking the "Starlet" would be no match for the "Play-Doh Man". John had prepared himself for any question Jill might ask him in their chat. She had no idea what questions he might ask; the Play-Doh Man had the upper hand. So let their chat begin. First, he said those three magic words to Suzie so she could go to bed and not stay in the room waiting for him. He knew his chat with Jill might take a while and it would not be fair to make her wait. She was ready to go any way from all their workouts and playtime together from today.

John looked down at Suzie and said, "It could be a while girl, time to go night, night without me. After she left the room, he began getting his computer ready to send Jill an email. Now that his plan was working, he could not miss this opportunity to have a chat with the "Starlet". John read Jill's email first before sending one of his own. It read as follows:

Starlet: Well, well, what do we have here? A mister knows it all. What makes you such an expert on all my movies and me? What do you know about the movie industry anyway, Play-Doh Man? Answer me that, if you can. Are you someone who can only criticize a person and not have anything to back it up with some real facts?

Play-Doh: Not an expert or a know it all. It is easy for anyone to see that your career has been sliding in a downward way for the last two years. All you have to do is check the box office receipts. Maybe it is time for you to get off your butt and do something about it by picking the right movie roles for a change. I think we both know what will happen to your career in the near future if you do not, there will not be one.

Starlet: Who in the hell do you think you are and are talking to, mister? That is, if you are a man? I am the one who is starring in the movies, not you. You might want to check your facts at who works for Planet Studios. I think it is I and not you. Unless you are willing to pay me what they do, go to hell.

Play-Doh: I know exactly who I am, a person who is trying to help you if you let me. I do have one question Starlet, have you been drinking tonight? There is no reason to curse at me, Starlet.

Starlet: My alcohol consumption is none of your business, Play-Doh. I am beginning to think you know nothing about my acting abilities. Nor even how the movie industry works.

Play-Doh: I believe you have many acting skills and hope one day you utilized them to their full potential. All you need is a different direction and a lot better material to work with while doing your movies. That is where I would be able to help you, Starlet.

Starlet: And who are you to help me? A person who calls himself the Play-Doh Man is going to help me. Please, tell me your grand plan.

Play-Doh: You have to ask nicely first, in order to receive my help. Otherwise you can keep on doing all those dull, put me to sleep movies you and your studio keep producing.

Jill, who already had a bad day with her meeting at the studio, was now experiencing something worse, her chat with this "Play-Doh Man; which was turning out to be pure hell and frustration because she thought he was playing games with her which she was not in the mood when starting this chat. She thought for a moment to turn off her computer and go to bed. Then forget all about this asshole and his smartass comments toward her. Jill's curiosity got the better of her and she decided to keep chatting with him to find out why he wanted to help her. While Jill was doing all this thinking, Play-Doh sent her another email.

Play-Doh: You are right about one thing Starlet, it is your business what you do on your own time. Drink as much as you like if it helps you cope with your present situation. We both can agree that box office receipts do not lie. Your movies have been declining over the last two years. Have you signed your new contract with the studio yet? I hope you have not before I get a chance to help you.

Starlet: After reading your last email and the horrible day I experienced and all your earlier criticism, I would be glad you are not standing in front of me right now, Play-Doh. If you were, I would kick you square in the balls and then tell you to go F… yourself Mr. Know it all. Are there any more comments you have for me?

He knew their chat was going in the wrong direction and needed to do something positive before Jill decided to end it. He wanted her to ask for his help, not threaten him with physical violence. Maybe by adding some humor of his own to calm things down might work. If he made Jill too mad, she would end their chat.

Play-Doh: If I were standing right in front of you, I would let you kick me anywhere you like, Starlet. That would be the best screen you would have done in years. Since I am not, how about you asking for my help, instead using such bad language and offering to do me physical harm. A real lady does not talk or act this way.

Starlet: Forgive me for my brief outburst. You have to understand that I have worked very hard to get where I am today. I do not think you have any idea of what I have been through to become a movie actor. Play-Doh, do you even know what it takes to make a movie, or stayed to the very end of a movie and read all the credits as they rolled up the screen; to see exactly how many people are involved in making one?

Play-Doh: Let me say first, thank you for your apology. Now to answer your question about making a movie and what is required of you and not everyone else. I believe your job requires you to memorize your lines from a movie script, and then repeat them in front of a camera. Never questioning anything or giving your opinion or insight while making the movie no matter how bad or how silly they might seem to you at the time because you are being paid to do it. In my opinion that is not acting, but only having conversations in front of a movie camera. That is why in your last six movies someone might call you a sellout to the system, a puppet for the studio to use. I do believe you have real heart and soul in your acting and might become something great if given the right material. Now, to answer your last question, no I have not stayed to watch all the credits after a movie ends. I thought we were chatting about your job performance and not anyone else.

Starlet: My studio still needs me; today they offered me a new contract. I am not someone's puppet to play with; I am though still a damn good actor.

Play-Doh: Then prove it, not to me, but for yourself. Stop letting the studio pull your strings and you pull your own for a change. How about taking on a roll that will show everyone what kind of an actor you really are. Instead of doing those dull movies the studio keeps getting you to do, why not try doing something brand new. They will only keep you until the public stops going to see your movies. When you are no longer of any use to them, they will get rid of you and find someone else to replace you.

Starlet: There is no reason for you to keep on insulting me. Remember, the studio is paying me to do those movies. The great roles are limited and hard to come by. You have to be lucky to get a chance to do one in your acting career.

Play-Doh: Maybe I have one of those roles you are talking about right here with me. If you asked me for my help, you might find out, or you can keep on working for that circus you call a studio. They will always have more dull material for you to do. Your studio never seems to run out of it.

Starlet: My studio is not some kind of circus. I think you should check your facts, mister. My studio makes money off their movies. At least I am doing movies, even if you think they are bad. That is why the studio offered me a new contract for next year.

Play-Doh: Yes, I heard for only one year. I thought your contracts were always for three years. I do not think you should waste your time working for those clowns. It is true their movies make money, but in the future, they are not getting any more of mine. Believe me, before I go see my next movie, I will check to see who made it. Even if the studio makes money off a movie, does not mean the movie is any good or worth seeing.

Starlet: Then what do you suggest I do? If I do not work for them, then who?

Play-Doh: Starlet, stop jumping though their hoops and jump through your own for a change. In order to do that, you will have to ask me for my help. I am the one who is trying to help you, not them.

Starlet: Now, what in the hell are you talking about? First puppets, then circus clowns and now jumping through hoops. I think it is time you tell me exactly who you are and why you want to help me. Funny words will not cut it anymore, Play-Doh. I am beginning to feel a little tired of this conversation. Describing my career as if I was working in some kind of a circus and not at a movie studio.

Play-Doh: You are right for the first time tonight; your career is in trouble, Starlet. There is still time for me to help you fix it. By asking for my help. I think it is time for you to run your own career for a change.

Starlet: Ok then, help me understand how you are going to help me. Tell me your great plan on how to fix my career. That is if you can, Play-Doh Man.

Play-Doh: That does not sound too sincere to me that you even want my help, and you call yourself an actor. Come on, show me what you are made of Starlet by swallowing some of your pride instead of that wine and ask me the right way.

Instead, Jill swallowed down the last of her wine that was in her glass before sending her next email response. She thought for a moment and then sent this to the Play-Doh man.

Starlet: Will you please help me "Mr. Play-Doh Man" to understand how you are going to single-handedly save my career and in the process make me a better actor, so maybe I can win an Academy award for my next movie performance. Otherwise, my career is doomed for the shitter without any of your gracious help.

Play-Doh: Much better, although we will have to work on your use of profanity in future conversations. I do not think a real lady uses such bad language. It could get you in trouble one day. All right, before I help you, go ahead and refill your wine glass. I am sure you emptied it before sending that last email.

Starlet: Hey, can you see in my room somehow? How did you know my wine glass is empty? Are you using your webcam to watch me right now?

Play-Doh: No. Lucky guess and no to the third question. Hope that answers everything.

Starlet: It did. Go ahead and tell me your grand plan while I refill my glass one last time for the night.

Play-Doh: Okay then, but I need you to think about what I am about to tell you before jumping to any conclusions. You need to let it sink in first before deciding to do anything. I suggest you sleep on it tonight. Because what I am about to tell you will be a big change in your life if you decide to do it. Are you ready for my advice and help, Starlet?

Starlet: Do not try to scare me now, fire away. I am ready and able to learn something new even if it is from you. So go ahead and teach me something, Play-Doh.

Play-Doh: I have four major points for you to think about, Starlet. Here they are and I hope you consider each one of them carefully before deciding.

1. First, fire your agent. She is not helping you or your career by working for both sides. The woman does not have a clue of your true potential as an actor. Going along and allowing you do all those bad movies proves the woman has bad judgment and only in this for the money. Your agent could care less if you become a better actor as long as she gets her commission.

2. Starlet, start doing the movie roles that appeal to you for a change. Something that has your heart and soul in each one of them for people to see. Movies that can portray it on the screen and you will feel it deep inside yourself while making them. I know somewhere in your mind you have thought about doing such a movie. One that could challenge your acting abilities.

3. In order for you to do what is in point number two, you will have to start directing and producing your own movies in the future. That means starting a new production company run by you. This will give you the control to make these types of movies.

4. If point number three is too much for you to handle alone, then get some more people involved that you trust to help make it happen. Well, that is all my advice to get your career back on track. I said it is a lot to take in. Well, what do you think of my plan?

Starlet: Have you completely lost your F...... mind? Open my own production company. Make my own movies with my own money. Now who has been drinking? Production companies take a lot of money to start up. Not to mention all the people and time to run them. You are way off about my agent, Miss Paul. She has been with me since the beginning of my career. Your help is so far-fetched and laughable; it is out of the question. I think you are insane for even suggesting your four points.

Play-Doh: Believe me I am sane. Remember, I wanted you to sleep on this before deciding. With your own production company, you will be in charge for a change. You get to make all the decisions about what kind of movies you want to make. The cost of freedom and creative change does not come cheap. You leave this world the same way you came, with absolutely nothing. When you are gone, someone else will spend all the money you have saved up over the years. Now let us discuss your so-called agent of fourteen years, I suggest you buy a pet; the animal you pick will be more loyal to you. Because the animal will love you unconditionally until it dies. Anyway, my source tells me that your agent has worked out her own deal with Mr. Bill Turner, even if you change your mind and not sign the contract tomorrow. You can always hire someone else to look out for your business interest. I would suggest an attorney rather than an agent to make sure all your legal business is also covered. If you give anyone too much control over your life, it could only lead to one thing; their best interest over yours.

Starlet: I do not believe you about Miss Paul. Who is this source?

Play-Doh: My source does not matter right now. Helping you before you make a huge mistake does. So answer me this, today at the studio did your agent come with you, or did she meet you there later? Did she stay behind when the meeting was over? Perhaps to discuss another client of hers with Bill Turner.

Starlet: Yes, she came in after I was already there and stayed behind when I left. How would you know all that?

Play-Doh: I told you, I have a source. He told me that Miss Paul is working behind your back to get you to sign that one-year deal. Her behavior at the meeting, confirms to me that she is playing both sides to get the best deal for herself and all the other clients she represents. Remember, you are only one of her many clients. This means her commission for each of your movies will be a lot more if you sign that new contract. Then some of her other clients will be working with you in the movies.

Starlet: I still want to know your source before I can believe anything about what you are saying. Miss Paul has never given me a reason not to trust her.

Play-Doh: That was in the past when your movies were making money. Now that they are not, things have changed for both of you. It does not matter who my source is, she will tip her hand at the meeting tomorrow. All you need to do is wait and see for yourself if I am telling the truth. Then you can decide who is really trying to help you, her or me. All I ask is that you keep an open mind and watch for the signs that something is not right.

Starlet: I am not sure what to believe after hearing all this. What I am supposed to watch for at the meeting tomorrow. Care to give me a hint since you have a source, and I do not. I hate to make the wrong decision and take the easy way out and stay their puppet if I missed the sign that everyone in the room was trying to screw me over, including my agent of fourteen years.

Play-Doh: I will help you with that part. At your meeting tomorrow, make sure to arrive twenty minutes early or late, so you are the first or last one in the room. Then sit at one of the ends of the table, to watch everyone in the room. Making sure Bill Turner and Miss Paul will to sit across from one another. Then you can see both their faces at the same time, to see any reaction they might have when you start asking your own questions. Trust me there will be a reaction and then you will see who is working for whom.

Starlet: Are you some kind of spy? The way you came up with this plan so quickly makes me think you might be one.

Play-Doh: No, but I have had some dealings with people like Mr. Turner and Miss Paul in the past. I suggest you sleep on all this and take something for that possible headache you might wake up with after all that wine you drank tonight.

Starlet: Layoff my wine drinking, Play-Doh. Remember, what I do on my personal time is my business. Thank you for the tip, I will take something before I go to bed. Will I be able to reach you tomorrow if I need to chat?

Play-Doh: Yes, I will be right here through the whole process if you need me. Since I started all this, it is the least I can do until it is finished.

Starlet: Okay then, I will contact you if I need your help. Thanks for trying to open my eyes, I will think about everything we discussed and consider it carefully. I am not sure what will happen tomorrow, at least you have warned me.

Play-Doh: You are welcome, Starlet. It has been a real pleasure chatting with you. I hope you have a good night's sleep and no headache in the morning. Good luck tomorrow at your meeting, in case I do not hear from you again.

They both ended the chat by turning off their computers at the same time. It was one in the morning at John's house and eleven in the evening at Jill's, both were past their usual bedtimes. The next day was going to be a long one for each. With Jill wondering what she was going to do at her meeting and John thinking about the same thing, knowing he could not help her from Oakland, TN.

John got up from his desk and went into his bedroom, exhausted from his long day and his late-night chat with Jill Amber Green. He got into bed with Suzie joining him by curling up at the foot of the bed by his feet. Soon both were fast asleep, with Suzie dreaming about playing fetch, and John dreaming about the Starlet. Knowing she was at a crossroads in her life and would have to make a major decision of what to do about it tomorrow at her meeting. At least he got a chance to warn her before it was too late.

Chapter 4

New Beginnings

Even after taking some aspirin before going to bed, Jill still woke up the next morning with a bad headache and a very dry mouth. Maybe that second bottle of wine was not such a good idea after all. She quickly tried to resolve the problem by taking even more aspirin and drinking a large glass of water. After getting dressed, Jill checked her computer to make sure last night was not some kind of weird dream and quickly found it was not. Seeing the emails were real and now she had a huge decision to make at her meeting in a few hours.

Before leaving, Jill decided to call Carrie to tell her about the Play-Doh Man and their chat from last night. After reaching her, Jill explained about the harsh message sent by Play-Doh. Then why she chatted with him last night. Carrie asked, "I thought you never chatted with your fans on the computer, Jill?" Jill said, "I never have before, but this man's message hurt and intrigued me at the same time, so I answered it by sending an email. One thing led to another and we chatted for a couple hours. He seemed to have an answer for every one of my questions, Carrie. As if he knew exactly what I was going to ask beforehand." Carrie said, "Sounds a little weird to me. Anyway you might know him?" "I don't think so. This man even knew about my meeting yesterday at the studio and certain things that happened during and after it. I tried to get his real name or a phone number, but he only wants to communicate on the computer by email." "Still sounds weird to me, Jill. I do like the part where you will only be talking to him on your computer, which sounds safe. I mean he still could be a dangerous person. Not knowing his intentions yet, it is best to be careful girl."

Jill hesitated and then said, "I believe he is trying to help me for some reason Carrie; by warning me about the studio and Miss Paul working together to take advantage of my current situation. I am not sure what I should do, that is why I am calling." "Why do you think Miss Paul is working against you?" asked Carrie. "Play-Doh said for her own financial gain and to get her other clients contracts signed at Planet Studios." "Do you believe him?" "I am not sure yet. He told me a way to find out for myself. What do you think I should do, sign for one more year or take Play-Doh's advice and quit?" "Jill, it is your life and career. I think whatever you decide, even if it is opening your own production company, I will support and help you any way I can. Look, you are stronger than you give yourself credit. If a total stranger believes you can do it than so do I." "Okay then, answer me this? What did you think about my last two movies?"

Carrie thought carefully before saying this, "I hope you do not take this the wrong way, but both were subpar and a little boring to me." Jill said, "Play-Doh said the exact same thing. I appreciate your honesty, Carrie. I know it was hard for you to tell me that." "It was, Jill. I have to say, the first ten movies you did were great. Each one was a little better than the last. For some reason, your last three went the opposite way. It could be the scripts." "That is a nice way to say I got lazy for choosing them." "Girl, I am not trying to imply anything of the sort. I know how hard you work, firsthand, from all our time on television together." "Anyway, Play-Doh said to get off my butt and do something about it." "I am starting to like this Play-Doh guy the more you talk about him. Hey, is he single?" "Why are you asking me that?" "Not for me, girl." "Carrie, will you please give up trying to find me mister right?" "Not till you are happily married like me." "I have to get ready for my meeting, any last minute advice before I let you go?" "Yes, if Miss Paul is trying to screw you over, than fire her ass in front of everybody, that way you have plenty of witnesses in case she tries to come after you later for more money. Like when you become very successful running your own production company." "So you think like Play-Doh, I should open my own company?" "I never said that, but it is always good to CYA in case you do." "Bye Carrie, call you when I have something to tell." "Good luck today girl, I will be waiting to hear from you and drive safe."

Before leaving her house, Jill wanted a quick bite and a quick chat with the Play-Doh Man to get some last minute advice he might have for her. Carrie was not much help and she had a few more questions answered. First, she heated up a raisin bagel and then headed for the computer to send an email to him. Jill typed on her computer while holding the bagel in her mouth, which was a sight the Play-Doh man was missing out with the Starlet multi-tasking by getting two things done at once because she was now in a hurry.

John's computer gave off a signal, letting him know he had a new email. He had turned on that feature in case Jill wanted to send him one, so he could be ready to respond back. Looking at the time, he knew she needed to leave soon.

Starlet: If you are there Play-Doh, I need your help. Please respond back if you see this. I only have a few minutes before I have to leave.

Play-Doh: Then let us begin. Fire away with any questions you might have Starlet; I am ready to answer them in short responses.

Starlet: I am not sure what will happen today. I still might take their offer, or quit my job at Planet Studios. Anything else you would like to tell me to help me make up my mind.

Play-Doh: At the meeting, ask anything that you need answered before signing your contract. If something seems strange or out of place, try to find out why. If they will not give you an answer, then push for one. I will give you some examples to use today.

Starlet: I have a pen and paper ready, fire away with your advice.

John sent her some examples to use on his next email and Jill wrote them down on a legal pad.

Starlet: Thank you for your help. I will take these questions with me and use them at the meeting at the proper time. Is there anything else I should know before I go?

Play-Doh: In the room, watch the people and their reactions while you are asking your questions, to see if they give anything away. Their faces will tell you all you need to know. You should leave now in order to get that seat at the end of the table. I suggest you watch Miss Paul the most. Your agent is the weak link, she is the one trying to betray you and this is something new to her. She will also be wondering why you are asking so many questions when you already decided to sign the contract yesterday. Last thing, search inside yourself for what you want to do, continue working there or move on to do something else. I will be here if you need me, good luck Starlet.

Starlet: That is a lot of good advice. Glad I decided to email you. I will contact you when I have any news. Bye for now and thanks for my list.

John had no choice but to wait for the outcome, even though he had a strong feeling what was about to transpire. He decided to call Michael and tell him to go ahead with the publication of his new book. His plan was coming together and he needed to be ready on his end.

After reaching him, Michael said, "The book will be ready for release next week. I might add ahead of schedule. Anything else you need me to do?" John said, "Nothing right now, but I will contact you know later today after I find out what has transpired, Michael. Talk to you soon."

The traffic was backed up which meant Jill was not going to be the first person in the room. While waiting, she played out the meeting in her head. It was like taking on a part in a movie, with Jill as the main character playing out a scene. The VP's and Miss Paul were the other characters in the scene opposite her. Jill was having some fun playing this game, while waiting for the traffic to start moving. Only this was not a game but her life that everyone was screwing with to have control over.

Instead of arriving thirty minutes early, Jill got to the meeting twenty minutes late. Miss Paul was sitting on one side of the table and the two VPs sitting on the other side directly across from her, leaving the seat at the end of the table wide open, which Jill quickly took. Ignoring Miss Paul as she was suggesting a seat next to her.

While one of the VPs pulled out Jill's new contract from his briefcase, Jill did the same with her legal pad from her large purse, with both of them setting the items down on the table at the same time. Jill could see a surprised look on all three of their faces after the legal pad was set on the table. All of them could see there was writing on the top page but could not make out what it said. Each knew now this contract signing was not going be as easy. Jill asked the VP to hand her the contract so she could read it over before signing it. Miss Paul told her there was no need to read it over, she had already read it and everything was in order. Jill ignored her agent and accepted the contract from the VP as he handed it to her and she began reading it over. Jill looked up now and then to gauge any reaction the three people might be having. She could tell by their faces that they were upset and wanted her to hurry up and sign the contract. When Jill finished reading the contract, she told the VPs there were a few questions she would like to ask. The VP sitting closest to Jill told her to proceed and ask her questions, which they would try to answer. Before Jill could ask her first question, Miss Paul gave one of her own for Jill to answer.

By saying, "Dear, what has gotten into you? Yesterday, you were ready to sign. Now, you have all these questions." "Yesterday was then, this is now. I have had a night to sleep on all of this. If you do not mind, I want to ask my questions. After all this is my life and what I will be doing for the next year." said Jill. Miss Paul did not have a comeback for that and let her proceed. Jill looked down at her legal pad and asked her first question without any more delays.

"If my next movie with these so called stronger cast members does poorly at the box office will my pay get cut again?" The other VP said, "If your next movie does not make our expectations, then yes, there will be another pay cut." "How much of a pay cut are we talking about?" "Not much, only ten percent." "Does that cut in pay include the entire cast and my agent, or only just me?" "Well, that will be a decision for Mr. Turner to make at the proper time. Why go into this now? Your next movie has not even been made yet." "Because, it says in this new contract that you can renegotiate my pay any time during the next year. By the way, I like to know who all these strong cast members that I will be working with." The

VP who handed Jill the contract said, "We do not have that information, Mr. Turner is the one who knows who will be in your next movie." "Then I suggest we get Mr. Turner in this room so he can answer my question." "I believe Mr. Turner has a very busy day, he might not be able to come." "Why don't you call him and find out or I suggest we reschedule this meeting for another time." The other VP got on his phone and called Mr. Turner to ask him to join them in the conference room at Jill's behest.

While waiting for Bill to come, Miss Paul asked Jill, "I do not understand what is going on with you dear? Why are you being so difficult?" Jill said, "I do not think asking who I will be working with in the future, is being difficult. Nor, asking if my pay will be reduced again if my next movie is not successful." "Jill, your fellow cast members will be decided when a movie is ready to be made. I do not see what difference it makes right now. I think you should stop causing trouble and sign this new contract before they change their minds and not offer you another year." "I think I will take my chances and ask Bill a few questions." Jill knew right then that Play-Doh was right, Miss Paul was working for the studio's interest instead of hers. She had gone this far, why not see it through.

Bill Turner entered the room with a very stern look on his face as he quickly walked over to the table and took a seat next to his VPs. Everyone in the room knew he was not happy being called into this meeting for a simple contract signing which Jill had agreed to do yesterday. Bill looked over at his VPs and waited for a response as to why they needed him in the room. One of the VP's quickly spoke up and told Bill all of Jill's concerns about her new contract and that she wanted to know the other cast members in her next movie.

Bill turned to Jill and told her three actors names that would be working with her in the next movie. All of them she recognized as being Miss Paul's clients. Jill realized the studio had plans of building up these three actors careers by giving them equal screen time in her next movie. Once again, Play-Doh had given her the right information. Over the next year, all these people in this room wanted to make whatever profits they could off her and then dump her like a sack of garbage not giving her a second thought. Bill went on to explain the reasons of why they picked these certain actors for Jill to work with to build up her image. Jill was not buying any of the information that was coming out of Bill's mouth. Now knowing the truth, she felt the meeting should end. Thinking, all these people were going to do was keep lying to her, including her agent who at the time was squirming in her seat. At least this was something Jill enjoyed watching. Knowing her agent had no idea what was about to happen next.

Jill had turned herself into a female Perry Mason asking all these questions which Bill had to answer and was not liking it one bit. Before ending the meeting, Jill decided to ask her agent one question, "What about your pay Miss Paul, does it get reduced if my next movie fails to meet the studio's expectations?" Miss Paul answered, "Why no dear, you know I am paid by commission up front. If you like, we can put that in your contract. I have faith in you and know your next movie will be a huge success." "That will not be necessary; everyone here has given me all the answers I require to make up my mind."

Miss Paul thought she had bluffed Jill into thinking she would take a pay cut in order to get her to sign the contract. She knew Jill would never ask her to put it in the contract because that meant the studio would have to re-write it. Which meant a delay and another trip she would have to make to sign the new version. Miss Paul stopped squirming in her seat and waited for Jill to pick up a pen so she could sign the contract and this would finally be over. She smiled at Bill thinking it was about to happen, which Jill caught her doing.

Now everyone at the table thought Jill was about to sign the contract. Bill looked at his VPs with a smile on his face, thinking this was a done deal. To speed things along, he said to Jill, "Now that you have your answers. I would appreciate your signature on the contract so we can go about our business of getting your next movie ready to be made." Jill looked at him and said, "I do not think that is going to happen. Right now, I feel like a victim in a room full of vampires ready to get the life sucked right out of me if I sign this contract. I think instead, I will quit my job here at Planet Studios before all of you can make that happen. Then, maybe you can suck the life out of each other without me being here to watch it happen."

Before leaving, Jill looked over at Miss Paul and said, "I no longer require your services as my agent and you are fired as of today. Go get you another client to suck dry, this one is done." While gathering her things, Jill told them to remain seated and not get up, that way it would be easier for them to start talking about her after she left the room. She walked out never looking back at any of them and no one said a word to stop her. Which proved once again, Play-Doh was telling her the truth about these people.

After reaching the lobby, a receptionist at the front desk stopped Jill by telling her she had a phone call, that it was Bill Turner on the other end. Jill took the phone from the receptionist, and spoke first before Bill could get a word out. "Go find another actress's career to put to sleep Bill. This one has decided not to work for you no matter what you try to offer me. I do wish you good luck with any future dull ass movies you decide to make. At least the blame cannot fall on me if I am not starring in them. If they fail to meet the studio's expectations, then they might want to fire your ass. Like you said, all they know is the bottom line, right Bill?" Jill handed the phone back to the receptionist while Bill was responding to all her comments. The receptionist explained to Bill that Jill had left and hung up the phone. Jill thanked her for doing it and then gave the receptionist her contact information in case she ever wanted a career change.

Jill hurried to her car and left the studio where she could get on her laptop to tell Play-Doh everything that had happened. After reaching a Starbucks, she sent an email to him.

Starlet: Well I did it, I am on longer an employee of Planet Studios and I fired Miss Paul before leaving the meeting. I even told Bill Turner off on the phone as I was walking out the front door.

Play-Doh: Sounds like a great start so you can begin running your own production company and make decent movies. I will be the first person in line to spend my eight dollars.

Starlet: I am on my way to see someone about doing just that. First, I wanted to thank you for your help in warning me exactly who I was dealing with and not wasting another year of my life at that place.

Play-Doh: It was my pleasure to do it. At least you have an opportunity to make a change for the better in your life.

Starlet: I still do not know why you are helping me. What are you getting out of this if we do decide to work together?

Play-Doh: A fair question to ask. First, I get to provide you with the material for your next movie with my new book. Then you can shape it into a movie script. Like what a kid does while playing with Play-Doh. When your movie comes out, you can give me credit by saying the material was from my book. That way we both profit, you by movie sales and me by more books sales. Now do you understand my reason for helping you?

Starlet: How do you figure that we will both profit? Is your book out yet? Is it any good? Will the movie I make be any good and make a profit?

Play-Doh: Many questions to ask at one time. You have to have faith, Starlet. My new book will be out next week and then you will see what type of sales it generates. Anyway, it will take you at least six months to get your new production company up and running, ready to make a movie. By then, I will have received most of my sales of the book. When my readers find out you are making a movie off the book, they will want to go see it. Now do you see my plan? Some of your movie fans will want to buy the book after seeing the movie. It is a win-win for both of us.

Starlet: It is, if your book is a successful one. If not, we can have a real problem on our hands by both of us losing a lot of money.

Play-Doh: At least by then you will know if my book is a success or a failure. You can always pick another script to do your first movie. I suggest that you watch the sales of my book, then decide if you want to use it or not. I am sure you can come up with a movie idea of your own.

Starlet: I will do as you suggested on all accounts. First, I need to find a lawyer to represent me and later look at some rental properties for my new company.

Play-Doh: Always good to have a plan ahead of time, Starlet. You will be receiving my new book in the next few days. Let me know if I can help you with anything else.

Starlet: I will do that. Now I need to go see my best friend and talk her into becoming my partner, not an easy task.

Play-Doh: After what you just did at that meeting, I think you can handle that job. How hard can it be to convince your best friend to come work with you again?

Starlet: Easy for you to say, you do not know Carrie the way I do. It might take some convincing. Chat with you soon, Play-Doh.

Jill called Carrie and told her she was on her way to see her to discuss something very important and that she wanted to do it in person instead of over the phone. On the drive over, Jill kept thinking about Play-Doh and why he wanted to help her. They had never met, but he still knew so much about her career and future movies that were not even out yet. This intrigued her the most about the man who calls himself the "Play-Doh Man". Now, thinking if she had not answered his message last night, she would have signed that contract for another year of doing even more bad movies at Planet Studios. By dodging that bullet, she has a chance at a new career, but needed her best friend's help to make it happen. Jill hoped Carrie would listen to her and not think she had gone insane with this bold new idea of making movies together with their own company.

Jill was at Carrie's kitchen table sipping coffee and telling her everything that went on at the meeting. Carrie listened intently, while Jill laid out all the details, including the part about firing Miss Paul and telling Bill Turner off before leaving the studio. Carrie said, "You had quite a morning, girl." Then Jill said, "You think? Play-Doh was telling the truth, they were all in it together." "Well, I have some news of my own. The television series I work on will not have another season. I too am out of a job." "Great, that makes things work out perfectly." "What? I do not see how both of us being unemployed helps anyone." "Then let me explain, I think it is time for both of us to have a career change. That is why I am here right now to ask you a very important question." "Then stop sipping your coffee girl, and ask your question." "I think it is time we made our own movies by starting a new production company as partners. Remember what you said to me, if I needed any help, just ask you. Well, I am asking."

Now Carrie was sipping her coffee while Jill explained why they should open a company together. Thinking her best friend had lost her mind by talking to this Play-Doh Man, and maybe needed medical help instead of hers. When Jill was finished, Carrie sat her coffee cup down on the table and replied to Jill's request by saying this, "You need to stop chatting with that Play-Doh guy. He is putting wild ideas in your head, Jill. We do not have a clue how to run a production company, or have any experience in making movies." "We have more experience than you think, Carrie. What we do not know we can learn over time. At least give my idea some thought before dismissing it." "You know, I will have to discuss all this with David before giving you an answer." "Of course, I can understand that. He is your husband and has a big say in what you do. I want you to think of all the opportunities we will have in working together again. Something I have missed a lot dear friend." Carrie smiled at Jill and reached out for her hand across the table with Jill met with hers.

Jill said, "With me directing and you producing, we are an unstoppable team. Not to mention all the people from your television show are now looking for work. There is a lot of talent out that we can use. I believe this is the perfect time to start our new company." Carrie said, "You have not mentioned anything about the material we are going to use for our first movie. Where will that come from? We need movie scripts to make movies." "That is where the Play-Doh Man comes in. He is supplying us with the material for our first movie, free of charge. It is in the form of a book that we will have to turn into a movie script. But I think we can afford to hire a few people to do that for us." "When does this book arrive?" "Within the next two days. He is sending a copy by FedEx, to my house. I can read it and if you decide to join me, I will get him to send two copies, that way you can read one. Then you can decide if you want to be my partner. How does that sound?" "If David does not mind me investing our money and Play-Doh's book is good and we can use it, then I see no problem in being your partner, Jill." Jill got up and gave Carrie a big thank you hug. Then she sat back down and started going over all the things they would have to do in the next two weeks to get their company up and running.

An hour later, Carrie said, "I hope this Play-Doh Man can back up what he has promised you. I mean, you have only known him for two days, Jill." Jill said, "He has been upfront and honest with me so far. I knew Miss Paul for fourteen years, and look how she turned on me to get a larger commission for herself and work for her other clients. Play-Doh knew exactly what the studio was trying to do and warned me before it was too late. Carrie, all he wants is for us to use his material and give him credit later." "Okay then, if you trust him, then I will too." "For some reason, I think he is no ordinary man, Carrie. I can feel something is different about him." "With the name like the Play-Doh Man, I would have to agree with you." "You talk to David tonight about what we have discussed and let me know your decision. I need to see a lawyer to make sure Miss Paul is out of my life forever, and ask him a few business questions about starting a new company. Call me later if you have any news and I will do the same with any updates I might have."

"I should know something tonight, I will call you then. Drive safe and good luck at the lawyer's office." They hugged and Jill left Carrie's house thinking she had convinced her friend to join her on this new adventure. The next two weeks will be busy ones, but Jill had plenty of time to get things done now being unemployed.

After getting home from the lawyer's office, Jill sent another email to Play-Doh to update him on what happened at Carrie's and other news of the day. He would become her sounding board and she would need him to get her company up and running.

Starlet: I took your advice and hired an attorney today instead of a new agent. I also went to see Carrie and asked her to be my partner in the new production company. She will give me an answer some time tonight. Here is my address so you can send me your book.

Jill did not receive a response right back from her email. Lucky for her, the phone rang, which gave her a break from staring at her computer screen. It was Carrie calling to give her an answer on the partnership. Carrie said, "I am in, partner." "Really, you are not playing with me are you, Carrie?" "No girl, I am not. David thinks it is a great idea and thought we should have done it sooner." "In that case, we can go see my new attorney tomorrow and have the papers drawn up to start J&C Productions and line up a real estate agent to see about renting office space." "I know there is a lot of work to do before we even start shooting our first movie. But I am ready to go to work, partner." "Yes, there is partner. I am glad you will be there to help me through it. I will call you tonight so we can discuss this some more. Right now, I need to chat with our other partner the Play-Doh Man." "Okay then, talk to you later."

While on the phone, Jill saw Play-Doh had sent her an email. She wanted to respond to him while he was reachable. She went to her computer to read what he sent.

Play-Doh: I am glad you are going to be jumping through your own hoops in the future. I am sending you my new book to the address you gave me. You should receive my book in the next two days with a few extra things to go along with it. One of them is add-ins, which are things I left out of my book. This is extra material you can use while writing your movie script.

Starlet: I will need two copies of your book, not one. Then my partner Carrie can also have one to read. I just found out she has decided to join me in starting my new production company to which we will be calling J&C Productions.

Play-Doh: Nice catchy name and easy to remember. Not a problem on the books, I will send you two of everything. Good to see you will not be alone in this process. I remember Carrie from the television show you two were in together. I assume she is someone you trust and has your back unlike your agent you fired today.

Starlet: You assume right on both counts. Tell me more about the add-ins you are sending me.

Play-Doh: The extra material I left out of my book. You can use them or not while making the new movie. I am also sending you all my notes on each one of your movies you have done. Please take time to read them and see if you agree with my conclusions on why some of your movies did not work. I think this could help you in making your first movie by avoiding the mistakes you made in some of your other movies. Only trying to help, not trying to criticize you or your work.

Starlet: I have never watched any of my movies before, but Carrie has seen all of them. I will read your notes about each one of them and draw my own conclusions. You have spent a lot of your time on me. Are you sure that I am worth it?

Play-Doh: I am still chatting with you and I believe you are worth it. Back to my package, there might be a few more surprises inside the box. I hope you get a chance to use them all.

Starlet: If the add-ins of yours are any good, why did you leave them out of your book?

Play-Doh: I want the book to be different from the movie you will be making. As you know, I like surprises. I think the audience should experience some, thinking they already know the outcome of the movie before seeing it. That is where the add-ins will work if used in the right way.

Starlet: Oh, I see your point. We put in the add-ins to surprise them. Once again, thank you for all your help over the last two days. Even if my company is not successful, you at least opened my eyes to the people around me about who they truly are. I do not know how I can ever repay you.

Play-Doh: You are very welcome, Starlet. You have repaid me in more ways than you know.

Starlet: How have I repaid you?

Play-Doh: I will explain that sometime in the future. How about for now you get some rest, you are going to need it. If you have more questions. You know where to find me.

Starlet: You are right about all that. I will not have much time to sleep when my new company gets started; and there will be a lot more questions for you in the future. Why not tell me your real name and a phone number to go with it. On the other hand, we could always Skype instead of emailing each other. That way I will not have to wait for you to email me back.

Play-Doh: I do not mind emailing you; after all, I am a writer. I think we should leave things the way they are for right now. I have enjoyed our chats over the last two days. How about you? Anyway, what is wrong with a little mystery in one's life?

Starlet: Yes, I have enjoyed our chats together. If that is what you want, I will email you when I need to talk again. Bye for now, Play-Doh.

Jill got off her computer and started compiling a list of everything she was going to need to do the next day. There was a lot of work for her and Carrie over the next few weeks getting their company up and running. She was hoping in the back of her mind that they would not run into any major problems while doing it.

Before going to sleep, Jill realized when Play-Doh's books arrived; it would have his real name on the front cover. Then she would know whom he was and if he was a good writer by doing some research of her own. If he was not, all of this could be for nothing and she would soon be job-hunting. A feeling deep down told her Play-Doh was for real. The man seemed to know what he was talking about these last two days. Jill went to sleep thinking about all this and the mystery man she had been chatting with, he had made her find new strength and confidence in herself.

John called Michael to give him an update about Jill and her decision to work with him. John said, "Well, it is official, I will be working with J&C Productions on their first movie." Michael said, "I guess that is good news. I wish I knew the whole plan of what you are up to, John." "You will when the time is right old friend. Now, how is my book coming along?" "Everything is ahead of schedule on that front. You have your copyrights, and we should have your book ready to go to print sometime next week. Soon enough for you?" "Everything sounds great. I have one small change I need to make. I want you to use Play-Doh Man as the author's name instead of my real name. I do not want Jill to find out who I am yet." "That could hurt our sales on the book, John. You might want to rethink this before it is too late. No one knows who the Play-Doh Man is, but they know who you are." "You will find a way to make it sell, Michael. I think people might be drawn to the funny name and buy my book." "I think you are taking a big gamble on this John, just so a woman cannot find out who you are." "Remember old friend, no one wanted you to publish my first book and they were wrong. Think of this as a challenge and we all know how you love challenges." "Okay then, I will make the name change on your new book. Anything else?" "One more thing, I need you to set up an account in that name for all sales of the book. In case Jill tries to find out who I am that way." "I will do all of it tomorrow, John. Anything else, the Play-Doh Man requires of me?" "Glad you asked my condescending old friend; I need you to send two copies of my book to Jill. FedEx them to the address I am emailing you. Also, I am emailing you everything else that needs to go with the books." "Not a problem, I am here to serve. I will take care of that and call you when I get your first sales numbers. I am hoping to have good news to report. Goodbye, John." "Thank you again for everything you are doing for me, Michael. I will tell you my whole plan soon." "All right John, I only hope you know what you are doing." "So far, so good. Talk to you soon."

John said night, night girl as he and Suzie headed off to bed. His plan to save Jill's career was in motion and they would be working together in the months ahead.

Chapter 5

J&C Productions

The next morning, Carrie met Jill at her new attorney's office to get a business license and to sign some other legal documents to begin their partnership. The next stop was to the bank to open a business account for the company. They decided to put five million dollars each into the joint account for company expenses. Both of them knew it was going to cost even more when they started shooting their first movie. While at the bank, they also applied for credit and business debit cards to use for future company expenses.

Next on their list was to meet a real estate agent about a building that was for rent. After doing a walk through, they signed a one-year lease. It was going to be the new home for J&C Productions. After that was done, it was time to see Jill's accountant to talk over some things with him about the new company and what they would need to do; such as payroll for employees, which business expenses they were allowed to write off as tax deductions. It was a short meeting to get Jill and Carrie knowledgeable of a few things to avoid making any bad business decisions right off. After that meeting, it was time to go shopping for furniture and office supplies to fill up their new offices. The two women found everything they needed and arranged for delivery next week. Jill was thinking ahead, in case the material Play-Doh sent was not any good, they could cancel their furniture order and the building they leased could always be rented out to someone else the next year to recoup some of their money.

After all the shopping, Carrie went to conduct a few interviews to try to find two assistants that could work for them. These assistants would run the day-to-day operations at J&C Productions when Jill and Carrie were out doing other things to get their movie made. When shooting started, the two would have to be at different locations shooting their new movie and someone had to be in the offices to answer the phones and greet any guests. Carrie knew the people she hired had to be trustworthy and able to make decisions on their own without having to ask Jill or her about every little detail. They would need to know what they expected out of them on the front end before they were hired.

Carrie had told Jill, she would handle hiring the personnel for the company. Jill's job would be to hire the right actors for their movie. They both could hire the people to shoot the movie and get it produced and distributed to the public to see. This would require press agents to help the movie get the proper advertising when the time was right. The two women were starting to feel the pressure now seeing the days were not long enough to get everything done.

After two days, Jill got her package from Play-Doh as promised. She could not wait to open the box to read the front cover of his book to find out who he actually was. She was disappointed after seeing the name Play-Doh Man at the bottom of the cover page. This man was trying to keep his identity secret from her and doing a damn good job thus far. She set the book aside and began pulling out the rest of the items inside the box. Which was another one of his books; two copies of a book called "How to start a new business for dummies", the ten add-in scenes that he mentioned in his email, a notebook that contained his reviews and notes on all her movies. The last item was a can of blue Play-Doh, which brought a small smile to Jill's face. Thinking, I got Play-Doh from the Play-Doh Man. At the bottom of the box was a note saying; I am only an email away if you need anything else, Starlet.

Jill made copies of the ten add-ins so Carrie would have a set. Then she phoned Carrie to tell her the box from Play-Doh had arrived and she was on her way to her house so they could start reading his book together. Jill said, "His book is over four hundred pages long. I think we should get started reading it to find out if we have the right material to make our movie." Carrie said, "I agree, so hurry up and get over here, girl. I will have the coffee ready and something to snack on while we read." "Well at least Play-Doh delivered what he promised. Now we will find out what kind of writer he is after reading his book." "Yes, now we know he is a man of his word, sending you that package." "Yes and he used Play-Doh Man as the author's name on the front cover. That man does not want me to know who he really is for some reason." "Does it really matter what his name is if his material is good?" "I guess not, but I would like to know who we are dealing with." "I think he will tell you when the time is right. So stop wasting time and get your butt over here so we can get started reading his book." "I am heading out the door. See you in twenty."

The two women set down in Carrie's living room, opposite each other on different couches. They decided to read the book and not talk about it until they were finished; thinking it was going to take at least four hours, if not more. As they began reading, all you heard in the room were pages turning while they immersed themselves in Play-Doh's book, called "Life's Consequences", a perfect title for a book with what these people now were experiencing. Jill and Carrie did not move from their seats, except to get more coffee or go the bathroom.

Neither spoke to each other over the next five hours while they finished reading the book.

Jill looked up at Carrie and said, "I know we can make a movie out of this, maybe even two." Carrie said, "I think maybe a television series down the road that could run for three or four years. This book has all kinds of possibilities we could expand on." "Let us not get ahead of ourselves, Carrie. We have not made our movie yet. First, we need to focus on getting that done. At least we know the Play-Doh Man knows how to write a great book. He picked something that I have a passion for but never did it in a movie, something that involves the fashion industry." "I have to say, you are right about this man really wanting to help you. He is a damn good writer and knows how to intrigue a person and keep them drawn in while reading his work. I do not know how you found this man, but please do not do anything to lose him. At least not until we have made our movie." "I did not find him it was the other way around. By him, sending me that harsh message. But I will not do anything to mess up this opportunity or our partnership, I promise."

"Carrie, can you find a screenwriter who can turn this book into a movie script we can use?" Jill asked. "Not a problem, I know just who to call. Do you remember the two brothers that worked on our television series?" "Yes I do, and Ron and Don will be perfect for this job." "I think we can get them at a reasonable price, since they worked with us before." "Okay then, call them tomorrow and try to hire them. We need a script, so I can start hiring the actors to go along with it. Then we have to pick the locations where we will shoot the scenes." "I will take care of it tomorrow. But we need to go over which parts of the book will be scenes in our movie." "I forgot all about the add-in scenes he sent." She handed a copy of them to Carrie to read, and she read hers, which took about thirty minutes. Each looked at each other, knowing they could use all of the add-in scenes in the movie.

Jill said, "Play-Doh told me if I need any more he could write them. That is, if we did not like the ones he sent." Carrie said, "And you found this man by answering a message he sent you?" "Yep, that about sums it up." "And you are sure you do not know who this man is?" "Carrie, you know everything that I know." "I have to say this is the damnedest thing I have ever heard of or been involved in." "I know, but isn't it kind of exciting?" "I have to admit, yes, it is."

Jill then handed Carrie the notes Play-Doh had written about all her movies he watched. Carrie read them because Jill had not seen any of her own work before. She never liked watching herself playing a part; she was self-conscious that way for some reason. Since Jill would not understand any of his notes, and Carrie had seen all her movies, it was only logical for her to read them. The notes stated why Jill's last three released movies had failed at the box office. Then Carrie read the notes of what he thought needed changing in each movie to make Jill's characters more successful in each movie. It took Carrie another hour to get through all of his notes while Jill waited patiently to find out what Play-Doh had said and her friend thought.

Carrie said, "This man is very insightful on what type of characters you should play and ones you should stay away from. I think he hit on everything that was wrong on the last two movies I saw. All the changes he suggested on each movie are good. If I did not know any better, I would think he might be in the movie business himself." Jill said, "So you think we have the right person to supply us with the material for our movie?" "Most definitely, this man is the right resource for our company." "Well then, I hate to tell you I told you so, but I was right about the Play-Doh Man. He has delivered as promised and I need to go home and thank him personally by sending him another email. I will call you later tonight with any updates, Carrie." Carrie told Jill goodbye and to drive safely home. She did not want to lose her partner suddenly in a car accident. With both her parents killed in one, she always reminded Jill to be careful while driving. Jill gave her friend a hug before leaving her house and promised her business partner she would drive home safely.

Jill got home and went straight to her computer to send Play-Doh an email to thank him for sending the package.

Starlet: I got your package today and Carrie and I have already read everything you sent.

Play-Doh: Well, what did you think of my book and all the other things I sent?

Starlet: We both loved your book and read it in one sitting. It took about five hours to do, but well worth it. Then we read your add-in scenes you sent and loved them too. I did not read the notebook you had sent about my movies. I let Carrie read them instead. After reading all your notes, Carrie said, you were right on every point of why my recent movies did poorly. That is when she questioned where I found you; not believing it was from answering a message you sent me. She thinks you are too unbelievable to exist and that you are involved in the movie industry in some way.

Play-Doh: You said a lot in your last email, Starlet. Waiting for it, I had thought you forgot all about me. Now back to your email, I think your friend Carrie sounds like a very special person and someone I would like to meet some day. So tell her I said so.

Starlet: Down Play-Doh Man, Carrie is happily married to David, a great man I might add. He is a wonderful husband and father and the two of them have been together for ten years and have a five-year-old daughter.

Play-Doh: Well, I guess the old saying is true; all the good ones are already taken.

Starlet: What did you mean by that, mister? Well, I am not taken and you would be damn lucky to have me and count your lucky stars if you did.

Play-Doh: Okay, if you say so. Now let us move on, did you like the Play-Doh I sent you?

Jill was a little upset that he was trying to change the conversation by bringing up that can of blue Play-Doh. She sent him this response to get back at him after he offended her with his comments.

Starlet: I would have preferred you sent me the color pink. It was my favorite color to play with when I was a child. I think blue is more of a boy's color.

Play-Doh: I figured you might have been a spoiled child while growing up. That is why I sent you my favorite color instead. Sometimes we have to be happy by what is given and not what we expect to have in our life.

Starlet: I made a promise to Carrie that I would not do anything to mess up our partnership or our involvement with you. Before I get mad, I believe you are right, it is time to move on. Why did you write your book about the fashion industry? Do you work in that business?

Play-Doh: Not hardly. No, I saw you give an interview one time, and the person asked if you were not making movies, then what kind of career would you like to have. That is when you answered; it would have to be something in the fashion industry.

Starlet: I remember that interview. It was right after I finished my first movie, eight years ago. You remembered that far back to a question I answered.

Play-Doh: The great thinkers have said, you remember what is most important to you no matter how much time has passed.

Starlet: So you are saying, I am important to you for some reason.

Play-Doh: Yes you are, Starlet. I plan to make a lot of money after this movie comes out.

Starlet: Oh, so that is all I mean to you. Someone to make you more money.

Play-Doh: For now, why complicate things. I have done my part. Now it is time for you to do yours.

Starlet: Yes, you have. Thank you for writing a book that I can use to make my first movie. You need great material before even thinking about making a movie. I always wanted to do a movie that involved fashion. Now I can because of you. You have changed my life in just one week, Play-Doh.

Play-Doh: Believe me, it has been my pleasure doing it, Starlet. If you need anything else, you know where to find me. I suggest you get lots of rest, I think you will need it in the following months. The real test will come after shooting starts on the movie. Hope you are up for it.

Starlet: All I can promise you is that I will do my best. Thank you for sending everything in that package. It should be enough to get J&C Productions up and running. Good night Play-Doh, chat with you soon with a progress report.

John turned off his computer and called his friend Michael at home. He began the conversation by saying, "You still up old friend?" Michael said, "Yes I am. Trying to get your new book ready to go to publication. What can I help you with this time the great Play-Doh Man?" "Just calling to give you an update. Jill received my book today and read it in one sitting. She loved it and all the add-ins I sent her. They have decided to make their first movie using my material." "How could she not? It is a damn good book, even if it is about the fashion industry and the main character is a woman. You included so many things which makes it a great book that can be turned into a movie and maybe later a television series." "I would have to agree with you on all counts. Now to the reason I am calling you, I thought it was time you knew my whole plan and not a few parts of it." "Please go ahead and tell me. For the life of me, I cannot figure out what you are doing with her, John."

Then John said, "Now before I do; please listen and do not comment till I am done." Michael said, "Ok then, I cannot wait to hear this." "After Jill finishes making her movie and it becomes a huge hit and her company a success, I will go meet her in person." "What the hell for?" "To see for myself who she really is, the actress on the screen or the person she can become but does not know it yet." "I still do not see what difference it makes if you chat with her on line, talk to her on the phone, or go meet her in person." "That way I will know if she is the one." "Sorry for all the questions, but the one what?" "The one I will spend the rest of my life with. Can I count on you to be my best man?" "John, it is all right to be infatuated with this woman. God knows we all have our fantasies. But to see you and her having a future together is a little far-fetched don't you think." "Let me worry about what is far-fetched, old friend." "You do know she has been involved with Johnny Mann for the last five years." "I have heard they keep breaking up not having a real connection between them. Except when he puts his hands to her face by slapping her around to get his way." "I have heard the same thing. But did you know about his black belt in Karate and that he has put quite a few people in the hospital after fighting with them?" "Should I be worried about that or have you forgotten what I have faced to keep you alive on this earth?" "No, I have not or what you lost because of it, John. That bear would have killed me if you had not come when you did. But that was an animal, not a man." "No difference if you know how to kill. It is all in the process you use by having a plan of attack. Let us not forget, saving you helped me create the JD character for my first book, which in turn has made us a lot of money. So let me explain something to you, Johnny or anything else in this world is going to stop Jill and me from being together. Now do you understand the situation?" "I know when you get your mind set on one thing no one or nothing in this world is going to change it." "You are exactly right on that point old friend."

Then John asked Michael for one more favor, "I need you to keep my real name a secret until I tell you differently. I might have to give Jill your phone number for some reason. So please do not tell her who I really am. Okay?" "Not a problem on my end. I will not tell her who you are; you have my word on it." "That sounds good to me. I think it will take them at least six months to make their movie. In that time, I will get to know Jill a lot better to determine for myself if she is the person I think she is and not some actor she plays in her movies. Thanks for all your help so far, Michael. I could not have done any of this without you." "If I had known your whole plan from the beginning, I would have kept my mouth shut and not been involved." "I thought as much, that is why I only told you parts of my plan and not the whole thing." "You can be a little sneaky when you want to be John." "You have no idea and neither does Jill, or that Johnny Mann with his black belt. Good night, Michael. Call you when I need another favor." "I am sure you will. Good night sneaky bastard. Call you when I have your sales numbers at the end of next week." "I think you and Jill should get together and work on your use of profanity. I believe you called me a little sneaky, not sneaky bastard." "Whatever John." "I will still be waiting to hear from you old friend."

John put the cordless phone on his desk and said the three magic words to Suzie as they headed off to bed.

Chapter 6

New Processes

J&C Productions opened its doors for business in the middle of May. With all the office hiring done, it was now time to go to work in making their first movie. In less than a month, the movie script needed to be ready and then Jill could hire the right actors to start rehearsing their scenes. Before that could happen, Don and Ron Wilson, the brothers that Carrie hired had to write a workable script, who at the time were having a few problems turning Play-Doh's book in to one. Not being writers themselves, Jill and Carrie tried to help them by coming up with new ideas for the brothers to use to put in the scenes. This led to all four of them working throughout the day and a few nights at J&C Productions to finish the script.

When there was free time, Jill and Carrie went out scouting location sites for shooting future scenes for the movie. Not having their own movie studio to shoot scenes at was a big disadvantage they would have to overcome. With location sites needing to be rented out to shoot on them at certain times of the day or night. Then came the permits that were required to shoot on the city streets and the traffic and people cleared from the area. First, Jill had to be finished with the script before all that could happen and their time was limited.

Making a movie was like any other business, having a process you followed and not jumping ahead or cutting any corners. After two weeks, the script was almost finished with only needing a few changes. At least now, Jill could hold auditions looking for the right actors to be in "Life Consequences". She decided to keep the name of her movie the same as Play-Doh's book. A perfect name for the material they were using.

In the meantime, John's book was flying off the shelves everywhere books were being sold even using Play-Doh as the author's name, Michael was using word of mouth and some good advertising tricks to make it happen. The first week's numbers were greater than John's first book he had written. Now Michael could tell John the good news about his book selling so well and a certain call he got from someone who wanted to buy the rights to his book and the huge amount he was willing to pay to get them.

Michael called and said, "John, your book is selling faster than I could have ever imaged. I guess you called it; the public loves your funny pen name, the Play-Doh Man. Now they are trying to figure out who you are and where you came from, writing such an insightful book about of all things, fashion." John said, "Then I suggest we keep everyone in the dark about who I am so even more people will buy my book. That way Jill has a real chance at making a good movie with good material, instead of what Planet Studio has given her in the past. I wanted this to happen before her acting career comes to an end." "Funny you should mention good material, John. A certain Bill Turner called me today to talk about buying your book rights and offered an extraordinary amount to get them. You do remember Jill's old boss from Planet Studios?" "I remember the man. He tried to put her career to sleep and almost succeeded. What was his offer?" "He offered five million dollars for the rights to your book. I told him that I would have to discuss it with the Play-Doh Man first then get back with him."

John did not respond immediately to what Michael had told him. He needed Michael to understand what he wanted him to do and why. John said, "Michael, you know that Jill is going to make her movie based on my book." Michael said, "Wait a minute John, you have not signed a real contract with her yet. Legally, you can still sell your rights to whomever you want." "Thank you for bringing that to my attention, Michael. I want you to immediately draw up a contract and fax it over to J&C Productions tomorrow. I will let Jill know it is coming." "What is the amount of money you want me to put in the contract for your book rights?" "Well, let me see, she can have the book rights and all creative authority for one dollar." "Are you crazy, John? You only want one dollar for your book. Do you know what I will make off that?" "A lot of questions for me to answer all at once Michael. You remind me of Jill by asking me so many. So let me try to answer you the way I do her. I am as sane as the day you met me. I am sure about the amount I want to charge Jill for my book rights. I believe your commission off this deal is twenty cents and I hope you will spend it wisely. To be fair, add in the contract, one kiss given to me when I choose. I hope now you understand this is not about money, but trust instead. Do I have yours?" "You hurt me for even asking that John. I will do as you asked. You do know this is going to piss Bill Turner off when he finds out Jill has the rights. He will want to hurt her in some way." "Then we will deal with him if and when it happens old friend. But for now, do as I ask, please."

Jill got home that night and wanted to go straight to bed without even taking her usual bubble bath. She was so tired from all the script writing and hunting the location sites, she could barely keep her eyes open. The work was harder than she had ever anticipated being before deciding to open her own production company. Instead of taking a bath, she took a quick shower and then checked her laptop for any new emails sent to her. She soon found one from Play-Doh, which said for her to respond back as soon as possible.

Starlet: What is the emergency Play-Doh? I just got home twenty minutes ago and I need to go straight to bed. I am dead on my feet and might go to sleep while chatting with you.

Play-Doh: Then I will make this quick. Bill Turner has contacted my publisher to offer me a large sum of money for the rights to my new book. Somehow, he found out that I have not signed a contract with anyone yet.

For a brief moment, Jill thought that Play-Doh was about to screw her over by selling his book rights to Bill Turner. Which would put Carrie and her out of business before they even shot the first scene of the movie. Her heart was beating so fast she had a hard time breathing, thinking about what was about to happen. Then a thought entered in her mind, if Play-Doh were going to sell his book rights to Bill, why would he tell her anything about it?

Starlet: What did your publisher tell him?

Play-Doh: That he had to talk with the Play-Doh Man about the offer. Now that he has, I told my publisher we had a deal first, which I intend to keep. Tomorrow, my publisher is going to fax a contract over to your office, for you and Carrie to sign in order to own my book rights. Of course, you will have to agree to all the terms and the one condition on the contract before signing it. Then fax it back to my publisher. In order for that to happen, I will need your fax number at your offices. Does all this sound fair to you?

Starlet: Yes, it does. If I like the terms, and that one condition you are talking about. I thought you only wanted publicity for your new book.

Play-Doh: You will like my terms, the one condition I am not sure yet. If you have any problems, just email me. We can always re-negotiate the contract online.

Starlet: How much did Bill offer to pay for your book rights?

Play-Doh: Would you believe five million dollars. I turned down his offer. I made our deal first, Starlet. Please remember, I will always keep my word with you.

Starlet: Five million dollars is a lot of money to turn down. Most people would have jumped at Bill's deal.

Play-Doh: True, but I am not like most people and do not care about the money. Since I helped talk you into starting your own company, I will keep the deal we made. I still have faith in you, Starlet. Now give me that fax number and you can go to bed.

Starlet: For some strange reason I am not tired anymore. Your first email has awakened me. I can chat a little longer with you. Here is my fax number so I do not forget to give it to you later (1-303-896-XXXX). Now, about that condition, what is it exactly?

Play-Doh: Remember, I like a little mystery. I think you can wait until tomorrow to find out. I do not want to ruin the surprise. Now tell me how is the movie script is coming along and finding the right locations for your shooting sites.

Starlet: Finding shooting locations are not the problem. Actually, they were easy to find. The script is another matter altogether. We seem to have hit a brick wall and are not sure which direction to take. There are only a few things we need to fix for the script to be ready.

Play-Doh: Tell me the problems you are having and maybe I can help.

Starlet: It is in the middle part of the book. We are trying to connect the first part and the last part to make it all fit together.

Play-Doh: Tomorrow, after you finish with the contract business, you can email me the problems while you are trying to work through them. I suggest you go buy some new laptops for you and anyone else who is working on the script. Write them off as a business expense. That way other people working on the script can email me also.

Starlet: I will go first thing in the morning to buy them. Then again, you could come here and help us finish writing the script in person. It might save us a lot of time.

Play-Doh: Nice try, Starlet. I like where I am just fine. Thank you for the invite. Remember, this is your project and your part to finish. I have already done mine.

Starlet: You do not have to remind me, Play-Doh. I know what is at stake, my business, livelihood and my future. I am beginning to feel tired again. I believe it is time to say good night. Thanks for everything and I will chat with you tomorrow.

Play-Doh: I have faith in you, Starlet. So keep up the good work and sleep well.

Jill needed to get off her computer so she could call Carrie and give her the news about Bill Turner trying to buy the book rights out from under them. After reaching her, Jill told Carrie the part about the contract with Play-Doh. That it was coming to the office by fax for them to sign tomorrow. Carrie said, "What do you think Play-Doh will ask for so we can keep using his book, Jill?" Jill said, "He would not tell me, but he did say I would like the terms. The condition was a different matter altogether. Carrie, what bothers me is Bill Turner is trying to buy the book rights we are using. He has found out what we are doing and is trying to stop us. I can feel something is not right. Why else would he offer so much money for this book?" "That is a lot of money. Almost triple what a studio might pay for book rights. I have heard your old boss usually gets what he wants no matter what the cost. I believe you pissed him off not signing that new contract and then telling him off before leaving the studio. Now he is trying to pay you back by putting us out of business before we even make our first movie."

Jill remained quiet, thinking to herself when Carrie said, "I think it was bad business on our part not to have signed a contract with Play-Doh to use his book." Jill said, "I have to agree with you. I told you we were going to make some mistakes along the way, Carrie. With everything going on, it slipped both our minds. I am glad Play-Doh does not care about money or we would be screwed." "You are right on that point. At least by tomorrow, it will be taken care of when we sign that contract. I hope Play-Doh does not change his mind and take Bill's offer. You have to agree, five million dollars is a lot of money to turn down." "Yes, it is. I still believe he will send the contract tomorrow. That still leaves Bill Turner to deal with. We need to be ready in case he tries something else." "There is no telling what he might do next, Jill." "Well at least we have the Play-Doh Man on our side and I think we can trust him. He still wants to help us get our company started." "If you say so, Jill. I will see you tomorrow morning at the office, partner." "Good night Carrie and give Molly a big kiss for me. Please tell her, Aunt Jill will come see her tomorrow night after work." "I will go do that right now. Get some sleep, girl. I know better than anyone that you need it." "Good night Carrie. See you tomorrow."

Jill got into bed, hoping everything would turn out all right tomorrow at the office. They have a lot invested in their company, and needed to use Play-Doh's book to make their movie. Carrie was right about one thing, they had no choice but to accept his terms and the one condition in the contract or close down J&C Productions. Without the book rights, there would be no movie and then no company.

The next day, Jill and Carrie showed up early at the office, waiting for the contract to arrive on their fax machine. Jill was trying to think positively, that Play-Doh was not going to change his mind and take the five million. She went about her day as if it was a normal one, and nothing out of the ordinary. Even though everyone there was told about the fax that was coming from Parnell Publishing Company and what it meant if they did not receive it today, with all their jobs depending on this contract being signed to stay in business.

Michael did exactly what John instructed him to do, even if it did hurt him to lose a million dollar commission. He had the contract drawn up and faxed over to J&C Productions for them to sign and fax back to him. He still did not understand John's reason for doing it, but he knew better not to question his friend any further on the matter. Knowing firsthand, John did not care about the money Bill had offered. There was something else at stake, John was thinking with his heart instead of his bank account. As John's publisher, he had no choice but to do his job and accept his twenty cents on this business deal.

A few hours later, the contract came through the fax machine. Everyone in the office was waiting to see what was going to happen next. Jill got up from her chair and went to the fax machine to get the contract so she and Carrie could read it over. They sat closely together as they read the contract, line for line learning the new terms and the one condition Play-Doh requested. They would still have to give him credit for using his book and would pay him one dollar for the book rights. The one condition being Jill giving JD a kiss he would remember for the rest of his life. Jill and Carrie could not believe the terms, and hurried up and signed the contract. Then, Jill told her assistant to make out a check for one dollar to Parnell's Publishing Company and then have it FedEx's to New York today.

Jill looked at Carrie and said, "I told you we could trust him. He has not let us down so far. I know he has a funny sense of humor. I guess that is why he calls himself the Play-Doh Man." Carrie said, "You are the one that has to kiss him, not me. I cannot believe he did not take the five million dollars. Anyone else in this business would have, Jill." "Carrie, unlike most people, Play-Doh is a man of his word. Something very much lacking in this world today. Now we can go back to work on the script, then I can hire our cast and we can start shooting our first scenes in two weeks.

With Play-Doh's help, they worked every day on making the changes needed until the script was ready. Jill, Carrie and the Wilson brothers emailed JD when they had questions or needing help fixing certain scenes. JD sat at his computer emailing his responses back to help them. Jill's first email to him read like this.

Starlet: Thank you so much for fixing that contract problem for me. I have already sent it and the one-dollar check back to your publisher. Please let me know when you want your kiss. I will abide by the condition. Making sure it is one you will never forget.

Play-Doh: Once again, you are very welcome. I will contact you later on that kiss you owe me. First, you have a script to finish, a movie to make, and an Oscar to win.

Starlet: Yes on the first two items, I do not think so on the third. Not to change the subject, but I did buy the new laptops today. I am glad we will be working together to fix this script. Will it be all right to start today?

Play-Doh: As a good friend of mine says, fire away. I will try to do my best.

Starlet: Are you mocking me Play-Doh?

Play-Doh: No, only having a little fun with you. So what is your first question?

The emails went back and forth to fix all the problems and the script was soon finished. On certain things in the book, John told them to pass on. The scene would be too hard to shoot and understand. It was better to move on to another one or use a different way to get their points across. He could see right off what Jill's problem was, trying to follow the book too closely while writing her script. John had to remind her the book was only the source, and she could change things to fit the scene she would be shooting. Explaining to her everything in the script did not have to be like the book line for line. That was when everyone started coming up with different ideas to put in the script. All Jill needed was a person looking outside of the room to show her how to fix certain things. Once again, the Play-Doh Man had come through for her. Finally, Jill could start hiring the other actors for the movie and set up a shooting schedule.

Michael had been stalling Bill Turner about his proposal to buy the book rights of "Life's Consequences" per John's request. John wanted to give Jill more time before he found out she was the one who had them and was about to start shooting her movie. John thought when Bill did find out. He would then move on and forget about Jill. Then she could start shooting her movie without Bill causing her any problems.

John was wrong on his thinking, when Bill did finally find out that Jill had bought the book rights and how much she had paid for them, it increased his hatred for her a hundred times over. He started plotting his revenge on how to put Jill out of business and teach her a lesson at the same time. Bill made another call to Parnell Publishing to talk with Michael about his offer. Their call was a bit one sided with Bill doing most of the talking.

"Mr. Parnell, you are telling me no to my five million dollars, because this Play-Doh Man sold his book rights for one dollar to a production company that has never made a movie before? Is this man insane and why did you let him make such a deal? How about your commission Mr. Parnell, you would have received one million dollars off my deal." said Bill. Michael said, "Yes you are right on all accounts, if we had taken your deal. You have to understand something; this particular author does not care about the money. He had already agreed to sell his book rights to the new company for one dollar and will not go back on his word. For some reason he has faith in this J&C Productions to make a great movie using his book." "This has to be the worst business deal in the history of all business deals. I have never heard of such a thing before in my life. Now I think the both of you have to be crazy, passing on five million dollars for only one dollar." "I guess it all depends on whose dollar it is, Mr. Turner. And I do not see how that is any of your business." "This production company you sold the rights to, I have never even heard of them. I think the two of you have made a huge mistake by not taking my deal." "Then we will just have to see how everything turns out, Mr. Turner. But if I am not mistaken, the co-owner of that production company was recently an employee of yours." "Really, who might that be?" "I believe her name is Jill Green." "She is the one who bought the book rights for one dollar?" "Why yes, she is the one. Can I answer any other questions for you Mr. Turner?" "No, you have covered everything. I will not waste any more of your time. Good day, Mr. Parnell." "Nice talking to you, Mr. Turner. Glad I was finally able to give you our answer about your generous offer we unfortunately had to turn down."

After talking with Bill, Michael was beginning to see why Jill had quit her job at Planet Studios and why John did not want to do business with him; Bill Turner was truly an asshole. The man wanted to get his way no matter what the cost. Michael thought Jill might be in trouble thinking Bill was not the type of man to let this go.

Jill was in her office when her assistant told her she had a phone call, that it was Bill Turner on the line. Jill thanked her assistant and then picked up the phone to answer the call by saying this, "Hello Bill, how are things going over there at my old studio?" Bill said, "You think you are so damn smart Miss Green; leaving us and opening your own production company. Let me explain something to you, making movies takes a lot more than being some actor. You have to be experienced in management and have a large bank account to stay in business." "Well, glad you care so much to give me a business lesson, Bill. I got all my experience and money from your studio over the years. I believe you left out one thing; you also have to have brains in order to make a great movie. I got mine from my parents and not from you. It also took a man called Play-Doh to help me realize what I am capable of doing if given the chance. I have the book rights and paid only one dollar for them, you do not. How do you think the public is going to react when they find out what you offered and what I paid to get them?" "Why should anyone care?" "I think it will be great publicity for my new movie, and J&C Productions needs all it can get before the movie comes out. I have to let you go now Bill; I have a movie to make, "Life Consequences". Good luck on whatever type of movie you decide to make." Then Jill hung up the phone before Bill could respond to her comments. The same way she did at the studio on her last day there. Jill thought their business was now over between them. Only she had no idea what Bill had planned next to pay her back by getting those book rights.

Jill quickly got on her computer and emailed Play-Doh to tell him about the conversation with Bill.

Starlet: You will not believe who just called me and why?

Play-Doh: Bill Turner, your old boss and new nemesis. He called my publisher again to find out if I would sell him the rights to my book.

Starlet: I guess there is no surprising you then. I am not worried about Bill Turner; he is a harmless executive bureaucrat. He might be mad at me now, but I think he will get over it soon enough.

Play-Doh: I knew he would contact you because he cannot believe you only paid one dollar for my book rights. Watch your back, Starlet. I think Bill is the type of man who will want some payback; especially the way you treated him in your last two conversations.

Starlet: Thank you for your concern and I will be careful. I think Bill only hurts people's careers; he will not do anything physically to me by getting his hands dirty. I still have a hard time believing you kept our deal instead of taking his. I want to thank you again for keeping our deal.

Play-Doh: I think this should prove to you that I do not care about making a lot of money. Now, my publisher is a different person altogether. He was upset with me for taking your dollar and not the five million. I mean, you cannot really blame him, there is a big difference between a million dollars and twenty cents; which was his commission on this deal. Enough said about money, how is your movie coming along?

Starlet: I finished casting this week and we will start shooting our first scene next week. I do not foresee any problems, except for maybe the weather not cooperating with our outside shots. I want get as much done as possible before the Fourth of July holiday. Then we can resume shooting a few days after.

Play-Doh: Sounds to me like you got everything under control. Let me know if you need help on anything, I am just a few clicks away.

Starlet: Will do, Play-Doh. Chat with you soon.

Michael called John and told him he had received the contract and a one-dollar check from J&C Productions. Being facetious, Michael asked John this question, "What do you want me to do with this huge check I got from Jill's company today?" John said, "Deposit it into my Play-Doh account, less your twenty percent of course." "I do not know how I am going to spend the twenty cents I made off this deal." "I guess you could buy a pack of gum, never hurts to have fresh breath." "Ha! Ha! The Play-Doh Man made a funny. Have you priced a pack of gum lately?" "I think in the end you will see everything will justify itself. After the movie comes out, a lot more money will come our way, Michael." "I know you have some kind of plan working inside that head of yours." "You know me too well old friend. Do me a favor and keep an eye out for Jill. I do not trust Bill Turner. I think he will try something very soon to hurt her." "I will keep my ears to the ground and let you know if anything happens. Talk to you soon Lone Ranger." "Thanks again Tonto, for everything."

John did not have his entire plan worked out yet; there was still the part about meeting Jill in person after she finished making her movie. Right now, he was more concerned about getting Jill's company and new career started so she could prove herself. This new project had given him something to do with his time and someone to help improve their life for the better. After all their chats, John thought Jill was that special person, even if she did not know it herself. That was something he wanted to show her in the near future after they met.

Early the next morning, Bill Turner called a special meeting at the studio with his two VPs to discuss Jill and her new production company. He was not going to let her walk out on him and start filming her own movies, making him look like a big idiot. Nor was he going to lose his job with some woman thinking she could make a fool out of him. Jill had no idea the trouble that was about to come her way and then put her out of the movie making business before it ever got started.

Bill told his two VPs that he wanted them to do in order to shut Jill's company down. Through one of his sources, he found out the entire cast she was using in her movie. Bill wanted all ten actors and their agents called in for an early meeting the next morning, not telling any of them what the meeting would be about, except it was a huge opportunity and that they would have a future at Planet Studios if they decide to attend. Bill gave his VPs the contact information of Jill's actors and wanted to see them tomorrow morning at seven a.m. The two VPs started making the calls to get everyone there per Bill's request.

The next day, Jill did not understand why her cast members had not shown up that morning. She wanted all of them to come in for a reading to get more familiar with their characters before shooting began next week. Feeling something was wrong, she decided to email Play-Doh to see what he thought.

Starlet: My cast members have not shown up this morning for the script reading. All of them are MIA. What do you think might be going on?

Play-Doh: That is very strange for all of them not to show up. Bill Turner could be involved in this some way. Have you tried to call them to see where they are?

Starlet: Yes, but no one is answering their phones. All my calls go straight to voice mail.

Play-Doh: Let me see what I can find out. I will email you back soon.

Starlet: Okay then, I will wait until I hear from you. If anyone shows up, I will email you back.

At Planet Studios, Bill was explaining his offer to all of the cast members and their agents; telling them to quit Jill's movie and come to work at his studio on a movie they were about to start filming. The studio was willing to pay each of them double what Jill had agreed to pay them and a one-year contract at the studio for any future movies would be included in their contracts. If any of them needed legal counsel in case Jill decided to sue for breach of their contracts, the studio would provide for it free of charge.

Bill said, "I want all of you to think this over and talk with your agents before deciding on taking my deal. I will give you fifteen minutes to discuss it amongst yourselves." He had a big smile on his face, knowing what a lot of them were going to decide. The deal he had put together was too good to pass up. Jill was about to lose enough of her cast and then her movie would be dead. J&C Productions was about to go out of business before it even made one movie. Then he could get the book rights of "Life Consequences" at a third of the cost he had offered. In Bill's mind, this deal was well worth the risk stealing Jill's actors.

After Bill left the room, the cast members and their agents looked at each other and could not believe what had been offer to them for the same amount of work. The only drawback was each of them would have to return the twenty-five percent of their pay back to Jill if they took Bill's offer. Everyone in the room was talking about the deal to double their salaries and receive a one-year contract with a major studio. An offer like this does not come around, but once-in-a-lifetime for an actor. That was why most of the agents were talking to their clients, telling them to take the generous deal. Planet Studio was an established business and J&C Production Company was not.

When Bill returned, eight of the ten actors decided to take his deal. He asked each of them to make out a personal check for the money they owed Jill for payment they had received from her. Then they could receive their new contracts and pay from him. He wanted each of them to sign a letter of intent, saying they were now working for Planet Studios, instead of J&C Productions on a movie project. The two actors that did not take Bill's deal left with their agents to go see Jill in person to give her the news of what Bill Turner was doing, stealing her cast members. Bill had a messenger waiting to rush over the checks and letters from the actors. She would know who was responsible for putting her out of business.

A messenger arrived at J&C Productions with a small box in his right hand and a clipboard in his left. After signing, tipping and thanking the man, she opened the box to find eight checks from her actors inside and their letters of intent to start working for Planet Studios instead of her. The two other actors, who did not take Bill's deal, showed up shortly after to find Jill reading all the letters. They apologized for what had happened and then explained how they turned down Bill's offer. Jill thanked them for their loyalty, but told them under the circumstances, they could go home for the day. She needed time to work things out and later contact them on what she was going to do about the movie.

Everyone there knew without the other eight actors, they could not start shooting the movie. Which meant she and Carrie would need to sit down and make some very hard decisions on what to do next. Before leaving, the two actors and their agents told her they did not understand why Bill was offering so much money to do one movie. Jill said to them, "He is paying me back for leaving his studio. He wanted the book rights to the movie we were going to make. Now by stealing my actors, he is trying to shut us down. Please, go enjoy your day off. I will figure something out and call you tomorrow morning on what we plan to do next. I know it looks bleak now, but give me a chance to work things out."

The two actors and their agents left the building, with Jill having no idea what she was going to do in finding new cast members. She called Carrie and told her to come back to the company. There was something she needed her help on. Carrie was out running errands at the time, but told Jill she was on her way back.

When Carrie arrived, Jill told her what Bill had done. Carrie said, "That man really hates you for walking out on him, Jill." Jill said, "Yes, I think you are right. Play-Doh warned me to watch out for him. I thought he was harmless and would forget all about me. I was wrong. Here is the note he sent with the actor's checks for the money we paid them. He also made them sign letters of intent, stating they now work for him instead of us." Carrie read Bill's note to herself. It said, "Try making a movie with only two actors. I think it is time you face facts, I put you out of business today. All because a washed up actor thought she could make her own movies. Now that I have taught you a lesson, please have some dignity to call it quits. See you around town "has been".

PS. You should have signed that one-year contract I offered you. Once again, you are out of a job. Signed Bill Turner.

Carrie could not believe what this man had written to Jill. She said, "Yes, you are right, he hates you. What are we going to do?" Jill said, "I do not have a clue. Even if we try to hire eight more, he will use the same tactics to steal them. We cannot compete with him Carrie. Bill can and will outspend us. Nor do we have the time to take the eight actors to court, to sue them for breach of contract, and make them return to work. Shooting was supposed to start next week, if we do not find a solution soon, we will start going over budget. I think we know what will happen then." "I do not know what we are going to do, Jill. Bill Turner has screwed the both of us. Well, I guess it was fun while it lasted. I mean we both knew this was a dream starting our own company. I believe it is time to cut our losses and close our company." "Maybe not Carrie, you have forgotten our most important resource in all of this. The Play-Doh Man will find a way to keep our business going. Let me contact him to see if he has any ideas on what we should do before making any hasty decisions." Jill got on her laptop and sent Play-Doh an email.

Starlet: You were right it was Bill Turner. He has stolen eight of my actors to work at his studio by offering them double what I was paying them. Also, a one-year contract to work at Planet Studios on future movies. Two of my actors turned him down. If I do not replace the other eight by next week, I will have to shut down the company.

Play-Doh: At least two of your actors kept their word and decided to stay with you. It would have been nice if they had told you about the meeting Bill invited them to attend. Maybe this would not have happened. I believe Bill does not want us making this movie, does he?

Starlet: I believe you are right on all counts. Why worry about something you can do nothing about. Bill out smarted me this time. He wants me out of business and found a good way to make it happen. He knows that I cannot compete with his money and can outspend me a hundred times over.

Play-Doh: There is more in this world than money and power. I believe everyone has a gift and should use it to the best of their abilities. You are trying to do that right now, and Bill does not want you to succeed.

Starlet: You are right about that, Play-Doh. He made sure to send me a nasty note to confirm it; along with my eight actor's checks for the money, I advance them. Got any more rabbits you can pull out of a hat for me.

Play-Doh: So all you need is eight new actors, to replace the ones Bill took from you.

Starlet: Yes, that about sums it up. If I try to hire any more actors here in town, Bill will try to steal them. Even if he just gets two or three of them to come work for him, I will not be able to shoot my movie, and he knows that. I think my dream is over, might be time to call it quits, Play-Doh.

Play-Doh: Quit, not the Starlet I know. The one I have been chatting with would not think of it. Do not give up so easily. Bill does not own the whole world.

Starlet: Not the whole world, only this town, and all the actors in it. Without a full cast, it will be impossible to start shooting the movie next week.

Play-Doh: I think it is time to think outside the box, Starlet. If Bill owns your town, then I suggest you go outside of it to find your actors. I believe they have a few in New York that do great theater work. Why not hire some of them.

Starlet: Play-Doh, I do not have time to go to New York and search for actors, it would take too long to find the eight people I need.

Play-Doh: Then let me give you my publisher's phone number so he can find them for you.

Starlet: How can a book publisher help me find the actors I need?

Play-Doh: You do not know Michael Parnell and all his connections in this world. He can make the impossible happen. It is like a game to him. He will be able to find your eight actors if they exist and are available.

Starlet: Well then, give me his number so we can put him to work on my problem.

Play-Doh: Here is his number in New York, 212-726-XXXX. Call him personally Jill, and then tell him which characters in the book you need to hire. He will be able to find the right actors that would be perfect for the parts you need. Hey, where did you go to college for your acting experience?

Starlet: I went to USC on a performing arts scholarship. Why do you ask?

Play-Doh: I thought you might be able to find some actors there to use in your movie. Why not tell the college you are giving auditions to find actors to star in your movie. Do you know anybody there that might be able to help you?

Starlet: My freshman drama teacher, he might be able to help me. He saw great promise in me the way you do. The other students called me the teacher's pet.

Play-Doh: For some reason, that does not surprise me. Now that you have options. I will tell you the way I did before all this started. Get off your butt and go to work. Making excuses is a waste of time for both of us. Forget about Bill and make things happen for yourself. I have faith in you, Starlet. You must have faith in yourself in order to succeed.

Starlet: I understand and will stop feeling sorry for myself and go back to work. Thank you for giving me a wake-up call Play-Doh. Chat with you soon when I have news from your friend Michael.

Play-Doh: Sounds like a good plan. I would keep all this just between you and your partner. It bothers me that Bill was able to call your entire cast into a meeting. How could he know all their names and contact information?

Starlet: I must have a spy in my company giving him the information.

Play-Doh: Exactly. Until we find out who, keep everything you are doing a secret.

Starlet: I will and thanks for seeing things I had not even thought of.

John called Michael to give him a heads up that Jill was about to call him. That she needed his help finding eight actors from New York to be in her movie. He asked his friend to do whatever he could for her in the short time span. Michael agreed to help after finding out what Bill had done. He would start looking for the right actors after hearing from her and would know which characters she needed to replace. They ended their call because Jill was on the other line waiting to talk to Michael.

John knew Michael would do whatever he could to help Jill find new cast members. Maybe Bill had won this round, but the fight was not over yet. In John's mind, this was a game of who could out maneuver the other. Only Bill was not playing fair and cheated by stealing Jill's cast members. He would remember this act and try to repay the man for what he had done in the near future.

Later that day, Jill got some good news from Michael. He had found her six actors ready to work on her movie that he knew could do the job. Michael gave her the names and all their contact information. He explained to her that the six actors were not famous people she might recognize but they could get the job done. At least that way Bill would not try to steal them. Jill thanked him for his help, but before saying goodbye, she tried to find out Play-Doh's real name from him. To no avail, Michael would not tell her anything about him. John warned him that she might try something to find out his identity. Jill gave up and ended the call, knowing Michael was not going to crack and give up any information about her mystery man.

With all the contact information, Jill and Carrie both started calling the people on her list to see if they wanted to come work on their movie. All six people agreed and the travel arrangements were booked for everyone to come to California the next day. Now Jill needed to find two more actors to have her eight. She was going to spend the next day at USC to try to solve that problem. At least things were looking a lot better than when this day started. Once again, the Play-Doh Man had saved her, which was starting to be a habit for him. Jill was surprised by how quickly his mind worked by coming up with solutions in order to get her out of trouble. He was helping her while that asshole Bill was trying to put her out of business. Jill had thought enough about that SOB, now she needed to start concentrating on getting her new cast together and start rehearsing scenes. This time the new actors contracts would be ironclad, there would be no escape clauses for Bill or anyone else to steal them. She was going to start shooting this movie and in the process, show Bill that he had failed to shut her company down. No matter what he might try to pull next, she had the Play-Doh Man watching out for her. It was good to know he was there whenever she needed help, which had been a lot lately.

Chapter 7

Soul Searching

While Carrie got the six new actors from New York settled in at their hotel, Jill went to visit her freshman drama teacher, Steven Seems at USC. He had been teaching there for twenty years. With it being June, the drama teacher's schedule was light, having only one class for the day, which gave him time to meet her for lunch so they could catch up. Jill had not seen him for at least fourteen years, being so busy with her television series and movie career, she did not have time to go back to visit her old college since graduation day. Now she was excited to see if anything had changed, including her freshman teacher she had not seen. Steven was always encouraging her to push herself while acting out a scene; immediately pointing out the mistakes she made so they could be corrected which helped Jill learn her craft and understand what she could do to improve it.

On the phone, Steven seemed excited about seeing his former student, and looked forward to having lunch with Jill. Knowing she was his most successful student so far in his long teaching career and wanted to hear all about her acting experiences over the years, behind the scenes, so to speak that Jill could tell him about. Then he could tell his future students some of what Jill shared with him, to show that dreams can come true if you work hard.

Jill agreed to meet Steven in his classroom before they went to have lunch. She wanted to catch up and see how things had been going with him, before asking for his help. After some small talk, they both decided to have lunch in the cafeteria, which was fine by Jill, saving her time instead of going somewhere off-campus. While eating lunch, Jill explained why she had really come for this visit. She needed his help in finding two young actors to fill her cast for a movie she would be shooting in a few days. She went into more detail telling him what had happened to her cast members with Bill Turner trying to put her out of business; she was looking for a young male and female actor to finish filling the cast. After hearing what the characters roles would be in the movie, Steven thought he knew the right two people Jill could use. Two very gifted students with raw acting talent for their age. The same way she was when he first met her and knew right then what she was capable of doing in the future. Jill smiled at her old teacher for the nice compliment. Steven wrote down the two students contact information and handed it to Jill. Saying that the two students were on summer break and in town at the time. She should not have any problem reaching them.

Before they left the cafeteria, Steven asked Jill why she was also directing this movie. He had never thought she was interested in becoming a director. Jill told him, me either until recently. I thought acting was all I ever wanted to do; until someone entered the thought of me running my own production company, which gives me complete control of making and producing my own movies. Jill thanked Steven for his help and invited him to come watch her direct some scenes on the new movie next week. He agreed to come if he could bring a few of the students with him to watch the process. Jill said, "Like a college field trip. It will not be a problem. Only let me know when and how many, so I can make all the arrangements. Okay?" Steven said, "I will, and thank you for the invite to lunch and hope it is not fourteen years until we do it again. I will call you next week to find out where and when you would like us to show up, Jill. It will be a pleasure seeing you at work directing for the first time and a great teaching experience for my students, seeing firsthand how making a real movie. I know the two actors I have selected for you will be able to meet your expectations. They are smart, quick studies, and have a true passion for our art of drama." Before leaving, Jill hugged Steven and once again thanked him for his help. He wished her good luck in making her first movie while saying his goodbyes.

Jill left the campus feeling a lot better than when she had arrived. With Steven's help, she thought she had found her last two actors. On the way back to the office, she called the two students and asked them to come in for an audition today at J&C Productions. Both could not believe it was actually Jill Amber Green calling them on the phone to be in her new movie. It took a few minutes to convince each one that it was not a joke, or some kind of prank, that Mr. Seems had given her their phone numbers. After hearing this, the two students agreed to meet with her later that day. Then, Jill called Carrie to give her the news about finding the last two actors that might be able to fill the cast. If they passed their auditions with her later that day. She wanted Carrie to have two more contracts ready for them to sign in case she did decide to hire them. Telling Carrie her drama teacher had assured her that his two students could fill the two parts with ease.

Carrie said, "Not a problem, Jill. I will get everything ready on this end. It sounds as if you found our last two actors. What are their names again? So I can put them on the contracts." Jill gave Carrie the information and told her she would be back at the office in about an hour. She then asked Carrie how the other cast members were doing. "All of them are checked in at the hotel. I will get two more rooms reserved in case we sign the other two. Before you called, I was about to leave and go pick everyone up and bring them back here to read over the script. But first, I wanted them to have a chance to unwind after their long flight." Jill said, "That was a good idea, Carrie. I think we all should be back at the office about the same time. If I am not there, go ahead and hand out the movie scripts for the cast to look over in the conference room. So they can get familiar with the first few scenes." "I will do that and see you there. But do not rush getting back here, drive safely girl." "I will Mother Goose. Looks like we are back in business, Carrie." Which before ending their call, Carrie agreed with her partner.

Jill stopped to get gas and stretch her legs for a bit. Then she pulled into a hotel parking lot to hi-jack their Internet in order to send an email to Play-Doh on her progress for the day. She typed and sent him this.

Starlet: Thanks to you and your source, I should have my movie cast filled today. I can start shooting the movie on time next week. Things are back the way they were before Bill pulled that stunt, almost shutting us down.

Play-Doh: Good to hear, Starlet. I have something else to tell you that might change your good mood a bit. Something you need to deal with today. My source and I believe you definitely have a spy, possibly being one or both of your assistants working for Bill Turner. I think it would be best to get rid of the spy today before anything else happens to give you another setback.

Starlet: Why do the two of you think it is the assistants? It could be an outsider and not someone who works with us.

Play-Doh: Not likely an outsider. That meeting was too well organized and done by a professional person. For Bill to have your entire cast and their agents called into a meeting, it had to be someone in your company.

Starlet: My partner Carrie hired the two assistants and both of them have access to that information. They mostly handle daily things while we are out of the offices. I do not have a clue of how to find the guilty party, Play-Doh.

Play-Doh: Then set a trap to find out. First, let Carrie know what you are about to do and why, but no one else. That way you will not tipoff either assistant before setting the trap.

Starlet: Well, that makes sense. Then what am I supposed to do?

Play-Doh: Here is the trap I would set. I think it will work to catch whoever is involved. Leak out some information that both assistants can hear and think Bill will want to know about immediately. Then the person or persons will try to contact him. That is when you catch your spy or spies in case both of them are involved.

Starlet: Sounds like a good plan, Play-Doh. It should work. Mr. Turner on the other hand is starting to be a real pain in my ass. I mean it is hard enough trying to make a movie without having to put up with all his dirty tricks. Thanks for all the tips and I will let you know how things turn out later today.

Play-Doh: Anytime, Starlet. I have to give some credit to my source. He came up with the idea you had a spy working in your company. I only came up with the plan to catch the person or persons.

Starlet: I think it is time we call your source by his real name, Michael Parnell.

Play-Doh: Maybe he is. Maybe he is not. Time will tell, but I will not.

Starlet: I do not have time to play with you right now Play-Doh.

Play-Doh: I know you are pressed for time, Starlet. You should be enjoying this process of making your first movie, not to mention running your own company, instead of dealing with Bill and his dirty tricks. I think you should try to relax.

Starlet: Easy for you to say. I have everything on my shoulders and the load is starting to be a heavy one, believe me. Like right now, I need to get back to J&C Productions to meet my new cast members for the first time, give auditions to two more later today, and try to catch a spy in the meantime. Chat with you later on sometime, Play-Doh.

Play-Doh: Yes, it does sound like you have a full day ahead of you. Good luck and good hunting Starlet.

After walking into J&C Productions, Jill went straight into the conference room to meet the actors from New York. She wanted to make sure they had everything they needed and to see if she could do anything for them. Jill saw all the actors looking over the script when she came into the room to introduce herself. The new cast members said things were going fine and they would be ready to start work on the movie next week. Jill told them it was good to hear, and she would be back in about thirty minutes to do a run through on the first scenes together. Then they could talk over any thoughts, questions or concerns they might have. She would go over the entire shooting schedule for their first day. The cast went back to reading the script while Jill motioned to Carrie that she needed to speak with her. They left the conference room and went to the front office area where the two assistants had their desks.

Jill began a conversation with Carrie, making sure it was loud enough for the two assistants to overhear. Jill said, "Carrie, the two new cast members that are coming in today will put our movie over the top with their performances. Just wait and see how good they are running through their lines during their audition. Do you have those two new contracts ready for them to sign?" Carrie was not sure what her partner was doing, but followed her lead. "I have the contracts ready like you asked, and two more rooms at the hotel are reserved in their names."

Now Jill's trap was set. All they had to do was wait to see who tipped their hand by getting on the phone to call Bill. Jill and Carrie went into her office and closed the door. That was when Jill explained her plan to Carrie of what to do next. Carrie could not believe that one of the assistant's she hired was a spy for Bill Turner. She had not known the two women very long, but thought both could be trusted.

Five minutes later, Carrie came out of the office and saw Jill's assistant on her cell phone at her desk. Carrie waited until the assistant ended her call. Then the assistant asked Carrie what she needed. Carrie said, "What I need is the both of you in my office to go over next week's shooting schedule, so bring your pads and pens and follow me. The two assistants did as Carrie asked, and followed her into her office, closing the door behind them.

The plan was to keep them busy long enough for Jill to check their cell phones to see what phone numbers were on them. Jill had kept Bill Turner's phone number from the last time he had called her at the office. She was about to return the favor and pay him back by catching his spy. Jill knew if his number appeared on either or both assistants cell phones; she would then know who the guilty party was and fire the person or persons today.

Jill could hear Carrie talking to the assistants as she went to search each woman's purses to find their cell phones. She pulled out each one to check the recent calls, incoming and outgoing numbers. Jill's assistant made a call to the same number that was on a piece of paper she was holding in her hand. It was Bill Turner's private cell phone number and she had hit pay dirt. The assistant also had Planet Studio's phone number in her call history. While searching the woman's purse, Jill found an envelope from the studio, but she did not open it to find out the contents. She had enough evidence and it was time to deal with the woman who almost put them out of business. Before that could happen, Jill had to make sure the other assistant was not involved. After checking her cell phone, the woman had no phone numbers connected to Bill Turner. Jill felt guilty going through this women's purse, knowing now she had done nothing wrong, but she had to be sure who was working for Bill.

After putting everything back the way she found it, Jill went into Carrie's office and asked her assistant to come with her. After the assistant came out of the office, Jill shut Carrie's door. Both of them went over to her desk and Jill told her to gather her things, she no longer worked for them. The assistant looked at Jill and said, "Why am I being fired? What did I do Miss Green?" Jill said, "For starters, you cannot have two bosses working at different companies. I know you have been spying for Bill Turner; his private number is on your cell phone. You just made a call to him a few minutes ago after hearing about the two new actors coming in today. Please leave now and tell Bill he should have been smarter than to call me on his own cell phone. You can go work at Planet Studios where you belong." "So you went through my purse?" "Yes I did. Now, will you get your things and get the hell out before I lose my temper."

The fired assistant gathered her things and left the offices. Jill went back into Carrie's office to tell her she let go the assistant and that they only had one working for them. Hearing this, Carrie's assistant was surprised at the news, and knew there would be a lot more work for her to do until someone else was hired. Carrie told her assistant, they would finish going over the shooting schedule later, and she could go back to her desk and answer any incoming calls. The assistant did as asked, and closed the door behind her, so Jill and Carrie could talk in private.

Carrie started apologizing to Jill for hiring that woman and for not checking her out more thoroughly. Jill said, "Not necessary, Carrie. No one knew what that woman was up to, except Bill Turner. I guess everyone has a price, and Bill found hers. At least Play-Doh and his source figured it out in time before anything else bad could happen. He suspected it had to be one or both of our assistants working for Bill in order to steal our entire cast. Someone had to give him all the contact information of our cast members and their agents. Let us not talk about this anymore. It is time to move forward and make our movie." Carrie said, "Sounds alright by me. Do you want me to hire you another assistant, or would you like to do it yourself?" "Our deal was you are the one who hires all the office staff. I will stick to our deal and trust your judgment. But do it soon, we do not want to lose the only assistant we have by overworking her." The two women laughed at Jill's comment and then heard Carrie's assistant talking to someone in the front office. It was the two students from USC to audition for Jill, hoping to get the parts in her movie.

Jill came out of Carrie's office and introduced herself to the two young actors. Even though they already knew who she was from television and her movies. Jill took them into her office so they could have some privacy while auditioning. Carrie asked her assistant to ask the other cast members what they would like for dinner. Already getting late in the afternoon, they might have to work into the night and would need something to eat before going over the movie script and running their lines.

The two young actors started doing some scenes from their drama class and Jill could see exactly what her teacher was talking about at lunch. These two young actors could play the two characters Jill needed and she decided to hire them on the spot. The two students jumped for joy with excitement, knowing they were going to be in a movie with the actor, Jill Amber Green. She was a legend at USC, and never imagined they would ever be working with her.

After signing their new contracts, Jill escorted her new actors into the conference room to introduce them to the rest of the cast. The eight other actors took a break from the script reading to introduce themselves to the two young people from USC. Jill wanted her cast to form a bond with each other and her, before shooting started next week. She thought this would make her job directing them easier and maybe get a better performance from them while shooting the movie. Being an unknown director and everyone never having worked with her or each other before, all of them needed to be comfortable around each other, or it would show while shooting the movie. Jill wanted them to become a small family before getting together to do a difficult job by making this movie. None of the cast members had never starred in a major motion picture except Jill and the two actors who turned down Bill's offer.

Later, Carrie and her assistant showed up with the food and everyone had their first meal together. After they finished eating, the cast members from New York started talking about past jobs they had done over the years. Jill remained silent, not bringing any of her own experiences into the conversation. She wanted them to have a chance to tell their stories in order to make them feel like they belonged in the room. Everyone there knew who she was and how much she accomplished in her career. The young actors from USC listened with amazement at each of the stories by the New Yorkers. It was their dream someday to do what all these people had been doing for a living, entertaining people all around the world.

It was past 9:00 PM, when they stopped rehearsing their scenes for the first day of shooting. Jill told them to take their scripts with them to the hotel, but do not let them out of their sights for one moment. She explained in more detail about Bill Turner and what he had tried to do in order to stop her from making this movie. Jill said, "Bill Turner thinks all of you are no real threat to him by doing only theater work and having two college students and two other actors to complete my cast. He wants us to fail in making this movie. I totally disagree, especially after listening and watching all of you rehearsing together on your scenes. You are as good if not better than any actors I have ever worked with in the past. Now, go get some rest and learn all your lines, next week we are going to show the world what some unknowns can do making this movie.

After the cast left for the hotel, Jill and Carrie stayed behind to talk a few things over before locking up. Carrie said, "What do you think of them? Can they do the job, Jill?" Jill said, "Yes, I believe they can Carrie. I hope they take my advice and get some rest because these people are going for one hell of a ride. Starting tomorrow, we need to hire the rest of the people to make our movie, Carrie." "Plus, another assistant for you." "You might think about hiring two before all this is over. For now, we need to go home and get some rest ourselves partner. Good night Carrie, and tell David and Molly hi from me." "I will, and drive home safely, girl." After Jill locked the front door, they walked to their cars and then drove out of the parking lot after finishing another long and hard day. Something the two women were getting used to doing lately.

When Jill got home, it was 10:00 p.m. her time. She was wondering if Play-Doh was still up and sent him an email.

Starlet: I know it is late, but I wanted to tell you that I caught my spy and fired her ass. Thanks to your help, everything is back on track. Also, please thank your source for me. Michael picked the right people I can use to make my movie.

Play-Doh: I decided to stay up in case there was any more trouble. Glad to hear everything worked out for you; and happy to hear my source found you the right actors. I hope this ends your trouble with Bill Turner. Now you can concentrate on your two jobs of directing and acting in your movie.

Starlet: My acting will not be the problem, Play-Doh. I know my lines and what to do in each of my scenes, directing this movie is a different matter altogether. I have never done that job before and everyone will see if I am doing a good job or not on my first day.

Play-Doh: You will be fine, Starlet. Look at how much you have already accomplished by starting your own production company. Listen, while directing your movie try to draw from some experiences of what other directors expected out of you while making all those movies, even the bad ones.

Starlet: I know you are trying to be funny by reminding me of my bad movies, but I can do without the snide comments, Play-Doh. Your advice is easy enough to follow; actually doing the job is a different matter. For the life of me, I do not know how you talked me into doing this.

Play-Doh: Deep down, you know directing your own movie is something you always wanted to do. It is all right to be a little scared, but after the first day of shooting, directing the cast will become a natural thing for you. The director's job is to control the actors and make sure the movie stays on track. So search inside yourself and find a way to make it happen. Get some rest, I know how busy your life is about to become. My source has explained all the things you are about to face in the next six months making your movie.

Starlet: You give great advice for a person who does not have to do the job. Good night Play-Doh and make sure you tell Michael thanks for all his help.

Play-Doh: Remember, I did my job by supplying you the material at a bargain rate price. I think it is time you fulfill your end of this deal by making a great movie; then I can receive my kiss from you. Please stop doubting yourself, and get off your butt to make it happen. Now get some well-deserved sleep, Starlet. I know first-hand you need it.

Starlet: After telling me all that, I will try to do my best. So thank you for your speech and all the things you have done in the past for me. I think that about covers everything. Except for when you will receive that kiss from me.

Play-Doh: You are very welcome, Starlet. If you need any more great advice, I am only an email away.

The next morning, John called Michael to give him an update on Jill's current situation with her cast members. After reaching him on the phone, he said, "Jill told me to thank you for finding those six actors for her. She said they are more than capable of doing the job." Michael said, "Not a problem, John. What are friends for but to help each other out when needed? What about the spy theory, was I right about who it was?" "Right as rain old friend. It was Jill's assistant doing the spying for Bill Turner. I did tell her a way of how to catch the guilty person or persons. After finding out it was her assistant, Jill fired the woman. Now hopefully this will end Bill Turner's attacks against Jill and she can start making her movie without having any more setbacks." "I would not count on that. Bill is going to hate her even more by finding his spy." "Then maybe we need to do something to keep him busy from bothering her. If he does not, I might have to take a trip to LA and talk to this man in person." "Only to talk, nothing else. Right, John?" "Oh, of course, only to talk. But if he cannot understand plain English then it might turn into a translation problem between us." "John, let me handle Bill. I have dealt with his kind all too often. I think you should keep helping Jill like you have been doing." "Fine, but keep me updated on Bill's attacks." "I will do that. But I want you to agree not to do anything rash." "Agreed. I will let you handle things until it is time for me to step in." "Ok then, John. Glad you agree with me on this. Even though, you could write any future books from prison." "Ha! Ha! Michael made a funny."

Then Michael said, "On another note, your book has sold over two million copies, John." John replied by saying, "See, I told you more money would be coming in soon. Now, since you brought up my book, I need you to have the paperback editions ready to go out by the first week of November." "Why is that? We just issued the hardback copies two months ago. We need more time to sell them before issuing the paperbacks, John." "Michael, I need the paperbacks ready before Jill's movie is released Thanksgiving weekend. That way we can sell more books before her movie comes out which in turn puts more money in your pocket." "Oh, I see your logic now. I will have five million copies ready to go out." "Better make it six million copies; I plan on giving away a million copies in movie theaters throughout the country that will be showing "Life Consequences" at them." "I know I have said this before, but have you gone insane old friend?" "Sane as the day you met me. And still need you to do as I have asked." "Well, you have been right about so many things on this book so far, I will do as you asked. But you do know, the publisher is supposed to be making all these decisions, not the writer." "On my next book, I will let you make every decision. Right now, I run the show on this one." "Understand perfectly, it is in your hands. Only give me enough advance notice on any other major decisions you might have like the paperbacks, so I can make it happen. Sound fair?" "Yes, it does old friend. Glad we could come to an understanding on this." "Not a problem, John. Publishing is a give and take business. But lately, I have been giving and you have been taking." "Do I have to bring up our special time with that black bear?" "No, you do not old friend. Remember, I was there and had a front row seat."

"Now, can we discuss the book tour's I would like you to go on?" asked Michael. Which John quickly replied, "You mean the book tour's you will be going on for me? I have already told you, if any came up, you would have to go in my place. I do not want the public to know who the Play-Doh Man is." "You mean Jill not knowing who you are?" "I will talk to you soon, Michael." "Okay then, no book tours." "Remember, I am the decision maker on this book." "How can I forget when you keep reminding me?"

John looked down at Suzie and said, "You ready girl?" Her head popped up from the floor, giving him her full attention. Then John said, "Outside, outside, get your ball." Suzie jumped up and ran to get her ball before heading to the front door to wait for her master to open it so they could go outside to play fetch together.

Chapter 8

Shooting Begins

Carrie started hiring the filming crew, set workers and everyone else so shooting could begin. The next week, Jill and the other cast members were taking their places so they could start filming their first scene together. Carrie sat in the director's chair whenever Jill had a scene in the movie to do. Now that the movie had officially started with the first scene shot without any problems, Jill held a short meeting with the cast and crew to explain what she expected out of each one of them while making the movie.

Jill said, "I will be counting on all of you to do your best work for me, if anyone has questions, concerns, or problems occur, please come see Carrie or me to get them resolved. I want everyone to throw out any egos; we are all trying for the same thing, to get this movie made right and on time. Okay then, since no one has anything, we can move on to our next scene, everyone take their places." Jill was in her director's chair at the time when she yelled out, "Begin scene". She wanted to be different from all the other directors and picked these two words rather than use the word, "Action" to begin shooting each scene. She would also use, "End Scene" instead of the word, "Cut".

Carrie was on the set to give Jill moral support and do anything that came up so Jill could stay focused on her job directing and acting in the movie. She would have a lot of free time until the movie was finished, then her job producing and editing the movie would begin. Right now, Carrie stayed by Jill's side watching the camera monitors looking at each scene that was shot and giving her opinion if they needed to do a retake. Jill valued Carrie's opinion and only over ruled her once the first day of shooting. She thought all the scenes shot that day were good enough not to do any more retakes with all the actors rehearsing them so many times before actual shooting begun.

With the first day and part of the night's shooting going so well, Jill started doing a few retakes to have different versions of a scene. When one of her actors suggested something new they might try, she reshot the scene and picked the best one to use in final production. Jill was taking Play-Doh's advice by using the actor's ideas and suggestions. With some of their ideas working, Jill decided to use the new scene instead of what they originally shot the first time around. The first day of shooting was a success according to Jill, by everyone working together. Now the making of the movie had become a reality and not a dream on pieces of paper you could only read and think of.

After getting home and ready for bed, Jill emailed Play-Doh to tell him how her first day on the set went.

Starlet: I have to say, my first day directing was exciting, Play-Doh. Better than I could have ever imaged. I am glad you talked me into directing this movie. I think it is more rewarding than acting in one. Being able to guide those actors and then see the results on the camera was amazing and exhilarating at the same time. It was like seeing the scenes come to life before your eyes.

Play-Doh: I am not surprised at anything you just told me. I believe you are a natural leader, Starlet. I could see that in all the interviews you have given over the years. Now back to your directing. I have some more advice for you if you want it.

Starlet: Sure, go ahead and fire away with your advice.

Play-Doh: Here goes, then. Please do not forget about the middle part of the movie. It could be the most important part, which is where so many movies fail. I have to say, not only in movies, but also in books, and in life itself. I think we both can agree that the movie has a strong beginning and ending. You need something in the middle to tie it all together. I wish someone had told me that before I started writing my books. More of my revisions are in the middle of my books than in any other part. My advice to you, concentrate on the middle of the movie, Starlet. Remember, you own the book rights and can change whatever you want.

Starlet: Well, how about putting even more pressure on me. Do you have any ideas of what I should do in the middle of the movie?

Play-Doh: Not a clue. You will come up with something; I have faith in you, Starlet.

Starlet: Good to hear, but that does not help me solve the new problem you have just given me.

Play-Doh: Maybe one of your cast members will get an idea of something you can try and then use.

Starlet: I will tell the cast members tomorrow and try to think of something on my own to bring everything together. I need to go so I can look over tomorrow's shooting schedule. Chat with you soon.

Play-Doh: Good night and sleep well, Starlet.

The next month, Jill was racking her brain trying to come up with something new to put in the middle of the movie. She had told her entire cast about finding a way to tie the beginning and ending with the middle. No one had any ideas at the time. Jill told them to keep thinking about it, and come to her if they thought of anything they could try by putting it in a scene.

Then one day on the set, the female actor from USC came to Jill with an idea that might work. Jill listened to the idea and decided to try it out by shooting a scene, then watching the scene to see if it worked. The scene worked perfectly, and Jill hugged the young actor for thinking of the idea and bringing it to her. Now they could concentrate on getting the last part of the movie finished. With only two months of shooting left, there was going to be a lot of long days and nights ahead. At least the middle problem was solved they did not have to worry about it anymore.

Bill Turner had heard about Jill's movie not having any major setbacks. Even after all his attempts to try to stop her, she was almost finished shooting her first movie. One of the VPs told him the numbers of what Jill had spent so far while making her movie. After looking them over, Bill knew she was not going to be able to release the movie. She would run out of money after paying all the editing and production cost, which meant there would not be any money left for distribution and advertising. Her movie was sure to fail but she did not even know it. Now he could relax and did not have to do anything else to stop Jill from making her movie, she had done it to herself. Bill thanked his VP for bringing him the good news and decided to buy him lunch. Which was a rarity for this man to do by picking up the check.

With only five weeks of shooting left, everything was going well, with no real problems coming up for Jill or Carrie to resolve. They were on budget and did not see anything to change that, until the reports of bad weather was coming to the area. The next week, it rained off and on for a solid week, keeping Jill from shooting her outside scenes having such sudden downpours. Even the television weatherman could not understand why the cloud fronts would not move out of the area.

While waiting for the weather to clear, the cast members had more time to rehearse their scenes until they had them down perfectly. They practiced each day to make sure that everything was ready when shooting could begin again. It also gave Jill time to get the ending of the movie just right, by making a few changes she thought would make a better ending. Jill held a meeting with her cast explaining to them that if the weather did not clear soon, she might have to cut some of the movie scenes to make budget. Not the big ending, it was going to stay in the movie no matter what. She thanked her cast for all the rehearsing they were doing, knowing they could be relaxing at the hotel or doing something else with their down time and appreciated all their hard work.

With the bad weather causing shooting to stop, Carrie had time to start working on the producing process of the movie with the scenes that were already shot and now ready for editing. Carrie started getting all the expenses of the movie together and everything else they would need to spend to market the movie. In order to find out the final cost and to make sure everything was covered. After looking over the figures, she soon discovered a major problem the company was about to have in getting their movie released. They would run out of money after the movie went through the editing and production process. There would be none left to spend on the distribution and advertising cost. Something that neither of them had thought about beforehand while making this movie. Now Carrie figured the distribution and advertising cost were going to run at least four million dollars, which they did not have in the bank to spend. If they did not find the money from somewhere, all their hard work would have been for nothing.

Carrie told Jill what she had discovered. Now both women were brokenhearted and did not have a clue of what they were going to do next. With nothing else to do at the office, Jill went home to think about the current financial situation. It was still raining when she drove home, which was supposed to stop the next day, according to all the news channels. Now that did not matter, finding the money to distribute and advertise the movie was all that she thought about.

After getting home, Jill sat at her kitchen table drinking her coffee, thinking that all the hard work by so many people was about to be for nothing. It was Carrie and her mistake by not figuring out the total cost of the movie before shooting began. Even if they both put up their houses as collateral, it would take too long and not be enough to cover all the cost. She started opening up her mail and soon found a letter from Mr. Bill Turner himself. Jill read the letter, "You forgot all about the distribution and advertising costs didn't you, "has been"? I decided to write you since you never let me get a word in over the phone. Too bad you do not own your own studio to cover the four million dollars you now need. Best of luck in finding the funding to finish your first and last movie "has been". With all that hard work, and nothing to show for it. Now who feels stupid? No contract, no job and now no company."

P.S. Call me if you would like to sell me your movie after shooting finishes. I am sure we can work out a fair price "has been". Signed Bill Turner.

Jill started crying knowing he was right, she did feel stupid. J&C Productions Company and their first movie were now officially over. All that was left to do was pack up the actors to send them back to New York and lock their office doors. She had hit rock bottom and called Carrie to tell her about Bill's mean letter. Carrie was angry after hearing about the letter and herself for not thinking of all the expenses they had missed. She kept on apologizing to Jill about how sorry she was that they were about to go out of business. Knowing there was nothing either of them could do to fix this huge problem.

Carrie said, "At least we have one hell of a tax write-off for this year, Jill." Jill said, "Wish I could laugh at that, Carrie. Now all I can do is cry knowing of how close we came to making our movie a reality and not a dream. This hurts me more than anything I have ever experienced in my life." "It hurts me too, I have not even told David yet. He is going to be very upset at me for spending so much money and not have anything to show for it. That is what I plan on doing tonight, how about you?" "I am going to email Play-Doh to give him the bad news. I know he will not be able to fix this problem. Goodbye, Carrie. Good luck in telling David tonight. He will understand because he loves you." With tears still coming down her face, Jill typed in her email to send to Play-Doh. Still multi-tasking but this time not in a good way.

Starlet: Our dream is over, Play-Doh. It was part my fault for not seeing the problem beforehand. The distribution and advertising cost of our movie is going to be about four million dollars, which J&C Productions does not have in the bank. Something Carrie and I had not figured out until today. With all the bad weather stopping our outside shooting, it gave Carrie time to run the numbers and found out that we are short the money to finish the movie. Even Bill Turner knew what it was going to cost. He was nice enough to send me a good-bye going out of business letter in the mail today. Saying he knew all along that I did not have enough money to cover my distribution and advertising cost. Also saying in his letter that I was, a "has been" and that he would buy my movie at a fair price.

Play-Doh: No way in hell does that man get your movie, Starlet. If you got the four million, then could you finish your movie?

Starlet: Yes, we could. Only Carrie and I are broke right now. Even if we put up our houses, it would not be enough to cover all the cost.

Play-Doh: Do not close up shop yet. Give me a day to figure something out for you. One more day will not hurt, will it? You have been waiting all week for the rain to clear out, wait one more day for me, Starlet.

Starlet: I appreciate your help, but I think this is a hopeless situation. Thank you for believing in me, Play-Doh. I have to accept my movie making days are officially over.

Play-Doh: With that attitude, you are probably right. I told you to keep your head up, did I not? What has happened to the Starlet I have come to know and love over the last six months? I want to chat with her and not you.

Starlet: It is hard to do that right now, knowing what is about to happen to our movie and my company. For you, I will try to stay positive. Wait a minute what are you talking about loving me? I mean we have not even met. You do not even know me well enough to say something like that.

Play-Doh: Need to go. I have a problem to solve. Chat with you soon, Starlet.

John quickly ended their chat after making that slip up, telling Jill that he loved her. He could tell how down she was while chatting with her. There was no need to complicate her life even more by explaining his true feelings toward her. The problem now was finding the money for his Starlet. Like always, he called the man who knew how to fix his problems, Michael.

John reached Michael at his office and asked him, "Michael, how much money is in the Play-Doh account right now?" Michael said, "Almost six million, why do you ask, John?" "I want you to send a five million dollar check to J&C Productions right away. Add a loan agreement with the check, stating that J&C Productions agrees to pay back the loan from the receipts of the movie that come in after releasing it nationwide. With an additional amount of one dollar to be paid as interest for the loan." "Now I know you are insane, John. It is one thing to help this woman with her career, but to loan her that amount of money and only receiving one dollar as interest. John, you should think this over before doing something so irresponsible." "If I do not help Jill now, the movie and her company will be finished. All this would have been for nothing, then Bill Turner wins and Jill loses. He found out she was having money troubles and will not be able to finish her movie. He even sent her a nasty note telling her that she was a "has been" and offered to buy her movie. My question is did you know all of this, Michael?" "I heard something about their money problems from one of my connections, but not about the movie offer. The only reason I did not tell you John, I thought you would overreact by doing something like this." "I believe we had a conversation about watching out for Jill and you telling me if any trouble came her way." "Yes, we did. But I did not think you would want to send her four million dollars." "You thought wrong. It is my money and I can spend it anyway I see fit. Send her the five million dollars instead of four." "John, I would think this over before doing it." "I have old friend. You made the mistake not telling me. Do not make another one now by not doing as I have asked."

Now, Michael knew John was serious about giving Jill the money. If he did not do as John asked, he would lose his friend and best author at the same time. "I will take care of everything today. Is there anything else you want me to do, John?" John said, "In the future, please keep me informed of anything else bad that concerns Jill. No matter what it is, let me know." "I will do that, John. The check and loan agreement will be sent FedEx to them today, Jill should receive it tomorrow morning." Their call ended without a goodbye. Which was a first for both of them. Michael knew now John was in love with this woman that he had never even met.

The next day at the offices of J&C Productions, Jill and Carrie were sitting in the conference room looking out the window. Seeing that rain had cleared out and it was going to be a nice sunny day outside. Only, it was still raining inside for the two women. Both were thinking there would be no miracle that would come out of the blue to bail them out. Later that day, Jill was going to tell everyone the movie was shutting down and the production company would be closing its doors. Jill said, "Thank you for agreeing to do this with me, Carrie." Carrie said, "It was a pleasure working with you again, Jill. We almost made our dream happen, finishing our first movie. I have not told David yet, hoping your Play-Doh Man can pull one more rabbit out of his hat for us." "I do not think he has any left. If he did, it would have to be a very large one. You were right; we came damn close to finishing our first movie together, Carrie. I believe even the Play-Doh Man cannot fix this. Four million dollars is a lot to ask anyone to find short notice."

After that statement, a FedEx truck pulled into the parking lot and came to the front door to make a delivery. The man was holding a letter package and needed someone to sign for it. Carrie got up and went to sign for the package. She returned into the conference room and then opened the letter package to see what it contained. After pulling out the contents, she was speechless, which gave Jill some concern. Carrie was now holding a check for five million dollars from the Play-Doh man.

She started screaming very loud, oh my God, that damned Play-Doh Man has done it again, Jill. He has single-handedly pulled our asses out of the fire by finding another very large rabbit to pull out of his hat." Jill said, "What in the hell are you talking about, Carrie?" She jumped out of her seat to see why her business partner was so excited and talking about. That was when her own eyes saw the check from Play-Doh and tears began forming in her eyes. She was hugging Carrie, while looking at the huge check that was in her hands, still not believing they now had more than enough money to finish their movie. The Play-Doh Man had come through for her once again.

Then Carrie pulled out the loan agreement that was also in his letter package. Carrie said, "Wait a minute, we might have got excited too soon, Jill. There is a loan agreement we need sign before we can have the money." Jill said, "I do not care what the loan agreement says, we need to sign it and fax it back to Parnell Publishing Company before Play-Doh changes his mind and rescinds his offer." "I cannot believe the loan is only going to cost us one dollar interest." "See I told you, there is nothing to worry about, Carrie. Play-Doh is only trying to help us. He has given his time, his advice, his information, and now his own money. Can we please sign now, or do you want to think about it some more?" "We can sign, sorry for ever doubting your special friend with the funny name."

The two women signed the document and faxed it back to Parnell Publishing Company. The funding Play-Doh had sent them saved their company and movie. With the weather clearing out, tomorrow Jill could start shooting scenes again. Right now, both of them needed to go to the bank and deposit that huge check so it would have time to clear. After doing that, Jill sent this email to Play-Doh.

Starlet: Received your check this morning and it is in the bank as we speak. We also signed the loan agreement and sent it by FedEx to Michael. Only wish I had the words to describe what I am feeling right this second for what you have done for us. I could give you a hundred kisses for giving us that loan with the tiny interest payment.

Play-Doh: One day when we do meet in person, I will give you permission to try. After all, you are an actor and should be able to pull off that scene without having any trouble. There could be some re-takes if your kisses are not to my satisfaction.

Starlet: Whatever you say Play-Doh. No script in the world could put it into words what I am feeling right now. You have come through for me so many times; that I will never be able to repay you for everything you have done for me.

Play-Doh: Never is such a long time, Starlet. Someday, you might have to make a hard choice in your life. Then we will see if you mean what you are saying to me right now.

Starlet: What do you mean by that, Play-Doh?

Play-Doh: Someday, but not today. First, go and finish making your movie. It is time to look forward and not backwards.

Goodbye, Starlet. Believe me, you are no "has been" in my eyes. I hope you believe it yourself.

Starlet: You mean our movie. We are partners now that we are using your money. However, there is a lot I need to do before shooting starts tomorrow. Thank you again Play-Doh, for the loan and nice comment. Chat with you soon, bye for now.

John got off his computer and took Suzie outside to play fetch. He had accomplished his job by putting Jill back in business. Now, he was back chatting with the woman he had fallen in love with. She would finish her movie and then they could finally meet in person. Which was the last part of his plan to put in motion.

Chapter 9

Finished Product

It took Jill less than a month to shoot all her scenes and finish the movie. With all the down time from the rain, she was prepared when shooting began again. Jill had a very detailed list of every shot she needed to make. Now it was time for Carrie to do her part and start editing the movie. She told Jill it should take by the end of October, no later. Then they could release the movie right before the Thanksgiving holiday, which would be the perfect time being a four-day weekend. Everyone was working together to make sure the dead line was met. Even Jill pitched in to help get Carrie through the producing process, by babysitting Molly when needed. She enjoyed spending time with her goddaughter, playing with a five year old was not hard work compared to editing a movie.

Later in the process, Jill spent a whole day watching them edit parts of the movie. Putting the scenes in the right places to tell the story, and leaving out the scenes that slowed down the flow of the movie. That was how Carrie explained to Jill about what they were doing with each scene and why. Some of the cut scenes could go on the DVD when it was out. Jill understood and trusted Carrie to cut all the unnecessary scenes. She had done her job on the movie, now it was Carrie's turn to do hers.

The week before the opening, Jill and Carrie went from coast to coast doing interviews and going to premiers for "Life's Consequences", in order to promote the film. Hitting all the talk shows, morning and night, to get the word out about their movie. Saying, they had made a movie that every adult, young or old would enjoy going to see. John watched Jill whenever she was on television, knowing exactly what she had gone through to make this movie become a reality. He was impressed at how well she handled herself when given a tough question to answer. It was like watching a completely different person all together answering all those questions. Telling the interviewer that making this movie had changed her life in so many ways. In John's mind, she was no longer a Starlet, but a serious player in the movie industry. He still could not help but be proud for what she had accomplished by directing and making her first movie by him pushing her in the right direction. Jill had come a long way since their first email chat together a mere six months ago.

Jill did not wait to give Play-Doh his credit until the movie came out. She made sure to mention something about him and his book, in all her interviews she had given. His name was to be in the credits before and after the movie. Jill made sure Carrie did that while editing the movie. All the interviewers asked Jill if she knew who The Play-Doh Man was. The public was interested in finding out who had written the book she was now making her movie about. Jill would only tell them what she knew, that he was a man of mystery and she only chatted with him by email. Sometimes, she would put in a few extras to make the interviews become more interesting. Trying to be a little mysterious herself, like the Play-Doh Man. At home, John got a few laughs from watching Jill answer the questions about him, knowing she had no idea about his identity. She was only doing what it took to get the word out about her movie. If she had to stretch the truth, it was all right by him.

Finally, the release date came with Jill and Carrie deciding to go see their movie, "Life Consequences". They went to their local theater and bought tickets to the last showing, to check out the reaction the audience might give while watching the movie. Both women came into the theater late as the opening credits were showing and the lights were off. They planned this so no one in the audience would recognize them. Jill and Carrie sat up front, two rows back from the screen, which were the only seats available. The theater was full, which was a good sign the two of them thought. During different parts of the movie, they got to experience the audience reactions and could tell they were pleased at what they were watching. Each knew right then their movie was going to be a hit.

After the movie was over, the lights came on while the last of the credits were still running. Jill and Carrie stood up and went to the front of the theater, to greet the audience. Everyone in the theater was surprised and elated to see Jill and Carrie standing there. Jill said, "Well, did everyone like it?" The crowd began to clap and cheer at what they had just seen. Giving the two women a feeling of accomplishment for all their hard work. Jill and Carrie told the audience if they wanted an autographed picture, to come see them. They had decided to bring stacks of their pictures, which were inside their purses in case this moment arrived.

It took them over two hours to get all the autograph pictures signed. Lucky for them, it was the last showing of the night. Otherwise, the theater would have had to postpone the next showing. The next day, a newspaper got wind of what Jill and Carrie had done and printed a huge article about their autograph session they held in the local theater. It was something few actors took the time to do in this busy world of making movies. Bill Turner saw the article in the paper; already extremely furious at how successful Jill's movie was opening night. He called a special meeting with his two VPs to discuss what he wanted them to do next. After a brief meeting, the two VPs had their instructions and went to carry them out immediately.

After leaving Bill's office, they had a conversation together about Jill. One VP said, "You have to hand it to her, she knows how to get free advertisement without having to pay for it. The newspaper article is only going to make even more people want to go see her movie." The other VP said, "Yes, you are definitely right about that. People will go see the movie, thinking they might have a chance to meet Jill in person. She is a lot smarter than we gave her credit for in those contract negotiations." "I believe our days here at the studio are numbered." "Yeah, I think it is time to get our resumes updated. You think Jill might hire us?" "No, I do not. But I think she would get a good laugh while interviewing us." "I guess we are screwed then. I think we should stay here until Bill decides to fire us. Which could be any day now."

For some reason, Bill could not find out who this Play-Doh person was and why in the hell he was helping Jill. He wanted to have a conversation with this man and stop all his participation in helping that woman become even more successful than she already was. He knew Jill had gotten the money from him to finish her movie. Bill decided to call Parnell Publishing Company later that day to see if Michael would tell him who this Play-Doh Man was and if he could talk to him about a business proposition.

The movie's numbers came out the Monday after the holiday. It was a huge success, grossing over sixty million dollars in the four-day weekend. Jill and Carrie could not believe their movie had done so well. After the word got out the public loved it, the next week's numbers were almost as high, grossing over fifty million dollars by word of mouth alone. Which meant, their movie had made over a hundred and ten million dollars in a week and a half. Both women had done very well in making, promoting and then selling their movie for the public to see. J&C Productions was definitely a company Bill was going to have to compete with in the future; these two women had discovered a new approach in making movies by using actors, from different occupations. Some were from theater, others did plays, and even by using two young inexperienced college students as actors, giving everyone a chance to make it in the movie industry. Jill and Carrie were willing to take chances on people when no one else even gave them a second thought. Hollywood did not work this way; Jill had changed all that, by making a very successful movie with her production company. Now actors no longer had to sign long-term yearly contracts with movie studios. They could pick which movies they wanted to be in and not the other way around. All the power had switched from the movie studios to the actors because of a company called J&C Productions.

The next month, everyone in the country was sending J&C Productions movie scripts, hoping they might use them for their next movie. It was a little overwhelming for Jill and Carrie to handle, but they did enjoy all the attention. Especially after most of Hollywood had written them off. Which might have happened, except for a man called Play-Doh and his generous five million dollar loan.

John's book had a surge in sales with the success of Jill's movie. Just like he predicted it would to Michael months ago. When his phone rang, he knew it was Michael, calling him. Michael said, "You were right again, Jill's movie helped to increase your book sales." John said, "Well, do not sound so disappointed my old friend. That means more money in your pocket. But increased sales had nothing to do with this, Michael." "I know helping Jill was. Right?" "Yes, that is the reason. However, this is not over yet. I still have to meet her in person." "Well, I hope you know what you are getting yourself into. Last thing I want to see in this world is your heart broken again." "We all make choices, I have to make mine."

Two months later, the movie had run its course and considered one of the best of the year. There was buzz about all the awards the movie might win in February, at the Oscars. A week later, the movie received four Academy Awards nominations. They were, for best screenplay, best director, best producer, and last for Jill as best actress in the part she played. Which was something John wanted to see her do and knew she was capable of if given the opportunity.

After hearing the news, Jill could not believe their movie was up for four Oscars. At the time, she was paying Play-Doh for their loan. She sent a check for five million dollars to Parnell Publishing Company. Since most of the movie's receipts had come in, it was time to pay back the loan. However, she did forget about the one-dollar interest payment, which was something else that slipped her mind. At the time, she was planning a weekend retreat next month for all the cast members. She wanted to show her appreciation for every ones hard work in getting the movie finished, by paying for a ski trip to Colorado. They all had earned some R&R after the job they had done and Jill thought they all could use a little vacation.

However, most of the cast was already back in New York where they lived, all six actors decided not to come. Some of them were already working on other acting jobs and told Jill they had seen enough snow in New York during the winter, they did not want to fly across the country to see even more. Jill understood and accepted their decision to decline her offer. The two young students from USC did accept and would be going on the ski trip. That left the other two actors who lived in California, but since they did not ski, they also decided not to go on the trip. This left the most important person of them all, the Play-Doh Man.

Two weeks before the trip, Jill emailed him an invite to come join them in Colorado for the weekend so they could finally meet in person instead of on line. He sent back an email that he would try to come if weather permitted him. There had been many flights cancelled in his area due to bad weather conditions. Jill emailed him all the information of the ski trip and hoped he could be there. All he had to do was make it to the ski lodge and she would reimburse all his travel expenses. The trip was the last weekend of January, in case he could join them to have some fun. He emailed back that he would do his best to be there to meet the Starlet in person. This got a huge smile on Jill's face after reading his last email.

There was no way John was going to miss the opportunity to meet Jill in person. Even if he had to drive to get there that weekend, John was going to be at that ski lodge. It was the last part of his plan, and then he would get his answer to what Jill was going to be in his life. Seeing for himself if they had a future and belonged together or not. His only problem was where to put Suzie for that weekend.

Jill was excited, thinking she and Play-Doh were finally going to meet. She wanted to thank him in person for all his help by talking her into quitting her job at Planet Studios to open a production company to make her own movies. However, he needed a special thank you for the huge loan he had given her. She knew how much this man was responsible for everything happening in her life recently. Jill called Carrie and said, "He is coming on the ski trip, Carrie. That is if his flight is not canceled from bad weather." Carrie said, "Maybe we should postpone this trip, Jill. Wait until there is better weather." "Are you kidding me? I have made all the reservations, Carrie. I think it is time we go enjoy ourselves. You know how much Molly is looking forward to going on this trip." "I know that full well. She has been asking me every day when we are going to leave so she can go play in the snow. This trip will give her something to tell her friends about in kindergarten. I do not think any of them have ever seen real snow before and I know David is excited about going. It will be our first getaway in almost two years." "Then it is settled, Colorado here we come in two short weeks."

A week before his trip, John called Michael to give him the news of his upcoming trip back to Colorado. John said, "Well, I am going to Colorado to meet Jill in person next week. Have any suggestions before I leave old friend?" Michael said, "It is about time you finished all this business with her, John. You know I want you to be happy and find the right person to be in your life. I only hope everything works out for you. Mainly what I cost you that day at the river." "Michael, it was not your fault and I never blamed you for that day. I know deep down you care about me. That is why you are my only true friend I have in this world. Wish me luck with Jill, I think I have some competition going against me. She now loves her new job that I have found for her. Being a director is a new passion in her life that she enjoys doing very much. If she wins an Oscar for it, I do not think I stand a chance with her." "I hate to be the one to tell you this, but you did tell me to keep you informed about anything pertaining to Jill. You have even more competition than you think. I heard she has invited Johnny Mann on the ski trip to Colorado. You will also be meeting him in person for the first time. It could be some kind of publicity stunt, since he is up for an award at the Oscars. But I thought you might want to know, John." "Thanks for telling me. I was planning to go a day early to scout things out before I approach Jill. Now I will definitely will, to see for myself what is going on between them. Johnny Mann or not, my heart will tell me if she is the one. Call you after I get there, bye for now, Michael." "Good luck and good hunting my friend."

John got off the phone and started packing for his trip. Knowing now that the black belt himself, Johnny Mann was going to be there. He decided to pack a few extra items he might need in case they had a run in with each other. Since the man had a reputation for getting into fights, why not oblige him with a few surprises. Suzie watched him pack his bags and for some reason knew, it was not going to be good for her. John had decided to leave Suzie at a dog kennel in town for the five days until he returned on Monday. The only neighbor he trusted was going to be gone the same week. He had no one else he could leave her with that he trusted. At least at the kennel, Suzie would have a chance to interact with other animals. Something she never got to do while living with him.

John knew he would have to make it up to her after getting back home. He took Suzie out so she could do her business before they went to bed. After coming back inside the house, John said the three magic words and they raced off to the bedroom. Since he was leaving soon, John let her win the race by getting under the covers before him. With it being winter, John did not use the central heat much and the house got cold during the night. He could not sleep if it got too warm, being so warm blooded himself, but he had plenty of covers on the bed which Suzie started getting under instead of staying on top when they went to bed. For some reason she only slept at the end of the bed, maybe she liked the way John's winter socks smelled.

Chapter 10

Time for R&R

It was early Thursday morning when John dropped Suzie off at the dog kennel. After checking her in and giving all his contact information to the woman who was working there, John told her he would be back in five days to pick Suzie up. She was not happy about her current situation, in a pen away from her master. She lay down at the fence and watched him drive away now going to the airport. John saw her in his rearview mirror and his heart broke, he had no other choice, knowing this was the right opportunity to meet Jill. It was time for the last part of his plan, which did not include Suzie on this trip. Otherwise, he might never get another chance to meet Jill in person and tell her how he truly felt.

While on his flight to Colorado, John daydreamed about their first meeting together. What he might say to her in person instead of an email. Being able to see what kind of reaction he would get while speaking to her for the first time. With his seat leaned all the way back and his eyes closed; John tried to relax on the flight while heading to Aspen, Colorado. The place where his grandfather had raised him since he was six years old and where he vowed never to return to after the tragic accident happened that changed his life forever. Now things have come full circle and forced him to return to seek a new future with a woman whom he thought could be his soul mate.

After landing in Denver, John rented a car and drove to the ski resort where Jill had made the reservation for the weekend.

His room would be reserved under the name of Play-Doh, the only name she had to use, still not knowing his real one. John arrived early Thursday evening at the resort, which was the day before Jill arrived. He walked inside to check-in at the front desk and saw a young man standing behind it, who was looking down at the computer screen. The desk clerk was checking on something and had not noticed him standing there. To get his attention, John said, "Excuse me young man, I believe you have a room reserved for me. The name is Play-Doh." The desk clerk said, "Why yes we do, Mr. Play-Doh. I see that you are a day early. According to my computer, your reservation is for Friday, check-in time is at noon sir." The desk clerk still had not looked up to see who was standing in front of him. He was typing something on the computer at the time, reading the information on the screen that came up.

John said, "I know my reservation is for tomorrow young man, but I was wondering if I could check-in now. I will gladly pay for the extra night." Then the desk clerk said, "I think you should …" He stopped speaking immediately after realizing the man standing before him, was John William Davis himself, the famous adventure writer. "You are John William Davis, the famous author who writes the JD adventure novels. I am a huge fan of your work, Mr. Davis. I have read all of your books so many times and wish I could write like you." "Calm down, young man. Yes, you are right. I am he. Can you please not announce it to the whole world? I do not want anyone to know I am here yet. Can we keep this quiet until I tell you otherwise?" "Not a problem, Mr. Davis. Now I know why your room was reserved under that funny assumed name. By the way, I am Rex Anderson. If you need anything, just ask and I will see to it personally, Mr. Davis." "Well, can I check-in now Rex?" "I believe I can arrange that. You will be in room #101 on the next floor. It is the first room on the left when you get off the elevator. Of course, there will be no charge for the extra day. I will not put in the computer that you have checked in yet. Only we will know that you have sir." "Well, thank you for that Rex. When will Miss Green be arriving?" "Tomorrow at noon is the time she is expected to check-in. But sometimes she comes an hour earlier to beat the weekend crowd."

John had to be careful how he phrased his next question to Rex. He did not want to raise any suspicion with him. Otherwise, he might not give him the answer. With Rex being a fan of his, he thought the young man would be glad to cooperate with him. John said, "Rex, you have been very helpful. I would prefer you to call me JD from now on. All my friends do, and now I consider you one. Mr. Davis sounds so impersonal to me." Rex said, "Thank you for letting me, JD. You do not know how much it means to finally meeting you in person. I have tried to come see you on many of your book signing tours. However, I have not been able to get away while working here. Now, it does not matter, you are standing right in front of me." John knew now he could ask this young man any question he wanted and did not hesitate doing so.

"Rex, could you tell me what room number Miss Green will be staying in tomorrow?" Rex said, "Miss Green will be in room #110, right across from yours, JD. She likes being close to the elevator, she always reserves that specific room when coming here." "What about Johnny Mann, does he have his own room, or is he sharing one with somebody?" "I am not supposed to give out that particular information about where our guests are staying and with whom. I think since we are friends, JD, it will not hurt to tell you. Mr. Mann is going to be in room #109, right next to Miss Green." "Thank you for the information. You helped me out, Rex. I think we can keep each other's secrets. That is what friends do." "All right then, here is your room key. The elevator is down the hall and on the right.

Do you need any help with your bags or ski equipment JD?" "No, just have the one bag; I travel very light when it is only me. Since I do not ski, there is no equipment for you to store. I want to thank you again for all your help Rex. It has been a long day and I think it is time for me to say goodnight. If there is anything, I can do for you to return the favor, just ask me. Okay, Rex?" "Will do, JD. See you tomorrow morning." "Nice to have met you Rex."

Rex watched his idol walk to the elevator and get on. He could not believe he just met John William Davis in person, and now gets to call him JD, and now considers him a friend. Rex was glad his boss called him to work the front desk tonight. Otherwise, he would have missed this opportunity to meet his favorite author.

JD went straight to his room and got unpacked. Then he decided to go fill his ice bucket and make himself a drink before going to bed. It should help him relax being anxious about tomorrow, meeting the woman he had been dreaming about for the last six months. He wanted to get to bed early in case Jill did decide to arrive before noon. While getting the ice, he checked where the other rooms were located on his floor. Jill's was right across from his, as Rex had told him, and Johnny was on the right next to hers. With the three rooms being so close together, there could be trouble in the future. JD would have to do some thinking on the current situation. Having Johnny so close was not part of his plan, and might cause a problem with him spending time alone with Jill.

After getting the ice and fixing a strong drink, JD decided to watch some television before going to bed. Then he would try to go to sleep and dream about his first meeting with Jill, and what he would say to her. At least by the end of this weekend, he would know if she was worth all the work and planning he had put in to help her. No more emails to communicate with each other, they would do it in person from now on.

The next morning, after having his breakfast, JD decided to take a walk around town to see how much it had changed over the years. After walking a while and doing some shopping in a few stores, JD returned to the resort to check on any news about Jill's arrival. When he entered the front lobby, Rex was standing there waiting to speak to him. Rex said, "A private matter JD, could you spare a minute?" JD followed Rex to a very large room off the lobby, which had a huge fireplace for all the guests to enjoy before going out to ski or returning from skiing to warm up and relax. There were couches and chairs all around the room, with a few tables to have drinks and food served. A server came in to take orders for any guests sitting in the room.

JD said, "Well, what can I do for you Rex?" Rex hesitated to answer him. JD told him to ask his question if he wanted to find out the answer. Rex said, "Here goes then. You said if I thought of something, that you would help me?" "What can I do for you Rex?" "I am trying to become a writer like you JD. I mean, I want to be a published author someday. Would it be too much to ask if you would read something I have written?" JD was relieved at the question thinking Rex was going to tell him that Jill was not coming, and had canceled her trip. "Not a problem, Rex. I have some free time now, bring it to me." Rex raced off to get his manuscript before JD could tell him the other things he needed him to bring. He returned a minute later with his manuscript in hand and gave it to JD. "I will also need a pen and paper, to make my notes while reading this Rex. It is an old habit of mine. I was going to tell you that but you raced off." "Sorry, I was so excited you agreed to read my work. I will be right back with both, JD." Rex came back with two pens and some paper and handed them to JD while trying to catch his breath from all the running back and forth.

"I need this while reading your manuscript to make any notes of where I think you need to make changes to improve your manuscript. That way you get my honest opinion of what I think. In addition, you will have my notes to go by if you decide to make the changes. Does that sound fair Rex?" Rex said, "More than fair and I promise not to bother you while reading it. Now I need to get back to the front desk before my boss shows up and fires me. I hate to lose my job fraternizing with the guest." "I can understand that. I will be in here reading your manuscript enjoying a drink. You better go back to work." Rex thanked JD for taking the time to read his manuscript, knowing he could have just said no. It meant a lot to him for doing it. "You might want to wait before thanking me. I have not read your work yet. Also, remember our secret. No one is to know I am here, right?" "You have my word on it, JD." "That is good enough for me, Rex." Then JD reminded him of the time by pointing his finger at his watch. Rex got the hint and raced off again for the front desk. He was pleased to find no one was there waiting for him.

JD picked a chair near the fireplace to sit in while reading Rex's manuscript. When the server came in, he ordered bourbon on the rocks and then continued with his reading. After a few pages, he started writing his notes of changes he thought would help. He knew now that Rex was a raw writer and needed to spend more time on his writing. JD thought this particular manuscript did not have good enough subject matter and material for Rex to try to publish. Being glad he had ordered a drink, he would definitely order a few more before finishing this manuscript. Not long after finishing his first drink and getting past the second chapter, JD told the server to keep them coming. That was when Jill arrived inside the lobby. JD could hear all the voices and he heard hers in the small crowd. The same voice he knew from her movies and interviews she did on television.

Jill and all her party arrived an hour early as Rex had told him. The small party consisted of five people, which were Jill, Johnny, Carrie, David and their daughter Molly. The two students from USC would be checking in later that day. While Rex was getting them all checked in; Molly decided to go exploring the ski resort without her parent's knowledge or permission. She being a precocious five-year-old, it was something all kids that age seemed to do while adults did boring grown-up things. Molly wondered into the very large room with the big fireplace and saw JD sitting beside it reading what looked like some kind of book. He was the only person in the room, so Molly decided to go over and have a talk with him.

The manuscript was in front of JD's face when Molly walked right up to him. She did not say a word to let him know she was there. JD could sense that someone was standing right in front of him. As he lowered the manuscript to see who it might be, there was little Molly staring back at him. She was holding a can of Play-Doh in her right hand. JD said, "Well hello there, little girl. What is your name?" The little girl said proudly, "Molly Smith and I am five years old." "Well it is a pleasure to meet you Molly Smith. My name is JD." "Those are letters, not a name." "Yes, they are. They are my letters that make my name. That is what I like people to call me. What is that in your hand?" "It is my Play-Doh. My Aunt Jill gave it to me to play with on this trip. She told me blue was not her favorite color. She always liked playing with pink." "Well, that was nice of your Aunt Jill. Would you like me to make you something with it?" "Like what?" "Name any animal and I will try to make it for you." "Make me a bear." "Okay, I will make you a bear. Let me have your Play-Doh." Molly handed the can to him and watched as he took out some of the clay. Then JD gave the can back to her, which she kept in her right hand. He pulled out his pocketknife and used it to sculpt the Play-Doh in certain areas. A few minutes later, JD had formed the Play-Doh into a miniature blue bear. He handed it to Molly and asked her what kind of sound does a bear make? "Garr," was all that came out of Molly's mouth. "That is right. Very good Molly."

Carrie entered the large room looking for Molly, and saw her standing in front of a stranger talking to him. By the look on her face, JD knew she was not pleased with what was going on. Carrie said, "Molly, what have I told you about walking off without telling me or your father first. Now come on and stop bothering this man so he can read his book. We need to go to our room and unpack, honey. JD said, "No harm done here. Believe me; I needed a break from my reading. Which gave me a chance to meet Molly here. She is a very smart little girl to be only five." JD then smiled at her and Molly returned a smile right back to him.

After a brief exchange with JD and Carrie introducing herself to him. Carrie thanked him for looking out for Molly until someone came to get her. Molly then said, "Look mommy, JD made me a bear out of my Play-Doh." She showed it to her mother and then made the bear sound like she did before. "That is the sound they make when they attack you, mommy." Carrie said, "Well, that was nice of JD to do that for you. Did you thank him?" "Thank you JD for my bear. And I will do my best not to smush him." JD said, "Good to hear, because if you do, he will not look like a bear anymore. Maybe you should let your mother carry your Play-Doh, that way you can use both hands to carry your bear." Molly took JD's advice and handed the can to her mother. Before leaving, Carrie also thanked him for making the bear for Molly and said their goodbyes. Then she and Molly started walking back to the lobby to rejoin the others.

On the way, Carrie was scolding her daughter for wandering off by herself. Carrie explained to Molly that she did not want her to be lost or hurt. Molly told her mother she would not do it again. She did not want her mother to punish her, by not taking her skiing later that day. Maybe even taking away her new bear that she was now holding carefully in both hands. She asked her mother were they still going skiing later today. Carrie told her it depended on how well she behaved until it was time to go.

Rex had everyone checked in when Carrie and Molly came walking up. He started handing out room keys and then asked if anyone needed any help with their luggage or storing any ski equipment. Jill spoke up, "Yes, we do with both." She then pointed over to the luggage carts across the room for Rex to see and there ski equipment outside on the guest rack with nametags attached. Rex said, "I will take care of it right away, Miss Green." He signaled for the bellhops to get all the luggage carts and follow the guests to their rooms. They quickly brought the carts over to the guests and waited until they were ready to get on the elevator. Rex told them to take care of the ski equipment when they returned down. Rex said it loud enough so the guests tipped the bellhops for doing both jobs.

When Rex asked if they needed anything else, Jill asked him if Play-Doh had checked in yet. He was also a guest of hers and she would like to know if he had arrived. Rex saw JD standing in the entrance of the big room, nodding his head no to him. Rex said, "No, he has not Miss Green. Would you like me to inform you when he does arrive?" Before Jill could speak, Johnny Mann decided to open his big mouth by saying, "Oh please do. She is dying to meet her Play-Doh Man. That is all she has been talking about this whole trip. It is beginning to give me a headache listening to all the stories about this man with the funny name. As if he is something special, after writing a bestseller she used to make her first movie. Maybe he is some kind of superhero for Jill to fantasize about." Jill said, "That is enough, Johnny. I think you made your point. You have not even met him, why talk badly about someone you do not know." "My point exactly. You too have not met him. For all we know he might be the biggest jerk in the whole world." JD heard everything, including the part about being the biggest jerk. Johnny Mann already took that job he thought. He was an immature, self-centered, whiny asshole, by first impression of the man. JD had run across a few of his types before in his life. He might be good-looking and famous, but from what he heard, he had no real personality or likable traits. He only cared about himself and everyone could see that except Jill. Even if they had started their movie careers together, it did not mean they had to go on every trip together. In JD's mind, Jill owed this man nothing; he was a nasty bug that needed stepping on. However, this was not the right time to meet her with Johnny around throwing a little temper tantrum. There would definitely be trouble if he decided to show himself to her. It was best to wait until Johnny was not around.

While Jill and her guests were making their way to the elevators, she looked over at JD who was standing there watching them. He had Rex's manuscript under his right arm, instead of leaving it in the room. She gave him a smile as she passed by him, and he returned with his smile and a slight nod back to her. Molly was waving at JD when she saw him. JD waved back to her as she walked by. Jill said, "Did you meet a new friend, Molly?" "Yes Aunt Jill that is my new friend JD. He is the one that made me this bear out of the Play-Doh you gave me." "Well, that was nice of him. I am glad you met him. That is why we are here, to meet new people in our lives."

Jill said it loud enough so Johnny could hear her. She wanted to pay him back for some of his nasty talk at the front desk. Then Molly said, "Do you know what sound a bear makes Aunt Jill?" "No, I do not. But I bet you do." "Garr. That is the sound they make before they attack you." "That sounds scary to me." "Oh, they are very scary and ferocious animals, Aunt Jill. If attacked, they would eat your whole body for dinner." "Molly, how do you know so much about bears and what they eat?" "Mommy lets me watch the animal channel." "I think I will have a talk with your mother about that. But I am glad you got a new toy from your new friend." "I met him in the other room that has a big fireplace. Then he used his pocket knife to make me this bear." Molly showed her Aunt Jill the blue bear. "He looks just like a real bear. Your new friend has a real talent."

Johnny knew exactly what Jill was doing, talking about meeting new people on this trip, meaning to meet Play-Doh. Now getting angry with her, she was going to pay for it in the near future. Telling her to keep on trying his patience, she would not like the results. Now having Play-Doh in the picture, it gave Johnny something to worry about as they entered the elevator.

JD walked over to the front desk to talk with Rex about why he nodded his head no. JD said, "Thanks for helping out by not telling Jill I was here. I do not want to make things harder for her, especially with Johnny Mann standing next to her. Do you understand my situation now?" Rex said, "I think I do. Johnny Mann is a very jealous person. If he knew you were here, he would find a way to start a fight with you." "In my opinion, he is a very self-centered person. I know all about his reputation. I want to tell Miss Green that I am here without him being around." "I understand perfectly JD. No one will know you are here until you say the word. I think you should know they are planning to go skiing later on today.

Miss Green has rented my brother's helicopter for the whole day to fly her and Johnny to Mount Elbert. When will you get to tell her?"

After hearing this, JD's mind switched to something else while listening to Rex. Even though he continued telling JD all about Mt. Elbert being the highest mountain point in Colorado, also that the skiing was the hardest to be attempted. Being from the area, JD already knew how treacherous the skiing was on Mt. Elbert. While growing up, he had been on that mountain hundreds of times with his grandfather, to teach him survive lessons in the wild. Rex kept on talking about skiing somewhere else that had bunny trails for the beginners. Thinking JD might want to try it out for himself. JD interrupted him by asking what kind of skier Miss Green and Johnny Mann were. Rex said, "Johnny Mann is an excellent skier, and I heard from his brother that Miss Green is pretty good. That is why Johnny wanted her to ski the mountain with him. The last time they were here, she did not want to go, but promised him the next time she would. Do not worry JD; they will be safe with my brother Mark. He is an excellent helicopter pilot and has never lost anyone on any ski trips before." JD said, "There is a first time for everything Rex. I do not doubt your brother's flying skills, but he does not control the weather, believe me, it has a mind of its own."

JD told Rex he needed to go to his room to check on something. He would be back in a few minutes. He handed his manuscript to hold to until he returned, but told him no peeking until he finished reading the whole thing. JD quickly headed for the elevator. His mind was racing about all the things that could happen to Jill before they got a chance to meet. He went inside his room without anyone seeing him. If Jill or any of her guests saw him going in that room, they would then know he was the Play-Doh Man.

After getting inside, JD turned on the television to the weather channel. He watched and listened about a storm front that was heading their way tonight out of Canada. He also saw there had been a smaller snowstorm two days earlier. Which dropped a few inches of snow. Being from the area, he knew how bad the storms got with no visibility with all the heavy snow and winds. Not to mention a big drop in temperatures during the night. You can easily die in a matter of hours from hypothermia. JD watched the weather channel for a few more minutes and then put two items in his jacket pocket. He turned off the television and checked the spyglass in the door to see if anyone was in the hall outside. It was all clear; he left the room and stood by the elevator waiting to go downstairs.

While waiting, Jill came out of her room with the ice bucket in her right hand walking toward the ice machine. She did not speak to JD, but gave him another smile as she walked by him down the hall. JD smiled back at her while waiting for the elevator doors to open. He could have introduced himself to her right then, but decided to wait having Johnny right across the hall in his room.

After getting on the elevator, JD was thinking about how beautiful Jill was seeing her up close. The movie screen did not do her justice. However, he could not think about that, he had to get back downstairs to ask Rex for another favor to warn Jill not to go on that ski trip. She would not believe him being a stranger, but maybe Rex could convince her to change her plans and go skiing another time after the bad storm passed.

JD walked up to Rex and asked for the manuscript. He was not about to ask him for a favor when he had not finished doing his own. JD said, "Rex, did the storm two days ago bring a lot of snow?" Rex said, "Not a whole lot. It was a small storm. I think we got almost two inches. We needed the snow; the bunny trails around here were pretty bare." "Did the storm pass over Mount Elbert?" "I think it did. Why all the questions about the past storm, JD?" "I think the ski trip to Mount Elbert will not be safe for Miss Green, Rex. If you got two inches, then the mountain got a lot more. I need you to warn her not to go for me. There is another big storm on its way that will hit earlier this evening." "Mark would not take them up if it was not safe to go, JD. I doubt she would listen to me. Not after booking and then paying for the trip, it is nonrefundable as long as the weather is clear for them to go. They have to go today or lose the five thousand dollars she paid for the trip." "Losing five thousand dollars is better than losing your life. Please warn her for me. You know why I cannot. With Johnny Mann being involved, she will not listen to me. I need you to try. Will you?" "I will try JD when they come back down to leave with my brother. Mark is supposed to be here in the next hour to pick them up." JD thanked him and returned to the large room to finish reading the manuscript.

This time JD decided to sit in a different part of the room to conceal himself and not be bothered while reading the manuscript. The server almost did not see him; JD ordered another bourbon on the rocks with his last one getting warm. He then began reading Rex's manuscript while waiting for his drink to arrive. Soon, Jill would come downstairs and have a difficult decision to make, whether or not to go on a ski trip to Mount Elbert with a huge storm approaching early that evening.

Chapter 11

Wrong Decision

O ne hour later, Jill and all her guests retuned downstairs to greet the two USC students and then go on their ski trips. After having a brief conversation with them, the two students decided to go to their rooms, so they could unpack their bags and then take a walk around town. Since neither had been to Aspen before, they wanted to do some shopping for souvenirs and see what the town had to offer. Everyone did agree to meet in the lobby early that evening in order to eat dinner together. David, Carrie and Molly were going skiing on one of the bunny trails nearby the ski lodge. Being Molly's first time on skis, she had to learn how to stand on them first before letting her try skiing down a little hill. Jill wished Molly good luck on the snow. Molly told Jill she was excited about going skiing and would see her Aunt Jill when she got back. Then she could tell her all about being on the skis and going down any hills. Jill leaned down and gave her goddaughter a kiss on the cheek goodbye. Then the three of them left to get their ski equipment. The two USC students had already left for the elevators, which left Jill and Johnny standing alone at the front desk with Rex.

JD watched from a distance while Rex was explaining to Jill about the bad storm that was coming down from Canada. It was not supposed to reach them until nightfall, but it could come sooner with the strong winds from the north. Rex wanted to mention it to her before she left with his brother, in case she might want to change her mind about going on the trip. Jill thanked him for telling her and then asked if he had heard from Play-Doh. Johnny overheard Jill asking about her invisible man and started getting upset about the attention she was still giving him. Rex said, "I still have not heard anything from him, Miss Green. There have been a lot of flights cancelled because of the bad weather." Jill thanked him for his time and information about the weather. Rex told both of them that his brother should be on his way to pick them up shortly. If they liked, they could wait in the large room with the fireplace until he arrived. To warm themselves up and he would gladly come get them when it was time to leave. JD had already left and returned to his seat in the large room.

Jill and Johnny decided to take Rex's advice and went into the large room that was off the lobby. The one with the big fireplace and JD, who now was sitting in the corner still trying to finish reading Rex's manuscript. They did not see him when they entered the room, Johnny lit into Jill about Play-Doh, which started an argument between them. Saying, he was tired of hearing his name coming out of her mouth every hour. He wanted her to stop from this moment on, or else. The desk clerk would let her know if her invisible man decided to show up. Jill asked him, "Why do you care? Are you jealous of him, Johnny?" Johnny said, "Of a writer that you have never met, please get serious. You do not even know his real name. I think you should concentrate on me instead of the invisible man who may or may not show up. I am the one who is here with you, not him. He did not even bother to call and let you know if he was coming or not." "You invited yourself on this trip Johnny with me owing you a favor. Play-Doh has not showed up yet, but he still could. Do not count him out; he has always come through for me when I needed him."

Over in the corner, JD overheard what Jill said. He was happy to hear all of it, including the part about Johnny inviting himself on this trip and not her and that she was looking forward to meeting him. All he had to do was get rid of this asshole and his plan had a chance to work.

Johnny was angry with Jill after her statements to him. He said, "See, this is why I lose my temper with you. All those smart-ass comments that keep coming out of your mouth. It makes me want to knock your f...... head off. He did not get to finish the last part of his sentence. JD had heard enough and was not going to let Johnny threaten her while he was present in the room. He made his presence known by clearing his throat, rather loudly. Jill and Johnny turned around to see him sitting in a chair over in the corner, behind them. Both being surprised he was there, thinking the room was empty at the time. Now wondering why he did not let them know sooner. Instead of listening to them, arguing with each other.

JD said, "Excuse me, folks. I could not help but overhear that the two of you are planning a trip to Mt. Elbert to go skiing. Is that right?" Johnny said, "What business is that of yours, mister?" "Well, it isn't. Except there is a bad storm out of Canada, heading our way. If I were you, I would think about going another time until after the storm passes." "But you are not us. We are not afraid of a little storm and some strong winds. We will decide whether to go skiing, not you mister. Isn't that right Jill?" Jill did not answer him. She was thinking about what the man had just told them about the storm and what Rex had said to her a few minutes earlier. Johnny thought Jill was about to change her mind and cancel their trip. He needed her on that helicopter and said this to convince her it was safe to go. "A little bad weather is what makes the trip more exciting, Jill. I want you to stop trying to scare her into not going, mister. Otherwise, you will soon regret butting in our business. I can guarantee you that."

Jill had a worried look on her face and was starting to doubt going on the ski trip. Which was exactly what JD wanted her to do. His plan was beginning to work getting her to change her mind. Jill said, "Maybe we should wait till the storm passes, Johnny. We can always go tomorrow." Johnny said, "Don't tell me you are listening to all this bull about a little storm. You know if we do not go today, that you lose your money for renting the helicopter. Five thousand dollars is a lot to lose, Jill." JD said, "I do not think you two understand the situation. The temperatures can drop to thirty below zero on that mountain. With all the cold winds and heavy snows, you will not be able to see your hands in front of your face. A person could die in a matter of hours. Believe me; Mt. Elbert is no place to be when a snowstorm hits. I think this room with that great big fire burning is a better place to be than trying to challenge a mountain and a storm at the same time." Johnny said, "How do you know so much about storms on Mt. Elbert? Are you a weatherman?" "No weatherman, but I grew up here as a young boy and have experienced many storms on that mountain. I just came back into town to visit a new friend. When I was younger----. Johnny cut JD off this time. "We have heard enough out of you and are not interested in your life story. Are we going or not, Jill? I hope you are not letting him scare you into changing your mind." He stood there waiting for her answer.

At the time, Jill was thinking if they should go or wait and see what the weather does. JD then said, "By the way, my name is JD and not mister. All I am saying, there is always tomorrow. Why not go skiing then when it is a lot safer. Look young man, you can go without her. I would be glad to keep an eye on her while you are skiing on Mt. Elbert." JD was looking over at

Jill when he said it, hoping to get a rise out of Johnny. Maybe a fight between them would be the only way to keep Jill from leaving. Johnny said, "Well, what do you want to do Jill? I am not going to leave you with this stranger. Either we both go now or not at all."

"Better to lose some money than your life. Then again, maybe the two of you are huge risk takers." Johnny said, "I have heard enough out of you, mister. I suggest you stop butting into our business and mind your own. Unless you would like a quick trip to the hospital, which I can gladly arrange. Do you understand?" JD said, "I have already told you, my name is JD. In case, you are hard of hearing and did not catch it the first time. I was only trying to help the two of you from making a big mistake." Johnny said, "Well thank you for that. By the way, this is Jill Green, the famous movie star from Hollywood if you did not know. My name is Johnny Mann I am also from Hollywood. Maybe you might have heard of us?"

JD had had enough of Johnny's smart-ass mouth. He did not want to fight him in front of Jill, but it looked like he had no other choice to keep Jill from leaving. It was time to teach him a lesson from a mountain man that he would never forget. JD said, "Why yes, I have heard of and also recognize Miss Green from her movies. I have to say the movie screen does not do you justice, Miss Green. You are even more beautiful in person." Jill thanked him for his nice compliment while blushing a little. Now Johnny was mad enough to fight the stranger. He could see Jill was enjoying all the stranger's conversation and attention toward her. He was competing with him instead of the Play-Doh Man. Not having a clue, they were the same person. JD said, "I cannot for the life of me seem to remember where I have heard your name before, Mr. Mann. I know it was not from the movies, I do not remember seeing you in one. Maybe you can help me out?" Johnny said, "I have only starred in a few movies, but my real talent is in music. I am even up for an Oscar for one of my songs this year."

JD could see he was on the edge ready to fight him. All he had to do was give him a little push to make him. JD said, "No, I do not remember any songs you have done. Oh, I know, I read about you in the newspapers. I believe you have been in a lot of fights over the last couple of years." Johnny said, "Yes, I have been in a few. Since I have a black belt in karate, it makes me a target for someone to try and challenge." "But I thought you were to avoid trouble being a lethal weapon, not try and find it. It seems to me you fight a lot wherever you go. Also, I read somewhere you like hitting on women from time to time, am I right?" JD looked straight at Jill after saying that statement. Her face was blushing red, turning quickly to embarrassment; she looked away from him in shame. He knew right then the stories were true; Johnny had slapped her around in the past. Which was something he wanted to know before fighting him. This would give him an incentive in the fight to hurt this so-called black belt. Only JD had to remember not to kill him in front of Jill. That might ruin his chance of being with her in the future if he had to go to prison for killing this SOB.

Johnny was mad enough now to kill JD instead of putting him in the hospital. He stepped closer to get into a fighting position. JD did not intend to come over to attack him. He knew that karate was for defense and not for attack. If Johnny did attack him, he would give him something he would never forget for the rest of his life. Johnny said, "I have heard a lot of talk come out of your mouth mister. How are you at backing some of it up? Why not get out of that chair and then we can settle this like men. I want to show you what a woman beater can do in person. Do not worry; you will be out cold in a matter of seconds. That is after I break a few of your bones first." JD said, "Well, if we must. However, I have to warn you. I have never fought a real black belt before, but I did fight a black bear once. Of course, you know that kind of fight is to the death. In the wilderness you do not stop fighting till one of you stops breathing, not knocked out or have a few broken bones." JD took off his glasses and put them on the manuscript that was on the side table. He stood up and put both his hands in his jacket pockets, waiting for Johnny's next move. "Whenever you are ready young man, come over here and get your surprise. I am dying to know if your black belt is better than the black bear I killed."

Johnny was not expecting JD to accept his challenge; now seeing him put both his hands in his jacket pockets. He did not like the way this fight was starting being unlike any of his others. JD was not coming over to face him. He would have to make the first move. Johnny had two choices; either back down and leave or go over and start fighting him. Johnny said, "What do you have in your jacket pockets?" "Well come over here and find out. Like I said, I am dying to show you." Johnny did move an inch; JD could have anything in those jacket pockets to use against him. Maybe a gun or a knife or both, it was too much of a risk for him to take. Johnny was starting to realize this JD person was not normal and maybe a little crazy. He did not sign up to be hurt or even killed on this ski trip. JD could have Jill for all he cared; he was there to do a job and nothing else.

Mark Anderson, their helicopter pilot for the day, walked into the large room, ready to take them on their ski trip if they were still going. They would have to leave now before the bad weather moved in. Mark had talked to his brother Rex about the storm that was coming and they needed to get in the air if they still wanted to go skiing on Mt. Elbert. However, if he got word on the radio that the storm was coming sooner, he would cancel the trip and not charge her for the day. Jill told Johnny that this was not worth fighting about. Johnny was still standing there ready to strike him if given the chance. Jill said, "Well, I am going skiing, see you outside if you are coming Johnny." She walked out of the room with Mark, both heading for the front desk to talk with Rex before leaving. Johnny said, "This is not over, I will be back later today to finish our business. That will give you time to get out of town, mister." JD said, "Good thinking on your part for not coming over here, you definitely would not have been going skiing now or anytime soon. But I am looking forward to you getting back so I can give you that surprise." JD was not going to back down to Johnny. He desperately wanted to get his hands on that son of a bitch who beat up Jill. Johnny left the room to go find Jill, so they could leave the ski lodge and this stranger behind.

JD sat down and started reading the manuscript again. He was thinking if Johnny had not been here, he could have easily convinced Jill to stay there with him by the warm fire. Especially after telling her, he was the Play-Doh Man. With Johnny being there, he would have definitely started a fight with him. JD did not want their first meeting together by him fighting Johnny right in front of her. He was getting tired of hearing people say how dangerous Johnny was by having that black belt in karate. Even if he had put a few people in the hospital, they were drunk at the time. Only one person in the world knew what he was capable of doing it pushed too far, his friend Michael. Seeing firsthand how John could turn himself into an animal to survive in a fight.

Rex came in the room to check on JD. He sat down and said, "I was worried that you might need some help with Mr. Mann. Therefore, I sent my brother in to break things up between the two of you. I was listening outside the room and thought you two were about to fight. JD, did you know that

Mr. Mann has a black belt in karate?" JD said, "Rex, if we are to remain friends, I do not want you ever to mention that again. Do you understand me?" Rex nodded his head yes. JD told him that he wanted to fight Johnny. Rex asked, "Why?" JD said, "I had a plan. If we fought, then Miss Green would not go on the ski trip. That way she will be safe from the storm. Rex, I have tried to make a plan before doing significant things in my life. Unfortunately, it does not always work out the way I want, but at least I tried." "Then I ruined your plan. I am sorry JD." JD saw Rex's head sink down a little by what he had done. He knew the young man was sincere about his apology and meant no harm in trying to help him. JD told him he had no way of knowing about his plan for Johnny. Telling him it was not his fault they went on the ski trip. Rex still felt bad that Miss Green left. If anything bad happen to her, he would blame himself. JD wanted to bring Rex's spirits back up, he decided to tell him a story that happened many years ago in his life.

JD said, "What I am about to tell you, few people in this world know about. You see, everyone who read my first book thought the story was pure fiction. Only, it was not. That book was about me growing up in this area and the story at the river did really happen. Now do you think I can handle myself in a fight with Johnny?" Rex said, "Now that I know you really killed that black bear. Then yes, I think you could fight Mr. Mann and win. Whatever happened to the man who the bear attacked first? Did he survive the attack like in your book?" "He survived and is now my publisher." "Michael Parnell was at the river that day?" "Yes, he was and is my best friend still today. We grew up together around these parts." "I am sorry about you losing your wife, Sarah. She seemed to be a very special person from what I read." "She was one-of-a-kind Rex. Or so I always thought." "What do you mean JD?" "Miss Green is like my Sarah. However, she does not know it yet. I will let you in on another secret, just between us."

Rex waited for JD's next statement. He had the young man's full attention, now. JD said, "I am going to marry Miss Green sometime this year." Rex said, "But the two of you have not even met." "Not in person, but online we did six months ago. I have a plan Rex; you wait and see if I can pull it off. I need you to keep this between us. Understand?" "I will not tell a soul JD" "I know my plan sounds crazy, but when you know, the heart always picks the one you are supposed to be with. You will find out someday my young friend." "I almost forgot, when Miss Green was leaving, Mr. Mann dragged her outside to leave with my brother. She came up to give me a message for Play-Doh. That she would be out skiing for the day, but before she could finish telling me the rest, Mr. Mann jerked her hard by the arm and took her away. He practically pulled her arm out of the socket while doing it. I could see she was in pain. I think Mr. Mann was very upset that she mentioned your name again. I believe he is jealous of you, JD." JD thanked him for the information; it could come in handy later when dealing with Johnny. Now it was time to discuss the manuscript if he had time. Rex said, "Sure, I am on my break right now."

Before beginning, JD told Rex he was only able to read three quarters of his manuscript. It was hard to concentrate, with all the interruptions going on around him. JD said, "I have some good news and some bad news. Which one do you want to hear first?" Rex said, "Give me the bad news first, JD." "This manuscript is not something you want to publish as your first book. You need to write about a subject that the public will want to buy and read. In my opinion, this will not sell. It needs a lot of work." "I appreciate you taking the time to read it, JD." "Not a problem, Rex. Now for the good news. You have an unusual writing style, my young friend. Which I have not seen in many years. The public would not understand it, but I do. I think with a few writing tips from me, we can get your first book published sometime in the near future." Rex was feeling down, but not anymore. JD had shot him back up by agreeing to help him with his writing. With JD's help, he was sure to succeed in becoming a successful writer.

Rex said, "How do I start?" JD said, "First, by reading all the notes I made on your manuscript. Then making the changes to your story to make it a better read. If you can do that, I think you have a good chance of becoming a published writer." JD handed Rex back his manuscript and the notes he had made. Rex thanked him for his help and would start working on it next week. He wanted to concentrate on his writing without having any distractions like his friend JD had experienced. JD agreed with him. It was best to wait until he was alone.

Now heading for Mt. Elbert on the helicopter Jill and Johnny were still fighting about Play-Doh and the stranger in the large room, which according to Johnny was the new man in Jill's life. He did not like any competition and was now facing two men that Jill had on her mind instead of him. Mark tried to ignore them and concentrate on his flying, so he did not crash and kill all of them. However, it was hard the way these two were yelling with each other. Even with his headphones turned on and theirs off, he could hear every word they said. Mark thought the situation might get violent, now with them pointing fingers at each other. He tried to defuse the situation by telling them to look out the window at all the beautiful mountain scenery they were missing. Both of them ignored him and kept on arguing, as if Mark was not even there flying the helicopter.

Johnny said, "Why did you invite me on this trip, if all you can talk about is this Play-Doh guy." Jill said, "I did not invite you remember? You invited yourself, Johnny. I wish you had not come on this trip. Especially if I had known this was the way you were going to act. You have never gotten jealous before, why now Johnny?" "You never gave me a reason before. Now you have two men in your life. Play-Doh and that stranger who said I beat you." "I guess all this is my fault then? Johnny, we both know what you have done to me in the past. I never said anything to you about all the flirting you have done while we were out together. I know that you have hooked up with other women after taking me home. It hurt each time you did it to me. So how about we forget about the past and try to have a good time skiing instead. Sound fair?"

Mark was happy to hear Jill say that and hoped Johnny would agree to do it. They turn their headphones on to find out how far they were from the mountain. He said, "We will be approaching Mt. Elbert in about five minutes. You two better get prepared to jump out when I give the signal. That means skis on and the door open ready to jump when I give the word." Johnny told Jill to put on her skis that she would be jumping first. He wanted to watch her while going down the mountain in case she got into any trouble. Then he would be able to help her. Jill got into position with her skis on, ski poles in her hands and the door opened so she could jump first. Johnny was ready with his skis on and would be right behind her. Mark was getting the helicopter into position to drop them both on the mountain when the call came on the radio from base camp. The storm of Canada was moving down much faster than everyone thought, except JD, of course. Mark said, "Hold up Miss Green, I am getting a message about the storm that is heading right for us."

The man on the other end of the radio told Mark if he still had passengers on board, he should return to base immediately. If not, he should get them back on board as soon as possible and then return to base camp. Mark relayed the message to Jill and Johnny that they needed to head back now. He would bring them back tomorrow after the storm had cleared at no extra charge. Johnny said, "No way man, we are already here at the mountain and are going skiing. That storm will not be here for hours. Look how clear the sky is, not a storm cloud in sight. Come on Jill, jump out." Jill was thinking and then said, "Maybe we should head back Johnny. JD said the storms are pretty bad on this mountain." She did not get to say another word, after she mentioned JD's name Johnny pushed her out the helicopter with all his force. She was not ready to jump out and now found herself falling toward the mountain at a difficult angle and not straight down.

After pushing her out, Johnny fell back into Mark on purpose; making him cut the helicopter sharply to the left and away from Jill. They were now flying down the opposite side of the mountain that Jill was on, and almost crashed before Mark could regain control of the helicopter. He yelled at Johnny for doing something so stupid and reckless by pushing Jill out before she was ready to go. Then landing into him, which made the controls of the helicopter do a hard turn to the left and almost making them go into a spin. It took a minute for Mark to get back around to where Jill was supposed to be. Mark hoped she was not hurt because of Johnny's actions. Johnny said, "She will be all right. I only wanted to go skiing before you changed her mind. That is why I came on this trip and pushed her out so we could go skiing."

Jill hit the ground hard and started rolling down the mountain like a human snowball. One of her ski poles went flying off her hand while gathering speed as she was traveling down the mountain. So was the loose snow from the last storm that came the night before. Jill had created a small avalanche effect for herself. When she did finally come to a stop, the snow was going to be right on top of her. While rolling, she tried to do something, but was unable to now going head over heels with her skis. Soon, both skis separated from her as she picked up more speed rolling down the mountain. The small avalanche of snow was gaining on her and she started to see and feel all the loose snow in the air all around her, but could do nothing to help her situation. The snow soon engulfed Jill's whole body making her come to a complete stop and knocked out from the impact. There was no trace of her to see from the air. There were two skis and one ski pole lying on the ground about sixty yards from where she had landed and started rolling. Mark returned to where he thought Jill might be and began searching for her.

They soon spotted the skis and the one ski pole but there was no sign of Jill. Mark said, "Where could she have gone so quickly? Maybe you should jump out and see what you can find on the ground." Johnny did not respond to Mark's question or statement toward him, he kept looking out the door for Jill. The search went on for a few minutes, and then Mark decided to call in Search and Rescue, so they could come help find Jill. After hearing this, Johnny explained to Mark that it was an accident, Jill jumped out too early. He was not to say anything different if he knew what was good for him. That before he radioed in the call, they needed to get their stories straight. Mark had witnessed a man push a defenseless woman out of a helicopter that was a friend. He knew if he did not go along with Johnny's story, it meant a trip to the hospital or maybe the morgue for him.

Mark radioed to Search and Rescue to report Jill's disappearance and that he was flying back to base to refuel. Then he radioed his brother to give him the news that Jill was missing on the mountain. In addition, Search and Rescue was coming to the resort to set up a base before going out to search for Miss Green. As soon as he landed and refueled his helicopter, Johnny and he would come to the resort and give their statements about what had happened. Which should be an hour from now.

Rex got off the radio and went straight to JD to give him the news about Miss Green. While walking toward the big room, he could not believe that JD's feelings were right about the ski trip. Miss Green was in danger, not from the weather but a supposed accident. She should have taken JD's advice and never left with Johnny Mann.

JD was having another drink while relaxing in front of the fire when Rex came into the room. The young man's face told him something bad had happen to Jill, because his face was white as a ghost. JD could only hope she was not dead.

A week before Jill's ski trip, Bill Turner held a special meeting with a certain person in his office. He made an offer the man could not refuse. They exchanged cell phone numbers and parted ways with Jill's future hanging in the balance. She had no idea Bill still held a grudge toward her and was going to use this person to get his revenge. He hated Jill that much and was going to use whatever means at his disposal to make sure she paid, even if it cost Jill her life. In his mind, no one crosses Bill Turner and gets away with it.

Chapter 12

No Rescue

Rex quickly told JD the news that Jill had gone missing on Mt. Elbert and Search and Rescue was on their way to set up a base at the resort. After gathering all the information, they will go search for Miss Green using his brother's helicopter; weather permitting. Rex had seen this done in the past, when one of the guests had gone missing on a ski trip. All of this JD already knew, but let Rex explain it to him without interrupting by asking questions.

Then Rex brought up the part about the storm, that it was coming a lot sooner than anyone thought. Rex said, "JD, how did you know the storm was coming early, are you a weatherman too?" JD said, "No, not hardly. After watching a weather report in my room, I knew the speed of the winds coming out of the north would cause the storm to arrive early. Remember, I have lived in the area before and know a little about the snow storms coming out of Canada."

JD was troubled about Jill's disappearance and with Johnny now coming back to the resort, not bothering to stay there and keep looking for her. After hearing the story of what had happened on the ski trip, JD knew Johnny was responsible for the accident and Jill's disappearance. Only he had no proof at the time and needed to hear more about what actually occurred on that helicopter before proving how Johnny was involved.

Rex told him something seemed wrong with his brother, he sounded scared over the radio while talking to him. That was when JD thought there might be a way to find out the truth about what really happened on the trip. For some reason, Rex thought his brother might be in some kind of danger. JD said, "I need your help, Rex. Miss Green and your brother's life could depend on it. What do you say are you willing to help me?" Rex said, "Of course, whatever you need me to do, JD." "Good, I am going to make out a list of supplies. I will need you to go buy for me. Remember to get everything on this list and bring it back to the resort as soon as possible. We do not have much time before I have to leave." "Where to?" "Mt. Elbert, to find Miss Green and save her life."

JD quickly made out the list of supplies and handed it to Rex. Then he gave him the money to pay for everything. Before they parted ways, both exchanged cell phone numbers in case there were any problems getting any of the items on their list. Time was running out for Jill, her Play-Doh Man might not be able to come through for her this time.

Carrie, David and Molly came back to the resort after their day of skiing on the bunny trails. They had no idea what was going on and went to their room to change clothes and rest before dinner. The desk clerk that was working at the time did not know Jill was missing or that Search and Rescue was on the way to the resort. Rex left without telling him anything per JD's instructions.

During his shopping trip, JD called Michael to give him an update on the current situation about Jill missing. He told him all about the events before Jill left the resort and now she had mysteriously gone missing on Mt. Elbert. He was going to need his help in finding her later that evening. Michael told his friend that his life was never boring. Then asked how he could help? John told him about his plan to find Jill. Using the GPS chip in her cell phone to track her exact position. Michael agreed with him, that his plan should work using Jill's cell phone. John told

Michael, it was the only thing he could think of with time was running out. He had to reach her before the full effects of the storm hit the mountain, sometime early that evening. It would be impossible to try to find her with the heavy winds and snows, and at night. Michael told John to call him back with Jill's cell phone number and her carrier. He would do the rest finding her exact location by going to her cell phone carrier's office to use their equipment to track her phone. JD told Michael as soon as he had the information, he would call him back.

Then Michael said, "I think it's time you reveal who you are John, especially under these circumstances." John said, "Not yet Michael, first I have to know who and what I am up against; the Play-Doh Man stays invisible for the time being. Who knows, I might get to spend some alone time with Jill on the mountain. That is if I get off the phone with you." He hung up and went back to shopping for his supplies. After finishing, he called Rex to see how he was coming along with his list. JD wanted to make sure he had all the items on both lists before returning to the resort.

Rex answered his cell phone, seeing that it was JD. Rex told him that he was getting the last item now. JD knew the last item on Rex's list would take some time to get. JD said, "So you are at Will Gary's hardware store then?" Rex said, "Yes, and I told Mr. Gary to make me a John Davis special bucket. He laughed when I said that to him and wanted to know where I heard about it. I told him I read about it in one of your books. I did not think you wanted him to know you were in town, JD. He is fixing the last part now." "Good thinking, Rex. You were right. That man can tell the longest stories, do not let him delay you." "Not a problem. I told him to hurry that I needed it done fast. Should be heading back to the resort in about five minutes." "Hey Rex, if Search and Rescue are already there, I want you to help them set up. I will come join all of you later."

"What about all the supplies, what should I do with them?" "Leave them in your truck for the time being. We will unload them later when it is time for me to leave."

JD got back to the resort before Rex or Search and Rescue. He went upstairs to his room to change his clothes and pack a few things in a sport bag to take with him on his trip to the mountain. Then he went back downstairs to warm up and wait for his meeting with Search and Rescue. JD went into the large room off the lobby and sat down in the chair that he used that morning. His cell phone rang and JD knew for some reason it had to be Rex calling him.

Rex said, "JD, I am finished and got everything you needed on the list. I have a question for you." JD said, "Ask it." "What will happen if Search and Rescue does not ask for your help? I mean buying all the supplies beforehand seems to me like it could be a waste of time and money." "I think you have forgotten our talk earlier today. You have to make a plan, and then wait to execute it, Rex. I can always return all the items and get my money back. I need to wait until your brother gets here at the resort and have him fly all my supplies and me to Mt Elbert. What I cannot do is waste any time in trying to save Miss Green's life. It is better to be prepared than not. Understand, Rex?" "I do now, sir. Sorry for asking such stupid questions." "If you do not ask questions. You will not get the answers and will not be able to learn anything from them my young friend." "Then I have one more. What if Search and Rescue will not let you take over their operation?" "Rex, I have been right about things so far today, let me worry about Search and Rescue. You need to get back here with those supplies and leave everything else to me." "I am pulling in the parking lot right now and see a lot of red lights flashing around the entrance of the resort. I will go help them bring in their equipment, like you asked, JD."

JD was sitting in the large room enjoying the huge fire by himself. He was trying to absorb all the heat his body could take before having to leave to go face those cold, wintery elements on Mt. Elbert, getting mentally prepared for his journey. Thinking to himself, he might even get a chance to visit his grandfather's gravesite while up on the mountain. After the wolves attacked and killed him in his tent, there was not much left of his body. The men that found him decided to bury the man on Mt. Elbert instead of bringing the remains down the mountain.

Even more emergency vehicles started coming into the resort's parking lot. Carrie could see many flashing red lights outside her window. She told David, something must be wrong for all those vehicles to come here with their lights on. Maybe they should go downstairs to find out what was going on, she had not heard from Jill since that morning when they left to go skiing. David agreed with his wife and all three left the room to see what was going on. After the elevator doors opened, Carrie saw four men entering the resort carrying a lot of equipment with them. They all had Search and Rescue written on the back of their jackets. A strange feeling came over her that she could not shake. She knew right then, something had happened to Jill and Johnny on their ski trip.

Jim Matthews was the man in charge of Search and Rescue, which was easy to tell by the way that he was barking out orders to his men. JD was the only one sitting in that large room off the lobby, enjoying the heat of that huge fire in front of him. While everyone else was running around like wild men, he sat with his eyes closed, preparing himself for the trip. It would be time to leave soon and he knew firsthand there would be no heat where he was going.

Jim and his three men were setting up the equipment when Carrie came in the room to speak with him. After introducing herself, Jim invited her to stay with them as they planned a rescue attempt to find Miss Green. David and Molly also joined them in that room to see how they were going to find Jill. Jim told Carrie that they needed to get all the information about the ski trip from Mark Anderson and Johnny Mann. Both men were on their way to the resort right now. Then they could decide what action to take in the rescue attempt.

Mark and Johnny came in a few minutes later and went into the room to talk with Jim. Johnny had told Mark exactly what he wanted him to say about what happened on the helicopter. That Jill had jumped before he gave her the signal. Making sure their stories sounding the same. That way he would not get into any kind of trouble with Search and Rescue or any other authorities. If Mark did not go along with his story, he would pay for it in the near future, was how Johnny had explained it to him. Mark knew then he did not have a choice and would have to help Johnny cover up the so-called accident.

Mark told the exact same story, which was Johnny's version. That Jill had jumped out of the helicopter before he gave her the signal to go. By the time he got back to where she had jumped, there was no sign of her on the mountain. Jim said, "Is that what happened, Mr. Mann?" Johnny said, "Yes it is. I cannot believe she jumped out too soon. Jill must have been in a hurry to get on that mountain to go skiing. She was out the door before we realized she had even jumped." Carrie yelled out, "You two are lying." She would have said something much worse, but Molly was in the room sitting across from her. She went on to say, "I do not believe that story the two of you are telling for one second. Jill would never do something so reckless and unsafe. But Johnny, I know for a fact, you on the other hand have many times."

Then Jim asked her to calm down, this was not helping them find Miss Green by accusing each other. We need to get the facts first before we can plan a rescue attempt to go find her. Jim asked Mark to show him on the map where he thought Jill might have jumped at and landed on the mountain. He walked over to the table and pointed to the spot where he thought Jill might have landed. Then Mark showed Jim where they both spotted her skis and the one ski pole from the helicopter. Jim put X's on the map to mark the spots of all three locations. Jim said, "Miss Green did not get too far down the mountain, did she? Are you sure there is nothing you two have left out?" Now everyone in the room was looking at Mark and Johnny, waiting for them to answer Jim's question. Johnny answered for both of them, "We are positive, that is what happened. Now, what do you intend on doing to find Miss Green?"

Johnny thought he would throw that question out to turn the attention back on Jim and not on him. Not knowing how long he could count on Mark sticking to his story. Johnny wanted to move things along before he got the blame for Jill's disappearance. Jim had no choice but to believe the two men. It could have happened the way they said it did. It would not be the first time someone had done something reckless by not following the safety rules.

Molly had heard what the adults were talking about and understood her Aunt Jill was missing on some mountain. What she did not understand was why no one was leaving to go look for her as her mother does when she wonders off. Molly thought she might not see her Aunt Jill again.

After hearing all the lies coming out of Johnny and Mark's mouths, Carrie was about to lose it. The story they both were telling did not make any sense. Jill was not a reckless person and always followed the safety rules while going skiing. Now this Jim from Search and Rescue was starting to believe their story, that it was all Jill's fault by jumping out of the helicopter too soon. She knew deep down, Johnny had something to do with Jill's disappearance and told everyone in the room. She was going to make him pay for what he had done to her best friend, even if it took her forever. Johnny ignored Carrie and her threats, as if she was not even in the room, which made Carrie even madder. Jim asked Carrie once again to calm down and let him do his job by asking the questions. Carrie asked him, "When do you plan on doing that, Jim? I do not see anyone going out to find Jill. What are all of you waiting for? Does Jill have to get herself off that damn mountain? All I see is everyone talking instead of doing something to go find her. If I am not mistaken, what is written on the back of your jackets means you are Search and Rescue, how about you go do some of that, Jim."

Jim told Carrie a decision for any rescue attempt would come soon. They needed a few more facts and a weather update before they go out and search for Jill. He called his office to find out when the storm would hit Mt. Elbert. He hung up the phone and gave everyone the bad news. Jim said, "I am sorry to tell everyone this, but the storm is moving faster than we thought. We will have to postpone the rescue attempt until the storm passes. It will be too dangerous to go now, we missed our opportunity."

Now Carrie was even more upset with Jim then Johnny. With Jim giving her another excuse, that they could not go search for Jill until the storm cleared. Carrie said, "What did you just say? We have to wait until Jill dies on that mountain, you are afraid of a bad snowstorm. I think before you took this job Jimbo, you should have realized how much danger that it involved. I believe your Search and Rescue Team are a bunch of useless cowards and do not have the guts to go save one woman's life who needs your help." Jim said, "I believe you said enough, Mrs. Smith. If you do not stop calling me Jimbo, I will be forced to remove you from this room." "Go ahead and try and see how much trouble that will be for you. Believe me; I am much worse than any snowstorm you have ever faced. Then again, if you do remove me, at least I will get to see you do something instead of standing around here doing nothing but running your mouth and making even more excuses of why you cannot go and save my best friend."

At the time, no one had noticed that little Molly had left the room. David went over to his wife to calm her down before things got out of hand. He stopped watching their daughter for that one moment as she walked over to the other room, where she met JD earlier that day. Standing in the doorway, she saw him sitting in a chair in front of the fire with his eyes closed. She walked over to see if JD would help go find her Aunt Jill when no one else would.

JD was not asleep, but instead resting his eyes while listening to all the people arguing in the next room about there not being a rescue attempt tonight. It was almost time for him to make an appearance and take over the rescue operation. While soaking up the heat he now heard someone crying in front of him. He opened his eyes to see Molly standing there, with tears rolling down her small red cheeks. JD asked her, "What is wrong, Molly?" Molly said, "My Aunt Jill is lost and no one wants to go find her, JD." "Why won't they go, Molly?" "Cause they are all afraid of a snowstorm coming. No one knows where she is. Everybody is fighting with each other. The Rescue Search Man told my mother to behave or he is going to take her away. I don't want to lose her too." "You mean the Search and Rescue man, who is in charge. He is the one who asked your mother to behave?" With more tears running down her face, Molly nodded her head yes to JD. Thinking her Aunt Jill was lost forever, and maybe her mother would be next.

JD picked her up and put her on his lap to calm her down by softly talking to her. He wanted her to stop crying. JD asked, "Do you want me to go find your Aunt Jill on the mountain?" Which Molly quickly responded by saying, "Would you, JD?" "Only if you can stop crying for me, and be a brave little girl. Something your Aunt Jill would want you to do. Be brave for her. Okay?" Molly was wiping the tears off her face with her little hands and then said, "I will try." JD handed her a handkerchief to help her wipe away the tears. She then blew her nose and finished wiping her eyes. She did not understand what brave meant until JD explained it to her. She wanted her Aunt Jill back with her at the resort, not on that mountain lost with a bad storm coming.

Carrie was still arguing with Jim about not going to find Jill. Johnny and Mark were still sticking to their stories about what happened on the helicopter. Then, she asked Jim what he planned to do next, if anything. Jim said, "Right now, there is nothing I can do. Look, if my team goes on that mountain now for a rescue attempt, more people will end up missing or dead. With the very strong winds and fast falling temperatures, it is too dangerous for a rescue attempt tonight. We will have to wait until the conditions are safer." Carrie said, "When do you think that will be?" "Hopefully sometime before daylight. I think the storm will be cleared out by then." "But it will not be safe for Jill by then. She will be dead if someone does not do something now." "Mrs. Smith, the temperatures could reach thirty below zero. It would be suicide to go under those conditions." "We cannot just sit here and wait for Jill to die on that mountain." "Well then, she should not have jumped out of that helicopter, or even went on the ski trip in the first place. Now I am being told she was warned about the bad weather coming by Rex Anderson and a complete stranger who is staying here at the resort."

Carrie was about to start yelling again when she noticed Molly was missing. She asked David, "Where is Molly, David?" They looked to where she was sitting and saw she was gone. He said to his wife, "She was sitting in that chair only a minute ago. When I came over to calm you down, dear." Then Jim said, "I wish John Davis was here to help us. He would be crazy enough to go out in this weather to find your friend." Everyone in the room heard him say it. That is when Carrie asked him, "Why don't you call him and get him here to help us?" That was when Rex walked into the room to find everyone talking about his friend. He went over, stood in one of the corners and listened while they kept on talking about JD. Jim said, "Even if I could find him and he was here, without Miss Green's exact location on the mountain, it would not do any good. We have to know where to look before trying to find her. Now can you see what we are up against?"

Jill was still out cold sleeping in her snow grave while all the other things were happening at the resort. The snow was impacted four feet deep all around her. She had a little room to move, which gave her a small amount of air to breathe while asleep. However, not for long if someone did not come, her air supple would run out soon. Then she would remain buried and not discovered until the snow melted around her sometime early in the spring.

Jim promised Carrie as soon as the storm cleared, he and a search party would go find her friend at first light. Carrie told him he needed to think of some other way to go find Jill tonight. Right now, she had to go search for her daughter. She looked over at Johnny and could tell he was pleased at the current situation. "You think this is over asshole, far from it. You will pay for what you did to Jill." Said Carrie. Johnny said, "I think you should find your missing daughter and let the professionals here do their job." Johnny thought no one would know the truth about what happened on that helicopter. Carrie and David started to walk out of the room to search for Molly, when she came walking in the room holding JD's hand, which surprised everyone except Rex. Knowing JD would pick the right time to make his appearance known. Rex was learning from his new teacher of how things work when you have a plan and then execute it. Search and Rescue had given up for the night and here JD stood, ready to go out and search for Jill.

Chapter 13

A Stranger Enters

*J*D and Molly were standing outside the room when they heard Carrie say she was going to search for her daughter. He decided it was time for them to make their presence known to everybody in the room. Since Jim and Carrie were calling out his name, he and Molly walked in the room before Carrie and David got a chance to leave. JD said, "I believe someone mentioned our names, Molly and I are here to see what all the arguing is about. Is there something you need me to do for you, Jimbo?" Jim looked over at JD and said, "Where in the hell did you come from you sorry old SOB? And where in hell have you been all these years?"

Carrie covered Molly's ears so she did not hear all the cuss words coming out of Jim's mouth. JD said, "I do not think that matters now. Would you like me to help find Miss Green or not? Molly tells me she is missing and no one wants to go in the storm and find her." That was when Molly said, "Mommy, JD told me he will go find Aunt Jill for us. He promised me. Right JD?" JD said, "That is right, Molly. First, Jimbo has to give me permission so I can go. Well Jimbo, what is it going to be?" Jim said, "If you are crazy enough to go on that mountain in that storm, please be my guest. You always were the craziest son of a bitch I ever knew, John. Hey, stop calling me, Jimbo. That nickname died off after you left some twenty years ago, no reason to start it up again." Once again, Carrie covered Molly's ears so she would not hear the profanity coming out of Jim's mouth. JD said, "Then I guess it is settled. I will agree to go as long as there is no interference from anyone. I run the rescue operation from here on out." Jim said, "Fine by me, John. Tell me what you need and I will provide it?"

Johnny was standing over in the corner, not believing what he was now seeing and hearing. That the stranger he met earlier today, was now taking over the search job to find Jill. Johnny said, "Who in the hell do you think you are coming in here making demands to take over this search? I do not think you are qualified to run this kind of operation." JD said, "I have been waiting for you to open your big mouth again Johnny. I think it is time we get to the bottom of all this and find out the truth about what really happened on that helicopter."

Rex, who was standing in another corner of the room when he told JD all the supplies were outside and ready to go. JD told him thanks for going to get all of them. He would let him know when to unload them. Johnny asked, "What supplies is he talking about?" JD said, "Do not worry about the supplies. You are in enough trouble, black belt." Then JD turned to Mark and started asking him some questions. He knew Mark would not lie to him in front of his brother. Rex was now staring straight at Mark as JD started questioning him about the events on the helicopter. JD said, "Mark, I want you to tell the truth this time, and not what Johnny told you to say." Johnny said, "He has told the truth about what happened today. There is nothing else he needs to add."

That was when JD told Johnny not to interrupt him again. If he did, black belt or not, he was going to send him to God without giving him time to repent all his sins. JD put both his hands in his jacket pockets so Johnny understood the situation he was now facing. No one in the room said a word, not even Johnny, who kept his big mouth shut and let JD continue. JD said, "All we want is the truth Mark, there is no reason to be afraid, tell us what happened on your helicopter." Mark saw that Rex was looking at him and nodded for his brother to do it. Now that someone had Johnny under control, it would be safe for him to tell the truth.

Mark told everyone in the room that Johnny had pushed Miss Green out of the helicopter before she was ready. Then he slammed his body into him, which made the helicopter fly in the opposite direction of Miss Green. When he was able to regain control and get back to the area, she was nowhere in sight. Johnny could not keep quiet any longer, with what Mark just told everybody, his story was definitely coming apart. Johnny said, "He is lying. I never pushed her she jumped on her own. It is my word against his. Let someone prove different." Carrie said, "If anything bad has happened to Jill, will you please send him to God, JD." JD said, "I do not think God wants him, how about the devil instead? I believe he will fit right in with the people down there." "As long as one of them gets him and he is no longer on this earth to hurt anyone else, it will be fine by me." Jim said, "When Miss Green is found Mr. Mann, we will have her side of the story about what happened. You could face criminal charges of reckless endangerment of another person. My advice to you is not to leave town, Mr. Mann. Not until this matter is resolved one way or the other."

JD told Mark thank you for telling the truth, and that he did not have to worry about any payback from Johnny; from this moment on someone would be with him. Not even Johnny would be stupid enough to try anything to harm him. Everyone in this room would know he would be the one responsible. Johnny stood there and did not say a word. He was trying to think of what to do next. JD tried to help him by saying, "I think it is time for you to leave, black belt. I believe you have done enough damage for one day." Jim backed JD up by saying, "I agree you need to leave Mr. Mann under these circumstances. We will see each other later after finding Miss Green." Johnny said, "You mean if you find her and if she is still alive and able to talk. Good luck with that search and rescue attempt, mister. I will see you later to finish our business." "Looking forward to it, black belt." JD replied.

Carrie rushed toward Johnny, but JD stopped her before she could reach him. JD told Johnny he was finished, the problem was he did not realize it yet. But the next time they met, he would." Johnny left the room and the resort to go find his comfort zone. Which was the nearest bar and female companionship for the night. In his mind, by the time they did find Jill, she should be dead somewhere on that mountain.

JD said, "Now that we got rid of the problem, we can work on the solution to find Miss Green. Is everyone ready for his and her job assignments? All of them stood there with their attention on JD, ready to do whatever he asked of them. First-order, JD told Mark to go get his helicopter and fly it back to the resort as fast as possible. They would be leaving from here to go to Mt. Elbert. With all the supplies outside, it would make it easier and save time. Mark and one of the Search and Rescue men left in a hurry to do as JD asked. Second-order, JD asked Carrie for Jill's cell phone number and her carrier's name. He wanted her to write them down on a piece of paper for him. Which she quickly did and handed it to him. JD got on his cell phone to call Michael with the information. Carrie listened to him call the information out, but did not know who he was talking to on the other end of the phone. Michael told JD that he would call him back as soon as he had Jill's exact location on the mountain. He would be calling Jill's cell phone company when their call ended.

While waiting for Michael's call, JD went over to the map to see where Jill left the helicopter. Then looked at the location of where Jill's skis and ski pole were on the mountain. Jim showed JD both locations that were now X's on the map, pointing them out to him. Third- order, JD told Carrie to go to Miss Green's room and pack some of her clothes for him to take on the mountain. For at least two days, and to make sure they were all for wearing in extreme cold weather. Then pack whatever else she thought Jill might need. Saying all of it had to fit in a small sports bag, no suitcases. Molly asked JD, "What could she do to help?" JD said, "You can go help your mother pack your Aunt Jill's clothes. Then bring down the can of Play-Doh so I can make you something special before I leave." Carrie and Molly went upstairs to start their job. JD told David to go get some wine from the resort bar. Something that Jill would like to drink, but make sure it was in a box and not in a bottle. David left to go get the wine. JD wanted to give him something to do to make him feel part of the operation.

Jim asked, "What is my assignment, John?" JD said, "It is coming, wait till after I get my next phone call." Then his phone started ringing, it was Michael, calling him back. Michael said, "Here is what I found out. He called out the coordinates to John, which was Jill's exact location of her cell phone. Her carrier had tracked it for him. John wrote them down and thanked his friend for his help. Michael told him to be careful. Which in turn, John told him he always was in this sort of situation.

JD went back over to the map to plot the position given to him by Michael. A few minutes later, Carrie and Molly entered the room, with a sports bag that contained Jill's clothes; David came in with the boxed wine. JD told them to put all the things on a table nearby and then come over to the map. He then explained to everyone that his friend on the phone had gotten

Jill's exact location using her cell phone. That the newer cell phones have a built-in GPS chip inside them. A satellite can track the phone as long as it is on and in her possession. I think Miss Green should be right here and pointed it out on the map to everyone as he put a big X and circled it to mark the spot. It was a little farther down the mountain than where the skis and ski pole X's were on the map. Jim said, "If that is where she is, why didn't Mark or Johnny spot her from the helicopter?" JD said, "I believe when she hit the ground and started rolling down the mountain, she caused a small avalanche of snow to follow her. The storm two days ago was enough to cause that effect. After the snow caught up with her, it engulfed her, and then stopped her movements by covering her entire body. Does everyone understand what I am talking about?" Carrie said, "You mean Jill is buried under a lot of snow?" "That is exactly what I am saying, Mrs. Smith. That is the reason why she disappeared so quickly and the only thing that makes any sense." Jim said, "Make sense to me; that has happen to a skier before on that mountain."

At that very moment, Carrie thought Jill was dead. Her head sunk down, and she closed her eyes as if to say goodbye to her best friend. JD quickly said, "I do not believe she is dead. Do you think I would have sent you upstairs to pack her some clothes if she was?" Carrie felt that part did make sense. Jill must be alive if JD wanted clothes for her to wear and a box of her favorite wine to drink.

JD said, "Now let me prove it to everyone. Has anyone tried to call Jill's cell phone yet?" No one in the room had even thought of the idea, not even Jim, head of Search and Rescue. There was a reason why JD was Jim's teacher years ago and not the other way around. Carrie quickly pulled out her cell phone to call Jill. Hoping to hear her best friend's voice on the other end.

Jill woke up hearing her cell phone ringing and vibrating inside her jacket pocket. After opening her eyes, she found herself surrounded and covered over by snow. When she reached inside her pocket for the cell phone and finally pulled it out, the phone stopped ringing. Jill knew it had to be someone trying to find her, but had no idea how long she had been asleep or all this snow had been on top of her. After looking at the screen, Jill saw it was Carrie trying to call her. She quickly pushed redial to call her back for help.

Carrie was leaving a voicemail message for Jill when Molly handed JD the can of Play-Doh. JD asked, "What would you like me to make for you this time?" Molly said, "I would like a mama bear and a baby bear to go with my other one, JD." JD pulled out some of the clay and start shaping it into two more bears for Molly. He would have them ready for her before it was time for him to leave. Carrie did not think that JD had time to play with clay. Not while her friend was missing on a mountain, presumably buried under some snow and might run out of air at any time and then die. She stared at both of them before saying how she felt about what was going on.

Carrie said, "Molly, please stop bothering JD, he is too busy right now trying to find your Aunt Jill." Molly said, "But he asked me to bring the Play-Doh down mommy." "I do not care if he did, honey. We have adult things to do right now. Your toys will have to wait until later." JD told Carrie to take a break in dialing Jill's phone number. He needed her to go out to his car and get a can of spray adhesive and a small wrapped box that was in the bag on the front seat. Then he added the word "Please" to get her to respond right then. Carrie reluctantly went outside to JD's rental car to get the items he needed. This gave JD time to finish the two bears for Molly without any more interruptions from her mother. JD asked Molly, "Where is your other bear?" Molly said, "Upstairs in our room. I do not want anything to happen to him." That was when JD asked David to go get the bear for him. He told Molly to go with her father to show him where the bear was in the room. David and Molly went with her telling him they would be right back down with the papa bear he made her.

JD needed both of them out of the room when Carrie returned. He wanted to have a private conversation with her about Molly. Carrie came into the room and gave JD the two items, then asked where David and Molly were. JD said, "Upstairs to get the other bear I made for her earlier." After hearing him tell her that, Carrie rolled her eyes at the fact. Then JD asked her, "Carrie, what do you think Molly is going to remember about this trip? That you got so emotional about her Aunt Jill going missing, which made her leave this room crying and then finding me in the other room. Or you not letting her have some clay bears that I am making for her right now?" Carrie was silent while listening to JD's questions. JD told her that children needed to feel connected to what was going on around them, if you shut them out and not let them be involved; then everyone loses the parent and the child.

While Carrie was thinking about what he just said to her, JD followed up by saying, "I am not going to tell you how to raise your daughter. So please do not tell her or me what I have time to do. Believe me, I am fully aware of the situation and will be leaving soon to go rescue your friend. I just wanted you to understand we only get a few childhood experiences while growing up. Can you remember a lot of yours? Please let Molly have this one. It will keep her mind off her Aunt Jill being missing.

Carrie was not pleased with JD lecturing her, but right now, she needed his help. JD began to spray the two new clay bears he had just made with the can of adhesive. Soon, Molly returned with the other one in her hand. Carrie watched them together as JD was spraying the last one with the can of adhesive. He then explained to Molly why he was doing it, in order to make all the bears hard and strong so she could play with them each day. Molly was watching him with excitement and thanked JD for doing it for her. She could not wait to pick up her bears and hold them. JD told her it would take one hour for them to dry. Then she could play with them as much as she wanted. Molly asked her mother to let her know when the hour was up. She began staring at her bears waiting for them to dry. Carrie told her daughter, she would let her know when the hour was up. Now understanding what JD was trying to tell her. This man had taken the time to do something so special for her daughter that she would remember for the rest of her life. What no one knew was JD also needed something to take his mind off Jill, wondering if she was still alive or not. First, the plan then the execution of it was JD's motto in life.

The answer to his own question came quickly when Carrie's phone began to ring in her hand. She looked down at her screen and recognized the number, knowing it was Jill calling her. She then screamed out who it was. JD told her to answer the phone and not to scream out anymore. Carrie said, "Hello, Jill is that you, girl?" Jill answered, "Yes, it's me partner." Carrie told everyone that Jill was alive under a lot of snow. Which JD had suspected but it was still good to hear she was alive.

JD told Rex to go outside, get all the supplies from both vehicles and put them together in one huge pile in the parking lot that his brother could access with the helicopter from above. He then asked David to take the sports bag and the wine outside and help Rex gather all the other supplies from each vehicle. David picked up the two items and went with Rex to start their job. Carrie was still talking to Jill when JD went over to ask some questions he needed answered before leaving.

JD asked Carrie, "What was Jill's current condition? How was her air supply? Did she have any broken bones?" Carrie started asking Jill all three questions. Jill answered back, "There is snow all around me, but I have some room to move and able to breath for now. I think my left ankle is broken. When I try to move my left leg, it sends a very sharp pain shooting up my leg. Carrie told JD everything Jill had said to her.

After that, JD told Carrie to put the phone on speaker, that way he could get his answers more quickly than having to wait for them. Carrie did and told Jill they were now on speaker. That she needed to answer JD's questions, so he could come help her. JD said, "Do you still have that one ski pole with you?" Jill said, "Yes, it is still wrapped around my right wrist. Why do you ask?" "If you start having trouble breathing, I want you to use the ski pole to punch a hole in the snow above you. While doing this, you must push at an angle above your body. Do not go straight up. It will only make the snow collapse around you more. Do you understand?" "Push at an angle, above my body, not straight up." "Also, you must push the ski pole, moving it side to side until you punch through the snow. Do not push and then pull back the ski pole toward you. Again, the snow will fall back on you." "I understand. This will give me something to do while waiting for someone to come find me." "How many battery bars do you have left on your phone?" "Two, no now it is down to one." "Try not to worry, I will be there soon. We need you to hang up now and not use any more bars, but leave that phone on. I am going to track you by your cell phone. It has a GPS chip in it. In order to do that, the phone cannot be dead or off. Do you understand?" "I understand. But please hurry, I am all wet and freezing in here." "On my way, be there soon Miss Green."

JD hung up Carrie's phone without giving her a chance to say goodbye to her friend. He told her they needed to save the battery in case he had to call her after getting on the mountain. JD asked her if they had the same cell phone carrier. Carrie said the phones were from the same cell company. JD told her he needed her phone; that he was going to take it with him. Carrie asked, "Why? Do you not trust me not to call Jill?" JD said, "No, it is not that. The reason I need your phone because it is the quickest way to track Jill's location after getting there by matching up the two phones. Since you two have the same carrier, only one satellite has to be involved instead of two. Do you understand?" "Now that you have explained everything to me I do." Carrie told him her number was the same as Jill's except for the last digit was a three instead of a four and handed JD her phone.

After JD suddenly hung up on his end, which Jill thought was a little rude of him, she put the cell phone back in her jacket pocket, but made sure it was still on, not wanting the phone to get wet and go dead before help could arrive. Unfortunately, she moved her left ankle while doing it. Which made her scream out in pain, but there was no one there to hear her. Jill knew her ankle was broken with all the pain she was now experiencing. Her eyes watered up and tears started rolling down her face as she tried not to move that foot anymore. Jill had to stay positive; she knew there was help on the way to save her out of the cold wet mess. Thinking this JD would tell her, I told you not to go skiing Miss Green, when he did get her out of this snow. Even if he did warn her more than once not to go on the ski trip. She would have to wait until her foot healed before kicking him square in the balls. Jill felt like the air was beginning to fade, she then pulled the ski pole forward and started her dig upward at an angle as instructed by the man she might kick in the balls sometime in the future. While pushing and twisting the ski pole, Jill tried to think of a reason why Johnny had pushed her out the helicopter without any warning. Even if he was mad at her, it did not make any sense unless he wanted to do her harm for some reason.

JD gave Molly a hug and told her goodbye. It was time for him to go outside and get everything ready to leave on the helicopter. Molly understood he had to go get her Aunt Jill off the big mountain. She thanked him for that and for making her, the two new bears and she would try to be brave like he asked. Carrie watched the two of them as JD handed Molly the gift-wrapped box and told her to open it. Molly did and saw a beautiful wood box that had her name craved on top. JD told her to put the three bears inside it when she was not playing with them. It would keep them safe for her and she would always know where they were. Molly showed her mother the box that JD gave her for the three bears. Carrie said, "What do you say, Molly?" Molly said, "Thank you, JD. I love it and my three bears you made me."

Carrie went over and thanked him personally for everything he had done, including making her realize she needed to spend more quality time with Molly. He was right; the little things do make a difference in a child's life. She did not know how to repay him for all his kindness. JD said, "Do not thank me just yet. Let me get your friend down off that mountain first. I am glad you understand what I was trying to tell you. Most people would not have, only taking it the wrong way before thinking about what I said to them was none of my business." JD and Jim went outside to get things ready to go before the helicopter arrived. In the parking lot, Rex and David had all the supplies in one pile for JD to inspect.

This time, JD started barking out orders instead of Jim. By giving out a few assignments to his men. He told two of them front and center as they waited for JD to tell them what he wanted them to do. JD said, "I want you two to go to McDonald's and bring me back two #12 extra value meals that are supersized with Coca-Cola as my drink and do not forget the barbecue and sweet-and-sour sauces; I want two of each with my order. Also, bring back some ketchup. If you want anything Jim, now is the time to speak up." Jim said, "Nothing for me, I have already eaten. I see you still eat fast food when you are in a hurry." "Yes, and I would like my food here before the helicopter arrives." "You heard the man, hurry up and go get his food. You two better not screw up his order, or you will be shoveling snow for the next week." The two men drove out of the parking lot to get JD's dinner. Jim's third and last man was standing there with them. JD told him to go get some aluminum foil and one-quart size Ziploc bag. The man left in a hurry to go get the two items. That left Jim and JD standing there alone. JD told him that he saved his assignment for last.

Jim said, "Tell me what you need and if I have it, it is yours." JD said, "Glad to hear it, I need all these items before I leave. Bring me one standard first aid kit, one pair of small binoculars, one satellite phone, one left calf contracture boot (medium-size), one flare gun with five flares, one two-way radio and one can of WD-40. You should have all those items on your truck, Jim." "Oh, is that all you need. Are you sure, there is nothing else I can bring you? Why only five flares and not six?" "No, five should do it. I have never used six flares on a rescue mission. By the way, where is your helicopter at?" "It was crashed on one of our rescue mission. You know all too well how long it takes to get the money to have it fixed." "The same state government bureaucracy, you are last on their list to receive any money." "Exactly. We always use Mark and his helicopter to fly our rescue missions when ours is down for repairs. Let me go get those items for you."

Now JD went over to the pile of supplies where David and Rex were standing. He wanted to check the sports bag to make sure Carrie packed a pair of snow boots for Jill. After seeing them, JD handed the left one to David for him to take inside with him. Explaining if Jill's ankle was indeed broken, she would not be able to wear the boot.

With the wind starting to kick up and the temperature dropping, JD thought it was time for David to rejoin his family inside the resort. JD told David as soon as he had Jill out of the snow and safe, he would call everyone on the satellite phone. David shook JD's hand wishing him good luck and thanking him for what he was doing. JD said he would do his best as they parted company.

Jim came over carrying two large sacks of supplies JD had requested and added them to the pile. Then JD added his sport bag and started getting dressed into his winter clothes. First, by putting on his coveralls and a hooded jacket. Then two pair of winter socks and freezer boots. He would wait to put on his freezer suit until it was time to board the helicopter. In order to move more freely while loading the supplies and packing everything up. Since Rex had read all of his books, JD knew he would get the right items on the shopping list he given him a few hours ago. He looked over all the items to make sure they were all there before packing them up.

Rex's List of Supplies

1. 5- Five gallon buckets in different colors. Which were white, blue, black, red, and orange.
2. 6- Lids for the buckets. The lids were screw on type and not regular push down. Easier to use in cold weather. Two lids were black. The other four matched the remaining buckets.
3. Three hundred feet of climbing rope. Six sets of rope, each in 50ft. lengths.

4. One winter tent that sleeps six people and came with a waterproof bottom floor sewn in. Lightweight that comes with a carry bag to travel in. Heavy-duty long tent stakes that are metal and not plastic.

5. Climbing gear (connection hooks, a hammer, one dozen climbing stakes, and one regular size harness).

6. Eating utensils- 2 plates, deep dish, 2 cups, 2 spoons and 2 forks. One small pot with lid. All in metal, no plastic items.

7. Two rolls of heavy-duty duct tape.

8. Two rolls of heavy-duty toilet paper.

9. The food was 6 bananas, 6 oranges, 6 energy bars, 6 granola bars, 6 packs of beef jerky, 6 packs of Slim Jim's, 2 cans of mixed nuts, 4 MRE meals of spaghetti and 1 box of Cheerios cereal. The drinks consisted of 12 cans of Boost- vanilla flavor, 12 bottles of water, 3-gallon jugs of water and a box of wine that JD added for Jill's consumption.

10. Two cans of steno flame. One box of matches. One roll of paper towels. One dozen garbage bags.

JD's List of Supplies

1. Two pair of coveralls. One for him, one for Jill.

2. Two freezer suits good for 30 below zero. One for him, one for Jill.

3. 12 pair of winter socks.

4. 6 pair winter gloves.

5. 2 sleeping bags.

6. 2 harnesses (One climbing harness and one shoulder harness for pulling).

7. 2 pair freezer boots for JD. Four pair of boot inserts. A pair of snowshoes.

8. 4 wool blankets. Two pair of snow goggles (anti-glare).
9. 4 Lanterns that were battery-operated.
10. 2 shovels (One trifold, and one regular. Both with short handles).
11. 3 Tarps. One large and two smaller sizes. Bungee cords all different sizes.
12. 1 raft, seats six people. Automatic blowup, no pump needed.

The two lists were about even in the number of things that JD needed for the trip. Only Rex had one extra job to do on his list. He had to take the two black lids to Will Gary's hardware store. Then Rex needed to ask Mr. Gary to make him a John Davis special with the two black lids, by using a jigsaw to make the two cuts inside the rim. The first lid he cut all the way around, inside the rim. With the middle piece saved and the rim part thrown away. Next, he cut the other lid two inches inside that made the cut out to be in the middle of the lid. Rex had no idea what the man was making, nor was he going to ask him, which would cause even more of a delay. This turned out to be the most time-consuming item on the list. Almost as long as getting all the other items. It was taking Mr. Gary a long time making the cuts, by stopping to tell Rex another story about JD when he was a boy. Rex was being polite by listening to him, but needed to get back to the resort with all the supplies, and find out what was going on.

JD unfolded and laid the large tarp out on the parking lot. Then he placed the raft in the middle of the tarp before blowing it up. Inside the warm resort, everyone was watching him from a nearby window. Molly was watching with her parents when JD waved and smiled at her, before pulling the cord on the raft to blow it up. The large raft suddenly blew up to full size and appeared like magic in a matter of seconds. Molly clapped with excitement seeing the raft become full size so quickly. JD began loading the buckets after putting what he could inside them, knowing what items he wanted in each colored bucket and then screwing on the lids. He left the tent in its storage bag and loaded it in the raft. He took the wool blankets and all the other loose items and loaded them in the raft. Next went the two sleeping bags, the two sports bags, and everything Jim brought him. He saved the black bucket for last. He told Rex to hand him a roll of duct tape, so he could fix the lid on the bucket. The lid had a hole in the center 18 inches across. JD duct taped the extra cut piece to the top of the lid. It fit perfectly inside the rim. He taped the two opposite sides of the loose lid to the screw on lid and showed Rex why he did it. JD was now sitting on top of the black bucket holding a roll of toilet paper in one of his hands. Rex began to laugh and so did Molly knowing JD was sitting on a commode he had just put together. After putting the toilet paper and roll of paper towels inside it, he loaded the black bucket into the raft. All the supplies fit, as if JD had done this job before.

Jim came over and said, "Do you think you will need all this? I mean we will be able to come get you after the storm clears, John." JD said, "It is better to be prepared than not. Remember Jimbo?" "I remember, teacher." Jim's third man came up and gave JD the Ziploc bag and a large piece of aluminum foil he had folded up. JD put both items in his pocket. He could now hear Mark coming with the helicopter, it was time to hurry up and finish before he arrived. He put on his freezer suit and then put his and Carrie's cell phone in his front pocket. He took out his Bluetooth and put it in his top front pocket; ready to use when he got on the mountain. Knowing he would be wearing headphones after getting on the helicopter, he made sure the cell phones were set to vibrate. JD then cut twenty feet of rope to use later for climbing out of the helicopter to reach the mountain. He put the two-way radio in the other front pocket of the freezer suit. Last part of his job involved tying up all the supplies and the raft. By bringing the four corners of the big tarp together that was underneath to tie them up and then put a connection hook on the end. This now made the object look like a very big bag. He told Jim that he would have to hook it up to the helicopter belly for them, while they hovered over the parking lot. Jim agreed to do it and then wished John good luck in finding Miss Green. JD pulled out the two-way radio and told Mark to land beside the supplies, but do not shut off the helicopter. They would be leaving soon for Mt, Elbert. Mark did as instructed and landed nearby waiting for his passengers to get on.

Finally, JDs food arrived with Jim's two men quickly running toward him. They handed him the food and told him they made sure it was freshly cooked. JD thanked them and told Rex to get in the front seat of the helicopter. It was time to leave; Miss Green had been under the snow long enough. JD waved to everyone and got in the back seat of the helicopter where Jill sat nearly three hours ago. Mark lifted off and hovered over the supplies while Jim hooked them up from below. While putting on his headphones, JD waved at David, Carrie and Molly as they headed for Mt. Elbert.

While JD was putting some chicken nuggets in a Ziploc bag, Rex decided to ask him, "Are those for you to eat later, JD?" JD said, "No, these are for Miss Green. I think she will be starving when I get her out of that snow and back to the tent. Hey, would you like my other fries and drink, Rex?" "Sure, I have not had a chance to eat since all this started." JD handed the two items to him. He then wrapped the Ziploc bag in aluminum foil and put it in his coveralls under his freezer suit to keep them warm. Then he started eating his own meal, while flying toward Mt. Elbert.

After he finished eating, JD put the two sweet-n-sour sauces in his coverall pockets with the nuggets for Jill to use later. He knew from her emails that she like dipping her chicken in that particular sauce. After cleaning up the mess from his meal, JD started putting knots in the piece of the twenty-foot rope, making them three feet apart. He tied one end of the rope to the seat support that was down in front of him. Then he put on his snow goggles that were around his neck. He knew they were almost at Mt. Elbert and Jill; he was now mentally and physically ready to go find his Starlet.

Using his headset, JD told Mark exactly where to drop him and the supplies. Which was a spot that had a small tree line. Mark asked, "I thought Miss Green was higher up the mountain?" JD said, "She is Mark. First, I need to set up camp before I can go search for her. You see how hard the storm is hitting, it will be worse when I get her out. Fly where I told you, by those trees, I can use them for cover against the storm tonight. Understand?" "I do now. Sorry for asking a stupid question, I now understand your reasoning." "Not a problem, I believe asking stupid questions seems to run in your family. But like I told your brother, if you do not ask, you will never know." Both the brothers smiled at each other after JD said that. Then Rex said, "Will Miss Green's air run out before you can reach her, JD? I mean, you might want to try to call her again to make sure she is still alive before going out on that mountain." JD said, "Not necessary, Rex. I told her what to do if she started having trouble breathing. Regardless, dead or alive, I am going to dig her out. First, I need to set up the tent, so I will have a place to take her that is warm. Her body could go into hypothermia after being under all that snow for three hours." "I can understand that. I have one more question before you leave, JD. How do you stay so calm while doing things like this?" "I learned a long time ago from my training with Search and Rescue that doing a rescue job taught me to prepare myself mentally and then execute it physically. I hope that answers your question." "First by having a plan. Right?" "You are learning, my young friend."

After hearing their conversation, Mark started to apologize to JD for lying about what happened earlier on his helicopter. JD cut Mark off by telling him there was no need. Eventually, he did the right thing by telling the truth. Right now, he wanted him to concentrate on the job at hand, getting him down on that mountain. JD opened his door and threw out the rope to begin his climb down when Mark gave him the OK signal. Mark said, "We are there, I am about ten feet from the ground. Whenever you are ready, JD. You can start climbing down. JD said, "Well, I will see the two of you when I see you. Wish me luck boys." Rex could not help himself and asked JD one more question before leaving, "JD, how are you going to get the supplies loose?" JD did not answer him; instead showed Rex a very sharp knife as he started climbing down a few feet and then stopping to cut the tarp loose from the hook underneath. Sending all the supplies flying down on the mountain, then he continued his climb down.

After getting on the ground, JD was in full action mode, moving as if he had a purpose. He did not take time to look up and wave to Mark and Rex. Now Jill was the only thing on his mind, nothing else mattered except finding her and getting her somewhere safe besides underneath that snow.

Rex pulled the rope back into the helicopter and then closed the door. They watched JD from above setting up the camp and could not believe how fast he was moving. Having everything out of the raft and starting to set up the tent in a matter of minutes. Both knowing JD would be going after Jill after the tent was set up and the gear to dig her out ready. Now that the storm was at full effect, Mark had no choice but to return to base. With visibility getting worse, Rex had a hard time seeing JD on the ground, wondering to himself what kind of hell had he volunteered to do. Only Rex did not know, JD grew up and felt at home on this mountain. He knew it better than anyone else did in the area.

JD hooked up his shoulder harness onto his body. Then rigged up the ropes on each side of the raft and put a hook on the end of the ropes. It was time to start the search; he connected himself to the hook and started pulling the raft to see if it would work. It did, so he unhooked himself to put the other things in the tent before leaving to keep them dry. JD then put the two shovels, two blankets, and two lanterns in the raft, before hooking himself back up to the raft so he could leave. He put his Bluetooth in his ear for incoming calls and started his climb up the mountain, hoping Jill would still be alive after finding her.

Chapter 14

The Search Begins

*J*ill heard the helicopter passing over her and then moving down the mountain and hovering nearby. After hearing that, she thought someone would be coming soon to dig her out of all the snow. At least while waiting, she was able to make an air hole with her ski pole, allowing fresh air to enter for her to breathe. The ski pole was now sticking out the hole, showing Jill's current position for someone to spot, thinking it was a smart idea on her part. She tried to relax and not move her left foot until help arrived to get her out. Then she heard the helicopter fly away down the mountain, and thought they did not spot her ski pole, and she would be stuck in this snow grave overnight.

Soon, Jill would get a very big surprise when JD finally did dig her out. He would explain to her, due to the bad storm causing poor visibility there would not be a trip on the helicopter for them until the next day. Instead, they would be staying on the mountain for the night in a tent and not the cozy ski resort room for him or a warm hospital room for her with cable television and nurses catering to her every need.

While heading up the mountain toward Jill's last reported position, JD called Michael to give him Carrie's cell phone number to use to track Jill's and his position, matching up the two GPS signals and getting them to come together. Michael was now at the phone carrier's main office when JD reached him. The owner was a good friend of Michael's and a huge fan of JD's books. He was more than glad to help anyway he could, even using his very expensive equipment for this rescue attempt.

JD kept in contact with Michael going up the mountain dragging the raft and supplies behind him. It was hard for him to see since it was night and wearing goggles to protect his eyes from the cold strong winds. Michael was letting him know if he got off course of Jill's current location, by telling JD which way to move, left or right to keep on track. Fifteen minutes later, JD was only a few feet away from Jill and spotted the ski pole sticking out from the ground, which had a pink glove tied to the top of it. The glove was waving around in the wind, letting whoever saw it her exact location. JD said, "I have found her, Michael. Jill left a sign showing exactly where she is buried." Telling Michael about the pink glove tied to the end of the ski pole. Michael said, "Did you tell her to do that, or did she do it on her own?" "It was all her idea, I cannot take any credit. Now you can understand why I feel the way I do about her. I have to let you go old friend so I can dig out the future Mrs. Davis. Call you in the morning with an update and please thank your friend for the use of his satellite." "Will do, John. I hope everything turns out the way you have planned. Talk to you in the morning."

After hanging up, JD stepped back about six feet away from the ski pole and started digging with the short handled shovel. He did not want to dig right on top of Jill and take a chance on hitting her. When JD reached three feet down, he started moving towards Jill's position. This took more time, but it was the safest way to do this job. There was darkness all around except for the whiteness of the snow; JD was using the two battery-powered lanterns on each side of him to help see while digging. JD tried to hurry knowing how long she had been under all that snow. The storm was hitting full strength, which made him dig even faster trying to reach Jill. The snowstorm with very cold winds were not going to stop him from finding her. At least all the digging was keeping him warm; he did not even notice the current conditions around him. This being his childhood playground, he was now officially back home and it felt good.

JD kept using the lanterns to check his progress in the new trench he was digging and was almost at the spot where Michael said she should be. He slowed his pace and a minute later spotted her ski's boots and knew then he had found her. He then dug around them and her legs until he had enough of her body to pull her out of the snow. Right away, he could tell she was freezing by the way her body was shaking in his arms. JD carried her out of the trench and put her in the raft. Which was only ten feet away from where he was digging. He wrapped her up in the wool blankets and loaded the two shovels and lanterns into the raft. Jill was looking around while he was doing this, wondering where the helicopter might be and why there was only JD and not more rescue people here. Thinking to herself this cannot be the only person sent to rescue her, a guest she met at the ski resort. What has the world come to, if that was the case sending this one man to rescue her?

JD hooked up the ropes to his harness and began pulling the raft back down the mountain to the campsite. Jill did not have a clue what was going on. She would have to wait for all her answers to the questions. Right now, JD was not standing around to have a conversation with her, he was moving so fast to get her out of the storm before she got any worse. Instead of walking to the campsite, JD started running down the mountain, dragging the raft and all its contents, which now included Jill Amber Green, to the campsite below. He made it there in no time, since the trip was downhill and a lot easier than the one going up, not knowing where he needed to go and start digging.

After arriving, JD carefully unloaded Jill, carried her into the tent and laid her down on one of the sleeping bags. Seeing she was in tremendous pain from her broken ankle, he elevated her foot by using one of the five-gallon buckets, laying the bucket down sideways and carefully putting Jill's left calf on top of it. By elevating her leg, it would stop the swelling for now. Later, he would have to remove her boot and reset her ankle. When her foot did warm up, the swelling and pain would be a lot worse.

JD then explained to Jill their current situation; that they would be spending the night on the mountain inside the tent. The helicopter had no good place to land and wait until he could find her under the snow. In the morning, they would travel to a pickup spot and then get on the helicopter to go to a hospital to have her ankle checked out properly. With the bad storm hitting now, this was the safest course of action to take. Then Jill asked, "Why not leave for the pickup spot now?" All Jill wanted to do was get off this mountain and not spend the night going camping with a stranger who told her not to come in the first place. She was visibly shaking while speaking to JD, freezing in her wet clothes. JD said, "Not possible in this storm. It will be too dangerous for the helicopter and its pilot to come back in these conditions. I believe you can wait twelve hours, and then you will be off this mountain. Do not forget, I warned you about coming here today." "I believe it is a little late to say I told you so, here we are stuck together."

JD reached inside his coveralls pocket to get the chicken nuggets out that he brought for her. He laid them and the dipping sauces down beside her. Then got her a bottle of water and one can of Boost for her to drink. He told her to eat the food and drink as much fluid as she could; he had to go outside to secure the raft for the night. Before leaving, he opened the can of Boost for her and told her to chew her food slowly. Saying it would be the only food she would get for the night. She did not listen and ate her food as if she had not had a meal in days, instead of hours. He left to go outside to secure the raft and put all the supplies away for the night.

JD found two trees with the right distance between them to tie the raft up. He turned it upside down and left one end at a 45° angle before tying it to the trees, leaving the other end of the raft on the ground. This would keep the snow out of the raft during the night. He gathered up the shovels and the two lanterns and returned inside the tent to check on Jill. The same woman who had not even thanked him for coming to save her and was trying to help her now. She was definitely not the same woman who he had been emailing over the last six months. That woman always thanked him for anything he did for her without ever asking. This woman needed a few lessons in manners, which he might be able to give her before this trip was over.

JD decided to call Jim on the satellite phone to give him an update on the rescue; that Jill was safe at a temporary campsite he set up for the night. After telling him all this, JD went on to explain the current situation that Jill has a broken ankle, which needed to be set soon, otherwise it could get a lot worse. In the morning, he would call so everyone could take turns talking to her. Right now, he needed to go to work setting that broken ankle. Jim understood the situation JD was facing. He would update everyone knowing Mrs. Smith was not going to like hearing the news she could not talk to Miss Green until morning. JD wished him luck with her and that exploding temper of hers. Jim said thanks and then told JD what a great job he had done in finding Miss Green. In which JD said, "Now comes the hard part, setting her ankle. You know how I feel about hearing bones cracking while setting them in place." Jim said, "Then you should have packed some earplugs or told me to bring you a pair. I guess you are not so perfect after all, John." "Call you in the morning, Jimbo." JD hung up before Jim could respond calling him by his nickname. Using one of Jill's tricks while talking to Bill.

JD returned to the tent to find that Jill had finished eating her dinner and the can of Boost was empty. Now, she was having trouble opening the bottled water with her hands shaking so much. JD reached for it and twisted off the top. Then he held the bottle so she could take a drink without spilling it all over herself. She wiped the excess from her mouth by using her hand and was now staring right at him, waiting to see what came next. Only meeting this man briefly earlier that day, she did not know what he had planned for her. All she knew was he had her all alone on this mountain for the night. Jill was not sure if she could trust him yet. A moment later, her thoughts turned into sudden panic with JD pulling out a very big knife.

JD quickly explained to Jill why he had the knife out, so he could get her left ski boot off and check the damage. With her foot swollen, there was no other way but to cut it off. She tensed up after hearing what he was about to do to her ski boot. Thinking he might hurt her some other way with the big knife that was in his right hand a few feet away. Their first real conversation together went like this after Jill pulled away from him and that very big and sharp looking knife.

She yelled out, "What are you planning on doing with that knife, mister?" JD said, "Like I said, your ankle is too swollen to get your boot off the regular way. I need to cut it off so I can see how badly your ankle is broken. Please let me take a look at it, and then I will know what needs to be done." "I think I can stand the pain until tomorrow. You do not have to worry about fixing my ankle, mister." "Like I said to you more than once, my name is JD. In case, you have forgotten from our conversation earlier today or talking on the phone about an hour ago with Carrie and me. If we do not get the boot off, your ankle will keep swelling through the night. Next, infection will set in by lack of blood circulation. Then you could get blood poisoning, and when we do get you to the hospital, there will be only one choice, cut off your ankle to save your life. Now Jill Amber, what is it going to be?" Jill moved her left foot back over to JD, so he could get her boot off. She did not say a word, now understanding the boot had to come off, otherwise she might lose her left foot or maybe her life. He told her to lean back and relax while he started cutting off the boot, but not to move her left foot. He did not want to cut her by mistake while getting it off.

Working quickly, JD got the boot off, but Jill had a few tears from all the pain she experienced having it removed. She was trying to be brave by not moving her foot or saying anything while he cut away the boot. Then he removed her sock and saw the bruised and severely broken ankle. It was not a pleasant sight, with her ankle turning outward in an awkward position. JD knew right then he would have to set it soon, which was not going be easy, while Jill was still awake. The pain began to increase with her ankle out of the boot and warming back up, feeling the full effects of the break for the first time. Jill said, "Please JD do something, it hurts really bad." Then she set up to look at it for herself, which almost made her gag. She turned away to keep from getting sick and throwing up her chicken nuggets all over him. He thought to himself, now she can remember my name when she needs me to do something for her.

JD told her the ankle had to be set in place as soon as possible, and then the pain would not be so severe. Jill asked him,

"Have you done this before?" JD said, "A few times in my life, but not lately. First, we need to get all your wet clothes off. You cannot stay in them, hypothermia could set in." Now Jill thought this was his way of making a move on her. She said, "I do not care about hypothermia. I am not taking off my clothes in front of you. I would rather freeze to death." JD said, "Then you will, believe me. Look at the way you are shaking right now. I really do not see what the problem is; I am only trying to help you stay alive. Plus, Jill Amber, I have already seen you naked before."

Now Jill had a funny look on her face, wondering when JD could have possibly seen her naked. JD helped her out by saying this, "Remember, you have done a few nude scenes in your movies. Think of this like one of those." "I got paid a lot of money to do them, and it was business." "So is this, trying to keep you alive. Unfortunately, I am not being paid and do not have any more time to waste arguing with you, Jill Amber. The clothes have to come off. Either you can do it or I will." "Does it include my underwear?" "If they are wet, then yes. We have to get your body temperature back up. That is why you are shaking so much. Do not worry, Carrie packed you some underwear in a sports bag, I brought with me." "I do not care if she did, my clothes stay on." She pulled away from JD, which caused her to cry out from the pain. "Okay then, you leave me no choice, Jill Amber. I will take them off for you." Jill yelled out, "Just you try mister and see what happens to you, broken ankle or not, I will kick you square in the -----. JD kept her from finishing her sentence. He already knew what she was going to say and could not waste any more time with this stubborn woman. He had work to do in trying to save her life. She would have to forgive him sometime in the future for what he had just done by knocking her out.

While Jill was yelling and threatening him, JD reached in his pocket, and pulled out his knuckle blaster stun gun and put it to Jill's neck, sending 900,000 volts through her body, immediately knocking her out and shutting her up at the same time. Now having peace and quiet, JD went to work by taking all her upper clothes off first, and then laid her down to start on the bottom ones. He carefully pulled off her pants, making sure not to hurt her ankle. That was when he made his discovery; the sudden smell hit him in the face. Jill had pooped in her pants while being under all the snow. That was why she did not want to take off her clothes in front of him, embarrassed by what had happened to her, while waiting for someone to come dig her out. JD knew it happened some time ago, the shit he now smelled had already started to dry which means it did not happen when he hit her with the stun gun. Sometimes while being shocked, people can lose control of their bodily functions. Now he had another job on his hands, and more explaining to do with Jill in the morning.

JD got the toilet paper and paper towels out of the black bucket. He used some of her wet clothes to clean her soiled area first. He also used the rest of the bottled water to get her bottom nice and cleaned. Then he put the rest of her wet clothes including the dirty ones he used as butt wipes, the toilet paper and a few paper towels all in a garbage bag, which he sealed up before throwing it outside to bury in the morning. Looking in the sports bag, JD got Jill some fresh underwear to wear and put them on her quickly, not taking time to sneak peeks at her naked body. Now it was time for the hard part, setting her ankle without causing any more damage.

First, JD turned Jill on her right side and then propped some of the buckets behind her back to keep it that way. He then put her left ankle over the top of his right thigh so he could pop it back in place. While doing it, JD could hear her bones cracking as the ankle went back into place. Last thing this man ever wanted to do was hurt this woman or cause her any pain. He thought she had experienced enough in her life by being with that asshole Johnny and dealing with Bill Turner. With the ankle back in place, JD put a pair of winter socks on her feet and then attached the calf boot to protect her left ankle from having any more damage. He moved quickly to open the two sleeping bags to make them into one big one for them to share. He felt her skin that was still very cold. Even knocked out, her body was still twitching. JD still had all his clothes on, including his freezer suit. From all the recent moving he was doing, and all the layers of clothes, JD was burning up. It was time to pull them off to start his last job before going to sleep. The only job he was going to enjoy and not hard to do, warming Jill's body up by using his hands and putting his warm body up against hers to get her body temperature back up. He could see how white and felt how cold Jill's body was being under all that snow in wet clothes.

After ten minutes of rubbing, JD had Jill's body temperature back to normal. He soon fell asleep, dreaming about the woman beside him, knowing he would pay for what he had done using that stun gun on her and removing all her clothes. For now, there was finally peace and quiet inside the tent. JD was starting to feel a real connection with Jill for the first time. Thinking everything he had done for her in the past was worth it, now beside the woman he had been dreaming about over the last six months. Even if she did need an attitude adjustment, thinking he might be the man to handle that job.

At the resort, Jim explained to everyone that John had found Miss Green; she was alive and safe with him at a campsite on the mountain. Right now, John needed to set her ankle and then get her body temperature back to normal. He would be calling in the morning then everyone could talk to her. So for now, please let John handle the situation without everybody trying to contact them. Carrie was not happy not being able to talk with Jill. She wanted to make sure everything was all right for herself and see if she could do anything for her. Like a good mother goose, she ignored what Jim had just told her, and tried to call Jill's cell phone by using her husband's cell phone, but only got Jill's voicemail. What she did not know, JD had turned all the phones off before entering the tent to set Jill's ankle. Then he got Jill's cell phone from her jacket and turned it off. JD did not want any interruptions while working on her ankle to set it in place. Jill needed her sleep to give her body a chance to start healing. Talking to everybody could wait until morning; he was the only one that came in this snowstorm to dig her out, not any of them.

With not being able to talk to Jill, everyone decided to go to bed. Then get up early in the morning, when JD's call came in. That is, everyone except Johnny Mann, who found out about Jill's rescue and had a much different plan for his night before going to bed. It was time to get some payback from Mark for double-crossing him, and he knew exactly how to do it. Knowing his helicopter would be the one picking her up tomorrow, Johnny needed to stop that from happening. Then Jill would give her statement about what happened on their ski trip. Now that she was alive and not dead like he planned, it could mean a lot of trouble for him. Not knowing if she was going to tell everybody that he suddenly pushed her out without any warning. Which could follow with him arrested for assault, which Jim had told him.

Johnny made a call to Bill Turner on his cell phone to give him an update of the current events. Bill told Johnny to keep him updated about Jill's accident and any rescue attempts. To do whatever it took to keep her on that mountain until he could arrange another accident of his own for her to have. Otherwise, their deal was off. Johnny understood and knew exactly what to do and told Bill not to worry. Jill would not be getting off the mountain anytime soon, which he could guarantee.

An hour later, Johnny arrived at the hangar where Mark stored his helicopter. There was no security around watching the area with the bad storm. This made Johnny's job of setting a slow burning fire to the helicopter's fuel tank very easy. When the helicopter did explode, he would be somewhere else giving himself an alibi. Now seeing that the fire was burning slow and steadily, Johnny left quickly and went to the nearest bar to set his alibi. After buying a round of drinks and finding the prettiest woman to start hitting on, the helicopter exploded at the hangar causing a lot of damage. Everyone at the bar ran over to the nearest windows to see what they heard. With the bad storm outside and heavy snow fall, no one could actually see what was burning, but knew something was on fire by the bright burning light in the distance. Johnny knew now Jill and that stranger would be stuck on that mountain indefinitely.

Johnny began acting out his part by asking, "What the hell is going on?" Word soon came, that Mark Anderson's helicopter was still on fire at a nearby hangar. Johnny acted so surprised at the news. He told everyone that he was just on that helicopter this afternoon. Johnny said, "I guess it is better happening now than when I was on earlier, otherwise I would not be around to buy another round of drinks for everyone." Everyone agreed and thanked him for the drinks.

A few hours later, Johnny and the prettiest girl in the bar left to go to the ski resort. After getting there, Rex spotted both of them getting on the elevator to go upstairs to Johnny's room. The same room Jill had paid for him to have on this trip. At the time, Rex did not know his brother's helicopter had blown up. That news came minutes later after getting a call from Mark, who sounded very upset on the phone, telling Rex his helicopter was on fire at the hanger.

Mark told Rex he did not know how the fire got started, but his helicopter was gone. Rex was feeling sorry for his brother and for JD and Jill getting off that mountain without any air support. Deep down, Rex knew Johnny had to be the one responsible for the fire. Wherever that man goes, trouble seems to follow. With no way to prove he had anything to do with the fire, Johnny would likely get away with it. According to Mark, no one saw how the fire got started. After seeing Johnny with his new roommate, the man had himself an alibi. The local girl would tell the authorities whatever story Johnny made up, knowing the man was a liar.

Even with JD turning off all the phones, Rex decided to leave him a voicemail about Mark's helicopter destroyed in a fire and that Johnny had a new roommate. Now, they would have to find another helicopter to come pick them up tomorrow. While leaving the message, Rex knew JD would make Johnny pay for all this before it was over. At the end of the message, Rex told JD to call him in the morning if he needed his help doing anything. Then like everyone else, Rex decided to go to bed.

While his pretty guest was in the bathroom getting ready for him, Johnny made another call to Bill, telling him the helicopter that was supposed to get Jill off the mountain had its own accident. It had suddenly caught fire and then blown up into many pieces. There would be no rescue in the morning; Jill would probably die on that mountain before another helicopter reached her. With of all the bad weather that was in the area, it would be hard to find one. Bill agreed with Johnny, arranging for another helicopter would take time. Then he told Johnny their deal was still on and would see him when he got back in town to sign his new contract. Johnny told him he would be there early Monday morning at Planet Studios.

The prettiest woman from the bar came out of the bathroom, now naked with a big smile on her face; she quickly ran over and jumped into bed with Johnny. She felt like the luckiest woman in the world being with such a famous person who was up for an Oscar and who had promised to take her as his date to the Academy Awards. Like so many women before her, Johnny would promise them anything to get what he wanted. He loved the game of screwing with their minds and then their bodies until he got tired of playing with them, then it was time to dump and run and find a new player. The only reason he never did that with Jill, she was more famous than he was and it would hurt his career. Instead, he used her to make his own connections to help further his career. Now that his future at Planet Studios was set, she would be out of his life forever. No more trying to keep her happy in order to keep getting jobs for himself.

After having sex a few times, Johnny went to sleep, knowing Jill was having a worse night than he was. Being in a warm bed with a naked woman that would do or say anything for him and there she was freezing to death on a mountain with that stranger. Johnny thought no one could last very long in those weather conditions. With tonight's temperature going way below zero, it would surely kill both of them. He went to sleep dreaming about the two of them frozen like two human popsicles.

Only Johnny did not know JD was not just an ordinary stranger, instead a man who prepares for everything and got some help from his friends. He would find a way to get Jill off the mountain without all of Johnny and Bill's attempts to stop him. Once again, Johnny had underestimated this stranger. Not knowing who or what he was dealing with, but would soon find out on their next meeting.

Chapter 15

Reasons to Live

As daylight broke, JD awakened and quickly decided to get dressed first before Jill woke up and began asking him many questions. Starting with what happened to her after being knocked out. He carefully separated himself from her body and he got dressed to go outside with all three cell phones with him. After walking a short distance from the tent, JD turned on all the phones to check for any messages. He had one voicemail on his phone from Rex. He listened to the message and found out about Mark's helicopter, that someone started a fire and blew it up. Finding out there will not be a pick up today unless they found another helicopter to use.

Before calling Rex, JD decided to check the raft, to make sure it was ready for use and not damaged from the storm. While Jill still slept, he made his call to Rex to find out more details about everything that had happened last night. He answered on the second ring and began telling JD the whole story of what he knew including the part about Johnny's new woman friend he brought to the resort with him late last night. He then asked JD what he could do to help them. JD told his young friend to sit tight; he would contact him soon with anything he might need him to do. First, he needed to have a talk with Jim, to see what Search and Rescue was planning of how to get them off the mountain.

After their call ended, JD knew just like Rex that Johnny had been behind the fire and explosion of his brother's helicopter. What he did not know was why Johnny wanted to keep Jill on this mountain. It could not be because he pushed her out of the helicopter; it had to be something more to it than that. Johnny could easily come up with another one of his lies to explain how Jill's accident happened. There had to be another reason for him blowing up the helicopter.

JD had to go to his source for the answer, Michael. If anyone could find out the reason, he would, with all his connections. JD called and found him working at the office, as if the man never slept. JD said, "Michael, I need your help finding out something for me. The helicopter we were going to catch a ride on today suddenly blew up last night. I believe Johnny Mann was the one responsible. I need to know who is pulling his strings and why?" Michael said, "It might take me a little time to find out, John. In the meantime, is there anything I can do to help you right now?" "Since you asked, do you know anyone important at Leadville Hospital?" "Will the Chief of Staff do?" "I would say very nicely old friend" "The two of us went to college together and he owes me a few favors. Every time that man comes to New York, he wants tickets to the top shows, saying if I ever needed a favor from him, all I had to do was ask. So just ask John and I will make sure you get it." "Well, Jill's ankle is broken worse than I thought. She will need surgery in order to save her foot. I think infection will set in and Leadville has the nearest hospital."

Michael said, "I will make the call after we are finished talking John, but how are you planning on making it to Leadville without a helicopter?" John said, "We will be on that side of the mountain by late tomorrow afternoon. I think we can make it to "Dead Man's Cliff" by this afternoon, if I run part of the way. After climbing to the top and setting up camp somewhere nearby, I will call you with an update of our current location. Go ahead and arrange to have two ambulances to meet us at the bottom late tomorrow afternoon." "Why two, are you hurt John?" "No, the other ambulance will be for Johnny Mann. I know he will show up to tell his side of the story. After I am finished with him, he will need the other ambulance for his trip to the hospital. I have a plan of what to do with Mr. Mann the next time we meet." "I hope it does not involve killing him, John. I hate to lose my best friend." "You mean your meal ticket." "John that hurt my feelings." "I am sorry old friend." "Hey, you have not even told me how last night went with Jill." "A gentleman never tells. Since you brought up Jill, in the future we will be using nicknames from now on. I do not want her to know whom I am talking to or why. You will be "Tonto" until I am off this mountain. Ok?" "Whatever you want "Lone Ranger" I will call you if I find out anything about Johnny. Consider the two ambulances being there tomorrow afternoon and I will make sure they wait until you arrive." "Thanks Tonto, I knew I could count on you."

JD started walking back to the tent to face his other problem, Jill. He knew by now she would be awake from being knocked out now only wearing panties and wondering where he had gone. A conversation JD did not want to have with her under any circumstances.

JD quietly entered the tent hoping Jill was still asleep, she was not. He saw her all balled up in one of the corners of the tent under one of the sleeping bags, starring right back at him like a scared animal. JD tried to act as if nothing was wrong and asked her how she slept. Jill was not going to play along. She asked, "Why in the hell did you knock me out, and why am I not wearing any clothes?" JD said, "Under the circumstances, I saw no other way to get the job done setting your ankle. You were not cooperating with me, fighting me at every turn. Believe me; you needed to be out when I set your ankle in place. The pain would have been worse than you were already experiencing. You are wearing some clothes." "Only a pair of panties. Still, it would have been nice to know beforehand that you planned to knock me out then undressing me. How about a little warning next time." "There was no time; I needed to get you out of those wet clothes and start working on your ankle, not wasting more time explaining every detail so you could decide if I could do it or not." "Now explain to me about taking off all my clothes." "With all the shaking, you were experiencing hypothermia. I had to get all those wet clothes off before you caught pneumonia and died. I did not want my trip coming to save you to be for nothing because of your modesty, Jill Amber."

While Jill gave him her funny look, JD continued by saying, "Now about the part where you messed on yourself, that is a different thing all together. I can see why you wanted to keep those wet clothes on, especially your underwear." "You think all of this is funny. Like some big fat joke you get to go tell all your friends about." "Look Jill Amber that could happen to anyone in your situation. It is nothing to be embarrassed about or ashamed of. It really does not matter that I had to change you like a newborn baby. I am not going to tell a soul. What happens on the mountain stays on the mountain." "Then why are you still joking about it?" "Well, I did do the dirty job wiping your ass, making sure it was nice and clean. While you slept like a baby through the whole process. Anyway, we would not want you to get any diaper rash before we get you to a hospital, would we?" "Ha, Ha, funny man. Now answer me about being in one big sleeping bag when I woke up. Where did you sleep?"

JD thought carefully before answering Jill's questions. He led off by saying, "I am sorry for knocking you out Miss Green. I should have warned you first. With your body being so cold in your wet clothes, I had to remove them and then clean you up. I put the dry panties on you and started rubbing your body in the right places to warm you. With me already burning up with all the layers of clothes I was wearing, it only made sense to put our bodies together, which warmed you up even faster. See it worked, you are not shaking anymore and your fever is gone. I slept right next to you all night in case you needed me. I hope that answers all your questions."

Jill was not happy with any of his answers, realizing they practically slept naked together last night. Jill asked JD, "What else did you do to me while I was knocked out?" JD knew exactly where Jill was going with that question. He said, "I only did what was necessary to help you, nothing else happened, you have my word on it as a gentleman." "So if I become pregnant, I know who to come looking for." "Believe me, you will not. I have four requirements before I make love to a woman. They are conscious and willing; need to be healthy and not sick and hurt; their human battery needs to be fully charged, trust me, I do not do things half way and last, they need to be in my heart. Do you understand everything I have just told you, Jill Amber?" Jill said, "I guess you do not sleep with very many women, do you?" "Now, who is trying to be funny? There are some fresh clothes in the sport bag if you want to get dressed. Remember, I told you last night Carrie packed you a bag. I suggest you put them on so I can check your ankle. I will come back in when you are ready for me to take off the boot and put on your pants and coveralls I brought for you to wear." "Where are we going to meet the helicopter?" "We're not, your good friend Johnny blew up the helicopter last night. But there is no way to prove he did it after setting up a very nice alibi for himself." "Now what are we going to do?" "You are going to get dressed and then we are going to have some breakfast and discuss the matter. I will be back in a few minutes to help you."

JD went outside to get things ready for them to leave. He already knew his plan of how they would get off the mountain if Jim did not find them another helicopter to use. Now it was time to put things into motion. With the weather clear, they could leave soon to reach "Dead Man's Cliff" by late afternoon. He wanted to stay on schedule in order to have Jill in the hospital by tomorrow evening at the latest.

With everything ready on the outside, JD returned inside the tent to help Jill finish dressing. She had her top clothes on, now waiting on him to help with the bottom half. JD removed the boot and then carefully put on her pants after making a small slit in the left pants leg so they would slide on easier. Then he put the protective boot back on her ankle and used some duct tape to put the pant leg back together around the boot. He helped her with the coveralls that had zipper legs, making them easier to put on. Jill helped by moving her body when necessary so JD could get the clothes on her without too much trouble.

Now that Jill was dressed, JD got out the bowls and spoons so they could have some Cheerios for breakfast. He poured the cereal in a bowl and then handed it to her with a spoon already inside. Then he got Jill a banana to eat either in the cereal or outside the old-fashioned way. Jill said, "I like my cereal with milk and sugar, not dry." JD said, "Well, I was going to give you a can of Boost to use, but let me fix that right up for you." JD took the bowl back from her and then got a can of vanilla Boost and poured half of it in her bowl. After mixing the contents up, he handed her back the bowl so she could start eating. "You are all set, anything else Jill Amber?" "Well, I usually have a glass of orange juice to drink with my cereal." "Well then, let me get you a glass." JD got two oranges and cut them in half with his big knife, the same one he used to cut her boot off last night. Jill watch him squeeze the four halves into a cup and then handed it to her. Jill did not say a word and started eating, while staring at JD who was across the tent from her eating his own breakfast.

After finishing her cereal, she asked JD, "So you think Johnny blew up the helicopter last night? Why would he do such a thing?" JD said, "I guess the same reason he decided to push you out of the helicopter yesterday for no reason. He told everyone at the resort that you jumped before the go signal. For some reason, I believe Johnny wants you to die on this mountain." JD saw by the look on Jill's face, Johnny indeed pushed her out. Jill said, "Yesterday was an accident. Johnny would not hurt me intentionally. You do not know him." "I am afraid, neither do you Jill Amber." "What do you mean by that?" "Let us test your theory about good old Johnny. I believe right now, he is in bed with a woman in the room you paid for. A very pretty woman I have been told." "You are wrong, you do not know anything. How could you, being up here on this mountain?" "Rex Anderson told me when I talked to him this morning and then find out about Mark's helicopter. He saw the two of them come in the resort last night and go straight to Johnny's room. You can always call Johnny's room to find out for yourself if you do not believe me. I am sure the pretty woman will answer the phone. Johnny is probably too tired after wearing himself out with her last night to do it himself."

JD reached in his pocket and pulled out two cell phones for Jill to use. One was hers; the other was Carrie's that he set on the blanket right in front of her. He told her Carrie's phone only had two battery bars left and she had only one. If she wanted to use them to check on Johnny and his new company. Then by all means, go ahead and call him.

Jill picked up her cell phone and called the resort. Rex answered the call at the front desk and recognized Jill's voice right away. Jill asked him to connect her to Johnny's room, which he did. When the woman said hello on the phone, Jill hung up right away. She could not look at JD and turned away in shame knowing now he was right. JD could see she was upset at the news. Jill said, "I guess this is where you say, I told you so again." JD said, "No, not this time. I see how much you are hurting. I am not the kind of person who takes pleasure in someone's pain and misfortune, Jill Amber. I cannot understand why you care so much for that man who treats you like this. Johnny is what I call a poor excuse for a human being. He only cares about himself and his own needs and no one else." "It was not always like that. There were many good times between us in the beginning. I guess things have changed now." "You are right about that. Must be nice for him to have things always go his way. What do you get out the relationship? I mean except getting your heart broken by him." "We have only known each other for one day. Why do you care so much about my wellbeing? What is in this for you, coming to save me?" "I made a promise to a five-year-old crying little girl that I would come find her Aunt Jill when nobody else would. I think we have talked long enough for the time being. You need to call Carrie before we have to leave. But remember, you only have a few battery bars left on those phones, I suggest you use them wisely." Before going outside, JD grabbed the satellite phone to call Jim, leaving Jill alone to make her phone call.

JD called Jim to tell him his plan for getting them off the mountain. That they were going to leave for "Dead Man's Cliff" and try to make Leadville the next day, sometime in the afternoon. Jim told JD to wait; they would find another helicopter to come pick them up. JD told him that they could not wait because of Jill's ankle. He had to get her off the mountain as soon as possible. If he did find another helicopter, he could send it to their current position. That was when Jim said, "Are you sure about this, John?" John said, "We leave in a few minutes, Jim. Call me if you have any news on a new helicopter. Otherwise, we will talk the same time tomorrow morning." "Well good luck and Godspeed my friend." "I will need it while climbing that cliff later today. It has been over twenty years since the last time I have did that climb. Hope to see you tomorrow afternoon Jimbo, goodbye." JD returned inside to check on Jill. At the time, she was on the phone talking to Molly. Telling her all about the rescue last night.

Jill said, "I will see you real soon Molly. Yes, I will tell him what you said, I promise. Now let me talk to your mother." JD pointed to his watch, which told Jill to hurry up and finish her call. He grabbed the dishes and the black bucket and went outside. Then Jill said, "This guy thinks he owns me, Carrie. He enjoys bossing me around and giving me orders." Carrie said, "Well, he did come and save you last night when nobody else stepped up. He was the only one that was willing to face that bad storm. Where is he right now?" "He took the dirty dishes and a black bucket back outside with him. I guess to clean them." "You do know the black bucket is the commode you get to use." "You have got to be kidding me. I am not using some bucket while he is around." What are you going to do, hold it until you get off the mountain? Good luck in doing that. By the way, what is JD's plan for getting the two of you off the mountain?" "Something about going to "Dead Man's Cliff" and then making it to Leadville by tomorrow afternoon. He said it should not be a problem if we leave soon. That is why he is rushing me to get off the phone now."

Then Jill's phone went dead. She called Carrie back on hers. Jill said, "Sorry, my phone went dead. I am using yours now. Carrie, JD thinks Johnny blew up the helicopter." Carrie said, "He probably did, Jill. He lied in front of everyone here about pushing you out of the helicopter. Later, Mark Anderson told the truth about what really happened. But only after JD threatened to send Johnny to God if he did not shut up and stop interrupting him, which Johnny did." "Why does this man care so much about what happens to me?" "I do not know, but I am glad he does. I thought I lost my best friend last night. Why not ask him, Jill?" Carrie's phone went to one bar, which told Jill she had to tell her goodbye before it went dead.

JD returned to see if she was ready to go. He needed to pack all the things up inside the tent to put in the raft, then come and get Jill. Last, he could break down the tent so they could leave. Jill told him she would be ready in a few minutes. JD asked if she needed to use the black bucket before they left and would help her if she did. He knew Carrie had told her what it was for in their conversation. Jill told him no thanks; she did not have to go right then. Maybe later she could experience that pleasantry with him. He smiled at her and told her to ask, he would help hold her while she did her business. JD knew she was going to have to use the bucket sometime while they were on the mountain. He started packing up the things in the tent and took them all outside.

Now off the phone, Jill got her things ready, a sports bag and the two cell phones. JD finished putting her coveralls on and then the freezer suit before carrying her out to the raft. He put the sports bags under her left ankle to elevate it and then gave her two wool blankets to cover herself. He then quickly broke down the tent and put it in its carry bag. Jill was surprised at how fast he worked getting everything done. Not knowing at the time, he had done it over a hundred times in his life while on camping trips on this very mountain.

JD put on his harness and then pulled out his toothbrush to brush his teeth before leaving. Then he got some bottled water to rinse out his mouth and toothbrush. Before putting away his toothbrush, he asked Jill if she wanted to brush her teeth before they left. Jill said, "I would like to, but Carrie forgot to pack me one. My breath probably smells pretty awful right now." JD handed her his toothbrush after putting toothpaste on it for her to use. She brushed her teeth and then rinsed out her mouth with some water left in JD's bottle. She handed the toothbrush and empty water bottle back to JD, but did not say thank you to him for letting her use his toothbrush. He felt she lacked having good manners and thought maybe it was time to teach her a little lesson from the mountain man.

JD pulled out his huge metal flask that had bourbon in it. He poured a small amount of the alcohol on his toothbrush to sanitize it. Then put both items away so they could leave. Jill was watching him do it the whole time and was not sure what he was up to with the little stunt. Jill said, "Why did you pour your liquor on your toothbrush?" JD said, "I think it needed sterilizing from all the germs in your mouth, Jill Amber. I do not want to catch any diseases." "So you are worried about my germs, mister?" "Well, I do not know what has been in your mouth lately, now do I?" "You mean like Johnny's tongue." "Not exactly, why don't we just drop it and go. We need to get started anyway." JD hooked up the ropes to the raft, connected them to his harness, and then began pulling the raft and all its contents. A couple minutes later, Jill figured out what JD meant and said, "Oh, I know what you meant now. You have a dirty mind, mister." "Better than a dirty mouth. I thought it might <u>cum</u> to you, Jill Amber. Most women would have dropped it and not given it another thought. But not you, I knew you could not, being the type of woman you are." JD looked back and saw Jill giving him that certain look she liked to give when she was upset about something. He knew what the look meant and for the first time enjoyed seeing it. He only had one more day to reach this woman. If she was even worth reaching. JD thought she was after all the time and money he had invested in her. He might as well have some fun while spending time with her in case things did not work out between them.

JD made good time to "Dead Man's Cliff", reaching it early that afternoon. He began getting all his climbing gear ready to make the climb. Now the hard part came, climbing to the top of the cliff and getting all the supplies and Jill up there with him. Jill saw the height of the cliff facing them and did not know what they were supposed to do next. She knew they were at a dead end, seeing the wall of the cliff going about 50 feet up, if not more. Jill said, "Why did you pull us here in front of this wall JD? Are we lost?" JD said, "No, we are going to climb up to the top of this cliff." "Have you forgotten about my ankle? I would not try to climb that if it was not broken. Also, I am afraid of heights." "You are not going to climb the wall; I am going to pull you up to the top after you hook yourself up to the rope and the connector. But first, I need to get all the supplies together and put them in the large tarp, I will tie them up in a ball so I can pull them up first; the raft and tent will be the next items and last but not least, I get to pull you up Jill Amber. All you have to do is hook each item up with the rope and connector that I will lower down to you. Then you hook yourself up last and I will pull you up. Do not worry it will be safe. You will be wearing my shoulder harness at the time. I can adjust it to fit you. All you have to do is to remember to keep your arms in on your chest, that way you will not slip out of it." "You are kidding me. I am not going to let you pull me up 50 feet in the air. Too many things could go wrong, you could slip and fall and the rope could slip out of your hands or even break while you are pulling me up." "It is the only way, or I could leave you here with the supplies. Help should arrive in about two or three days. Then you will be facing the same thing with the helicopter, you will have to use a rope and a harness to get you aboard because there is no place to land around here. I will not drop you; the rope can hold 400 pounds. Trust me; it will not break while pulling you up. You do not look that heavy to me, but they say looks can be deceiving." Jill gave him the same look again, which he ignored while switching out of his harness. JD put on the climbing harness and then adjusted the shoulder harness to fit Jill. She was not happy with the current situation, but had no choice but to go along with JD's plan.

Before starting his climb, JD asked if she needed to use the black bucket. She said, "No, I am all right for now. Just be careful not to fall and kill yourself. I would die here if you did." JD said, "I am glad that you care so much for your own safety. It really touches me, Jill Amber. It will take me about forty-five minutes to reach the top. Then I will need to tie knots in the rope to help me pull all the other things up. One knot every three feet on the rope should work. After one hour, I will lower the rope with a locking hook on the end for you to connect the items for me to pull back up. Any questions before I leave?" "Have you ever climbed this cliff before?" "Many times, I am the one who put the climbing spikes in the rocks many years ago. I know exactly where to hook up to them. If the spikes are loose or rusted, I will have to drive in new ones. Well, I better get started; see you later at the top." "Like I said, please be careful and try not to get yourself killed, JD." "Like I said, your concern for your own well-being touches me, Jill Amber." JD got that look from Jill while enjoying the banter between them before leaving to start his climb.

All Jill could do was sit and watch him make the climb up. She was seated close by the supplies so when JD did lower the rope, she could do her part. Like he said, JD made it to top in about forty-five minutes and then soon after lowered the knotted rope so she could get started hooking things up. First, the tarp of supplies, and then came the raft. JD untied the supplies and then loaded them back into the raft. This gave him time to rest in between pulling up the rope with the items. Next, he got the tent up and tied it to the back of the raft. That way everything would be ready to go, when he had Jill with him at the top. Now it was Jill's turn for the ride up. He lowered the rope so she could hook herself up. Jill said, "Don't drop me JD. That is all I ask." JD told her to keep her arms in on her chest and close her eyes if she was scared. She did both while being pulled up. He had to lean out a little so Jill did not hit or rub up against any rocks while being pulled up. He then began to pull her up quickly which only took a matter of minutes for her to reach the top. After unhooking Jill and taking the harness off, he loaded her back into the raft and then switched out the harnesses. Putting the climbing harness away and the shoulder harness on himself.

JD wrapped Jill in the blankets and told her they would need to find a suitable campsite before dark. They needed an area that had some trees for cover against any storms that could hit during the night. He hooked up to start pulling again when Jill told him not to leave. She now needed to use the black bucket. JD asked her, "Do you have to go one or two?" Jill said, "Both, does it really matter?" "Not to me, but it might to your butt. A piece of blanket you have around you will =help keep your butt warm and comfortable while sitting on it. Also it will keep your butt from getting an imprint of the lid top on it." "I am glad my ass concerns you." JD then cut a part of the blanket that to use to go on top of the bucket. He took out the bucket and the toilet paper before removing the centerpiece that was on top of the lid and placed the blanket piece over it to cut out the center of the blanket. Now that piece was hanging over the bucket, but the 18-inch hole on top was visible. That way Jill's butt would stay warm and imprint free while using the bucket.

JD got Jill out of the raft and helped by taking off the bottom half of her clothes. He pulled them down to the ground while she leaned on him for support. After getting her pants and panties down, he lowered her down on the bucket while wrapping the rest of the blanket around her to keep her warm and give her some privacy. He stood behind her to make sure she did not fall off. While sitting on top the bucket, Jill tried to hurry to do her business. Being naked from the waist down and exposed to the cold weather was not a fun experience she enjoyed having right now. Thinking to herself, she should have done it in the tent before they left when JD asked. Soon she wiped herself and told JD to help her off the bucket. He lifted her up to help her put her clothes on. Then he put her and the black bucket back in the raft. Jill said, "Do I have to ride with that right next to me?" JD said, "Why not, after all it does belong to you. I will clean the bucket later after I have used it. Do not worry, the lid is on tight, nothing will spill on you. I am sorry I forgot to bring adult diapers for you to use, Jill Amber." We do not have time to waste discussing this, move away from the bucket if you like."

Jill did exactly that, moving as far away as she could from the black bucket while giving JD her funny look. JD thought she was being silly and ignored her and the look, thinking Jill liked having her way a little too much. He knew this kind of life was not for everyone. She was trying to get on his nerves and it was beginning to work. He began pulling the raft faster to take his mind off Jill and her stupid hang-ups and funny that look she likes to give him.

In the raft, Jill was making whipping sounds and moving her right hand back and forth as if she held an imagery whip, cracking it to make JD go even faster. While looking back at her, JD said, "Glad you have found a way to entertain yourself, Jill Amber." Jill said, "Less talk more work. Now mush doggie, mush." As she cracked her imagery whip one more time at JD's back." JD thought that at least Jill did go to the bathroom in front of him, which took some courage on her part. She could have done it in her clothes again and make him clean her out of spite. Then he would have to take a very long look at that gorgeous body as payment for doing the job.

While daylight was running out, JD kept searching to find a suitable campsite, but getting tired, he decided to take a break to get something to eat. Jill joined him in having a quick snack. JD had some beef jerky and two energy bars while drinking bottled water. Jill ate two granola bars and skipped the beef jerky and energy bar. She drank a can of Boost instead of having water. She was not as hungry as JD; sitting in the raft while he did all the work pulling her, it did not require much energy on her part.

Jill decided to find out more about the man who came to save her. She asked him, "Why did you come last night, JD?" JD said, "I have already told you, Molly asked me. But aren't you glad I did or would you rather me put you back where I found you?" "I think there is more than Molly asking you." "I volunteered when no one else did. They were going to wait until the next morning after the storm passed. I could not let you die there if I could help you. Since I knew the area and trained the man who is in charge of Search and Rescue, who better?" "You risked your life to come save me. That is what I do not understand." "I will make a deal with you, when this is all over and you are safe, I will explain everything to you. I promise. First, we need to get you off this mountain and to a hospital. Now that we have some time, I want to take a look at your ankle."

Jill looked away as JD took off her sock to see her foot. Which looked better than he expected, but she still needed to go to the hospital and have it checked out. It could be worse since he could not see what was happening on the inside of her foot and ankle. He put the sock and the calf boot back on Jill's foot. Jill said, "Well Dr. JD, what is your diagnosis?" JD said, "You will live, but I think you will need surgery on your ankle. They can fix it properly and give you antibiotics for any infections you might have. We should make it in plenty of time before they have to amputate your foot." JD grinned after saying it to her.

Jill changed the subject by asking, "How did you learn so much about the mountain and all your survival skills, JD?" JD said, "My grandfather taught me a lot of things while growing up here. My parents gave me up for him to raise when I was eight. The man had an interesting way of teaching me things. He would show me how to do something and I had to do it right the first time. Otherwise, he would beat me until he saw blood. I soon learned to do things the right way, after a few beatings that is." "I'm sorry that happened to you JD. Your grandfather does not sound like a good person to me. That is no way to raise a child. To beat them because of making mistakes." "It is also not a way for an adult to go through her life either."

Jill knew he was talking about Johnny and the times he had beat on her. She decided not to respond to his statement. JD broke the silence, "I do not understand why women put up with someone like that. I had no choice and had to live with my grandfather. All you have to do is walk away and never see Johnny again." Jill said, "You do not understand our relationship JD. Sometimes I get lonely and need someone in my life. He has always been there for me. That is why I have put up with the way he treats me." "I hope that changes soon. Remember, he is the one responsible for your current situation. However, this time he made a mistake, by involving me. Blowing up that helicopter last night will cost him dearly. The next time we meet, he is going to pay for keeping us on the mountain." "I would be careful JD; Johnny has put many people in the hospital, he is a very dangerous man." "So am I." Jill thought JD was no match for Johnny, being a black belt and seen firsthand what Johnny could do to a person in a fight. She did not know JD already thought out a plan for the next time they met. Johnny would never see what he had in store for him until it was too late.

JD hooked himself up to the raft and started pulling again. He left out the mixed nuts for Jill to eat later if she got hungry. Jill said, "Well thank you; I like all of these except for the Brazil nuts. Never acquired a taste for them." JD said, "Most people do not. They only put them in the can to fill it up and they are the cheapest nuts. Remember, do not throw any nuts out, we do not need to leave a food trail for any animals to follow. Jill was not listening to what JD told her. She was too busy opening up the can of nuts to eat some. JD started pulling and she was sitting back eating the mixed nuts and throwing the Brazil nuts out in the snow. To get them out of the way of the other nuts she wanted to eat. JD had no idea at the time what she was doing. He was too busy trying to find them a campsite before the next storm hit. With the winds picking up and snow starting to fall, he needed to find a tree line for cover.

After a mile of steady jogging, JD spotted a small group of trees and headed straight for them while Jill was still eating and throwing out the big nuts. Before reaching the trees, Jill put the lid back on the can but there was no Brazil nuts left inside, they were all in the snow behind them. Now any wild animal could track them by the trail of nuts.

JD set up the tent and took in the necessary supplies, then came out to get Jill to bring her inside the tent. The raft was the next, by finding two trees to tie it up for the night to keep the snow out. Then he put the black bucket underneath the raft for him to use later. JD made sure Jill was comfortable before leaving her to go gather some rocks. Jill did not know what he was up to but said she would be all right until he came back. JD told her he had a little surprise for her when he did.

After returning, JD set up a tarp right above the tent opening as a little roof. Then he put the rocks underneath it into a small circle and put two cans of steno in the middle of them. He lit the two cans and placed two plates on top of the cans to get hot. Later, he got out the MRE meals and poured them in the plates to heat up. Jill still did not know what he was doing. JD told her to put her gloves back on, because their dinner plates were going to be hot. He said, "I have cooked us some dinner, Jill Amber. You will be having spaghetti with wine to drink." He pulled out the box of wine from one of the buckets and showed her. It was her favorite wine that was in a box. Her eyes lit up after seeing the box in JD's hands.

Jill ate her dinner fast but sipped her wine slowly, enjoying every drop. Later, Jill asked JD if he wanted any wine. JD told her no, he never liked the taste of it. The wine is all yours, but you do not have to drink the whole box tonight. You can always save some for another time. Jill said, "Why, we should be off this mountain tomorrow right?" JD said, "Yes, we should. I was only thinking about the bathroom situation, Jill Amber. Do you really want to take a piss in the middle of the night during a snow storm?" "I have been meaning to ask you, why do you keep calling me, Jill Amber?" "I believe it is your name that is why." "No one else has ever called me that before. Not even my mother and she is the one who named me." "I always seemed to get your full attention after saying it. Would you rather I call you a cougar instead. That is what they call a woman who dates a much younger man, right?" "I do not know why you keep coming back to Johnny." "My point exactly Jill Amber, why do you?" "He understands me by having the same kind of job and lifestyle. I think deep down he cares about me." "That is pure crap and you know it. If he did, where is he then? He only cares about what you can do for his career or if you will pay for everything. That is why he hangs around you. Let me give you a piece of advice, Jill Amber. Find someone that cares about the person you are on the inside and the one on the outside. Who sees what you have to offer them besides the money and fame of being a movie star. Otherwise the relationship does not have a chance of working." "I guess since you have all the answers you have been married before. But I do not see a ring now, did she leave you?"

Jill hurt JD with that last statement but he answered her question anyway. JD said, "I was married once a long time ago. And yes she did leave me when I did not do the right thing." Jill said, "No one special in your life now?" "I have someone, her name is Suzie. We have a true respect for each other. That is what matters most in our relationship." Jill felt a little sad, JD had someone special and she only had Johnny part-time in her life. She stopped asking questions and kept on drinking her wine. JD was not going to tell her Suzie was his dog. She would have only laughed at him not knowing how special she was in his life. He also wanted to see the reaction on her face with his answer. Now seeing she was hurt, he should have told her that he was Play-Doh.

JD asked her, "More spaghetti, or are you full?" Jill said, "Full of food, but I can still drink some more wine." She had already drunk half the box, and was getting drunk. Not feeling any pain from her ankle at the time. This was why JD did not cut her off; wanting her to have another good night sleep before heading out in the morning. The next night she would be having surgery in the hospital. Only JD did not know Jill loved to talk a lot when she got drunk. Now getting late, she did not want to go to sleep, but instead talk to him about her feelings and her past relationships. Including her failed marriage, which was something JD did not want to hear about. To him the past was irrelevant because nothing could change it. He thought you should learn from your mistakes and move forward.

JD asked her if she needed to use the black bucket before going to sleep. Jill said, "No, I am fine right here with my wine." She laughed after saying it to him, thinking it was funny. JD knew his mistake right then, no more wine on camping trips with Jill. Camping and drinking do not mix well with her. Instead, better to have an email chat with her when she got drunk at home, you can end them at any time. JD tried to get her to lie down and close her eyes, but as usual, she was not going to cooperate with him and kept on talking to him. Even after he turned his back to her, so he could try to go to sleep. It did not work; she decided to start singing a song to herself to keep her company. Finally, JD said, "If you do not shut up woman and go to sleep, I will be forced to take action that you will not like." Jill said, "What are you going to do, hit me with that knuckle shocker and knock me out again." "No, something much worse than that. You will force me to "Call the Ducks". Believe me; you do not want me to do that." "I don't care who you call JD. We are having a party, the more the merrier I say." "Okay then, you asked for it." JD was on top of his sleeping bag at the time, still with his back to her. Then a sound went through the tent, sounding something like a duck. Jill was not sure what she just heard. Then the sound came again and then again. Jill looked over at JD and realized he was farting. A sound she had never heard come out of someone before. JD was snickering to himself after doing it. Knowing in a matter of seconds, Jill would get the full effects of what he had just done.

The smell hit her like a tidal wave, as if someone had literally taken a shit right in front of her face. The smell hit her nose and mouth and she was unable to speak or breathe. JD was downwind and still had clean-air to breathe while Jill was choking and searching for some clean-air of her own. Jill said, "My God, what in the hell did you just do, shit on yourself. I literally cannot breathe JD." JD said, "Now you know what I went through after getting your clothes off. Look Jill Amber, stop talking and breathe out of your mouth. I told you, the ducks would shut you up." "It is like having shit in your mouth. I have to get some fresh air." "How do you know, had shit in your mouth lately?"

Jill did not answer him. Instead, she crawled to the front of the tent when JD blew out one last fart right in her face. "Had enough gas, I mean guests for tonight or should I call for some more?" "You are dead inside JD. I have never smelled or tasted anything like this before. I think I am going to be sick and throw up on you." "Stop complaining, it is only air that you are breathing right now laced with the nice smells inside me. The odor will fade away soon and then we can go to sleep, right?" Jill reached the tent opening to get some fresh air to breathe before gagging. After taking a few deep breaths, she looked out to see something moving about fifty feet away. Jill said, "Look JD, there are two doggies up here on the mountain with us. How did they get up here?" JD's eyes popped wide open knowing those were not dogs Jill was now looking at outside the tent. Instead, it had to be wolves looking for food and they were it.

Chapter 16

Able to Survive

JD jumped up and went into his full action mode knowing there was not a lot of time before the wolves attacked them. First, he got Jill away from the tent opening and closed it up tight. While doing it, he saw the two animals outside that were stalking them from a distance. Jill did not understand what was going on to make JD so active. Still feeling the effects of the wine, she watched him get dressed and asked what was such a big deal about two wolves, anyway? JD said, "There are probably more than two, the ones we saw are only lookouts. They are checking out the situation for the rest of them before they attack us." Jill said, "We have not done anything to them. Why would they attack us?" "Jill Amber, like any wild animal, they are hungry and we are their dinner."

Jill had seen wild animals in a zoo and on television, but never up close. Now she was going to have a front row seat to all the action from the wolves and JD who was preparing to go outside to face them. Wondering to herself if both of them were about to die.

JD hurried and put on his hooded jacket and then the coveralls. He then put a fresh pair of inserts in his boots and put them on. After reaching for one the buckets, JD pulled out the duct tape and a flare gun with some flares. JD said, "Jill, you are going to have to help me." She watched him tape up his wrists and forearms with the duct tape. He got out his knife so Jill could use it to cut the tape when he asked. JD started taping around his neck and stopped whenever Jill needed to make a cut. He told her why he was taping these areas, so they will have protection from the wolf's huge teeth while biting him. Jill finished helping him get ready but still did not know his plan. JD showed her how to aim and fire the flare gun. Then he showed her how to reload it with another cartridge. There was four cartridges plus one that was already in the gun for her to use. He also gave her the knuckle blaster, in case the wolves got past him. Jill said, "What are you going to do after getting outside, JD?" JD reached inside the sports bag and pulled out something that was inside a hand towel. After taking the towel off, he laid the new knife down which had a funny looking attachment on the handle. There were two plastic ring holes on the handle attached to the middle of it. "What are the two holes for?" JD showed her by putting his first two fingers of his right hand through the holes while holding the knife. Then he started spinning the knife back and forth to change the position of the blade in his hand, going upwards and then downwards in one quick motion. The knife could spin quickly in his hand without dropping it. Jill said, "Oh, I see now. What are you planning to do with it?" "I cannot wait till they come in here to eat us, there is no room to maneuver inside this tent. Because you are hurt and would only get in my way. Outside, I will have plenty of room to move around and fight them." "To do what, exactly?" "To kill the wolves before they come to kill us. Eaten alive by wolves is not something you want to experience, trust me. I know you drank a lot of wine, but you will still feel their teeth tearing into your flesh."

Jill started visualizing in her mind what if they did attack her and eaten alive by wolves. It was not a pretty thought to have even being intoxicated. Still, she did not want JD to go outside and kill the wolves. Jill said, "Maybe they will not attack us, just give up and go away JD. Those are God's creatures and have a right to survive." JD said, "I believe so are we, last time I checked. I think you should go outside and explain things to them. I am sure they would listen to you. Then you will become their dinner. Look, right or wrong, they will kill both of us if I do not go out there Jill Amber. Now listen up while I show you once again how to fire and reload the flare gun."

Jill watched him and nodded her head as if to say she understood what to do. JD told her to save the last cartridge for herself. Not knowing how many wolves he was going to face, she might want to use it on herself, by putting the gun in her mouth and pulling the trigger. She said, "You want me to commit suicide?" JD said, "Yes, with the flare gun or you could use the stun gun on yourself. Either way, you do not want to be awake while the wolves eat you. I am only telling you this as a last resort. If there is no other option, I would suggest you do one or the other." "I cannot do that JD, just give up and kill myself. No way in hell mister. So I suggest you go outside and make those wolves go away instead." "I will do my best, but you have to understand what we are facing. Wolves are very smart and sneaky animals. They carefully plan their attacks beforehand and will not give up in a fight. They also work as a team and not individually. If you fight one of them, you fight them all. Last, they are very committed especially when they are starving and need food. I hope you do not think any less of me after this is all over." "What do you mean by that?" "I am sorry you have to witness the fight. I guess there is no other way under the circumstances. Now I have to become like them, a wild animal in order for us to survive. It will be a bloody fight, so you might not want to watch. But if you do, know that I am only doing this to save us." "I still do not know what you are trying to tell me JD." "Then let me try to explain it to you in a way that you will. Did you ever watch any of those old black and white Tarzan movies while growing up? The ones that had Johnny Weissmuller and Maureen O'Sullivan in them." "I saw some of them. Why do you ask?" "Do you remember when Jane got into trouble; she would do her jungle call for help. Then Tarzan would call back to her to let her know he was coming to save her. He would swing halfway across Africa in order to reach her." "Yes, I remember. The film went into a faster speed so it looked like he was coming from miles away. Swinging from vine to vine and then reaching her just in time to save her." "And when Tarzan did, he would pull out his big knife and say his famous lines at the animal. Which sometimes the animal would leave, but other times they would stay and fight him. I think it all depended on how hungry the animal was if it stayed to fight him. When I get outside, I will not have time to talk to them about leaving. Only a quick death is what they will receive from me. I will have to go all Tarzan on them. Now do you understand?" "Yes. But I wish there was another way instead of killing them." "Me too. However, life does not work like that in the real world. Sometimes we have to do things we do not like Jill Amber."

Jill lowered her head in disappointment, knowing it was time for JD to go outside to start fighting the wolves. He had to end the threat that faced them and she knew there was no other way. Now all alone, she wondered if JD and her were about to die.

JD told Jill the wolves were not like any stray dogs you might find running around in your neighborhood. If given the chance, they would kill you by chewing your throat out. I guess it is time. Jill said, "Please be careful JD. Try not to get yourself killed." JD said, "I should be all right, they were not that big from what I could see. I only hope that two are all I have to face. I will run to the big tree, in between them and the tent, and then wait for the wolves to come attack us." "Why the tree and not out in the open?" "The tree will protect me from an attack from behind, to watch my back so to speak. That way one of them cannot sneak up behind me while I am fighting the other one. There could be even more wolves than the two we saw. I do not want to get very far from you in case there are a lot more. A pack of wolves could number as many as ten animals, including their young."

Jill's eyes widened when she heard the total, thinking she might have to face a few wolves herself. JD told her to stay away from the opening. That she needed to lie on her stomach and be ready in case one of them tried to get inside. He also told her not to shoot him by mistake with the flare gun. Only fire it as a last resort for her safety. Moreover, to make sure she hit the wolf and not the tent. He did not want her to catch the tent on fire in the process. That would only add to the problems they now faced. Jill gave him that special look of hers, showing her disappointment in him.

Jill told him she understood and scooted back to get on her stomach. JD said, "Well, I guess it is time. I have made them wait long enough." He put the knife in his hand and started moving to the opening to leave. Jill asked him more questions to stop him. "Why aren't you wearing the freezer suit? It could also protect you from them. And why only one knife and not two?" JD said, "A lot of questions for me to answer all at once Jill Amber. Nevertheless, I will try. The wolves will tear up the freezer suit during the fight. I need it to stay in one piece while pulling you in the raft tomorrow and I need to move freely while fighting them. The reason I am not carrying two knives, I am planning to use my left arm as bait. When a wolf grabs my left, I will knife him with my right." "All that makes sense. I guess you know what you are doing." "I have done this a few times in my life."

Jill was only stalling him; she was scared and did not want him to leave her alone. JD told her to call Jim if he did not make it back alive. To use the satellite phone in the morning to reach him and explain everything that happened. Jill put her hand on JD's arm and told him not to die; his job with her was not finished yet. JD felt for one moment she was going to thank him for all he had done for her and for having to go out now to face the wolves. The only thank you he got was giving her the mixed nuts, which caused the problem they now faced.

When she did not thank him, it further pissed him off. Something he needed as an incentive for the job he was about to partake in. He had not killed an animal since the black bear. Now Jill gets to see the other side of him he wished would never surface again. Knowing he was good at killing things and never showed any fear no matter what he faced in his life.

JD went outside and closed the tent opening behind him. He sprung up from the opening and sprinted to the tree to put his back against it. The wolves were not where he had seen them earlier. They went back into the woods to plan their attack. JD stood ready for them whenever they decided to come out and face him, head on or from one of his sides. With both his arms taped from his elbows to his wrist for protection. He looked over at the tent to check on Jill and saw she was in the same position he left her in. With the lanterns on inside, he could see she was still lying on her stomach. JD called out to her to be ready, the attack would happen soon and have both weapons ready to use. Jill had forgotten about the knuckle blaster, it was lying down next to her. She put it close by her, ready if any of the wolves got inside the tent. Then she called back to JD saying everything was ready. Now he could concentrate on the wolves that were in front of him. He still did not know how many or where they would come out to attack him. The only advantage he had was the knife in his right hand. Using his speed and strength to give him a chance to kill them quickly during the attack. He stood very quietly as the snow fell on top of him, waiting for them to show their faces. He could hear them moving in the woods in front of him. Pacing back and forth trying to decide where they would come out to charge him, building up their courage before exposing themselves in the open. JD had picked the perfect spot to fight them. They had no way to sneak up on him now.

Jill was watching from inside the tent, wondering why the wolves had not attacked yet. JD had been outside for at least ten minutes, but still no sign of the wolves. She did not like all this waiting, so she called out, "Maybe you scared them off, JD." JD said, "Be quiet Jill Amber. They are still here somewhere in the woods in front of me. I need you to be silent so I can hear them." Jill did what he asked even though she thought he was being rude to her again. Now all she could do was watch and wait like JD. She did not want to see the animals killed or even JD for that matter.

JD knew the attack would come soon. By running straight for the trees, it had confused the wolves. Now with him standing there waiting for them to come out to start the attack, the wolves were building up their courage. It reminded JD of the fight he almost had with Johnny by waiting for the attack to come to him, which he had planned before the fight began. Knowing he would have the advantage over him and not the other way around.

While waiting for the wolves, JD thought if Jill and he had gone to sleep earlier, they would be the wolf's dinner right about now. In a way, Jill had saved their lives by getting drunk and keeping both of them awake. Funny how things work out in life even if you do not plan for them.

Suddenly the two wolves shot out of the woods at the same time, but from different locations. They were ten feet apart heading straight for him. He stood ready to greet his new friends that were running full speed to his location. JD saw the wolves were only a few years old, weighing about ninety pounds each. He had his left arm out and ready so one of them would try to grab and bite it. While his right hand was hidden from them down at his side, with a knife ready to be used on them. The knife had an eight-inch blade with a double edge and extremely sharp. The blade was black in color; it had no reflection for the wolves to see in the moonlight. Not that it mattered, since the wolves had committed to the attack, there was no going to stop. They kept coming straight for him as Jill was watching inside the tent. She was scared for JD now seeing the two animals running very fast to attack and try to eat him. She flinched at the sight, while JD stood like a statue waiting for them to arrive. Jill kept watching the attack, not knowing what she was about to witness.

JD knew exactly what he was going to do after the first wolf reached him. Lucky for him, one of them was a faster runner then the other. The first wolf did as expected, biting down on his left arm and started tearing at it with his strong neck muscles. Pulling JD's arm back and forth to get him on the ground. Instead, JD used all the strength to lift the wolf off the ground. Now the animal no longer had a surface to pull from. It was hanging in the air trying to tear at his arm. JD quickly drove his knife under the wolf's mouth into the back portion, where the neck met it at the top. The knife went into the wolf's throat and quickly entered its brain in a twist motion. The wolf instantly released its grip on JD's arm and hit the ground dead from his knife strike. It was over in seconds. Now the other wolf was on top of JD and it grabbed and bit down on the arm that held the knife. He was lucky with the first wolf but not the second one. JD had to find a way to get him off in order to use his knife. While trying to fight the second wolf, he saw another wolf approaching the tent. It was twice the size of the one that was on his arm and looked a lot older and wiser, he waited until JD was occupied fighting before exposing himself. JD knew Jill was going to be in big trouble by the way the wolf was stalking her from outside the tent. Even with the weapons he left for her to use, it was not going to be enough to stop that huge animal. He needed to hurry and kill his wolf if he had any chance to save Jill from that beast.

Jill had no idea what was approaching the tent, the huge wolf was moving silently to the front of the tent for the attack. He could smell Jill inside and decided to charge the opening, tearing at the material with its huge teeth. Jill jumped when it did, scared at what was trying to get in to eat her. Now she understood what JD was trying to tell her about these animals. A few seconds later, she fired the flare gun right at the wolf and the tent opening. The flare hit the wolf in the neck and started burning its fur, which made the wolf retreat from the opening and put its neck in the snow to stop all the burning. Rubbing his neck deep in the snow so it could start the attack again. Nothing was going to stop this wolf from reaching Jill and killing her.

The huge wolf returned and started tearing at the opening, trying to get his head inside to reach Jill. After some more tearing and using his strong legs and shoulder muscles, the huge wolf's head was inside the tent. Soon he would be on top of Jill having her for dinner. Jill got the flare gun reloaded and fired it at the wolf. This time the gun misfired and nothing happened. She dropped the gun down and had the knuckle blaster ready to use on the wolf when he got inside. If it did not work on the wolf, she was going to use it on herself when the wolf started attacking her, she was not brave like JD, and could not be awake while the wolf ate her. JD had left his other knife with her to use. However, what chance would she have using it against this huge animal? Jill thought Johnny was going to get his wish; she was going to die on this mountain after all.

JD decided to drop the knife, by opening up his hand and shaking it off to the ground. Then he could use his left hand to kill the wolf. He quickly moved to reach down with his left hand to pick up the knife. Only this time, there was no time for him to put his two fingers through the ring holes. It took two quick strikes to kill the wolf that then released his grip on JD's right arm. He started running toward Jill and her uninvited guest.

Jill saw up close how dangerous and vicious this animal was staring right at her with its dead black eyes. She only hoped JD would be coming soon to help save her one more time. In about five more seconds, the wolf was going to turn her into grandma like in "Little Red Riding Hood". Jill moved to the very back of the tent not giving the wolf a chance to bite her as he was trying to push his huge body through the opening. The wolf was almost in enough to reach her. With one more good push and tear at the opening, he would be on top of her, chewing out her throat. Jill could even feel his warm breath inside the tent, thinking the end was near. The wolf was eyeing its prey, knowing he would be sinking his teeth into this helpless victim soon. Jill decided to close her eyes, not wanting to watch herself eaten by this huge wolf. She held the knuckle blaster against her neck, ready to use it on herself when the wolf reached her. Knowing if the flare gun could not stop this animal, the blaster would not either having only one chance to knock it out.

JD arrived in time to grab the wolf's hind legs out from under him and pull the huge animal out of the tent. He could not believe how big this wolf was he had in his grasp. It weighed at least one hundred and sixty pounds, if not more. The largest one JD had ever seen or heard about in his life. The wolf was surprised at what was happening to him, losing the use of his back legs and then dragged out of the tent away from his dinner. JD was talking to the animal as if they were old friends going to have a play date together.

Jill opened her eyes and saw the wolf was now gone out of the tent. Once again, JD had arrived in time to save her without any regard for his own life or safety. Anyone else might have looked at the size of the animal and hesitated to take the wolf on with only a knife. JD was not like anyone Jill had ever met before in her life.

Before releasing the hind legs, JD cut the left tendon of the wolf's leg. Cutting the hind leg made it hard for the wolf to stand or run away. Now it had no true balance and something to worry about, the man standing in front of him with the knife. If the wolf tried to leave, JD would be able to track it by the blood trail. The animal was not going to leave until JD was dead and he had Jill for dinner.

Jill was sitting inside the tent, watching the fight unfold before her eyes. JD showed no fear while waiting for the wolf to attack him. Soon they began circling each other, sizing the other one up, looking for an advantage before the fight began. Jill felt it was like being at the movies with a front row seat to all the action. She too was waiting for the fight to begin.

Now losing a lot of blood, the wolf would have to make his move soon. JD had to be more careful not to rush the attack because of the size and age of this animal. The wolf was bleeding and limping while following JD in a circular motion. JD decided to stop and wait for the wolf to attack him and in the meantime have a little fun with the animal for Jill's benefit. He called out the <u>Tarzan movie line</u> to the wolf to see what would happen. JD said, "Ungula Waa" many times to the wolf. Jill could hear him do it inside the tent. She knew he was doing it for her benefit. Trying to make the wolf leave so he did not have to kill it. The wolf was watching as JD was saying the words and showing him the knife in the process. JD saw the wolf's eyes and knew it was not going to leave. He prepared himself for what was going to happen next by taking a very deep breath in the frozen air.

The wolf leaped up at JD with his one good hind leg. JD put his left arm out to block the attack and then drove both of them to the ground. While going to the ground, he put his left arm deep in the wolf's mouth and started using his right hand that had the knife to stab the wolf repeatedly in the neck.

Jill let out a scream when she saw the wolf jump up to attack JD. Now she was seeing what JD never wanted her to witness. He had turned himself into Tarzan and got as vicious as the wolf he was now fighting. By stabbing the wolf many times, the way Tarzan did with the rhino that was trying to kill Jane. JD stabbed the wolf at least a dozen times or maybe more with Jill losing count. He did not stop until he knew the wolf had stopped breathing and was finally dead. Then he rolled off the wolf, got up, and walked away a few feet to fall face first in the snow, fully exhausted from the fight.

Jill was now a little frightened of JD by what she had just witnessed by the death of that animal. He had changed himself into an animal and no longer a man. She was not sure what to do or say to him when he came inside the tent. Jill decided to wait until he talked to her first to see what JD had to say about what she just witness him doing to those animals.

JD had blood all over his coveralls and gloves after the fight. He was now lying in the snow to get some of it off. Also to get some rest, giving him a chance to calm down and return to being human again, and to have the right mindset before going to check on Jill. He knew she would not understand his actions and might hate him for what he had just done. The blood turned the snow red underneath his body. He soon got up to go check on Jill, not knowing her current condition.

After reaching the tent opening, JD poked his head in and said, "I am sorry you had to see that, I hope you are not scared of me." Jill said, "I have to admit, I am a little bit. You became exactly what you described to me earlier. A complete animal and not a human being." "I know I did. Only, you cannot have any mercy in that kind of fight. I wish there was another way to handle things. But if we had waited, they would have tracked us down in the open." "I understand now, they would have killed us." "Exactly, or maybe just you." Jill gave him her look again after that statement.

He asked her if she was hurt in any way by the big wolf. Jill said, "No, the wolf never got close enough to bite me. I think the flare gun is broken. I reloaded the gun and tried to fire it, but nothing happened." JD said, "It is a cheap gun, I am not surprised. I am glad you are not hurt. Now, can I have my knuckle blaster back?" Jill still had it on her hand and forgot it was even there and JD did not want her to use it on him or herself by mistake. She handed it back to him and he put it in his pocket and asked. "How close were you to using it on yourself before I came?" "To be honest, it was heading for my neck when you grabbed and started pulling that wolf out of the tent." "A good thing I made it in time before you did." "Yes, I would have to agree. That is until I saw what happened between you and that wolf. I should have done as you suggested, closed my eyes." "I only know one way to attack in a fight for your life. Never stop until the threat is over, not before. I learned that the hard way once. If you like, we can never speak about this again." "I think it would be best JD." "I understand. It will not be brought up again." Jill nodded her head in agreement with him.

To change the subject, Jill asked JD to help her use the black bucket before she went to sleep. A few minutes later, JD lifted Jill off the bucket and then helped pull up her panties and laid her down on the sleeping bag. He got one more jab in before leaving her, by picking the black bucket up using both his hands to carry it. Pretending the bucket was too heavy to carry only using one hand. Jill said, "Very funny, JD. Will you please take that bucket outside?" JD said, "I cannot believe all of this came out of such a small woman. You really should not take in so much air while eating Jill Amber. That is what causes you to have gas and this unpleasant odor we are now experiencing." "I think you are not the one to talk about anyone's gas or odor, mister. Remember all the ducks you called earlier tonight." JD did not comment and left after Jill called him mister again.

JD fixed the tent opening by using one of the small tarps. He returned inside and started gathering up some food and water to put in one of the other buckets to take with him. He went outside and got the raft ready to carry the dead animals. He opened the other small tarp and put it down in the raft with the bucket of supplies. Then he got the three dead wolves and put them in the raft. After putting on the shoulder harness, JD went back in the tent to tell Jill where he was going and why.

JD told Jill not to wait up for him. That he was going to get rid of the dead animals by dumping them off a nearby cliff, as it would be a lot faster and easier than burying them. Jill said, "Not a problem, you killed them, you can get rid of them. I will stay here and try to get some sleep while you are gone. By the way JD, I have to say, it is never boring being around you. May I ask what you have planned for us to do next?" This time he gave her one of his funny looks while not answering her. He had not planned any of this and only got one thank you from this woman since pulling her out of the snow. Not even one after pulling the wolf out of the tent before he had her for dinner. Maybe he should have stayed at the resort sitting in front of that big fire instead of coming to save an ungrateful woman who only cares about her own well-being.

JD quickly hooked himself up to the raft and started his journey. On the way, JD had a theory he wanted to check it out. Wondering to himself why there were no females in the pack that attacked them. The next day would be the hardest on him pulling the raft with all the hills and he hoped to return to get some sleep before daylight.

While jogging and pulling the raft, Michael called JD's cell phone. He stopped to put in his blue tooth to answer the call and then began pulling again. Michael said, "How are things going, Lone Ranger?" JD said, "Terrific Tonto. You will not believe what I am doing right now." "Not a clue, so why not just tell me to save time." "I am pulling three dead wolves in the raft to go dump off a cliff. They tried to attack Jill and me about an hour ago. First, I am on my way to a cave to check on something. What are you up to tonight?" "Wolves, where in the hell did they come from?" "I do not know exactly, but one of them has a silver back." "The wolf that killed your grandfather?" "It has to be, the wolf is the biggest one I have ever seen, Michael. Now, what news do you have for me?" "Nothing much except Bill Turner is the one who is pulling Johnny's strings. He is going to sign him to a big contract when he gets back in town. I heard it is a ten movie deal at his studio." "Well, now everything makes sense. This entire calamity happening to Jill had to be by someone who had true hatred for her. With her movie being a huge success, I guess he wants her out of the movie making business forever. Did you get everything set up at the hospital and the use of the two ambulances?" "It is all taken care of John. A surgery team will be on standby at the hospital and the two ambulances will be at the base of the mountain at three o'clock tomorrow. Anything else I can do for you?" "You have done more than enough, Tonto. Thank you for everything. I wish Jill were more like you old friend. She still has not thanked me for anything I have done for her except giving her a can of nuts to eat. I will call you tomorrow to let you know how things are going. Bye, Tonto and thanks again." "Good luck Lone Ranger and I am glad it was you who got "Old Silver Back"." JD did not tell him Jill was not around him at the time. He wanted to use their nicknames for practice, even though Michael probably had figured it out for himself.

After their call ended, Michael thought Jill was not worth the time John had spent on her. Never thanking him was inexcusable, even if she did not know he was the Play-Doh Man. Now thinking to himself if he ever got another chance to speak to her again, he was definitely going to give her a piece of his mind. She has to realize the world does not revolve around her needs and no one else's. Michael thought about a television show he saw as a kid that had an Ice Queen in it and Jill reminded him of that woman by her actions toward John.

Three hours later, JD returned to the campsite to find the tarp on the tent opening did not hold with all the strong winds. He quickly put the raft away and took off his shoulder harness before going inside the tent to check on Jill. She could not go to sleep with the temperature inside the tent feeling like a freezer. Jill was shaking under all the blankets trying to stay warm until he got back. He hurried to get the opening fixed and then took off his clothes to get Jill's body warm. He checked her forehead, it was warm and her fever had returned. Jill told him she tried to fix the opening when the storm hit but could not when the tarp blew away on the outside. So she got under the blankets to stay warm until he got back. JD opened the sleeping bags and crawled in with her. His body was very warm from all the work pulling the raft and doing a few errands along the way, then running at a steady pace on the way back to keep himself warm in the storm.

Like the night before, he intertwined their two bodies and started rubbing Jill's body to raise her temperature. Jill said, "What in the hell do you think you are doing, JD. I did not ask you to come and warm me up. I am only wearing panties and a t-shirt." JD said, "Your fever has returned, I need to get your body temperature back up to break it. The same way I did last night, by rubbing your body in the right places. You will soon know exactly what I did last night after using my knuckle blaster on you. So be quiet and try not to move, Jill Amber. Let me do all the work and take care of you."

Jill did not say another word to him. JD's warm body felt so good next to hers. He was like an electric blanket covering her entire body. Soon she stopped shaking and her temperature was back to normal. She fell asleep shortly after JD stopped rubbing her. JD put both his arms around Jill's waist and rested his hands on her stomach before falling asleep next to the woman that was in his heart. He had only five hours left until daylight broke. Time never seemed to be on his side on this trip. With no more distractions, both were sound asleep with the wind blowing outside. JD was dreaming about her and only God knew what Jill could be dreaming about, maybe her next box of wine she was going to drink. With only one day left with her, his time was about up. Not being sure if he would tell Jill tomorrow he is the Play-Doh Man or wait until they were off the mountain.

Chapter 17

A Small Bond Forms

The five hours passed by like a quick flash, as if JD closed and then opened his eyes as his watch alarm went off and he saw daylight inside the tent. His mind and body still felt exhausted and thought one more hour of sleep would not hurt. He set his watch and dozed off dreaming about the woman next to him. Jill was sound asleep next to him and had not moved all night or even when his alarm went off. She also needed more rest after the busy night they both had and the day they would soon face. It felt so right, having her sleeping next to him, something JD hoped would happen for the rest of their lives. At least this time, Jill would not wake up mad at him, asking a whole bunch of questions.

The next hour went by as quickly as the first five, with JD's watch alarm going off waking both of them up this time. Jill wanted ten more minutes, she asked JD to hit the snooze on that alarm she was now hearing. JD turned off the alarm and got up, but let her get ten additional minutes. He needed to get dressed then go outside to pack up everything so they could leave after making some very important phone calls.

After JD got dressed to leave, Jill said, "Don't leave me JD, you are my human blanket that keeps me warm." JD said, "If it was up to me, I would stay here next to you all day. Unfortunately, we have to get up and start our trip to get you off the mountain. You have a date with a surgeon late this afternoon, remember?" Jill reluctantly started stretching in the sleeping bag and then made a pouty face at him. She sat up and started putting on some of her top clothes. JD would help her with the bottom half items later. Before going outside, he checked her ankle and found it was worse than the day before. She definitely needed antibiotics for her foot. After seeing it, Jill also knew she needed surgery. JD told her to cheer up; she would be off the mountain today and rid of his enjoyable company to rejoin her friends. After a brief hospital stay, she could go home and continue living her busy life. Jill said, "I do not think you should be mean to me our last day together, JD." Jill was nervous about going to the hospital and having her foot surgery. She did not like hospitals or doctors, which had involved too much physical and emotional pain in her past. JD asked how she slept and felt, which Jill replied; "I slept great and feel okay, except for my ankle". JD checked her forehead again to make sure her fever was gone. It was, by him keeping her body warm the rest of the night.

Outside, JD got the raft and put it in position to be loaded by the tent opening. Then he got his harness ready to wear, the black bucket, about twenty feet of rope, the trifold shovel and put everything in the raft. All the items he needed to load except for Jill and their sports bags of clothes. She would be the last item he would load before leaving the campsite.

JD called Jim on the satellite radio to get today's news and any updates. Asking him first about any weather changes he might need to know about before breaking camp to leave. Jim answered his call with some great news. They had found another helicopter to come get them off the mountain. It could be at the resort by ten o'clock this morning and could reach them an hour and a half later. JD asked him, "How did you manage that?" Jim said, "Out of the blue a man called to volunteer his helicopter to pick Jill up and take her to the hospital. Unfortunately, the helicopter only has room for one passenger. You will have to hike down the mountain by yourself." "Who is this man you have been talking to Jim?" "He lives in California, someone Jill used to work for, a Bill Turner who is the president of Planet Studios". JD's mind was racing full speed after hearing his name. He knew if Jill got on that helicopter, she would not make it to any hospital. This had Bill or Johnny's name written all over it. Their last attempt to do her harm without any witnesses present. "Jim, tell Mr. Turner no thanks that everything is taken care of and we do not need his help. We will be in Leadville this afternoon and I have already made arrangements to get Miss Green to the hospital."

Jim did not understand why John was refusing the man's help. He thought John was putting too much on himself in getting Jill off that mountain and told him so. Then JD explained to him that Bill Turner was Johnny's new boss. He was the one who orchestrated the whole thing by trapping Jill on this mountain. If she got on that helicopter, we would never see her again. Probably having the pilot push her out accidentally on the way to the hospital. JD told him exactly what he wanted him to do, call Mr. Turner and explain to him that Jill will be in Leadville at three o'clock this afternoon. The use of his helicopter will not be necessary; Jill will be holding a press conference when she gets there. JD also wanted Jim to get Carrie and her family to Leadville so they could wait for them to arrive at the base of the mountain. If Bill asked anything else, tell him that is all you know. Jim said he would take care of it and would see JD in Leadville.

JD called Rex next; his young friend was going to have a major part if his plan had any chance of working. After today, Jill's problems with Bill and Johnny were finally going to end. JD reached Rex and told him what he needed him to do. Rex agreed to help, so JD explained his whole plan to him. He was to go to Leadville and wait there at the base of the mountain for his signal. First, by a phone call and second with a wave from him to put his plan into motion. Rex told JD he would be there ready for his call and signal. He would get his brother Mark to help him with the heavy lifting. JD thanked him and said he would talk to him later to see how things were going. Finally, JD called Michael, for some more assistance. "Hey Tonto, I need your help once again. Bill Turner tried to send his helicopter to pick up Jill today. I knew it was some kind of trap, so I declined his offer." Michael said, "I think that was a good idea, Lone Ranger. I see Bill Turner is still up to no good. I do not understand why that man wants to harm Jill." "Well that is the reason I am calling you, after today Bill and Johnny will not bother her ever again. I need to put some real fear in them so to speak." "Whatever you need, Lone Ranger. I am here to help." "Good to hear, Tonto. We will be at the base of the mountain by three o'clock this afternoon. Is there a way you can arrange some press to meet us there to cover the story of Jill's rescue? That way she will be safe from any more harm from those two knuckleheads." "Let me make some calls. I will call you back to let you know what I have come up with, Lone Ranger." "Sounds good, Tonto. I need to go eat my breakfast and get Jill ready to leave. Talk to you later on today."

JD returned inside to find Jill on the phone talking with Carrie, about seeing her late this afternoon in Leadville. JD motioned to her for the phone so he could talk to Carrie. After Jill handed him the phone, JD said, "Carrie, JD here. I have asked Jim Matthews to let you and your family follow him to Leadville today so you will not get lost. He will be coming to ask you with the trip being a little tricky from where you are now." Carrie said, "That will be great, JD. Thank you for thinking of us and for saving my best friend's life. I have not had a chance to tell you yet. I will do a better job when I see you in person today." "You are very welcome on both counts. Here is Jill again." JD handed her the phone and started to get some things ready for breakfast. Jill continued with her conversation as he was working. Soon the phone went dead in the middle of the conversation. JD told her it was time to eat anyway; she could talk to Carrie later when she saw her in Leadville. Right now, it was time to eat their breakfast and get ready to leave. They ate the same meal they had the day before except adding an energy bar this time.

While eating, JD explained to Jill about the offer for the helicopter, but that he had turned it down. Jill had a shocked look on her face after learning there would be no helicopter. She could not understand why he had done that, unless he enjoyed pulling her in the raft up and down the mountain for the hell of it. Jill said, "Why in the hell did you do that, JD? We could just wait here for the helicopter to come pick us up." JD said, "The helicopter only has room for one passenger. I will not be able to come with you, and it belongs to Mr. Bill Turner. Would you like me to call Jim back and get that helicopter for you?" Jill's face turned ghost white and she looked very scared. "I guess I made the right decision. Your good friend Bill wanted me to hike down the mountain by myself and leave you all alone in his helicopter. That is why I declined his offer and told Jim to call Bill back and tell him that I started this job and intend on finishing it without his help. I will get you off this mountain without any more harm coming to you, I promise." "You made the right call JD. I know you are here trying to help me and I trust your judgment. Bill Turner is a snake and has no morals. I almost worked for him but instead started my own production company. I know exactly what kind of man he is and what he is capable of." "Glad to hear it then. I think there is some hope for you yet." They both smiled at each other while eating their cereal.

Then their conversation began again with JD saying, "Did you hear that Bill Turner intends on signing Johnny to a ten picture deal with a huge signing bonus?" Jill said, "No, I did not. How did you find that out?" "Rex told me about the story. It was in the newspaper he was reading yesterday." "I see, that means Johnny now works for Bill." "Have you had enough to eat or do you need more?" "I guess that was enough." "Make sure, this will be the only time you get to eat today. You cannot eat anything before having surgery. Which should be sometime early this evening." "I guess another banana and an energy bar would not hurt then."

JD handed them to her and waited until she was finished eating. Now he had one more job to do before they could leave, by pouring out the rest of the food they had left on the tent floor. JD was unwrapping all of it and cleaning up any trash he caused. Jill watched him but did not know what was going on, she asked, "JD, why are you wasting all that food?" JD said, "I'm not wasting it, the food will be eaten by someone else very soon. Get your things together so we can go." JD poured the last of the Boost into a partial gallon jug of water, making it a little more than half full. Then he cut off the top of the jug and left it on the tent floor. He poured some water in both deep-dish plates and left them with the food and the Boost shake he had made. It looked like a big mess that a six-year-old child would make instead of a thirty-seven-year-old grown man. Jill was still confused at him and his behavior but stopped asking questions. She now had her things together and was ready to go. JD loaded the sport's bags and the rest of the bottled water into the raft. Jill knew now this was all they were taking with them. JD loaded Jill into the raft, hooked up his harness, and then began pulling the raft without looking back at the campsite. After a few minutes, he began sprinting when they came to a hill, so he could make it to the top.

After reaching the top, JD came to a stop and unhooked his harness from the raft. He pulled out his small pair of binoculars to look down at the campsite. After about ten minutes, some objects came into view of what he had expected to see. He then handed the binoculars to Jill and told her to look down at the campsite. She refocused them and saw a huge wolf going into their camp. Behind the wolf were three little wolves following, her pups. All of them went inside the tent, knowing there was food for them to eat. Jill lowered the binoculars and looked at JD. She asked, "How did you know about them?" JD said, "Something was bothering me last night after the attack. There were no female wolves, only males. There is always at least one in the pack. Anyway, I knew about a cave three hundred yards from our camp and had a feeling she might be there with her pups, which explained why she did not join in the attack. Last night I visited them before dumping the other wolves off the cliff. I went in quietly and used my knuckle blaster on her when she charged me. I wanted to leave some food behind for them. She was weak from hunger and from nursing her pups, so it only took one quick blast. Then I made the pups a Boost milkshake and played with them for a few minutes. Later, I cut up one of the dead wolves so the mother would have some fresh meat to eat. She needed to get her strength back before taking her pups out of the cave. Only, she does not know her mate was her dinner last night. Since he was the biggest and had the most meat on him, he was the right choice to cut up."

Jill went back looking through the binoculars as JD said, "Also, I saw one the pups this morning. He poked his head out of the woods when I was getting things ready to leave. I knew his mother was there watching me. She would not let him go wandering that far away from the others. She must have had enough to eat last night, not coming out of the woods to attack us. That is why I hurried up so we could leave and let them eat their breakfast I made for them inside the tent." Jill asked, "How did you get them to come to our camp site this morning, JD?" "The same way you got the three wolves to come last night, by throwing Brazil nuts out in the snow. Last night I left a trail for them to follow to our camp. Knowing they would come this morning to see what happened to the rest of the family. Anyway, when I saw all of them missing in the can you were eating, I had figured out what you had done with them even after I told you not to do it. I used all the Brazil nuts out of the other can we had left. For some reason Jill Amber, you never seem to want to take my advice. Look what that has gotten us, a weekend on the mountain together."

Jill's head sunk down in shame for what she had done. By causing the wolves to attack, while searching for food and was responsible for their deaths and almost hers and JD's. JD took his hand and put it on her chin so he could lift her head back up and she could look at him. He told her she was the reason why they still were alive by getting drunk and keeping them up last night. If they had gone to sleep, the wolves would have been on top of them sometime in the night. She had saved their lives by spotting them when she went to get some fresh air from his odors.

Jill said, "That does not change the fact that I almost got us killed, JD. I am responsible for the deaths of those three wolves. Those baby wolves no longer have a father or two brothers and it is my fault." JD said, "Yes, but we are alive and have saved four wolves from dying on this mountain. It all equals out in the end Jill Amber. I believe the huge wolf that tried to eat you was the same one that killed my grandfather two years ago. They found his body and saw two sets of tracks running away from his campsite. The tracks were very deep, but definitely made by the wolf I fought and killed last night, which was "Old Silver Back". The other set of tracks had to be his mate and she probably was pregnant at the time. The other two wolves I killed last night would not have been born yet." "JD, anyone else would have killed the mother wolf last night if given the chance. Especially knowing it had killed their grandfather. You chose to let her live. Why did you do that?" "She is an animal and only kills to survive. Those three pups need their mother and will not survive without her. My grandfather knew the risk when he went camping alone. I am not a heartless person and I try to think of all the consequences beforehand. Life has its cycles; those wolves have a right to survive. Even if I was not close to my grandfather, I respected him. He lived and died on his own terms, in the wild." "Now I understand why you left all the food inside the tent. You are giving them a chance to survive." "Exactly, but they will have to find their own food in the future. I have done all I can." "Do you think they have a chance to live up here?" "Better than they did yesterday. With all the food I left at the cave and in the tent, they have a decent chance. The mother wolf knows the area; she will be able to find some more food now getting her strength back. Well, I guess it is time for us to leave. You have a doctor's appointment to make this afternoon." "Don't remind me, more pain I get to experience in my life."

JD hooked up and started pulling the raft while Jill kept watching the little pups going in and out of the tent, thinking to herself that JD had a good heart in helping those animals. After killing her mate and her two sons, he took the time to try to save the rest of the pack. What kind of man would do that? Not the savage she saw last night fighting that huge wolf. It had to be the man that was now pulling her down off this mountain and kept on amazing her by his actions in the two days they spent together.

Later on, Michael called JD to give him the news on his progress with the media. Michael said, "Lone Ranger, the media will be there at two forty-five in full force. The local newspaper and two television networks will be covering the story, waiting to interview Jill. Sound good?" JD said, "That will work perfectly, Tonto. Good job and thanks for all your help. Call you back with the outcome when it is all over." "Before you go, have you got a thank you from the Ice Queen yet?" "No, not yet. I did get one from her best friend Carrie and her five-year-old daughter, Molly. I think we both know life is not perfect, right Tonto." "I guess, but she needs to learn a few things. I think you should tell her who you really are." "Let me handle things on this end. You stay out of it, Tonto. Understand?" "Okay then, Lone Ranger. I will let you handle it. Good luck with her, I think you are going to need it before all of this is over."

Jill said, "Who is Tonto and are you the Lone Ranger?" JD said, "A close friend of mine. We use our childhood nicknames sometimes on the phone. Having a little fun while talking to each other. Don't you and Carrie do the same thing; have funny nicknames for each other?" "No, we do not have any nicknames, just our own. Anything I need to know about that call from Tonto?" "All in good time, Jill Amber. I will tell you about it later. I have a plan that will take care of everything today. All you need to do is sit back and keep your leg elevated to keep the swelling down. Enjoy the sights and the ride while I drag your butt off this mountain. Okay?" "I will do exactly that after I use the black bucket. Can we please stop and pull over?" JD was just getting into good stride when she said that. He stopped and helped her go to the bathroom, which was only doing number one this time. Soon they were back on their way, heading for the top of the mountain.

Before starting again, JD made a call to Rex on how things were going on his end. At the time, he was in his truck with his brother Mark, driving to Leadville. Rex told him he would be there at the bottom, set up and ready to go on his signal. JD went over his plan exactly what he needed Rex to do after getting a signal and then reaching him and Jill. That way Rex would understand all the parts to it and why. Rex said, "I understand and will handle everything you have just told me. JD, I think you should know Johnny will be there, he has rented the equipment and is in a truck following me as we speak." "That is what I want him to do. Good job, Rex. See you later on this afternoon at the trees." "JD, I hope everything works out, for all of us." "As long as you do your part it will my young friend."

While dragging her, JD asked Jill if she was excited to see Carrie, David and Molly later on today. Jill said, "Of course I am. They are the only true friends I have in this whole world. I mean except for you now." JD thought he was just a friend. Well at least that was a start. Jill said, "I forgot, Molly told me to tell you, thank you yesterday, for saving her Aunt Jill. I guess it slipped my mind." JD said, "That is okay. I figured she had when I overheard that part of your conversation with her. She is a very special child, I like her a lot." "Molly is my goddaughter and I love her like she is my own." "Do you ever spend some time alone with her? I mean just the two of you." "To be honest, not much. Running my new company keeps me very busy." "I have to say, these are important years in her life. The ones she will remember spending with you while growing up. If I were in your shoes, I would take at least one day a month out of your busy schedule to spend with her." "I will try to do that in the future, JD. Not that it is any of your business how I spend my days." "All I am saying is you could have died this weekend and what would Molly have to remember you by? That you are a very busy person who loved her, or a person that took one day out of the month to spend time with her, showing how much she really loved her goddaughter. Jill's head sunk down again, she was ashamed not spending any real quality time with Molly except when Carrie needed a babysitter. JD was right in what he was saying to her, even if it did hurt hearing it from him. JD looked back to see Jill's face. He said, "You still have time to change things by looking toward the future and not your past events. Try thinking about all the things you would like to do with her that will be special, and she will remember doing with you. Believe me; it could shape the person she will become as an adult." Jill started thinking about all the things JD said and was wondering how to change her past choices to improve her future ones.

After a few hours went by, Jill asked JD how much longer before they reached Leadville and the base of the mountain. JD told her in about two more hours, they would be at the top to make their descent to the tree line. It was going to be a fast slide in the raft down the other side of the mountain to a small group of trees before reaching the base. He began jogging again to make sure they would make it on time. Every time they came to a top of the hill, JD would stop and unhook himself. Then he would tell Jill to move up to the front of the raft while he pushed it from the back. When the raft started moving downward, JD quickly jumped in and joined her as they rode down the hill together until it came to a stop. Then he would hook himself back up and start pulling the raft again.

There were not many hills, but JD took advantage of every one he could find to use. This made the trip go faster and he could save his strength from all the pulling. Soon there was only one more hill to climb before going over the top to the other side, where everybody would be waiting for them, including Johnny Mann. The black belt that JD would finally have to fight in order to give him that special surprise.

Chapter 18

Mountain Man vs. Black Belt

*J*D pulled them almost to the top and stopped before reaching it, wanting to stay out of sight. They were about fifteen minutes early, which gave him time to rest and make his phone call to Rex to put his plan into motion. Now it was time to tell Jill exactly what was going to happen after reaching the top and then afterwards when they came to a stop at the trees. JD said, "Jill, first we are going to the top so everyone can see us down below. This will give Rex enough time to get into position before coming to pick you up. After I wave to him, I am going to push the raft so we can start sliding down the mountain to a group of trees, about two hundred yards from the base. That is where Rex will come to meet us on his snowmobile and take you back down the mountain. There will be an ambulance waiting at the base that can take you to the hospital. Also Carrie, David and Molly will be there to go with you for support and to make sure you're safe."

Jill listened to JD's plan without interrupting him, but now thought it was her turn to ask some questions. Jill said, "Where will you be after Rex takes me down with him? And why aren't you coming with us?" "You never seem to run out of questions, do you Jill Amber? I need to stay behind and wait for someone." "And who might that be?" "Johnny is also down at the base with a snowmobile and thinks he is going to pick you up and bring you back down with him." "Why is he down there and why would he think that?" "I arranged for the media to be down there waiting to interview you. Johnny is trying to do damage control for himself by using them and you. If he is the one that brings you down, the press will take many pictures of the two of you and report that he is some kind of hero for getting you off the mountain. Instead of being responsible for you being left on it to die. Then he and Bill can go back to the way things were before all this happened. Since their plan failed in getting you out of the way, they have to cut their losses and accept this instead, to save face." "Do you really think that Johnny and Bill tried to kill me?" "Yes, I do. If given another chance, they would try again." "What can I do to stop them?" "By letting me handle things now. I will be waiting for good old Johnny by the trees, so there will be no witnesses. All this ends today, Jill Amber. I can promise you that. No more Johnny or Bill to worry about in your future." "Then please make me a promise, JD." "If I can, I will." "Don't go all "Tarzan" on Johnny and kill him. Like you did with "Old Silver Back" last night with your knife. He is not worth ruining your life for, by going to prison. If you kill him, they will send you there." "I thought Johnny is a very dangerous person who can take care of himself." "I know now what you are capable of, he does not stand a chance against you especially the way you plan things out in your head. Johnny reacts to situations without thinking about them ahead of time. So please do not waste your life on him. He is not worth it, JD." "I will only do what is necessary in order to stop him. Nothing else, I promise. Okay, I think it is time to call Rex to let him know to warm up his snowmobile. Then we can go to the top and have some fun sliding down this mountain in this raft, going really fast."

JD called Rex on his Bluetooth while he was pulling the raft to the top. He cranked up his snowmobile and got into position ready to take off. Johnny was over with the media giving them an interview when he heard Rex start his snowmobile. He was trying to explain what had happened to Jill two days ago on their ski trip. Carrie and her family were waiting with Jim a short distance away. Mark was over talking to one of the EMTs at the time, they knew each other from a past rescue attempt.

Suddenly everyone looked up at the top of the hill and saw JD and Jill appear. Jill was waving down to Carrie and her family, letting them know she was all right. JD got into position and then waved at Rex. This was the signal for him to get started riding up toward them. Leaving Johnny behind still talking to the reporters. Rex had a good ten second jump on Johnny as he ran over to his snowmobile and started after him trying to catch up. Rex was full throttle, racing up the hill and now ruining Johnny's plan to bring Jill back down with him, in order to be the hero. Johnny yelled at Rex to stop or he would face the consequences. Rex ignored him and his threats; he kept on riding toward the trees knowing JD had plans for Johnny behind them, which nobody would be able to see. All he had to do was make it there first, and then JD would take care of the rest.

A few moments earlier, JD unloaded the raft so he could spray the WD-40 on the bottom of it to make the surface very slick. After loading everything back in, including Jill, he started pushing the raft hard down the mountain before jumping in and sitting behind her to enjoy the ride down. The same way they had been doing all day when given the opportunity. Those were just practice hills for this one, to get the feel of the raft going down, to gauge the speed and direction they would be moving. This ride in the raft was a lot faster with this hill being much larger and steeper than the smaller ones. By using the WD-40, the raft was increasing a lot of speed and much harder to control. Jill yelled back to JD asking him how they were going to stop before hitting the trees they were heading straight for. Knowing they would crash soon if they did not slow down. JD yelled not to worry that he had a plan to stop them. At the time, he was using the trifold shovel by putting it in the snow at the rear of the raft, in order to steer it to the far right side of the trees.

Rex was heading for the trees on his right side. The opposite end where JD and Jill were going. The plan was after reaching the trees, he was supposed to turn left and keep driving the snowmobile to the other side to meet them. JD would be waiting with Jill in his arms to help load her on the snowmobile. They would leave and go back down to the base without giving Johnny a chance to get her. He would stay behind to have a little talk with Johnny before coming down.

Johnny was on a newer snowmobile and gaining on Rex while heading up the hill. However, there was no way he could catch Rex before reaching the trees, he had too much of a head start. He did not have a clue about what was going to happen after getting behind those trees. JD planned for everything to happen too fast for him to do anything about it.

Before reaching the trees and crashing into them, JD pulled out his knife and punched a huge hole in the raft. Letting all the air out by deflating it. Which made them come to a complete stop. JD immediately jumped up and then picked Jill up into his arms, waiting for Rex to arrive. He could hear him in the distance heading for the trees. Moments later, Rex made a left turn and went full throttle heading straight for them, as he saw JD holding Jill, waiting for him to arrive to carry her down. When he pulled up, JD loaded Jill on the back of the snowmobile. Seconds later, Johnny made the same left turn and drove straight for the three of them. JD patted Rex on the back and told him to leave. Jill said, "Remember what you promised me, JD." JD nodded his head yes at her while she was grabbing around Rex tight before pulling off. Jill looked back and saw JD going into his action mode. She knew right then Johnny was heading into trouble and did not have any idea what JD had in store for him. Johnny was about to get a life lesson from her new friend the mountain man and it was a damn shame she did not get to stay and watch him get what he deserved.

Johnny arrived too late to take Jill down with him. She was already heading back down the mountain with Rex, where all the press was waiting to hear Jill's story about what really happened to her. Johnny's plan had failed with JD pulling this stunt on him. Now he was going to make him pay for it with his life. They were all alone with no witnesses around; it was the perfect time. Johnny did not know this was exactly what JD wanted all along, to get them alone to explain things to him in mountain terms.

JD went over to the deflated raft and positioned it in a certain way. Then he pulled out the rope and cut it into two pieces. One piece about six feet the other was about fourteen feet in length and laid them on the ground to use later. Johnny was getting off the snowmobile and taking off his helmet before heading toward him. JD unhooked his harness from his body and let it fall to the ground. He stepped away from it and waited for Johnny to arrive. He was now smiling at Johnny, which made him even madder and exactly what JD wanted. JD said, "What is the matter black belt, did I ruin your plan to rescue Jill and be a big hero in the public eye. You do know that only happens in the movies. I guess you and your new boss Bill Turner will have to come up with something else to do to save face. My plan seems to spoil all of that for you." Johnny said, "Don't worry; you won't be around to see it. I believe you said something about sending me to God. Let's see who goes to see him first." "Come over and get your surprise I have been saving for you black belt."

JD stood perfectly still waiting for Johnny's attack, not moving an inch. His chest was wide open as an easy target for Johnny to punch with his fist. Johnny made his karate sound

"Kaiya" and drove a punch straight in the middle of JD's chest by using his right hand with all his force in the punch to try to kill JD hitting him in the chest. This knocked JD back a few steps from the blow and both men could hear bones being broken from the impact. Only they were not JD's bones but instead Johnny's, in his right wrist and hand. He had hit JD's metal flask dead center with his fist, and in the process broke two bones in his hand and fractured one in his wrist. The next move was JDs, he jumped up and came down hard on Johnny's right knee with his left foot, caving it inward, breaking his knee. Now with only one good leg to stand on, Johnny fell down to the ground in tremendous pain. He was screaming and trying to grab his knee at the same time, but was unable to with his right hand and wrist being broken. Johnny started screaming at JD for breaking his knee. He was helpless to defend himself and at JD's mercy. JD could easily kill him without any trouble, but instead had other plans for good old Johnny.

JD asked, "Johnny would you like something for all the pain?" Johnny said, "Hell yes, go get me some help. There are EMTs at the bottom of the hill. I need them to come up here and take me to the hospital. I think my hand and knee are broken." "I did not hear please come out of your mouth or do not send me to God JD, either. Which would be very easy for me to do in your current condition." Johnny swallowed his pride, and gritted his teeth to tell JD please on both counts. "I will get you some help, but first we need to have a talk about Jill. Would you like some bourbon for the pain while we do?" He pulled out the big flask and opened it for Johnny to take a drink. Johnny's eyes widened when he saw it, knowing that was what he hit when striking JD's chest. The impact to the flask broke his hand and now had his fist imprint on the front of it. Johnny took two huge drinks from the flask, while JD held it for him. JD started talking to him about Jill and his current situation.

"If you or Bill try anything else or go near Jill again, I will hold both of you responsible. I will hunt you both down like animals and kill you. Do you understand me, Johnny?" "Yes, I hear what you're saying. I will explain it to Bill when I talk to him. Now will you please go get me some help? I need something for all this pain." "Would you like another drink before I go to hold you over till I can get some help?" Johnny nodded yes, JD held it down to him and he took another huge drink. Johnny asked him why he was not drinking. "I never drink and drive. Especially when I have a passenger riding behind me. I think we will go down together to see the EMTs, Johnny." Johnny had a puzzled look on his face after hearing what JD just told him. JD quickly pulled out the knuckle blaster from his jacket pocket and hit him in the neck with it, knocking him out cold. Then JD poured some bourbon on Johnny's jacket and put the flask inside of it. To make it look like it belonged to him. He then picked Johnny up, carried him over to the raft, and threw him down on top of it. JD got the black bucket and opened it to pour Jill's urine on Johnny's pants to make it look like he pissed himself. Then he wrapped him up tight inside the raft and tied the smaller length of rope around him to keep him that way. Now he looked like a neat tight package to deliver to the EMTs down at the base of the mountain.

JD used the longer length of rope to tie Johnny up behind the snowmobile and started riding down the mountain dragging Johnny with him. Thinking the press was going to have a field day with this story. A Hollywood star drinking and then crashed into some trees and broke his hand and leg. Luckily, there was a nice man there to bring him down the mountain and save his life. Not only did JD get the chance to save Jill on this trip, but also Johnny. JD thought life was good in his world, because this time his plan worked out perfectly.

Jill was already down at the base with everyone gathering around her asking questions, which were coming at her too fast to answer any of them. Unfortunately, the press would not slow down and kept on asking Jill even more questions. Rex had helped her off the snowmobile and the EMTs came over with a gurney to put her on it. Only, Jill was not going to leave for the hospital until she knew the outcome between JD and Johnny. She had to know JD kept his promise and was safe before leaving. She stalled by answering some of the reporter's questions about what had happened on her ski trip and on the mountain.

Molly soon ran over to give her Aunt Jill a huge hug and kiss to welcome her. Carrie and David fought through the small crowd to do the same. Rex moved out of the way to give them room to reach her. He had done his part and wanted to watch for JD coming down the mountain. Soon everyone spotted him riding the snowmobile dragging something behind it. He arrived, calling for the other EMTs to come over and help him. Two of them were standing around waiting for something to do anyway. JD said, "This man has been in an accident, he wrecked his snowmobile into the trees and knocked himself unconscious. I think he might have a few broken bones." They ran over with another gurney while JD was cutting the ropes to unwrap the raft around Johnny. After arriving, the EMTs could smell the strong urine odor on him. "I think he pissed himself during the crash. I smelled some liquor on him and his breath while wrapping him up to bring down. When will people learn not to drink alcohol before riding a snowmobile? Only bad things can happen, like with this guy."

The press was around taking pictures of Johnny in his present condition, while writing down everything JD was saying to the EMTs. This was going to make a great story for tonight's news. This turnout was better than JD could ever have hoped for, his friend Michael had come through for him as promised. After this story hit, Johnny and Bill's careers in the movie industry would be over and Jill would be safe from them forever. The EMTs loaded Johnny on a gurney and then put him in the back of the ambulance so they could leave to go to Leadville General Hospital.

All the reporters stayed with JD to get more information about what had happened to Johnny Mann behind those trees. They forgot about Jill for the time being. Something JD wanted, it was also time for her to leave. He wanted Johnny in their sights and not Jill. JD told them to wait with their questions. He would answer them shortly. First, he wanted to make sure Miss Green got on her way to the hospital. JD walked over to Jill and told the EMTs to load her inside the ambulance; she should be ready to go to the hospital. Jill looked at JD but could not react at how glad she was to see him with the press being all around her. She said, "Thank you for keeping your promise, JD. It means a lot to me." JD said, "Not a problem. I am glad I was able to do it. It is a shame that Johnny drove straight into those trees and hurt himself. I guess drinking and riding snowmobiles do not mix either." Jill smiled at his comments, knowing he had given Johnny his injuries but left him alive. At least he finally got a real thank you out of her even if it was for keeping Johnny alive.

The EMTs finished loading her up and drove away. Molly asked JD if she could get a hug and a kiss from him. Since he rescued her Aunt Jill, just like he promised. JD bent down to get his payment from her. The first real thank you he had received for saving Jill's life. At least someone cared about what he had done to get her back safely. Then Carrie and David thanked him too, saying they would never be able to repay him for saving their dear friend. JD told them they could, by going to the hospital to be with Jill in her time of need. She was scared of hospitals and needed her friends nearby and not to leave her until she was ready to go home. That would be payment enough for him. They did as he asked and said their goodbyes and left for the hospital.

JD told the press to wait one more minute to interview him. He had to make an important phone call first. JD called Michael to let him know how things had turned out. The press started asking Rex, Mark and Jim some questions while waiting for JD to make his quick phone call. The reporters were trying to cover all angles of the story by talking to the people who were involved in this successful rescue of the beloved Miss Green.

JD called Michael and gave him a quick summary of how his plan had worked out. Then he asked for one more favor; call the Chief of Staff and tell him not to operate on Johnny first. His injuries were not as severe as Jill's and hers were two days old. Michael promised to make the call to him as soon as they finished talking. JD told him Johnny had drunk a lot of bourbon anyway and would have to wait to have surgery. Michael knew he did not have the complete story and would have to wait until JD told him everything else later. He knew the press was around and John could not talk freely over the phone. JD would call him back later when he was alone.

After finishing his call, JD walked back over to the press to make some statements about what had happened to Jill and her so-called accident on the ski trip with Johnny Mann. JD made it seem there was no accident with all the bad blood between Jill and Bill Turner, the man who now holds a new contract for Johnny's movie career. Then he told the press that he had smelled liquor on Johnny and he should not have been riding that snowmobile. He could have killed someone or himself. Johnny was lucky that he was around to help him in his time of need. Now it would be up to the studio to bail him out of this trouble. For some reason Johnny never pays for any of his bad behavior. JD said, "I guess with people like Bill Turner being around to bail him out of trouble, who can blame Johnny for doing whatever he wants. I believe some people in Hollywood have their own set of rules and are not held accountable." The press was listening and writing down all of JD's statements. This interview was going to be in the paper and on the evening news stations tonight. The major networks might pick up the story and air it all over the country. Jill would now be safe in the hospital with her friends. This story was paying Bill back for all the bad deeds he had done to Jill and with Johnny Mann and his involvement in Jill's accident. JD was going to let the press draw their own conclusions. He made sure to steer them in the right direction during the interview. John thought Planet Studios might want to cut their losses and fire Bill after this interview aired. Finally, he had turned the tables on Bill and Johnny; Jill would never have to worry about them ever again.

Before ending his interview, JD made sure that Jim and Rex got credit for all their help in the rescue. It was a team effort and the rescue would not have happened without everyone's involvement. At the end of the interview, a reporter asked JD if he was going to write a book about all of this. JD said, "Well that depends on my young friend, Rex Anderson. If he agrees to write it with me, then the answer would be yes." The reporters looked over at Rex and waited for his answer. Rex could not believe what he had just heard JD say to the press. Rex said, "It would be my pleasure to co-author a book with the famous John William Davis." "You got his answer. There will be a tell-all book of these events coming out soon. A book that will have both of our perspectives of what went on this past weekend. That is all the questions I am willing to answer at this time. If you will please excuse me, I need to go get some much needed rest from this hard ordeal."

The reporters had enough information and rushed off to get their news story in on time so everyone could see and read about it tonight. JD helped Rex and Mark load the snowmobile in the back of the truck and then he went to say goodbye to Jim and thank him for all his help. He returned his satellite phone and binoculars, but told him he had to leave all the other supplies back at the camp to save time. It is about three miles up the mountain and then back down another eight to the campsite. If he wanted, he could show him on the map where to go pick all of them up. Jim said, "What, a broken flare gun with a few flares, John. I am glad you and Miss Green made it safe down off that mountain in one piece. Especially since your grandfather did not two years ago." JD said, "Speaking of that, I had a run in with "Old Silver Back" last night in our camp. You do not have to worry about him attacking anyone else; he no longer walks this earth." While shaking hands goodbye, Jim wanted JD to tell him all about his encounter with the wolf. JD told him it would have to wait for another time; he was too tired. He walked over to Rex's truck and got in the back seat to leave for the ski resort. His job was finished here; all he wanted to do was sleep for the next ten hours, then go home the next day and pick up Suzie from the dog kennel.

On the way, JD made a small list of things he wanted Rex to go get for him in the morning, including his breakfast items. The list consisted of a copy of his first book "Life in the Wild", three cans of Play-Doh with the colors being white, pink and brown. One toothbrush that was pink and a small box to put all the items in. The breakfast items were two big man meals from McDonald's and a large pot of black coffee. He handed the list and some money to Rex and asked him if he could go get the items for him first thing in the morning. Rex said, "Not a problem. If I cannot find your book, I will give you one of mine, JD." JD said, "I will make sure you get another copy that is autographed by me. Now that we got that all worked out, what is happening on the helicopter situation Mark?" Mark said, "The insurance company is going to pay me, but only at a depreciated value of the helicopter. Which means I will be out at least ten thousand dollars on that plus another ten thousand from loss of business till I get my new one." "No you won't, I am going to loan you the twenty thousand dollars before I leave to go home. You can pay me back when you can and I will not charge you any interest for the loan. You okay with that, Mark?" Mark said, "I cannot do…. JD cut Mark off and explained to him he could and would take his offer. After all his and Rex's help today, it was the least he could do by helping him out; so he might as well accept his offer. Mark finally agreed to his kind offer and told JD that he would have his money back before the year was out. "That sounds okay by me. But do not over extend yourself." Mark nodded his head yes to him, understanding what JD meant.

Michael called JD and told him that they were prepping Jill for surgery and would be operating on her ankle and foot within the hour. That S.O.B. Johnny will have to wait until her surgery is over to have his. JD thanked his friend and then filled him in on the rest of the story about what actually happened to Johnny. Michael got a kick out of hearing what JD had done by wrapping him up with Jill's urine. Thinking all that worrying about his old friend was all for nothing, JD knew how to carry out a plan if given the time. JD told Michael that he would call him after he got home, and then they could discuss the next book he was planning on writing. Michael liked hearing that part knowing John would be working on another book. He looked forward to their call and told his old friend to get some well-deserved rest.

JD told Rex and Mark he was going to take a nap while they drove back to the ski resort. They could wake him when they got there, but he was going to sleep now. He dozed off, dreaming about last night after his fight with "Old Silver Back", and what had happened on the trip to go get rid of the dead wolves.

While heading for the cave, John decided to take a quick detour and go visit his grandfather's gravesite. Jim had told him where they decided to bury him on the mountain instead of bringing down the remains, not having much left after the wolf attack. Seeing he loved Mt. Elbert so much, it only made sense to bury him there, keeping him up there forever.

John went right to where Jim had showed him on the map the night before. He walked up to the gravesite and saw it marked by a wooden cross, put together with two sticks. Only the top part had broken off because of rot, which made the cross look like the letter "T" instead. John said a short prayer to himself and then pulled out the knife he had used to kill the three wolves. He drove the knife deep into the top of the wooden "T" to make it back into a cross again. He had an extra knife with him and could spare that one for his grandfather's grave marking.

Now starting back on his journey, JD was thinking about the last time the two of them had a conversation and what they had said which made him decide to move out of his house and never talk to his grandfather again. John had gone to his grandfather to ask for his grandmother's wedding ring to give to Sarah, the girl he was going to propose and hoped to marry. His grandfather refused his request and said he would not be at their wedding. He told John to go buy his own damn ring since he was now a grown man and did not need his help anymore. The two of them parted ways and never saw each other again.

That was eighteen years ago. Even after Sarah died, John's grandfather did not attend her funeral.

After the death of John's grandfather, Jim sent the diamond ring and a letter his grandfather had written to Michael Parnell, knowing John and he were best friends. Michael made sure John got both items, giving them to him personally. The letter asked John to forgive him for the way he treated him while growing up. The beatings he had received over the years were the only way he knew how to raise a young boy to make him into a man. John was sorry for not making amends with him before his death. At least he has made his peace with him now, even if he was not there to see it.

After approaching the cave opening John stopped pulling the raft and unhook his harness to go inside to check his theory. After entering the opening, he sense right away he was not alone, now hearing the heavy breathing in the darkness only a few feet away. John reached inside his pocket and pulled out the knuckle blaster ready to use it on whatever came out of the darkness to attack him. He heard a growl and then something leaped out of the dark straight for him. As he suspected, it was silverback's mate that he now saw on the ground and knocked out by his knuckle blaster. Soon, three more small figures came to check on their mother, who was out cold at John's feet.

Chapter 19

Time to Heal

After arriving at the resort, JD went straight to his room and put the do-not-disturb-sign outside on his door handle. With everyone at the hospital in Leadville, he did not have to worry about anyone seeing him going into Play-Doh's room. After taking a very hot shower, JD got into bed and went right to sleep. He slept eight hours straight before getting up to use the bathroom; then slept another two hours before waking up to eat his breakfast.

Exactly at six a.m., Rex was knocking on JD's door bringing his breakfast to him. He also had all the other items that were on his list. JD told Rex to have a seat while he ate, they needed to discuss a few things. First, by going over how they would write their new book together. JD told Rex he wanted him to write his part of the book about all the things that had happened at the resort, also the people who were involved when the guest arrived, then Jill's ski trip and finally her rescue. Ending with his part at Leadville on the snowmobile to come get Jill. Rex understood exactly what JD wanted him to write about, starting with their first meeting together at the front desk at the ski resort. JD would write about his experiences that led up to the rescue and the time he spent on the mountain with Jill, by getting them both down safely.

Rex liked JD's idea of how to write their book and could not wait to get started writing his version of events. He told Rex they could fax the chapters back and forth while they were writing each chapter. This would make sure everything was covered and his young friend did not get off track like the way he did while writing the manuscript JD had read. After the writing of all the chapters was finished, JD would put their book together and send it to Michael. Both of them exchanged contact information and found out when the best times to call or email each other to discuss the book while writing it. Rex thanked JD for this huge opportunity and left him so he could finish eating his breakfast. Knowing he wanted to go to the hospital to visit Jill before returning home.

Before checking out and leaving for the hospital, JD got the can of brown Play-Doh out and started making some animals for his little friend Molly. After finishing them, he sprayed each one with the adhesive and set them aside to dry. Then he did the triple "S", which in man terms was taking a shit, a shower and then shaving, which most men do to get ready before going out for the day. He got his one bag packed and then called the airline to check on his flight back to Tennessee, which was going to be delayed a few hours with all the weather. After doing all that, the clay animals were now dry and it was time for JD to go check out and say his goodbyes to the two brothers who would be waiting for him downstairs.

After getting off the elevator, JD went over to Mark and handed him a check for twenty thousand dollars. He shook his hand while saying good luck and goodbye to him. Then JD went over to Rex and told him he had appreciated everything he had done for him and would never forget it while shaking his hand. Before leaving them, JD had one more piece of advice for each. He told Rex to get busy writing his part of the book; they were now on the clock. He told Mark to always tell the truth in the future especially when someone's life depended on it. Both brothers agreed to do the thing JD asked while he walked out of the resort.

On the way to Leadville, JD got a call on his cell phone that changed the entire day he had planned. The caller was the veterinarian at the kennel where he had dropped Suzie off. He told JD that his dog was not well, Suzie had not eaten anything in the last three days and she would barely drink any water. She had lost all her appetite and they could not get her to eat. JD asked why no one had called him sooner. The vet told JD that he thought she would snap out of it. For some reason all she wanted to do was stay at the same spot at the fence when you left her with us that first day.

JD thought this man was an idiot and hung up on him. He knew right then what was wrong with Suzie, she was waiting for her master to return and take her home. After calming down, JD called the vet back to get more information about Suzie's current condition. Explaining to the man their call had dropped with all the mountains around, JD asked the vet to continue where they left off. The vet said, "Well like I said, your dog does not want to leave the fence unless she needs some water. Otherwise, she stays right there waiting for you to return." JD asked, "Is that where she is now?" "No, we moved her inside yesterday when it started raining. I have been feeding her through an IV ever since." JD thought this vet was not a total idiot. "I will be there first thing in the morning to pick her up. Please keep a good watch on her till then." "Not a problem Mr. Davis, we will see you then." JD thanked the vet for calling and put his phone away while driving even faster to the hospital in Leadville. Knowing Suzie's condition had been his fault, leaving her in a strange place with strangers. She probably thought he had abandoned her and was never coming back. JD re-thought his plan of how he was going to spend his day at the hospital.

First stop at the hospital was to check on Jill. Then tell her who he actually was, her Play-Doh Man. Then say goodbye to

Carrie and her family. Last, have a visit with good old Johnny to explain his current situation. Then make his flight and go home to get Suzie out of that kennel. JD had another very long day ahead of him, which got worse after hearing the news about Suzie, giving him something else he had to deal with.

Inside the hospital, JD found out what room Jill was in at the nurses' station. Carrie met him in the hallway outside her room. She gave him an update on her condition by telling him, "Everything went well with her surgery, but they had to put some metal screws in her ankle because of the break being so severe. The doctor said she should make a full recovery in about two months. They also had caught the infection in time and had it under control." JD was glad to hear the good news; his day was not all bad. He asked, "Carrie is she awake so I can go see her?" Carrie told him she was still asleep with all the drugs they had given her for the pain. That she might be out for a few hours. After hearing that, JD asked Carrie to give her the package and the card he brought, if she did not mind. He could not stay much longer needing to get to the Denver airport in time to make his flight. A family emergency had come up and he needed to get home to take care of it. However, he did want to say goodbye to Molly and David before he left. Carrie told him that they were in the lounge playing with her clay animals until Jill woke up later today. Carrie took the card and a package from JD and told him she would make sure Jill got them when she did wake up. He shook her hand, said goodbye and thanked her for doing it for him. JD said, "I wish I could stay around to do it in person. I really wanted to see her face when she opened the box and read the card." Carrie understood and wished him a safe trip back home. JD left for the lounge to say goodbye to his little friend and give her some more clay animals he had made for her.

JD found Molly playing with the bear animals at a table by herself. Her father was nearby in a chair reading a sports magazine. He went over to the table and sat down to talk with her for a few moments. Molly was happy to see him and said so. JD opened up his bag and gave her all the new animals he made that morning, plus the extra Play-Doh that he had left over. She was very excited to get the gifts and then showed them to her daddy by holding them up for him to see. There were four wolves made out the brown clay and one dog made out of the white clay. JD said, "Molly, the four wolves are the mother and her three baby wolves. These are the ones that your Aunt Jill and I saved on the mountain yesterday." Molly was listening, while JD was telling her all about them. Then she asked him about the white dog. Why did he make that one for her? "This is Suzie, she is a German shepherd dog I have at home and is a very smart dog for her age like you are Molly. Right now she is very sick so I have to go home and try to save her." Molly said, "Why is she sick, JD?" "Well, I left her in a place she was not used to and she thinks I will never come back to get her." "Why did you leave her, JD?" "So I could come here and meet your Aunt Jill in person. Which at the time was very important for me." "Why was it so important for you?" "I care a lot about her and wanted to tell her that in person, Molly." "Do you love my Aunt Jill, JD?"

JD thought about her question before answering it. He also felt Molly had a lot of Jill in her, by asking him so many questions, one after another. JD said, "Yes, I do Molly. Very much I have to say." Molly said, "I love her very much too, like you do JD." "I am glad we both do, Molly. Now, I have to leave so I can do the same thing for my Suzie. She is in trouble and needs my help. I am very sad that I cannot stay to be here with you until your Aunt Jill wakes up. So I made you a clay Suzie, to remind you of me and why I had to go." "Can I give you a hug and kiss goodbye before you leave JD?" "I will not leave until you do, Molly." Molly went over to hug and kiss

JD for all his help in getting her Aunt Jill back and for the new toy animals, he had made for her. Molly told him she was going to miss him very much. JD told her they might see each other again someday. At least he hoped they would. Now he needed her help so her Aunt Jill could get better a lot sooner. By minding her parents when they asked her to do something. Molly promised JD she would try, just for him. JD gave her one more hug and left her at the table to play with all her new toys. He went over to talk to David before leaving, to say his goodbyes and thanked him for watching out for Jill until she was ready to go home. They both shook hands and JD left the lounge now going to the nurses' station again for one more room number.

JD soon found out Johnny's room number, which was not a problem after the nurse recognized him from the TV interview she had watched last night on the news. The nurse knew JD was the one who had saved Johnny after he crashed his snowmobile. She gave him the room number and pointed which direction he should go, but told him Mr. Mann might still be asleep. JD told the nurse he did not mind waiting until Johnny woke up. He thanked her for her help and started walking toward Johnny's room for their last meeting together.

Johnny was resting very comfortably when JD entered the room to have their talk. Now seeing him asleep after having his knee surgery earlier that morning and having all those drugs in his system, it was going to take some work to wake the black belt up. Luckily, JD was up to the task and did not care how much pain it caused Johnny by waking him. JD began shoving Johnny's right shoulder using his right hand. After a few hard shoves, Johnny's eyes popped wide open, finding JD hovering over him, which totally surprised him. Knowing this was not going to be a friendly visit, his first reaction was to reach out for the signaling device to call a nurse for help. JD stopped him by grabbing his right hand. He explained to Johnny that he was not in any real danger at this moment. That could change very quickly if he did not hear him out. He wanted to explain to him about his situation with Jill in the future.

JD said, "Glad to see you are ready to listen to me black belt." Johnny said, "Well, since I have no choice in the matter, go ahead and tell me what you came to tell me. But make it fast, I am in pain and still need my sleep to start my recovery." "All I need is your word that you will leave Jill alone in the future. No more attacks or schemes against her, then I will be on my way and out of your life forever." "I told you on the mountain I was not going to bother her anymore." "Yes, but you did not give me your word." "What if I do not give it to you?" "Then you will see what I am really capable of. Right now, you only have a couple of broken bones. Which is nothing compared to what I have planned for you if these attacks do not stop." "You do not scare me old man. Go to hell with all your threats." "Maybe later in my life, but let us get back to you and your current situation. Exactly what your life will become if you do not agree to do as I ask. You see, what you do not know is, Jill made me promise not to kill you on the mountain and I kept my promise. As you can see now, we are no longer on the mountain and Jill is not here to save you this time. Give me your word or you will force me to take action." "What else could you possibly do to me? You have already ruined my chance to work at Planet Studios." "I will become the hunter, Bill and you will become the hunted." "Now you're threatening me?" "No threat, pure fact black belt. Do not be surprised to see me again in the near future, standing over you like this. Believe me; we will not be talking then." Johnny was thinking about JD's last statement before asking him some questions.

"Look, I do not understand why you care so much about Jill's well-being? You only met her a few days ago." JD said,

"The why does not matter, your word to me does." "Explain to me why and then I will give you my word." "All right then, have you ever heard stories about people who do harm to others for their own personal gain." Johnny looked puzzled at what JD said. "Like finding a better person to spend your life with then getting rid of your girlfriend or wife by killing them off. Then collecting the insurance money on them so you can have a better life for yourself and new significant other." "Yeah, things like that happen all the time. So what?" "Well black belt, I am the opposite of that kind of people, I find someone in need, I think of their safety and well-being before my own. What can I say; I am a giver not a taker black belt." "What makes Jill that person?" "With all the things Bill and you have been doing to her. Now do I have your word?" "What difference would it make to give it? You do not believe me about all the things that happened before." "I know you are the one who was responsible for pushing Jill out the helicopter, then blowing it up later that night. The only reason to do those things was to keep her on that mountain to die by natural causes. I believe you have some kind of life insurance policy on her somewhere that she signed but did not know what it was at the time, or you got travel insurance on the both of you before going on the ski trip.

Johnny saw JD meant every word he had just told him. Now, he was in fear for his life by this crazy mountain man and was not sure what to do next. Johnny said, "I think it is time for you to leave before I start yelling for help." JD said, "Go ahead and start yelling, you might get a few words out before I break your other knee and hand. Being an ex-search and rescue person comes in handy sometimes. Lucky for you we are in the hospital so they can quickly fix you right back up with even more surgery. Anyway, it would be your word against mine, and everybody around here thinks I saved your life yesterday when you crashed that snowmobile. You should have not drunk so much." "Yeah, you tricked me into drinking all that booze." "You always blame someone besides yourself, black belt." "I don't think I will give you my word. After I heal up, I want another shot at you old man." "Really and why do you think I will wait till then? Look how things turned out the last time we spent time together." JD moved closer and eyed his injuries after saying it. Then reached inside his pocket making sure Johnny saw him doing it. Which at the time he was thinking JD had that stun gun with him and did not know what he might do to him next.

JD said, "What you have to understand black belt is I am willing to pay the ultimate price with my life to protect Jill from the likes of Bill and you. Are you willing to give up yours? By trying to hurt her in the future. Your movie deal is over, time to move own and let all this go." Johnny said, "You ruined that for me when you broke my knee. The doctor said I will have to use a cane for at least one year maybe more." "You started the fight by breaking your hand with that karate punch. I only broke your knee in self-defense. At least I knocked you out to save you from all the pain you were experiencing." "I still blame you for all my injuries. You tricked me by having that flask in your coat pocket. You planned the whole thing ahead of time." "True, but something had to be done to get your attention. You have to understand Jill is off-limits. Remember, you attacked me first. I only reacted by your actions punching me in the chest. I think we both can agree I outsmarted you with me standing here and you are lying there. Hopefully, that should tell you something black belt." "And what would that be?" "That I am better at this than you are. Give me your word so I can leave you to recover." "You have cost me a hell of a lot." "If you do not give me your word, it's going to cost you even more." "I am not giving you shit, asshole." Johnny turned his head away from JD and closed his eyes. JD kept talking to him anyway.

JD said, "True enough, shit does come out of assholes, but I am not here for you to give me a health lesson. I will give you a life lesson instead. I hope you listen to me black belt; your life will depend on it. The next time I come to visit you, it will not be so pleasant. I will not listen to any excuses or lies that might come out of your mouth. When I wake you up the next time, it will be with my knife and not my hand. Before you die, you will beg me to kill you. I have field dressed many animals in my life, in my mind, you are not any different from any of them. You have a nice life black belt, what is left of it. For some reason, I feel you do not have a lot of time left on this earth." JD turned to leave when Johnny asked him to stop. He said, "You have my word. I will not go near Jill or bother her again." "Thank you black belt. Now was that so hard?" "No, but you still have not answered my other question." "Which one? You have asked so many I have lost track." "Why are you Jill's savior?" "You have not seen the real Jill like I have black belt. The real person underneath that is more beautiful if given the chance to appear." "That does not answer a damn thing." "No, but it does tell you what you have lost in your life. Jill is no has-been, far from it. Her best work in the movie industry is yet to come. I can see her true potential and will try to help her achieve it." "What makes you think you can?" JD looked at him and said, "That is what the Play-Doh Man does. He shapes people into what they can become in life if given the opportunity."

While Johnny's eyes widened after hearing those words, JD turned and left the room leaving the injured man knowing he was the Play-Doh Man. The man Jill could not stop talking about on the ski trip. The man she was secretly in love with even though she had never met him before. Which was the reason Johnny had taken Bill's deal, he was jealous of this Play-Doh Man and wanted to hurt Jill because he lost her to a complete stranger.

JD left the hospital and drove straight to the airport feeling somewhat satisfied by the job he had done. He was not able to tell Jill who he really was, but at least he got some satisfaction by telling Johnny. Now it was time to go home and save Suzie, that was his current mission. It was tearing him up inside by leaving her behind to go on this trip. He started driving faster to the airport in order to make his flight in time.

Jill woke up later that day and found Carrie asleep in a chair across the room. Her neck was in a sideways position in the corner of the chair. She called out to her so she would wake up. Carrie did, and got up to go see what Jill needed. Jill said, "Nothing, I thought you might get a stiff neck if I did not wake you up. Sleeping in that chair with your head turned sideways made my neck start hurting." Carrie said, "Thanks, it feels a little stiff and sore now. Hey, your friend JD came by earlier this morning to see you. Unfortunately, you were still asleep at the time." Jill said, "Where is he now?" "He could not stay; his flight home left about an hour ago. JD told me he had some family emergency to take care of. Then he told Molly about a Suzie needed him back home to help her get well." "I should have figured it was something like that. Suzie is his girlfriend he told me about on the mountain." "Oh I see he has a girlfriend? I thought that maybe the two of you made a connection with each other on the mountain. I mean the way the both of you were looking at each other it was obvious. I could tell something was going on between the two of you." "Well it does not matter now; he is going back home to be with her and not staying here to see me. Now is he? Anyway, I have you guys to help me heal, Carrie." She hugged her friend and then went to get David and Molly so they could visit with Jill now that she was awake.

Later, after David and Molly left to get them something to eat, Carrie remembered about the package JD left for her to give Jill. Carrie said, "Jill, JD left you this package and card." Jill asked her to bring it over so she could open them. First, she opened the package and set the card aside for later. After getting the box opened, she found three items down inside it. She pulled them out one a time to show Carrie. First item was a pink toothbrush. Jill said, "You forgot to pack me one during the rescue. I had to use JD's on the mountain. I will tell you that story another time." She laughed after saying it. Second item was a book by John William Davis. It was called "Life in the Wild", which at the time Jill did not know why JD had given it to her. Carrie said, "JD stands for John Davis, the famous adventure writer." Jill said, "I guess he thought I would have time to read it, since I am going to be laid up for a while." "Well, it will give you something to do, Jill." The third item she pulled out was a can of pink Play-Doh. She held it up to show Carrie and was not sure why he gave her this last item. Carrie told her not to forget about the card, it might explain everything to her. Jill opened up the card and began reading it aloud. The card said, "I hope you like all my gifts. It was all that I could come up with at the time. Everyone can always use an extra toothbrush. The book was my first one, it tells about my early life while growing up in Colorado. The can of Play-Doh was a gag gift like when I sent you the blue one. I wanted to get you the right color this time. Since I sent you a can of blue the first time. I wish I were there to see your face right now, your Play-Doh Man.

Jill laid the card down in her lap. She and Carrie were in total shock that JD was the Play-Doh Man, her email friend she had wanted to meet on this trip. The shock soon turned into sadness, Jill started crying not being able to talk to him before he left. She wanted to ask him so many questions, but could not. It was too late; he was on his way back home to be with his Suzie. Jill had missed her opportunity and her heart was breaking not being able to tell JD how she truly felt. Carrie held her friend while she cried; knowing JD had hurt her more than the broken foot Johnny had given her. Jill could not understand why JD did not tell her after all the time they spent on the mountain together. It did not make any sense to her. Jill said, "We went through so much Carrie, why would he not tell me. It had to be because of Suzie and he did not want to hurt me." Carrie did not know what to tell her friend, so she kept silent while Jill was crying on her shoulder.

JD got home and caught up on some things like his mail and emails on his computer. He was going to pick up Suzie first thing in the morning and wanted to have everything ready for her. He even stopped to buy her a new doggie bed, knowing she was not going to be able to jump up on his bed being so weak. Later, he would have to break her altogether of sleeping with him. Right now, his focus would be getting her better.

The next morning, JD arrived at the kennel and paid his bill. Then he found Suzie in one of the rooms lying on a table. After seeing him, she tried to get up but could not being so weak from not eating anything for the last four days. JD went over to her and started petting her on the head, trying to get her to snap out of the current condition. He fed her a few treats while speaking to her very softly, saying how sorry he was for leaving her behind. A few minutes later, he picked her up and carried her out to his truck to take home, where she belonged. They spent the next few days and nights together until she grew stronger.

After a few days, Suzie was back to her old self, playing and running with him outside in the yard. John knew things were going to have to change between them. Suzie needed to become more independent without him for her own good. He would have to do it gradually over time and not shock her all at once the way he did leaving her at the kennel.

The next week, John tried to email Jill to see how she was doing after returning home, but for some reason he never got any response from her. He decided to wait until she tried to contact him. He needed to start working on his new book anyway. Not wanting to fall behind by letting Rex finish his part before him. Not to mention, having to put both parts of the book together made his job a whole lot harder. The book had to come together in a certain way so the readers could follow and understood what was going on to make it a decent read. With two different styles of authors writing it, John had a lot of work ahead of him putting this book together.

Rex kept up his end by finishing on time with his part of the book. His chapters only needed a few rewrites; they finished writing the book in about two months. Now it was time for Michael to decide to publish what they had written. If he liked it, he could publish the book without any further delays from him. John promised Michael could make all the important decisions on his next book.

Michael loved the book written by the two authors. Using Rex as co-author made this new book very different from any of the books JD had written before. He could not wait to get it printed and out for the public to see how well it sold.

Jill decided not to have any more contact with JD again. She refused to answer any of his emails, not wanting to get involved with a man who was already in a relationship. No more playing third wheel for her, she had enough of that with Johnny and his past girlfriends. No matter how much it hurt her, she was going to ignore his emails in the future. She even decided not to read John's book he had given her, instead put it on a shelf in her house to collect dust. Since he hurt her by not telling the truth, she was not going to waste her time reading his first book. Now that the Academy Awards were coming up, she had to focus on getting ready to attend them, by finding something to wear. With two Oscar's nominations, Jill thought she needed to go, even if she did have to wear a protective boot on her left foot. This should have been the most exciting time in her life, but there were a few things missing. Jill did not have anyone special at the time, so she attended the Academy Awards without an escort. Carrie and David were there to support her if she needed them.

That evening when they called out the nominees for best director, Jill got nervous when she heard her name. The person said, "The winner is, Jill Green for "Life's Consequences". She was so excited and then walked slowly up on the stage to accept her award. She thanked everyone that was involved in making the movie and helping her earn this great award. Everyone that is, except Play-Doh, the man who started it all was never mentioned, neither was John Davis for saving her life, enabling her to hold the gold statue in her hands right now for all the world to see.

Later that night, it was time for the best actress award to be announced. Jill was not nervous this time, thinking she did not have a chance to win a second Oscar. Then the person called out her name as the winner. She was shocked and everyone could see it on her face while walking toward the stage. This time making her acceptance speech, Jill had some tears starting to form in her eyes. Once again thanking everyone that helped her win this prestigious award except for John. He had been the man who started all of this, by making Jill challenge herself and reach her true potential as an actor and now as a director on this film.

John was at home watching Jill on the television win her two Oscars. He was proud of her and not hurt by her not mentioning him either time while making her acceptance speech. He knew for some reason she was upset at him by not answering any of his emails. John did not blame Jill; he should have been honest and told her who he was on the mountain. Michael called him and said, "That would be just like "The Ice Queen" to forget about the one person who was responsible for her winning those two Oscars." John said, "I hurt her, Tonto. She will never forgive me for not telling her who I really was on that mountain. I had my shot and blew the whole thing. I should have taken your advice and told her who I was at the resort or on the mountain. Now, I am too late. You know full well I do not care about any of the credit for those awards, I wanted her." "She is not worth it, Lone Ranger." "You got one thing right; I really am the Lone Ranger now. Only, you are wrong about her, she is more than worth it. I found that out on the mountain, Tonto. We are heading off to bed, talk to you tomorrow."

After getting off the phone, Michael felt bad for John, wishing he could do something for him. If given the chance, he was not going to let his friend suffer any more by that "Ice Queen" in the future. John deserved better from her after all he had done. If given the chance, he was going to tell Jill exactly what he thought and felt about her treatment toward John.

John went to bed with a little sadness in his heart; feeling all alone even with Suzie being right there with him. This time he let her sleep in the bed wanting the company, instead of her doggie bed on the floor. John had lost Jill and knew it tonight. She would always be in his heart but not in his life.

After the Academy Awards were over, Jill went to a few after parties to celebrate her two Oscar wins. She talked to some people and later sat at a table with Carrie and David to enjoy the rest of the night with her dear friends. Still, something was missing in her life, that special someone to share this experience with should have been JD. Jill looked sad and Carrie wanted to know why. This should have been the happiest time in her life, not a sad one. Jill told Carrie she was just tired from the evening and carrying around her two Oscars. They both laughed at her explanation. Jill then told Carrie she was going home to get some rest, with her foot starting to bother her. She told them to stay and enjoy themselves as she got up and walked out of the room with both Oscars in her hands, but did not have the one award she wanted most of all. She would have traded both those statues to have JD standing beside her right now. She realized he was the man who was in her heart. She missed him so much, but he belonged to another woman and her name was Suzie.

JD could not fall asleep, thinking about how things could have been different if he had been truthful on the mountain. Thinking life sometimes does not work out even if you do have a plan. Now he had to accept the way things were and move on. Even if he thought they belonged together, he had missed his opportunity to be with her. What he did not know was that Jill felt the same way he did. Now two hearts were broken that night and neither one of them knew how the other one was feeling at the time.

Chapter 20

Two Hearts Join

The next day, Jill called Carrie to set up a play date with Molly, wanting to spend some quality time with her goddaughter. By taking JD's advice and hoped it will become a regular thing between them in the future. Carrie told her it would be fine; she could clean the house while they had their playdate together.

After arriving, Jill asked Molly what she wanted to do today. Molly said, "Let's play with my Play-Doh, Aunt Jill." They went to the kitchen table to build different things out of the clay. Later, Molly went to get her special box that JD had given her at the resort. She wanted to show her Aunt Jill, since she had never seen it before. After placing it on the table, Jill could see the box had Molly's name engraved on top of the lid. "JD made this special for me, Aunt Jill. I love my box and my friend JD." Jill said, "Why do you love him Molly?" "He kept his promise to me and saved you on that mountain. I was crying and he picked me up to wipe away all my tears. Then he made me a promise to go find you when no one else wanted to go in that bad snowstorm. He also told me he loved you very much before he left to go home and save Suzie. I told him we had that in common with each other." Jill gave Molly a hug after hearing her say it.

Jill was remembering the time on the mountain she spent with him, while listening to Molly talking about JD. She wished things had turned out very differently between them. Now seeing how special JD was to not only her, but to others as well. Then she heard Molly say that JD loved her. Jill asked Molly, "Are you sure JD said that he loved me?" Molly answered her, "Yes, Aunt Jill. JD told me so at the hospital. Let me show the other bears he made me to go with my first one." Molly pulled them out to show Jill. She watched and listened as she called out their names while showing them to her, one animal at a time. Then Molly pulled out all the wolves he made for her. Jill saw all four of them; which was a mother wolf and her three pups. This brought back memories of their last day on the mountain together. The last clay animal Molly pulled out of her box was a white German shepherd dog to show her. Jill asked, "What is the dog's name Molly?" Molly said, "Suzie, the same as JD's dog he has at home. She got very sick and he had to leave to go home and save her, Aunt Jill."

Jill could not believe that JD had done it to her again. By not explaining things, making her think that Suzie was a woman instead of a dog. He never bothered to mention that part on the mountain. Jill did not know whether to be happy or angry at the news. Not understanding why JD had misled her by not saying whom and what Suzie really was. Perhaps, it was a plan he had to keep her in the dark for some strange and stupid reason.

Jill went to Carrie and told her what she found out from Molly. After hearing about it, Carrie wanted to know what she was going to do. Jill said, "I do not know yet, Carrie. I cannot believe Suzie is a fucking dog and not a woman. This man has my brain all twisted up in knots." Carrie said, "I can see that you are frustrated girl, but I think you need to calm down." "No, what I need to do is go home and figure all this shit out for myself. Maybe make a plan of my own like he always does before facing something important in his life. Please explain to Molly that I had to go. I will make it up to her later."

"Remember to drive safe and call me later with what you plan on doing about John."

After getting home, Jill decided to email JD to get some answers. Unfortunately, she did not know he was out of town at the time and had his computer turned off. While waiting for a response from him, she decided to sit down and look over the book he gave her in the hospital. She wanted to find out exactly who this man really was, since the book was supposed to be about his early life, maybe she could learn something about him she did not already know.

A few hours later, she finished reading most of the book and understood a few new things JD went through earlier in his life. After checking, he still had not answered her email. Jill picked up the book from the back cover to put away, when she saw something written inside the back page. It was some contact information of JD's publisher in case someone wanted to write to him. Jill remembered then that Michael Parnell was Play-Doh's publisher. She got her contact book and looked up Parnell Publishing Company's number to have a talk with Michael and get some answers about John.

Michael answered the phone and said, "Michael Parnell here, how can I help you?" Jill said, "Well, I hope you can. This is Jill Green and I need to get in touch with John Davis, would you happen to know a number where I can reach him? It is very important that I talk with him." "Why, does the "Ice Queen" want to jump on his heart some more? I think you have done enough damage to my good friend for one lifetime Miss Green?" "What, I do not know what you are talking about. I am the one who needs some answers. That is why I am trying to reach him." "Well then let me explain a few things to you about the way you treated John. By you never thanking him for saving your life on that mountain. Of course, we can always talk about all the things he did to help get your company started. How about you not mentioning his name when you won those two Oscars. John saved your life and your career, but you do not have the common decency to open your mouth to say thank you to him Miss Green. He told me so; please do not try to deny it." Jill was getting pissed at this man's attitude toward her. She called for a phone number to talk with John, not have Father Michael give her a sermon on past events. He was quickly becoming the first person on her list she wanted to kick square in the balls. She even pictured doing it in her mind while Michael kept preaching to her over the phone. Which was a nice sight to see. That would shut him up from making all the smart-ass comments toward her. Simple science, not being able to breathe makes you unable to talk.

Michael said, "Are you still there Miss Green?" Jill said, "Still here. Just thinking about something I wanted to do while letting you finish before I got started. My turn now, your dear friend was not very honest with me. I think he has some explaining to do himself. How about telling me how special his relationship with Suzie is in his life. Making me think she was a woman instead of a dog. Not to mention all the names he uses instead of his real one. It is hard to keep up with who John actually is each day." "I told John to come clean and tell you who he was before everything got out of hand. I think by now, you know John does things on his own terms. Anyway, he was going to tell you everything after rescuing you. Then you were very rude to him and did not appreciate anything he was trying to do for you. His plan changed, he decided to get to know you first, then tell you he was the Play-Doh Man. Hoping the two of you could have a big laugh together. Then things at the hospital did not work out right, with you still being asleep and he finding out Suzie was sick. This made him return home before he could tell you everything in person." "So you are telling me, he left me to go take care of a dog?"

"Look Miss Green, Suzie is not just some ordinary dog. You will know that the first time you meet her. John did not lie to you; they do have a special bond between them by taking care of each other. Something else you will see after meeting her. Anyway, John blamed himself, by leaving her behind to come meet you. He had no choice but to come home and try to help her get better. May I ask why you want to talk with John now? You have shut him out of your life for the last few months." "Look, I need some answers to some personal questions. After reading most of his book, I decided to contact you in order to find him." "Which book would that be?" "Life in the Wild", I only had time to skim over it." "What did you think of what you read?" "Did all those things happen to John that were in the book? I mean like the bear attack at the river, did John really kill a bear?" "Yes to all your questions. We decided to leave out the part that the woman who was killed was his wife, Sarah." "Oh my God. He lost his wife that day at the river?" "John was right about you, Miss Green. He told me, you do ask many questions at one time. Yes, he lost his wife by saving mine first instead of hers. Please let me tell you the whole story." "I have time, please continue Mr. Parnell."

Michael told her the story about the three of them being on a camping trip together so Sarah could get to know him better. On the morning of the bear attack, he and Sarah got up early to eat breakfast, but John was still sleeping in. After we finished eating breakfast, the two of us decided to go wash the dishes down at the river. John had told me to always take the gun whenever entering the woods or going to the river, with bears in the area searching for food. That morning, I had forgotten about the gun when we left. Later, John woke up and found us gone. He knew by the dishes missing where we were. Then he found the gun I left behind. He went into action mode by taking the gun and running toward the river to come find us.

Jill said, "I know all about his action mode. A saw it first-hand on the mountain when the wolves attacked us. Please continue, Michael." Michael said, "Sarah and I were cleaning the dishes when a bear came out of the woods and charged us. The bear knocked Sarah into the river and then jumped on top of me. She started floating downstream unconscious, while it had me pinned down on the ground. It was about to start eating me when John came charging out of the woods. He was yelling and firing the gun at the bear. He fired two times, missing once. Then fired two more times before the bear got off me and went toward him. He could see Sarah floating down the river while shooting at the bear." "That was when John made that split second decision?" "Correct, I lived and she died." No one spoke for a moment.

Michael said, "John should have left me and gone after Sarah to save her. Instead, he stayed to make sure I survived. That was when the bear knocked the gun out of John's hand and started his attack going up on his hind legs. Standing ready to jump on top of John the way he did with me, by using his weight and size against him. Only that was not going to happen. John knew exactly what to do, he went ape shit with his knife on that bear, stabbing it over and over again in the right spots." Jill said, "I call it going "Tarzan" instead." "Great analogy, Miss Green. I never thought of calling it that. I forgot for a moment, you saw him do it before on the mountain. Well then, you know how John gets when he is trying to protect someone. Anyway, he soon killed the bear and went after Sarah downriver. He knew I was still alive by me moving on the ground. John found Sarah about a hundred yards downriver against the bank. Unfortunately, he was too late and she drowned. I am the one who got to live that day knowing maybe he could have saved her." "It was not your fault, Michael. I mean, John did not stop the bear with the gun, how could you." "John has to live with his choice; he saved me instead of his wife. Thinking he had time to save both of us. I still do not know today if he regrets making that decision or not. I wish things had turned out differently. I would have given my life to save hers. Believe me; the pain John went through was not pleasant. If he had not started writing, I do not think he would have made it after losing Sarah. It gave him something to do to get over his loss. Now do you understand John's and my relationship, knowing what we have been through?" "Yes, but I still need to talk to him about our relationship." "I think you need a plan like John always seems to have. Here is his address, why not go see him in person instead of over the phone. You can think about what to say to him on the flight there." "Give me the information, but do not tell him I am coming, Tonto."

Michael laughed when she called him that. He gave her John's address, wished her luck before saying goodbye and said he would not tell John she was coming to see him. Now everything was in her hands. Jill thanked him and asked him one more question before they hung up. Then she called and booked a flight to Tennessee for the next morning. Thinking tomorrow, she will go see her Play-Doh Man and find out the answers to all her questions. Jill called Carrie to update her on the news and that she was going out of town for a few days and she would have to run their company. At the time, this involved reading over movie scripts to try to find their next project to make into a movie.

Jill arrived the next day at John's house and drove up his driveway seeing him sitting on the front porch. While she was getting out of her rental car, JD and Suzie stayed seated on the front porch waiting for her to come to them. He was sitting in a chair with Suzy lying down beside it, both looking straight at her with curiosity on their faces. While walking up toward them, Jill carried a bag in her hand that had one of her Oscars inside sticking out between the handles. She was a little nervous coming to see him but needed to get the answers why he had sent her that first message and why he cared so much about her well-being.

JD was a little surprised seeing Jill standing in front of him holding that bag with the fancy hardware. He had not turned on his computer yet, so he did not know about any email Jill had sent him. He decided to break all the tension between them by sending Suzie to make friends. He whispered a command to her and she got up from the porch and went to Jill. First Suzie sniffed Jill's hand and then started licking it to show her she wanted to be friends. Jill started petting her on the head, trying to get some of the dog saliva off as JD began speaking to her from the porch.

"Well what brings you to our neck of the woods, Jill Amber?" asked JD. Jill said, "I believe I still owe the Play-Doh Man one dollar interest for the five million dollar loan he gave me. I forgot to add it to the original balance, which was a total oversight on my part. So I thought it would be a good idea to pay it in person in order to keep my credit in good standing." "You did not have to come all this way to pay me that dollar, mailing it would have been all right. Anything else bring you here?" "I also came to get some answers, John William." "I see you have been talking to Michael. I asked him to stay out of this. Is he the one who gave you my address?" "Yes, after I called him for the information and got a sermon from him instead. First, I found out Suzie was your dog from Molly when we were playing with her clay animals. Then after reading some of your book you gave me, I decided to call Michael and find out how to reach you, since you never answered the email I sent two days ago." "I am sorry, but I just got back home yesterday.

I have not been on my computer for a while since you never answered any of my emails I sent you. I hardly check my emails anymore." "Well it does not matter; I am here now ready to get the answers from you in person, John William." "Go ahead; ask me anything you want to know."

Before asking her first question, Jill petted Suzie some more trying to get her courage built up before beginning this serious discussion. Her first question, "Why didn't you tell me who you were? My God, I think I had a right to know." "I was going to tell you so many times, but something always happened to stop me." "Like what, exactly?" "Well for one thing, Johnny being at the ski resort with you. If I had told you then, a fight would have broken out and I might have killed him in front of you. Not the way I wanted our first meeting together to go." "How about on the mountain, you had plenty of opportunities there, we were all alone." "You are the one that stopped me then." "Explain to me what you mean." "Like you not thanking me for saving your life, but thanked me for not taking Johnny's. There were a lot of other little things in between." "Keep going mister, what other little things?" Jill was back to calling him mister again, something JD hated her doing more than anything. She asked for it, so he let her have everything that had built up inside him waiting to let it come out. "Let me see, setting your ankle, dragging your ass up and down the mountain, feeding you, warming your body up on two occasions to break your fever. There was holding you while you were going to the bathroom, dressing you, undressing you, cleaning your ass, dragging "Old Silver Back" out of the tent before he took a bite out of you, the list goes on and on. Is that enough, or shall I continue.

Jill was upset at herself remembering the way she had treated him on the mountain. John could see the disappointment in her eyes and she was truly ashamed of herself. He said, "Look, the Jill I got to know on the computer was a very gracious and thankful person. The one on the mountain was not." Jill said, "Only because I did not know who you were or what was going to happen to me on that mountain. Then we got off on the wrong foot so to speak by you using that knuckle blaster on me. Let me tell you from first-hand experience, that damned thing really hurts." "I know it does, but I had no choice at the time, you have to agree, it does the job." "I guess it is according to who is being knocked out, John William." "I see your point, Jill Amber. Believe me; when I put your ankle back in place you needed to be unconscious. It was so severely broken, when I went to set it, my stomach got sick from listening to all your bones going back in place. If you have been awake at the time, I could not have done the job. That is why I had to knock you out." Jill was starting to understand some of the things he was telling her.

"Why did you really send me that message eight months ago? I want the truth, John William." John said, "I hate to see someone waste their God given talent in life by throwing it away, never reaching their true potential. Jill Amber you have a gift, I wanted to give you a chance to use it by directing and acting in a real movie, not the garbage your studio was making you do. I believe that piece of hardware you are carrying in your bag proves my point."

While looking down at the Oscar, she said, "I brought this one for you. I won this one for best director. I know you were the one who is responsible for me winning it. I am sorry for not mentioning your name that night in my acceptance speech. I guess I deserved being called the "Ice Queen" from your friend yesterday." "I think I need to have a long talk with Tonto in the near future." "Please do not blame him; he is your true friend, John William. At first, I wanted to kick him in the balls the same way I did with you. Later, after he made me understand your relationship with each other, I know he really cares about you. Not because you saved his life or are his best author. Michael considers you his true friend in life and only has your best interest at heart. Everyone in this world needs one." "Like Carrie being yours." "Exactly, John William." "Well, I see you did read some of my first book." "Yes, and I'm sorry you lost your wife by the choice you had to make, saving Michael's life instead of hers." "I guess you know all about me, then?" "A lot more than I did on the mountain. I have learned you have special people in your life that you care about and put them before yourself." "Without Michael's help, I never would have been able to find you on the mountain in time. Then get you the proper medical attention later after we got off. He has always been there for me when I needed his help, no matter what I ask him to do." "With you saving his life from being eaten alive by the bear?" "No, not just that. When we were kids growing up together, he was always Tonto and I was the Lone Ranger. We always looked out for each other no matter what the cost." "You sure do have a lot of names John William." "And you have given me another one today by calling me that, Jill Amber." Jill smiled at him for the first time since she arrived. She moved on with her next question.

"Why not tell me Suzie was your dog?" asked Jill. John said, "At the time, you would have laughed. Remember, we were talking about special people in our lives, not animals. You not knowing how special she is and why, it would not be fair to Suzie. Her only being a dog and not a person, you would have laughed at me. Now that I know how you feel about animals, like on the mountain when you did not want me to kill the wolves, I probably should have told you." "I still do not know why all the secrets. I hope this is not some kind of game you are playing with me now." "Not a game, but a test in life. I wanted and got the opportunity to get to know the real Jill

Amber Green on the mountain and not the Hollywood made up version in the movies. To get to see the real you on the inside and not the one on the outside."

Jill had her funny look on her face after hearing that from JD. He tried to explain it to her in Hollywood terms so she could understand. JD said, "Do you know who Rita Hayworth was?" Jill said, "Of course, she was the lead actress who played in the movie called "Gilda"." "That is right, Jill Amber. However, did you know she was married two times and then divorced in a small amount of time in each marriage? I heard both her husbands wanted to be married to the movie actress and not the woman in real life. The men had a false belief that they had married Gilda and not Rita. Do you understand now what I am talking about?" "Yes, I do. You wanted to know the real me and not the made up version in the movies." "That is right, Jill Amber." "Well, do you know the real me?" "I think deep down I do." "You took a big risk not being honest with me, John William. Maybe ruining any chance, we might have to be together. Trust is something I take very seriously. Can you understand that?" "I know now it was a huge mistake on my part not telling you who I was on the mountain. I wish we could have spoken at the hospital before I had to leave. At least now you know the reason why." He reached down and petted Suzie on her head. She had returned to the porch to her original spot by John's side.

Jill asked, "What happened to her?" John said, "When I left her at the dog kennel to come meet you, she thought I had abandoned her and blamed herself. She lay down at the fence for two straight days waiting for me to return, barely drinking and not eating at all. She was slowly dying, waiting for me to come take her home. It was my fault for being so close to her and not letting her have some independence from me, which I am now rectifying. I am truly sorry for not being honest and telling you who I was and hope you can forgive me, Jill Amber." "I am truly sorry for not thanking you when I should have on the mountain and at the Academy Awards. Not only did you save my life, but you also changed it in so many ways. I do not know why you did all those things, but glad you did. I am a better person, not to mention still being alive. I do not think I will ever be able to repay you, John William." "Let us test that by you coming up on the porch and sitting with us. We will not bite you, I promise." Jill walked up on the porch to join them and sat in a chair next to John out of Suzie's reach just in case John was mistaken about his dog and she was the jealous type.

Then she asked him another question. "Which one of your names would you like me to use since you have so many, John William? Jill asked. JD said, "John will be fine. I only use JD when I travel on trips for book signings. Play-Doh Man was a screen name I made up to get your attention on that message I sent you. As you can see, it worked with you sitting next to me now." "Yes, it got my attention. That is why I made up my screen name "Starlet" before sending you my email. Now for my next question John, what do you want out of life and am I supposed to be in it with you?" "I see now why Michael gave you my address." "Father Michael only has your best interest at heart, John." "Father Michael and I are going to have a long talk very soon about my personal life. Now, back to your question. I believe it is time we talked from our hearts, to get our true feelings about each other out in the open. I think we need to be truthful with each other and I will start by saying this. I am looking for a very special person to spend my life with who will come to me each night and puts her arms around my waist and gives me a hug, while resting her head on my chest. Then she will look into my eyes and say "We got through another day together my love, cannot wait to see what the next one brings us". Then we kiss as if we have not seen each other for years. Cherishing that moment like it was our last. Can you understand everything I am telling you?" Jill listened to every word, but did not know how to respond to what John just told her.

John continued by saying, "I found that very special person on the mountain in Colorado buried under four feet of snow with a broken left ankle. I loved her then, now and will forever. I can only hope she feels the same way about me some day." Now tears started pouring out of Jill's eyes and rolling down her flushed red cheeks. The same cheeks that had drawn John to her the first moment he saw her at the ski lodge. What a sight those red flushed cheeks made then, but were now wet from all her tears.

Jill was crying because no man had ever spoken to her from his heart before, she was on unfamiliar ground. It was the only thing she could do at that moment, wanting to hide her feelings from John, there was no place for them to go but out. John got up from his chair and kneeled down in front of her. He put both his hands on each side of her face to wipe away the tears. Telling her everything was going to be all right and she could stop crying. He held her face, still removing the remaining tears by using his thumbs to wipe them away. Unveiling those pretty cheeks below, while smiling at her the whole time so she could truly see how he felt about the very special person in front of him.

Jill said, "I do not deserve such …." John leaned in and kissed her to stop the words from coming out of her mouth. He did not want anything negative to ruin this moment. The kiss was long and deep, something he had been planning to do for a long time and now got the chance. They began to melt into each other, holding tight for dear life. Both had traveled a long way to be together. John was thinking this kiss could be their last, so he made it count. Now making sure Jill knew exactly how he felt about her, leaving no doubts. John got up and went back to his chair before continuing the conversation.

"I know we have not known each other very long, Jill. Only the time on the mountain and all our email chats, I knew you were the one that I wanted to spend the rest of my life with if given the chance. Now it is your turn, Jill Amber. How do you truly feel about me?" "I know you are a special man John, I have seen it and now felt it from that kiss. To be honest, I do not feel the same way you do and it could take more time for me. Can you understand that?" "I have plenty of time if that is what it takes. Did you reserve yourself a hotel room somewhere near by?" "I did not have time to find one; I came here straight from the Memphis airport." "Then it is settled, you will be staying with us. Do you have any more bags we need to get from your car?" "No, just the one. I learned how to travel light by bringing only the bare necessities from a special man I met in Colorado. I did bring my own toothbrush that you gave me." "Good, sounds like I'm rubbing off on you." "Only the good parts, not the bad." They both laughed at Jill's joke. "Now, about that dollar you owe me." "Oh yeah, I have it in my bag down there on the ground." "How about I trade it for another kiss. If I remember correctly, you promised to give me a kiss that I would never forget." "Believe me; my kisses are worth more than a dollar." "I am only going by what you told me, Jill Amber." "I also owe you a kick in the balls. Which would you like first." "I think it would be in my best interest not to accept either debt from you right now. How about I cook you dinner instead?" "Sounds great, let me go get my bag." "No need, Suzie will get it for you. Watch this."

John called out the command for Suzie to go fetch Jill's bag and she jumped up off the porch running straight for it. She picked it up off the ground using her mouth and returned to the porch waiting for John to open the front door for her.

Which he did while calling out another command, sending Suzie to the spare bedroom with Jill's bag. She returned downstairs to get her treat. Jill was amazed after seeing what she had done and started to realize what Michael had told her; that Suzie was a special dog. John said, "She can do a lot more than that. Trust me." Jill said, "I believe you. She could come in handy on shopping trips or doing things around the house. I guess real talent runs in this family." "Well, we do not have any trophies to show off like our guest, but we do our best to make our visitors feel welcome." Jill elbowed him in his side as they were walking down the hallway in the house. "I hope you can stay long enough to find out more about our talents, we would love to have you." "I think you have a good heart and soul, John." "Hey, that sounds like a good title for a book, mind if I use it?" "Go ahead, be my guest. Glad I could contribute something while being here." "I think you can contribute a lot around here, Jill Amber. Do not sell yourself short." John gave her a devilish look after saying his statement. "Slow down there cowboy, this relationship just started." "Oh, are we in a relationship now?" "After your heart to heart speech and that long kiss you gave me, I would have to say yes we are."

Meanwhile, Suzie was getting a little impatient with the both of them waiting for her treat. Finally, John gave her one and told her what a good job she had done. While in the kitchen, Jill asked, "What are we having for dinner and do you need any help?" John said, "A southern meal of chicken, mashed potatoes, corn on the cob and homemade biscuits with iced tea to drink. How does all that sound?" "Chicken, huh. I hope you will not be "calling any ducks" while I am here." "Do not worry, the chicken will be baked and not fried this time. There will be no duck calling for at least two days, I promise." "Good, that is when I was planning on going home. I get to miss all those pleasant sounds and odors your body seems to make." Again they both laughed. Remembering their time on the mountain before the wolves attacked. The two days they spent there seemed a whole lot more with so many things happening to them that they never expected.

After eating dinner and cleaning up the mess, they decided to go in the living room to talk before going to bed. Eventually, John brought up his visit with Johnny in the hospital. John said, "I visited your friend before I came back home." Jill said, "Which friend would that be?" "Johnny Mann, right after his surgery." "May I ask why you did that?" "Well, I was not able to see you being so heavily sedated and asleep. I had an hour to kill before I had to leave and decided to go check on Johnny to see how he was doing. Anyway, something was bothering me and I needed to ask him a few questions." "Wasn't he also asleep after having his surgery? And what questions did you need to ask him, John William?" "Yes, he was sound asleep. After a few hard shoves, he woke up with me standing over him. Now about the questions I needed him to answer. Something was bothering me as to why Johnny wanted to keep you on that mountain. Did you ever sign anything for him, but were not sure what you were signing?" "No, I never signed anything." "Then I suspect he took out travel insurance on the both of you before that ski trip. Which would not require your signature but only his. If you died on that mountain, he could collect the insurance money from your death. I knew he had done one or the other when I asked him that question and his eyes gave him away. The good news is the policy is only good for that one trip."

John continued by saying, "Anyway, before leaving him I explained his situation in regards to you. He gave me his word not to bother you again." Jill asked, "So you are telling me I lost Johnny as my friend." "No, I am telling you, you are trading that piece of shit for me and I promise not to kill you for any insurance money in the future. How does that sound?" "Sounds alright by me. I never thought Johnny would ever go to such extremes and kill me for money. I guess you think you know someone but you do not." "I bet you never thought a person would send you a message that would change your life, but here we are." "Again, I cannot argue with your logic, John William. I am sitting on your sofa having this conversation with you."

John decided to change the subject and not discuss Johnny anymore. Instead, he wondered what Jill had planned on doing for her next movie. Jill told him that Carrie was looking over manuscripts to find one while she was gone. Then Jill asked John what book he was currently working on. John told her that he and Rex were working on a book together about the weekend at the ski lodge, which they finished last week. Jill asked, "I guess I have a part in this new book?" John said, "A major part, and I hope you do not mind. I did it more for Rex than for myself. He wants to be a writer and I am trying to make that happen." "After all you have done for me; I do not have a problem with you doing that for him. As usual, you are thinking of someone else before yourself. I think it is time for me to say good night. I am a little sleepy from that long flight. Do you mind showing me where the spare bedroom is, John?" "Not a problem. Night, night, girl." Suzie jumped up and raced to John's bedroom while the two of them watched. "It is a little game we have played since she was a pup." Jill nodded her head as if she understood what he was telling her. John told her he would explain about it tomorrow.

They went upstairs and John showed Jill the bedroom she would staying in which had a full bathroom connected to it. He wished her a good night's sleep, and if she needed anything, his bedroom was straight down the hall, giving her that devilish look again that she ignored. She thanked him for dinner and letting her stay at his house for a couple of days. John told her it was his pleasure in having her and said his last good night.

About forty-five minutes later, John's bedroom door started opening which made Suzie growl at whoever was doing it. John told her to be quiet; he knew it had to be Jill. She was standing in a doorway only wearing a T-shirt and panties. Another beautiful sight John got to experience with this woman, thinking he must be dreaming. John said, "Do you need something, Jill?" Jill said, "Yes, my human blanket to keep me warm while sleeping. I cannot seem to go to sleep without it. Can you help me find it, John?" John raised the bed cover so she could come join him. She pulled off her T-shirt, letting it drop to the floor while climbing into the bed. His body covered hers with his chest to her back and both his arms wrapped around her body, pulling her close to him, letting Jill feel his body heat. Another thing she had missed from him while being off the mountain. She asked, "How does your body stay so warm?" "DNA my dear. I have always been warm blooded since I can remember. That is why I love going up on the mountain in the winter." "John, I am conscious, healthy and my battery is fully charged. Got any ideas what we should do about all that?" "I believe there was one more thing I require, Jill Amber." "You are also in my heart, John. I was fighting the fact and have never felt this way about anyone before. This is very new to me. I …." John turned Jill over on her back and once again did not let her finish the sentence. He started making love to her as he had dreamed of doing so many times before.

Soon after, Jill's panties hit the floor. Suzie left the bedroom, giving the two humans some privacy. Jill was making her sexual sounds too loud for her ears to handle so she decided to go and sleep in the guest bedroom since no one was going to use it tonight. John and Jill made love well into the night and the following morning. Jill had never felt so at peace with someone before and John had not since being with Sarah. They both were missing that special someone and finally found each other.

The next day, after having breakfast, making love and a short nap together, John showed Jill his office where he did all his writing. Then all the books he had written and a few awards he had won. He put the Oscar that Jill had brought him on the shelf next to them. Then he showed her a picture of Sarah, Michael and him on the day they went camping together. They sat in his office and talked for a while about that day and other things in John's life. Next on the agenda was to give Jill a tour of his property while playing with Suzie along the way. Jill could see how smart and obedient she was. She called out some commands and Suzie responded to each of them; understanding what they were and obeying each one. John was surprised she responded to them, only knowing Jill the one day.

When lunchtime rolled around, John decided to take his two girls into town. He gave Jill a quick tour of what was in his small town and then they made a stop at the local bookstore. John knew the owner, Mrs. Olson, and introduced her to Jill. The elderly woman was a big fan of John's writing and had all his books in her store. Recently losing her husband, John would go in the store to check on how she was doing. While John looked around the store, Mrs. Olson and Jill started having a conversation with each other. Later, Jill decided to make a purchase, all of John's books that were in a boxed set. Mrs. Olson gave her a store discount and told Jill to come back without John next time. Then they could talk more freely without him being there. Jill agreed and then autographed a magazine for her she appeared in recently. Then John, Jill and Suzie went to have their lunch before returning to his house.

In the two days, Jill enjoyed the time she spent with John and Suzie. Now having received all the answers she came for and a few extras by now being in a relationship with John. Unfortunately, it was time for her to go home and help Carrie find their next project if she had not found it already. John could tell she did not want to leave but had to go help run the business he helped start.

Before leaving for the airport, John asked her to come into his office. He had a couple things to give her to take back home. Jill followed him in and stood in front of the desk, waiting for whatever John was about to give her. John was sitting on the other side of the desk. He reached into one of the drawers and then pulled out two items for Jill to take with her. Which was a manuscript with a small wrapped box on top of it. John said, "The manuscript is mine and Rex's new book we are publishing next week. I wrote this one in a movie script form for you. I believe you will not have to hire any screenwriters this time around." "How did you know to have this ready? We may not have ever spoken to each other again." "Always good to have a plan and be prepared than not, Jill. I had faith one day we would be together. If not, I would have sent you the manuscript to use anyway." He told her to open the box. Jill unwrapped the box and looked inside. She found a diamond ring shining back at her. She looked up at John in shock and was speechless, not knowing what to say to him. "I know this is quick, but will you marry me, Jill Amber?" She did not say a word, but only stared at him and then back down at the ring. Once again, this man had her mind twisted in knots, not able to think. "You do not have to answer me right now. Think about it first. Then let me know your answer. I wanted you to know how I truly felt before you left. I am serious about us and know you will be in my heart till the day I die."

Jill had a few tears coming down her face. She wanted to say yes right then so badly, but did not. John handed her his handkerchief to wipe her face. He told her not to be sad but glad she had someone in her life that really cared about her. Even if they are not together, every second of every day did not mean they do not love each other any less. Jill told him she would think seriously about everything he said and give him an answer the next time they were together.

Jill put the two items in her bag to take with her back home. Jill said, "It is a very beautiful ring, John." John said, "The ring was my grandmother's and I got it when my grandfather died on our mountain. The only thing the man had left that was worth anything. Now I want you to have it." "If I decide no, I will make sure to return it to you." "That sounds fair to me, Jill Amber."

Even with the two gifts, Jill was still sad about leaving John more than ever. She wanted to say yes to his proposal and start spending her life with him. Only right now that was out of the question and they both knew it. John said, "Read the movie script and decide if you want to use it or not for your next project. We can use the same terms as the last time." Jill said, "Then let me go ahead and pay you the dollar up front this time. In case, I forget to do it later. Okay?" She handed him a dollar and he put it in his shirt pocket. John said, "Payment received in full, thank you Jill Amber. I will make sure Father Michael receives his twenty cents as his commission." This time they both laughed at John's joke.

Before leaving, Jill gave Suzie a good rub down to say goodbye. She went over to John and gave him a kiss that he would soon not forget. John said, "That was the kiss you were talking about in your email, wasn't it." Jill said, "Yes it was. Now we are even on great kisses." "Why haven't you kissed me like that before?" "I owed you that one and it will be the last one you get until we see each other again, John." "No kick in the balls before you go?" "No, we might want to have children someday. I would not want to be the cause if we could not." "I guess I am safe then." "For now, but who knows, things could change." They both laughed while walking out to her car. John gave her a big bear hug before she left. Jill told him she would call him after getting home. John asked her to call him after she landed and email him when she got home; he had missed their chats. She agreed to do it. He waved and Suzie watched while Jill drove away. John said, "Don't worry girl, she will be back to see us. I know it in my heart." Suzie looked up at him while he was talking to her.

They went back into the house so John could call Michael to give him the news. He needed a best man if he was going to marry Jill. The woman he knew and not the Hollywood actress everyone else saw on the movie screen. That woman they could have and keep. He wanted the one that left his house going to catch a flight to California.

Chapter 21

Time to Leap

*D*uring the flight home, Jill read the movie script that was all about John and her experiences before and during their time on the mountain. While reading, Jill was making notes of any changes she wanted to make to improve the manuscript. Something else she had learned from John. When she finished, there was the material for a new movie her company could turn into a movie. Jill could not wait to let Carrie read the new manuscript and see what she thought.

As usual, Michael was in his office working when John's call came in. He answered his phone not sure, how this conversation was going to go. Either they finally worked things out, in which case he would not be mad at him for giving Jill his address and her showing up unannounced. They did not and John was calling him for interfering in his business, then firing him as his publisher and ending their long friendship together. Michael picked up the phone to find out which was about to occur.

Michael said, "Michael Parnell here, how can I help you?" John said, "I think you have helped enough, Father Michael. But since you asked, let me think about that question for a moment." "John, before you do anything rash for butting into your business, let me explain why I did." "Go ahead, I am all ears and cannot wait to hear your reason or reasons when I specifically told you not to interfere." "I know you did. Look, Jill called me in order to find you. After having a conversation with her, I thought it was the right thing to do. The way things were going, you two might never have gotten together to resolve the issues between you. I had a talk with Jill and decided to give her your address; telling her the conversation she wanted to have with you should be in person and not over the phone." "She told me about your talk and thought it was more like a sermon you were giving her, Father Michael. I wish I was there in person with you right now instead of over the phone." "John, if you are going to fire me then just do it. I know what I did might seem wrong to you, but I thought the two of you should have a chance to work things out before it was too late. What is this Father Michael crap? I see Jill is giving out the nicknames now." "Only fitting after what you put her through and calling her the "Ice Queen". After hearing that, she wanted to kick you in the balls, even pictured it happening in her mind while listening to you keep on preaching to her." "Really, are you sure this woman is the right one for you?" "More than ever now. Also, you were right about everything you did to finally get us together." "Well why did you not say so in the first place? I thought you called to fire me." "And then who would be my best man? Of course, if you are not up for the job, I could always call Rex. I know for a fact he would jump at the chance." "You do and I will never publish anything either one of you write in the future." "Just having a little fun with you old friend. I gave Jill my grandmother's wedding ring when I proposed to her. It is on her left hand heading for California as we speak. She has not said yes to my proposal, nor did she say no. She wanted time to think about it first. I think you should clear your schedule next month for my wedding if you want to be my best man. If I know Jill, things will happen very quickly when she makes up her mind." "I will be ready to come whenever you need me, John." "Glad to hear it. Now, how is the book coming along? Will it be ready to release next week?"

Michael could rest easy; he still had John as his number one writer. Now asking business questions, something John had never done before, always letting him call with any updates. Michael said, "Everything is ready on my end. All I need is a title to put on the front cover of your new book." "Well, how about "Heart and Soul" as the title?" "I like it, John. The title fits the book perfectly. I am glad we decided to wait until you came up with the right one. With that title, more women will buy the book. You have out done yourself this time, John." "Jill was the one who came up with the title and let me use it for my book. All the credit goes to her. I gave her a manuscript based on the book to read on the flight home. She will let me know if it will be her next movie project." "I am sure she will love it with the story being about the two of you and how you met. If she decides to use it to make her next movie, will it be with the same terms as last time, John?" "But of course, Father Michael. One dollar that you get twenty cents of I might add. I have decided that will be your punishment for butting in my business. Jill even paid me the dollar up front this time. I will mail your two dimes tomorrow." "Don't bother, John. Consider it your wedding present from me. This time I get to come out ahead financially." "All kidding aside, I want to thank you for sending her to me. I finally got my "Starlet", Michael." "Well I hope she says yes. No more being the Lone Ranger. Call me when she agrees to marry you." "Hey, you could get ordained and marry us. Then you will be Father Michael for real." "Goodbye, John." This time Michael hung up on John, not liking his joke one bit.

After landing, Jill called John to tell him she arrived home safely and loved the script, but thought a few changes might improve their story. This peaked John's interest and told her they could chat about it later on the computer. Jill told him that she was going to stop by Carrie's house on the way home to give her the manuscript to read. Their chat would have to wait until she got home. John told her to drive safe and that he loved her. Jill looked down at the diamond ring on her left hand and said she loved him too and said goodbye.

Jill arrived at Carrie's house with everyone greeting her at the door with lots of hugs and kisses from Molly first and then Carrie and David. Carrie told Jill they were about to eat and told her to come in and join them. All of them went into the dining room and started having dinner, while Jill talked about her last three days at John's house. Later, showing her left hand and the nice engagement ring that was on her finger. Carrie was the first to say congratulations, while Molly was asking everyone what the pretty ring meant. She explained to her daughter that Aunt Jill might marry her friend JD. By finding the right man to be her husband and then spending the rest of her life being his wife, if she decides to marry him. Molly asked, "Well Aunt Jill is JD going to be my uncle?" Jill said, "I do not know yet Molly. I have to think about it first." Carrie could tell her best friend was eventually going to say yes. Which now left her with some doubts where their company was heading if she did marry JD. Jill saw Carrie's face and had a feeling why she was worried. She put her at ease by saying, "If I do marry John, he wants me to keep working at the company making movies. After all his help showing me what I can do by directing and acting with the right material, he thinks I should continue doing it to see where it takes me." Carrie said, "I knew there was some kind of connection between the two of you. Jill, you fell in love with him on that mountain." "You are probably right, Carrie. We have only spent about a week together; it will be best not to rush into anything like marriage. John wanted me to think it through before answering his wedding proposal, which I intend to do. Thank you for dinner, but I need to get home so I can email the Play-Doh Man to discuss all the changes I made to his manuscript. We have a lot of work ahead of us if we are going to make John's manuscript our next movie. First, you need to read it tonight and tell me what you think. Then we can move forward by signing cast members and deciding on shooting locations. Jill got up and said her goodbyes and left to go home.

After arriving home, Jill went through her mail and found a particular letter in the stack. She opened the letter and learned it was from Bill Turner. Jill sat at the kitchen table the way she did the other time he sent her one. The letter was telling her that he wanted to call a truce between them. Saying how sorry he was for all the bad things that had happened between them. Not taking any blame of course, but said he would no longer do anything underhanded to her in the future, that she had his word on it. Now wandering if she could believe the man could keep his word and why all of sudden this change come over Bill to write her this letter. It had to be something very serious for him to not only give up, but to send this letter saying he was no longer a threat to her. Then it started to make sense, John must have talked to him on her behalf the same way he did with Johnny. Now Jill had another question to ask her fiancé on their next email chat. She went straight to her laptop to get that answer.

Starlet: I am now at home and found a letter sent by Bill Turner. Would you happen to know anything about it? I think we both know Bill is not the type to say he is sorry for anything he has done to anybody.

Play-Doh: A week after we got off the mountain I made a call to have a talk about his situation with you.

Starlet: Situation?

Play-Doh: Situation!

Starlet: Please explain what you did, John.

Play-Doh: I told him that your health and well-being would now involve me. In very clear terms, if anything should happen to you by his doing then I will have to act on your behalf.

Starlet: I see. So does that mean you would go "Tarzan" on him?

Play-Doh: Yes, in a heartbeat. I wanted him to understand that I protect what belongs to me no matter what the cost.

Starlet: So I belong to you now.

Play-Doh: In my heart you do. Now back to the evil villain. I told him that it was in his best interest not to bother or contact you in the future. Otherwise, he ends up like his friend Johnny, having his own hospital visit in the near future with his own broken bones.

Starlet: You would honestly do that to protect me.

Play-Doh: Yes, once again in a heartbeat. I believe if you hurt someone, expect to be hurt back. Trust me; I know how to hurt someone who deserves it.

Starlet: I think you are a peculiar and interesting man, both at the same time. I still love you even if you are a little off-balance at times, John William.

Play-Doh: Right back at you, Jill Amber. Now, tell me all about those changes you made to my manuscript. What did you add and what did you take away?

Starlet: I think you will like all my changes; they will tickle your heart and touch your soul, John William. Anyway, your manuscript needed a woman's touch. Since there is a woman as one of the main characters, her part of the story should be in a woman's viewpoint, what do you think? I do have two Oscars proving my point.

Play-Doh: One Oscar, I have the other here with me. Knowing what I do about you, I will probably like all your changes, Jill Amber. Michael is going to use the title you gave me for my new book.

Starlet: Good, I love "Heart and Soul" a lot better than what you had before, calling it "Search and then the Rescue". Carrie is going to read your manuscript tonight, but I know she will love it. I cannot wait to start making our movie.

Play-Doh: Now we really are partners in the movie making business.

Starlet: More than that, John William. We will be partners in life and in business unless I decide not to accept your marriage proposal.

Play-Doh: Well then, hope you understand why I had my talk with Bill and Johnny to protect our future together.

Starlet: I understand, now that you have explained things. I love you John William.

Play-Doh: I love you too and always will Jill Amber.

They ended the chat agreeing to do it again tomorrow night. Finally, an actress and writer were now in a relationship together. This was going to be a fun ride for these two soul mates in the crazy world they lived in.

The next day, Jill went into her action mode, something else she had learned from John. With Carrie loving the manuscript, she had so many things to do and was up to the challenge. After making one movie, the second movie should be a lot easier by not making the same mistakes like on the first one. This time, her cast would not be stolen or a spy being hired to cause any delays. The word soon got out; Jill had another movie under production, which Bill Turner read about in the newspaper. Even after writing that letter agreeing not to bother Jill again, he had no choice but to try something to save his job at the studio.

One week after Jill left to go home, John got a call from someone he did not expect. He answered his phone and found Carrie on the other end. She wanted to talk to the "Play-Doh Man" himself, to thank him for all he had done for her best friend and their company. Carrie said, "I wish you had told me who you were in the hospital before you left. I could have thanked you properly, John. May I call you John?" John said, "Of course you can, Carrie. Now to answer your other question. I wanted to tell Jill first before anyone else knew. I think you can understand why." "Yes, I sure can with the two of you being in love with each other. I called to let you know how grateful we are to have you in our lives. I believe you have changed Jill's life for the better. Believe me when I tell you this, she is a changed woman after you gave her a new purpose in life. Something that was always missing for her." John thanked Carrie for calling him and told her to call whenever she felt like talking to him.

As they continued to talk, John asked Carrie about Molly and if he could talk to her. Carrie put Molly on the phone to talk to John. She called him JD instead of John. She began telling him how much fun she was having with the clay animals he had made for her and wanted to know when they were going to see each other again. John said, "Hopefully very soon Molly bear. I am waiting on a decision from your Aunt Jill. Then I will know. Wish me luck on her decision." Molly told her mother that JD called her Molly bear and then laughed. Then Molly got back on the phone and asked JD, "About you marrying my Aunt Jill?" "Yes, that is the one." "I hope she says yes JD. Then I can call you my Uncle JD." This time JD laughed and then said, "Yes you can, Molly. I hope that will happen." "JD, what are the most ferocious animals in our country?" "Well Molly, there are about four of them and you have two made out of your Play-Doh, which are the bear and the wolf." "What are the other two?" "I would have to say the wolverine and the cougar, which is sometimes called a mountain lion. Why are you asking me, Molly?" "I was wondering if you could make them for me. Then I will have all four of them in my collection." "It would be my honor to make them for you. I will get your address from your mother and send them to you. How does that sound?" "Great JD, I will be looking for them in the mail and thank you for doing it for me. Let me put mommy back on the phone so she can tell you where we live. Bye for now, JD." "Bye Molly bear."

Carrie got back on the phone, and gave John their address and thanked him for doing it for her. Telling him that Molly loved playing with her clay animals every day in her room. John told her it would be his pleasure to make the clay animals for Molly, and then thanked Carrie for calling. After hanging up, John thought how lucky Jill was to have this family in her life. The same way Michael was in his. He went to bed thinking about his "Heart and Soul", which was Jill Amber Green. After saying night, night, to Suzie, they raced off to his bedroom. John won this time by him getting a head start on her; then jumping under the bed covers first before she even got in the room.

The next day, John got another surprising phone call from someone he never expected to hear from in his lifetime. It was Bill Turner with a business deal he thought John might be interested in hearing. Bill offered him six million dollars for the rights to his new book on the best sellers list. John said, "No thank you Mr. Turner. I already sold the book rights to Jill Amber Green for one dollar. I believe you are too late once again. I think it would be in your best interest, to never have any contact, including writing letters, to either one of us in the future. Since I did not make myself clear in our last conversation, I hope for your sake I have now. I know everything you have done to Jill, even if I cannot prove it. Unlike Miss Green, you cannot hurt or outspend me. Please do not make me come to Hollywood and explain how I truly feel about you in person. I have given you an ultimatum, now it is up to you what will happen." Bill did not respond to anything John just told him. Instead, he hung up the phone. He got the message by finding out firsthand, that John did not care about money, but instead people that were in his life. John knew Bill's days at the studio were numbered, being desperate by calling him and then offering so much money for his book rights.

Jill was sitting with Carrie at the offices of J&C Productions working on the manuscript of "Heart and Soul", when they got a phone call from Michael. After saying hello to him, Jill decided to put the phone on speaker so Carrie could hear the conversation. He was calling to let them know the news of Bill Turner calling John to buy his book rights. Michael said, "I just found out from John that Bill Turner tried to buy the rights to "Heart and Soul" for six million dollars." Jill said, "That man always wants what we already have." Carrie said, "I wish your old studio would just fire him. Then maybe we would never hear from him again." Michael said, "Well, John turned him down of course. He went on telling them about the conversation of what John told Bill. To never contact him or you Jill, in the future. Otherwise, he will have to come to town to see him in person. That was when Bill hung up on him. I do not think Bill will be bothering you any more ladies." Jill said, "I hope you are right and he got the message. I would not want John coming into town to go "Tarzan" on Bill. That kind of publicity is something none of us need. All three of them broke out laughing. Michael said, "You are right about that, Jill. You know firsthand how John gets when someone he loves is in trouble. There is no stopping him then. I thought you might want to know since John probably will not tell you about the conversation." Jill thanked him for calling.

Jill told Carrie she would have a conversation with John, to make sure he did not over re-act and do something drastic to Bill by putting him in the hospital. Even if Bill got the message from John to leave Jill alone. Carrie agreed with her and thought it would be a good idea, knowing that good communication is the key to having a good marriage. Carrie went on to say, "Even if I do dislike Bill and think he deserves a good beating, I would not want to see John going to jail beating up that piece of garbage. There are other ways of dealing with Bill. Jill said, "Like having another hit movie? I think that would take care of Mr. Turner permanently. The studio would have no choice but to fire him." "I agree, so we better get back to work and make it happen."

Jill sat there thinking about the man who had started all this for them and the one she would soon be calling her husband, the "Play-Doh Man". How lucky she was for him entering her life. She returned to work selecting the cast members for the upcoming movie. Unfortunately, for Bill, he had no idea what was in store for him. With all these true professionals working together and enjoying their jobs, they were going to end his career in the movie business very soon.

Jill got all her cast members signed and under contract. She decided to shoot the mountain scenes of the movie at Mt. Elbert. She booked the ski resort that Rex worked at for a month before the snow started melting. In this movie, Jill would have hire more stuntman and use computer graphics for the fight scenes with the wolves. Not having much time, Jill kept in contact with John emailing him throughout the day and night. She too also missed having their chats instead of talking to each other on the phone. Neither one of them brought up the marriage proposal. Both knowing it was not the right time to have that conversation with so much going on in their lives, with Jill making her movie and John promoting his new book by going on book tours. John knew Jill would give him an answer when she was ready. She wore the engagement ring every day on the set, never taking it off. In her mind, she had already said yes and accepted his proposal, but wanted to tell him in person and not over the phone or by an email. It was an important decision and she wanted to do it the right, John deserved that from her.

Since John did not do any book tours on his last book, Michael made sure he had plenty to do on this one. Rex also attended as many as he could to promote their book, which made John happy. This gave his young friend the opportunity to show his true potential in writing and then promoting his first book. Now Rex could start his own writing career. A dream that would come true after meeting John. Maybe John had a gift of spotting talented people, only needing the right person to show them how to use it. First with Jill and now with Rex. Some people go through their life never knowing what they are capable of achieving. But not Jill and Rex, they knew what they could do and were doing it now, with Jill directing and acting in the right films, also allowing Carrie to now produce films and help run a production company with her best friend. Then came Rex who wanted to be a writer like his idol and was on his way. All in all, not a bad year's work for John. He had changed their lives for the better and his in the process, finding some new friends and the love of his life.

The next month, John and Suzie were sitting outside on the porch when a delivery truck pulled into his driveway heading toward the house. Suzie jumped up to attention, in case there was going to be any trouble. John told her to steady herself, and let them find out what was going on first before they went on the attack.

After backing the truck up to John's house, two men got out that John recognized from town. He knew they worked at the local furniture store and were the deliverymen. They both went over to John and the driver said they were here to take out the old furniture from his house and put it in the front yard. Then they would unload the new furniture and bring it in the house. Finally, they would load all the old furniture on the truck and take it with them. John said, "Sounds like you two men have a lot of work ahead of you. The only thing is I did not buy any new furniture. Did you girl?" Looking down at Suzie when he said it. The driver said, "I know you did not Mr. Davis. The woman that is following us made the purchase and is the reason we are here."

Then the driver pointed to a car that had pulled into John's driveway. Jill quickly got out of her rental car and started giving orders to the two deliverymen. Letting everyone there know who was in charge by saying, "Daylight is burning boys, let's get this done." Jill went into her action mode and took the two men in John's house to show them which furniture to take out to the front yard. While walking in and out of the house, Jill spoke to John using quick and short sentences. At the time,

John had returned to the front porch with Suzie to get out of everyone's way and listen to Jill as she walked by him.

She said, "Yes John William, I will marry you." Showing him that she was still wearing the engagement ring on her left hand. She left him to think about that. Next thing she said, "The wedding ceremony will be here this Saturday, which is in six days." She left him again. Then she said, "Carrie and her family will be staying here. That is why I bought the new furniture. Your friends can stay in town." She went back in the house to help the men. The last thing and most important thing she said, "Sorry this is so quick, but so was your proposal. I am pregnant, you are the father and we are having twins. Any questions?"

John could only sit there with his mind all twisted up in knots from all the things Jill just told him, like he had done to her after receiving his gifts in the hospital and later finding out Suzie was a dog. John was in shock from all the news hitting him at once, which Jill did on purpose to pay him back. He even saw a small smirk on her face after telling him about having twins.

Now he was to be a husband and a father all in one sitting. He nodded to her and said, "No questions. Whatever you need from me I will do." Jill said, "Good, call your people and give them the news. I will finish up with the deliverymen so we can start planning our wedding." She left him to go back to work. Then John said to Suzie, "What have I gotten us into girl?" Suzie got up and gave him a quick look before going into the house to find Jill, abandoning her old master on the porch. John thought he had that coming. Suzie was now looking out for herself. Jill was the new master of the house and John's reign had ended.

Later that evening after dinner, Jill gave John a medium-sized box to open. John said, "My first present from you, Jill

Amber." He opened it up and saw cans of air fresheners they were all different kinds and brands. Two bottles of Bean-O and two boxes of Gas-X were also in the box. Jill laughed at him while he was looking all the contents over. Jill said, "I did not know what would work best, so I brought all this so we can try them out while you are "Calling the Ducks"." "I see you came prepared for any situation." "I have learned it pays to be prepared, John." "You are right about that. Now I do not feel guilty about eating all that fried food yesterday." "At least I have weapons this time to fight the ducks." They both laughed and started cleaning up the dirty dishes before going to bed. With only five days left before the wedding, both of them were going to need their rest.

The next day, Carrie, David and Molly came to John's house, to help them get things ready for the wedding. John was excited to see Molly and they played with Suzie while the others did some things in the house. The groom's job was to show up and say his vows, ending with I do and then kissing his new bride. Jill had all the hard work to do and John was glad she was in charge of everything that involved their wedding.

This visit gave Carrie and David a chance to get to know John better while being in his home. To find out more about the man Jill has fallen in love with and was about to marry. Later in the week, Rex and his brother Mark arrived for the wedding. Michael also flew in the same day to fulfill his job as best man. John decided to take everyone out to dinner on him, so everyone could get to know one another.

Every day before the wedding, Jill had everything running like clockwork, with Carrie's help of course. She was going by her checklist the way she did while making a movie. Only this was her wedding and she wanted it to happen without having any problems. With everyone pitching in, the ceremony went as she planned, with no problems occurring. The wedding was held on John's property with Molly as the flower girl and Suzie as the ring bearer in the ceremony. John had taught her how to carry a small pillow in her mouth and then walk down the aisle to bring the rings to them. Carrie was the matron of honor and Michael was John's best man. During the ceremony, Michael could see his friend was truly happy in marrying Jill. John was right when he told him that she was worth it. Jill was the right someone, John could spend the rest of his life with and love each day. Everyone had a great time at the reception and most left the next day to give John and Jill some time alone. Michael and Rex stayed in town, there was going to be a book signing later that week. Only John had not mentioned it to Jill yet.

The day of the book signing, the two of them were sitting on the porch. John looked at his new bride and said, "I need you to go somewhere with me and not ask any questions." Jill said, "Let's go." Which told John she trusted him completely. John told her to get in the truck while he went to get her a pillow and blanket. Jill was thinking John was taking her somewhere maybe to have sex in the truck somewhere out in public, thus the pillow and blanket. Instead, they drove into town and stopped at the local bookstore, seeing a large crowd of people inside and out. After getting inside the store, Jill realized this was a book signing for John and Rex's new book "Heart and Soul". They walked over and sat down with Rex at a table. He was surprised to see both of them thinking only John was coming. Then Michael came over to talk with them. Michael said, "You did not tell me Jill was coming? When the word gets out and it will, we will run out of books, John." John said, "Look old friend, Jill is my wife, where I go, she goes. Remember, I agreed to let you make all the decisions on this book. Now show everyone that great problem solving skill you have by coming up with a way to fix our problem." Michael got on his phone and started making calls to all the bookstores in Memphis to have more books delivered. Luckily, there was a few bookstores in the area. When the bookstores found out Jill was going to be at the book signing, all of them agreed to bring their copies of "Heart & Soul" to him. He could have their books delivered to the store within the hour. Another problem solved by Michael who had the right connections and knowledge to fix whatever came up. Something John knew he could do and would all along.

When word did get out, more people came and lined up outside the store, trying to get in to buy the book and get all three autographs. Later that evening, all of them took a thirty-minute break to get something to eat and stretch their legs before going back to meeting the local people and signing their books. With three of them, autographing the books it took a lot longer to finish. When it was time for the bookstore to close, there were still a lot of people waiting outside. They came a long way to get their autographs and were disappointed it was going to be for nothing. John went outside and told the people to hurry up and buy a copy of the book, that they would stay around outside in the parking lot to sign everyone's copy.

After the store closed with record sales for Mrs. Olson, people formed a line to John's truck to get their book signed. John, Rex and Jill sat on the tailgate of his truck under a parking lot light to sign them. Later, John went and got the pillow for Jill to sit on and the blanket to wrap her up in to keep his wife warm. It was midnight when they finished signing all the books and left to go home. While driving home, Jill asked John if he would mine doing her a favor. John told her to ask away. After spending all that time at the book signing, how could he refuse any request she asked of him? She then asked, "Could you help show the stuntman how you go "Tarzan" while fighting with wild animals? I think it will make the movie more authentic if it is done the right way." John said, "If that is what you need, I will be more than happy to help you. But this time Suzie gets to come on the trip." "Agreed. You can even bring her on the set with you each day. I know she will behave herself and not cause any problems. I think I got the better of this deal John, only having to spend eight hours to help you. You are going to spend at least a week helping me film those fight scenes." "Not a problem, Michael has arranged another book signing in LA. Rex is flying in for it. I guess I forgot to tell you about it." Jill leaned herself into John and went to sleep while he drove them home. She was not even upset about the other book signing, knowing it was going to help Rex with his new career. They did not have much of a honeymoon, but at least they were now together and not apart.

They went to LA the next week to start filming the scenes. John taught the actors and stunt men how to go "Tarzan" on the trained animals. He made sure the scenes portrayed what actually happens in real life. Jill was still going to have to use some CG in order to get the kill scenes closer to what actually happened and not to have any animals harmed in the process. John's book signing went on for two days instead of one, with LA being a much larger city than John's hometown. Now Rex's career was well on the way. It was up to him where it would end up; he would write his next book without any help from John.

Finally, it was time to have their talk about where they would call home. John said, "Well, my state is a little too far from where you work and all your friends. I can write from anywhere. Your state has thirty-six million people, which is a little too crowded for my taste after spending a week here. How about a compromise with us living in Colorado. We met there and fell in love and it was my home growing up. As a bonus, it only has three million people living there and we already know a few of them. You will not be too far from Carrie or your company. I have not even mentioned all the mountains and beautiful scenery to grow up around while raising our family. Well, what you think Jill?" Jill said, "You are right, we met and fell in love on that mountain. I think it would be a great place to buy or build our house and raise our children, John." John told her he would go check out some places he thought might be ideal to build a house on; that she could check out some real estate possibilities on the Internet. Between the two of them, they should narrow down where to build or buy their home. Jill thought John had picked the perfect place to live by choosing Colorado. She started planning to sell her house in California that week. John did the same thing in Tennessee. He left the next day to find out exactly where they would live. Jill stayed behind to finish filming the movie. Then it would be ready for the production process that Carrie and David were going to handle this time together.

The following week, John and Jill bought a piece of property where they decided to build. It would take time to sell their houses anyway. Jill wanted to design a house that would fit both their needs for now and in the future. The construction started on the home and was finished the same time as the new movie "Heart and Soul" came out, which was in December. Jill planned a huge Christmas party for their family and friends, one week before Christmas and her due date, to celebrate the movie, the new house and the holidays. Once again, John was right with the movie being a huge success and the book sales increased with people enjoying the experience of reading the book and watching the movie, to see any difference between them.

John made sure Rex got all the extra money from the sales of the book. Michael understood why and arranged it by setting up an account for Rex at his publishing company. He knew without Rex's help during the crisis, John and Jill might not have made it off that mountain. He also was becoming a better writer with John's help and deserved the extra money.

Carrie, David and Molly stayed over the holidays to help Jill during her pregnancy. She was due any day and needed help doing things around the house. Carrying twins was hard on her and Carrie was glad to help. John and his little friend Molly spent their free time playing with Suzie each day waiting for the babies to arrive. On one of the playtimes, John asked her, "What do you think of my dog, Suzie? Is she fun to play with?" Molly said, "I love her very much. Suzie can do all kinds of tricks and I wish I had a dog just like her and not the Play-Doh one you made me." "I know the one I made you cannot do any tricks. Maybe one day you will have a real dog that you can play with." "I hope mommy and daddy will let me have one. I wrote to Santa Claus to send me a dog just like yours, JD. That way I can play with it every day and teach it new tricks. I will give my dog a treat the way you do with Suzie after she does her trick. Then hug my dog around the neck while it licks me all over my face." "Sounds to me you have everything all worked out, Molly." "Just need Santa Claus to bring me my real dog, JD." JD laughed after hearing that from his little friend. He would make sure to give Carrie the breeder information where Suzie came from in case she wanted Molly to have a dog.

Jill went into labor Christmas Eve night, she and John went to the hospital. Michael came into town to be with his friend to celebrate the birth of his children. Carrie, Michael, David and Molly waited in the lounge while Jill and John were in the delivery room. She was in labor for over six hours before the birth of the twins finally happened. They had a boy and a girl born at 12:10 and 12:15 a.m. on Christmas day. Two of the best gifts Jill could have ever given John as Christmas presents. They were healthy and Jill was doing fine after the births. She had finally given him something very special, a family that wanted and loved him, something he never had before in his life. With both his parents giving him up to his grandfather as a punching bag to beat on while growing up.

John was so nervous becoming a father. Uncertain what kind he would be until he held his children for the first time, the feeling went away. He knew right then everything would take care of itself. All he had to do was to be the best husband and father each day by putting them first in his life instead of himself. That is what he thought while holding his children with Jill fast asleep next to him. She was exhausted from the delivery and needed her rest. John could not believe how lucky his life had turned out over the last two years. Now being a husband and a father with a beautiful family to share his life.

The next day, it was time to name the babies. Jill said, "I have a great idea of what to name them, John. How about William and Amber, after the both of us. Since they are part of us, why not have our names." John said, "I love the idea. William and Amber will be their names. That way I will not call you Jill Amber anymore and you will not call me John William. It will be too confusing for the children when they get older. I knew I married you for more than your good looks and great body, dear. I am just glad we have one each and not two of the same." "And why is that?" "Easier to tell them apart, I will never get them confused." "I would hope not. If you do not know the difference between a boy and a girl, we are in a lot of trouble, mister." They both laughed at each other's funny statements, which seemed to come at the strangest times. This time John did not mind Jill calling him mister, knowing she was doing it only to have a little fun with her husband.

While resting in the hospital bed holding the twins, Jill was thinking about how her life had changed over the last two years. Being married to a wonderful man with twin babies, who was now living in Colorado in a house she helped design. In two short years, Jill had opened a production company, directed, and starred in two movies, for which she won two Oscars. Now having a nomination for a third Oscar, for best director in the second movie. She had a great life with a great man to share it with her. Finally with her life was on track, she was living in a dream and hoped it would never end with her answering a very harsh message from a person calling himself the "The Play-Doh Man".

Chapter 22

The Ultimate Union

*W*hen the Academy Awards night came, Jill was not able to attend. The twins were almost two months old and she decided to stay home with her family. John knew how much it meant to his wife and did not want her to miss this experience. There was a camera crew at the house to film her reaction if she won the Oscar for best director two years in a row. They would do it live, via satellite if Jill won to show the world a real-time reaction and hear her acceptance speech to whomever was watching.

That night Carrie had two nominations for Oscars for the film "Heart and Soul", for best producer and supporting actress. Her daughter Molly also got to star in the film playing herself. Which gave her knowledge and recognition in the industry, being only six years old. Later that evening, Carrie won an Oscar in the category of supporting actress and in her acceptance speech she thanked Jill first and then her family for the award. Jill was at home while her best friend won and accepted the award. She was so proud that the industry acknowledged her hard work on the movie and picked her to win. John and Jill were excited watching the Academy Awards at home and they were going to get even more excited in a few moments. With Jill's name, being announced as best director for the field. She made her acceptance speech holding the twins, showing them to the world for the first time. Making sure this time to thank John first for winning the award. Wishing she could be there to accept it in person, but as everyone could see, she had her hands full at home. Jill wished everyone had a great night and enjoyed the rest of the evening at the awards. The audience cheered and clapped after she gave her acceptance speech, seeing how happy she was with her family and new life in Colorado. It had changed so much for her in such a short time, with all the Oscar wins; her new company had proven to be a huge success. All the other motion picture studios had to take notice and accept there was a new player in town. J&C Production's was that new player.

A few months later, Jill got a call from Planet studios to set up a meeting with her, to talk about merging the two companies into one. Jill said, "I will discuss it with my husband and partner and get back with you." The Board of Directors at the studio said they would be waiting for her decision. Jill talked it over with Carrie, David and John who all agreed it could be an advantage for them to merge with the studio. This would give them less responsibility and more resources in making future movies. As a bonus, more time to spend with their families. Only having to make one movie a year, instead of two could make a huge difference in their lives. John told Jill and Carrie to go to the meeting and see what they had to offer. Now that Bill Turner was no longer there, maybe it would be worth listening to what they have to say. John decided to get Michael's attorney to go with them. The man was a real hellhound for business deals. He would make sure the studio did not try to pull anything underhanded in the deal. Jill called Planet Studios and agreed to have a meeting with them. The two women left the next day to hear what they had to offer them by merging the two companies.

After hearing their proposal then talking the deal over, Jill and Carrie agreed to the studio's offer. Which was more than fair for everyone involved. With so much competition in

Hollywood, it made sense to merge the two companies. As long as J&C Production were able to keep their creative influence on all movies that involved them and made sure it was in the business contract. The studio had no problem with the terms. They wanted Jill and Carrie because of the four Oscar wins between them over the last two years. Both women were happy with the deal; it meant more money and less work and financial responsibility on them. They also could close down the company building to save money, with the studio providing them with offices on their lot and sound stages to shoot their scenes. Instead of going out to find shooting locations all around the city. Which meant, saving a lot of money and time on those two items alone.

Jill was proud of what she and Carrie had accomplished with a new business deal with Planet Studios. She could not wait to get back home to tell her husband the good news. Already missing him and the children so much, only being gone for that one day. Jill only felt complete when she was at home, being a wife and a mother, not a director or a Hollywood actress. She knew what her job was and did not mind or complain at any time while doing it. With John and Rex supplying her with the movie material how could she fail? David was also included in the new business deal with the studio. He would be doing some production work with the new movies to finish the process. David had learned the job on the last two films and enjoyed doing the work in that field to get the movie finished. Everyone was satisfied with the way things had turned out at the meeting.

After losing his job at Planet Studios, Bill Turner got another job at a smaller studio. Only it did not last long, he got caught embezzling money from the company. He was arrested, prosecuted for his crimes, and sent to prison for five years. John thought the man got his just reward and finally went where he belonged, not able to hurt anyone but himself.

That same month, Johnny Mann was killed in a bar fight. A man shot him to death instead of trying to fight him with his fists. Jill's two enemies were now dead or gone and not to be heard from again.

Rex wrote his new book, which Jill was going to turn into her next movie project. He would only accept one dollar as payment, just as John had done with his books. Rex knew who helped him get his writing career started and was not going to forget it either after having some success. Now Michael had another star writer at his publishing company thanks to John. He no longer complained about his commission being so low, with Rex only charging Jill a dollar for his book rights. He was used to getting the twenty cents on these deals. Michael had become a better man and was now engaged to an actress of his own he had met on the set of Jill's latest movie she was directing. Michael thought since John married one that made him happy, maybe he could have the same thing, by getting married and starting his own family. Rex was also engaged to a woman he met on one of his book tours. He felt an instant connection with the woman and decided to pursue it with John giving him that exact advice one day when you find that special someone. That he would know if she is the right one to be in his life. Then show her how you truly feel no matter what the cost or how foolish you think your actions might be. John did not want Rex to make the same mistake he made by not being up front and honest with Jill from the beginning.

John got an idea of a very different kind of book he wanted to write. After finishing it, he sent the short story for Michael to read and then publish. He only wanted one copy made and sent back to him. Michael did not understand why, but did as his friend asked. He had one printed up and mailed back to John. After receiving it, John hid it in his desk to use in the near future when the right time came. John called Michael to thank him for doing it for him so quickly and would explain later why he wanted the book printed. It was a plan he had come up with for the twins and Jill. Only he had to wait until the twins got a little older before he could read the book to them. Michael said, "What does Jill get out of the book?" John said, "That is a personal matter I cannot discuss with you old friend. I will tell you all about it after I use the book and see if my plan works out. Hey, but right now I am working on my new book "The Interventionist", which should be finished sometime next month. I hope you like it, being so different from my usual upbeat subject matter." "I'm sure it will be good like all your other books, John. You really know how to tell a story. That is what matters the most in my opinion." They said their goodbyes. John then went to work on his new book to have it finished in time before Thanksgiving. He wanted to spend all his time with his family during the holidays, being the twins first Christmas.

After finishing "The Interventionist", John let Jill read it first before sending it to Michael. She could not believe he had written something so different from his usual material. John told her he wanted to create a new character with different subject matter that no one would expect. Bob was a new character he could write a whole series of books about without running out of material, the way he had done with the JD character. Jill said, "That should not be a problem in your character's line of work. You should never run out of ideas or stories for him to do in future books." John agreed with her and said, "Not that we need the money, but "The Interventionist" will keep me writing for years to come. You know how much I love being a writer. I only hope the public likes the idea and can relate to my new character." "He is different, I have to say that much. When will you send it to Michael, so he can give his opinion on your book?" "After the holidays and his wedding. I wanted him to have an open mind when he reads it." "Good idea, he will need time to read and understand your new character. But I think it will sell, John." "Me too, I am glad you like it. I even gave Rex the idea to write about a character opposite of mine. He is trying it out to see if he can. It could help out both of us in the future, as far as books sales and maybe movies go." "That is what I love the most about you, John William. Always looking out for someone else and having a plan working in that head of yours." "You know me, always trying never stopping Jill Amber. Now what's for dinner?" "We are having soup and bread, tonight." "No duck calling then?" "I have learned in the last two years without any meat in your body, you cannot call them." "How about a little meat for me and I take the Bean-o?" "No way, nothing works for your gas. Too bad you cannot earn a living passing that." "I wish. Then Bill Gates would not be the richest man in the world, I would." They both laughed and went to have dinner without any fear of any ducks called later that night.

Chapter 23

The Bedtime Story

The next three years seemed to fly by in John and Jill's lives. The twins were now four years old and growing like weeds. John was busy writing books about his new character Bob, "The Interventionist", and Jill was still directing at least one movie each year. Both of them were so busy it did not leave much time for each other with all of the twin's needs. They were always wanting their parent's attention, whenever and however they could get it. John and Jill did work out a system to balance out work time and family time. Taking turns with each other, while doing family responsibilities and chores. Jill was gone 3 to 4 months out of the year to direct her one movie, but John could find time to write whenever he was not busy with the children. He loved spending time with William and Amber every day because he was able to teach them new things to learn. That is what he cherished the most about being a father.

Everything seemed to be working out in their lives and in their friend's lives also. Michael was married and had a baby girl named Annabelle. Now if John called him, he would find him at home instead of at the office working, because that was where his priorities were. Rex was also married and had a baby boy he named John, after his hero and good friend. John was proud of him and pleased at what he had done with his life, becoming much like himself. Being a good husband, father and writer all at the same time. Even his brother Mark was doing well with his helicopter business, with Jill using his helicopter to film all the mountain scenes in the movie "Heart and Soul"; he made a lot of money. He was able to pay John back the loan ahead of time with interest. He even brought another helicopter and hired a pilot with business being so good. The movie industry even decided to make more movies with mountain scenes in them, meaning more business for him. Now everyone was having some success and enjoying their lives because of a certain mountain man had entered in them by chance. Even though John did not want any of the credit, each person let him know how special he truly was every time they were around each other.

When Jill and John were home together, they took turns in getting the twins ready for bed. First by getting their baths, brushing their teeth and then reading them a bedtime story while they were in bed. This routine helped them go to sleep each night without any complications. John always loved it when it was his turn to read to the twins. Sometimes he would read them a classic or he would make one up in his head to tell them. William and Amber liked the made up ones the best. Their daddy would make funny sounds and faces while telling them the story and he could get a reaction from his children by making them laugh. It tested his imagination and spontaneity while making up the stories. This kept John's mind open to all sorts of possibilities that sometimes helped him with his own writing. While experiencing writer's block, telling the children stories sometimes helped John overcome it by having fresh ideas pop in his head. Thus giving him new ideas of how to fix his problem by coming up with new ways to write about his new character in his current book.

Unfortunately, Jill saw story time in a different way. She being so tired at the end of day looked at story time being another job and not a joy spending time with her children the way John did. Only doing it to get her children to go to sleep, then she could relax. Jill always wanted to hurry up and get it over with when it was her turn. She having so much to do in her day, there was never enough time to enjoy the important things in life. This was about to change for her with what John had planned earlier by having Michael print a certain book for him that had been locked in his desk for three years. Now it was time to put his plan into motion by using the book to teach Jill an important lesson in the process of spending quality time with your family.

Jill got the twins bathed and dressed for bed. Then she made them brush their teeth and got them all tucked in ready to hear their story, making sure they went to the bathroom first. That way she would not have to start reading the story all over again. She had learned that lesson the hard way once before. John was downstairs in his office doing some writing at the time. Suzie was at his feet, laying down waiting for the signal for them to go to bed. John knew at any moment Jill was going to call him upstairs.

Jill went over to the kid's bookshelf to pick out one of the books to read to them. Not sure which one to get, she asked the twins what book they wanted her to read tonight. William said, "I want you to read this one, mommy. It is our favorite, right Amber?" He opened up the nightstand, pulled out a book and handed it to his mother. Amber said, "I love our favorite book." The book was one that Jill had never seen before. She looked at the cover to read the title, which was "Mountain Man meets Wine Woman". Jill said, "William, where did you get this book?" William said, "Daddy gave it to the both of us last week. He has read it to us a few times, mommy." Jill said, "Did he now?" She sat down and started reading the book to them but William and Amber made her stop. Both of them told her she was not reading it right. Amber said, "No mommy, you have to use the funny faces when you read it." William said, "Yeah that's right and don't forget the funny sounds. That is what daddy does while reading it to us and why we like it so much." Jill said, "I am sorry, but I do not know how to do the funny faces and sounds. So why don't I go get the one who does." Jill went over to the bedroom door to call John. She said, "John honey, we need you up here." John said, "Coming dear. Let me turn off my computer and the lights and we will be right up." He and Suzie went upstairs to find out what Jill wanted. Even though he knew, his wife had probably found the book and needed his help to read it the right way for the kids. Now it was time to have some fun with his family, something they had not done in a while.

John got to the kid's bedroom and found his book lying on the seat of a chair by the twin's bed. Jill was sitting in another chair across the room waiting for him to arrive. He ignored his wife, went straight into character, sat down in the chair and opened up the book to start reading it to the twins. He called out the command and Suzie jumped on the bed with the twins so she could hear the story with them. John started reading the story using funny voices and later funny sounds when it was time to use them. John had the twins laughing and giggling with him as he read on. Suzie popped her head up a few times after hearing John make his funny animal sounds. The story was about how John and Jill met and survived on the mountain. This story was in a fairytale type version, instead of an adult one. With John adlibbing a lot throughout the book.

Jill did not like the story at first because of the title, but then saw how excited her children got while listening to their father read this story. She even began to laugh at the way her husband was telling their story. John was making it seem funny and exciting at the same time. He even put in the part about "Calling the Ducks". William started making fart sounds by using his hand in his armpit while flapping it. Amber said, "That part of the book is disgusting by having farts blown in someone's face." Jill was now having a good time seeing the bedtime story involved the whole family. She was beginning to understand why her husband had written the book. The whole family had something to enjoy while spending time together. Even if some of the story was not true by John using his imagination. It made it seem more exciting and fun to hear.

After he finished reading the story, John reached down to kiss his children good night and told Suzie to stay with them. She liked sleeping with the twins anyway. He walked over to Jill and put his arm around her waist and they started walking out of the room, while turning off the lights as Jill said her good nights to them. The twins were going off to sleep, dreaming about the story of the "Mountain Man meets Wine Woman". Not knowing it was about their parents and how they fell in love with each other that one weekend. They would tell the twins about it when they were a lot older and could understand what really happened on that mountain between them.

John and Jill were walking toward their bedroom with their arms around each other. John said, "Are you ready for your bedtime story, Jill Amber?" Jill said, "What kind the story did you have in mind, John William?" "Well how is your battery tonight?" "Fully charged after hearing that story." Then it hit her, why John had read the story in front of her. Remembering him doing some of her household chores throughout the day. "I cannot believe you would use our children in order to have sex with me, John William." "What, do you honestly think that I planned all of this to have sex with you? I think you give me too much credit, Jill Amber. What kind of man do you think I am?" "A man who always has a plan way ahead of time is the kind of man I think you are. Is that why you did some of my chores today?" "Of course not, I was just trying to be helpful, that's all. Did you like the story or not?" "Very much. I cannot believe you got Michael to make that children's book for you." "Well you know Tonto, always willing to help when called upon. He is a good friend and I am going to have to find a way to repay him for doing it. Now let's go to bed so I can tell you your bedtime story, Jill Amber." He looked into his wife's eyes and knew his plan had worked. "Okay, I want to hear it, John." John knew that Jill would look at doing the bedtime stories in a different way from now on. Even if she did not know the book was written three years ago which John was not about to tell her. Now about to have sex with his wife was a bonus for all his hard work and planning for just the right time to use the children's book. He did not want his marriage to become like so many others, with no surprises left to experience. John was going to make sure that did not happen with his. He was already working on his next plan in his head for Jill and him to experience together.

Going to bed with his wife in his arms, John thought to himself, what a great feeling he had when a plan works out perfectly. He had two healthy children and a wife that loved him. What more could a man ask for or need. Jill said, "I am cold, where is my human blanket to keep me warm?" John said, "Right here beside you dear ready to cover your body all night to keep you warm, my Jill Amber."

This story has ended, maybe another one to come for the Play-Doh Man and the Starlet in the future. With their two hearts and two souls joined together to face whatever comes their way.

About the Author

First time author James Peevey has worked in the warehouse industry for over thirty-five years. He grew up in Memphis, Tennessee and lives in the surrounding area. He believes that love can come to people in many different ways and forms, which is why this book was written.

jamespeevey@att.net

Printed in the United States
By Bookmasters